***She had never been inside
a bigger house.
Or a darker one.***

Standing just inside the threshold, the tall man hovering behind her, she tried to peer into the blackness. Ahead of her a hallway seemed to stretch forever into the dark.

She had no idea where the tall man had taken her. They had driven northward for what seemed hours, the high-rises of Manhattan dwindling into suburbia, the suburbs thinning out into country. When she asked him where they were going, he had only repeated, "My place."

She didn't like being taken to an unspecified destination. Now that they'd arrived, she liked it even less.

"Any lights in this place?" she asked, trying to keep the nervousness out of her voice.

Behind her she heard a hollow scrape. Match light flared over her shoulder, then bloomed into a deeper glow. The tall man had stepped in front of her, a silver candlestick in one hand. Behind him, his looming shadow wavered on the dark-papered wall.

"Come," he said. .

D1475224

DYING BREATH

JON A. HARRALD

POCKET STAR BOOKS

New York London Toronto Sydney Tokyo Singapore

For
Bruce Kawin
———

A Pocket Star Book published by
POCKET BOOKS, a division of Simon & Schuster Inc.
1230 Avenue of the Americas, New York, NY 10020

ISBN: 0-671-69029-9

First Pocket Books printing August 1992

10 9 8 7 6 5 4 3 2 1

POCKET STAR BOOKS and colophon are registered
trademarks of Simon & Schuster Inc.

Cover art by Don Brautigam

Printed in the U.S.A.

Acknowledgments

Heartfelt thanks to Dr. Paul Woolf and Dr. Michael Gewitz, New York Medical College, and to the members of the New Castle Police Department.

Once we were—but now no longer are—blessed spirits; because of our pride we all were driven from Heaven; and in this city of yours we have seized the rule, because here we find confusion and sorrow greater than in Hell.

—Niccolò Machiavelli, *Carnival Song: By the Devils Driven Out of Heaven*

Prologue

Stoneham, New York
Wednesday, October 26
8:05 A.M.

She had been born and raised in the city, but whenever Beth Richardson thought of the fall, she had always pictured the suburbs, as if its sights and sensations—trees blazing with orange, children bounding into leaf piles, the smell of wood smoke curling through the neighborhood—had been part of her own past. Now she was there. Three months before, in early July, she and her family had made the move northward to Stoneham, and though the summer had been rich with its own country pleasures, she had waited impatiently for this, her favorite season, to arrive.

Everything about October in Stoneham gave her pleasure: the cardboard figures of wart-nosed witches and capering skeletons taped to the display windows of the village merchants; the brightly painted wooden placard in front of the Town Hall, announcing Saturday's Halloween parade; the ears of Indian corn hung, like a Christmas wreath, on the front door of her neighbor's eighteenth-century colonial.

Even the sight of the two fat pumpkins sitting on her own front steps, awaiting the creative efforts of her husband Martin (the family's official jack-o'-lantern artist), made her inordinately happy—though at the present moment, as she stood in the foyer buttoning the sweater of her six-year-old son, Chris, her pleasure was somewhat dampened by the noisy squabble taking place between her two other children. Her oldest child, Danny, almost twelve, was accusing his sister of having stolen his Nerf football from his closet.

"I did not!" Amanda shouted indignantly. "I haven't even seen your stupid ball for months!"

"*So?* So that just means you took it months ago and never gave it back—"

"I did not take it!"

Danny jabbed her in the chest. "*Borrowed* it, then—"

Reaching over, Beth swatted at Danny's hand. "Don't do that to your sister! Amanda, button your sweater. That's enough, I don't want to hear it. You're going to miss the bus if you don't hurry. You don't have time to fight. Come on now, everybody, give me a kiss." She received a peck from Amanda and nothing from Danny, who was still stewing about his ball, and in any event, was several years past the age of kissing Mommy good-bye. Chris, who was not yet sure about this school business, gave her a brief, desperate hug.

"Love you! Have fun and work hard!" she called, shooing the three of them out the door. The sky was a deep fierce blue, unstained by clouds or the haze that passes for sunlight in the city. What a gorgeous day, she thought, holding the front door open with a hand as she inhaled the fragrant coolness of the morning. Her glance shifted to her three children zigzagging across the damp lawn, wetting their sneakers, and her heart stirred with happiness at the sight of their sturdy little figures.

The moment they reached the road—their part of Stoneham had no sidewalks—they began to chase each other in a ragged circle, laughing riotously when Chris, unbalanced by the weight of his Ghostbusters backpack, went tumbling onto the edge of their neighbor's lawn and landed in a leaf pile half as tall as himself.

"Hey, you three! Cut it out," she called after them. "Get going or you'll be late!"

Danny pulled his kid brother to his feet and started rapidly down the road, while the two younger siblings followed him at a pace only slightly more brisk than a dawdle. But Beth had secretly sent them off with time to spare. She watched them until they rounded the curve in front of her

4

neighbor's house and were lost to view. Then, smiling, she turned away from the door.

Returning to the large, airy kitchen, she settled down contentedly at the half-cleared table. Now that Chris was in school all day, she was filled with a luxurious sense of leisure, of having—for the first time since the birth of her oldest child, nearly twelve years before—time to spare. She poured herself another cup of coffee and picked up the local newspaper.

After scanning the front page, she turned to her favorite feature: the Police Blotter. Reading it religiously was one of her guilty pleasures, partly because it functioned as a kind of local gossip column: "10/19, 9:25 P.M. Smith Street woman calls police to report loud domestic argument in neighboring house." "10/17, 11:05 P.M. Family dispute reported to police by Adams Road resident." Mostly, however, the weekly Police Blotter provided her with a profound sense of security. With its record of vandalized mailboxes, shoplifting arrests, and missing dogs, it served as an official confirmation of the fundamental safety of the world she and her family lived in.

At that moment, however, even the Police Blotter couldn't capture her full attention. Not with that Sara Lee pecan-and-raisin coffee cake sitting on the table mere inches away from her left hand. She knew she should not have a second piece. Twenty pounds overweight and just starting a new diet, she said aloud, "Willpower, kid." But it was no good. She sighed again and resignedly cut herself another piece, imagining the disapproval of her husband. Well, it's just a tiny slice, she rationalized. And I've got that workout class later—that'll probably burn up six hundred calories right there.

At precisely that moment, four miles to the west of the Richardson home, Jerry Waller, Danny's sixth grade teacher, eased his nine-year-old Toyota into his parking space behind the Willow Brook Elementary School. A husky forty-six-year-old, with thick salt-and-pepper curls, a full beard, and a fondness for plaid lumberjack shirts—the proud badges of his countercultural past—Jerry was, as he liked to think of himself, a born teacher, whose early arrival that morning was only one small sign of his dedication to his

5

work. His colleagues would not start appearing for another fifteen minutes, but Jerry had driven to school beforehand in order to put the finishing touches on the scale model of a seventeenth-century Salem village he and his class had spent the last few weeks constructing.

To be perfectly honest with himself, he had to admit there was another reason he had left home early that day. A bitter quarrel with his wife—a dispute over the amount of time and attention she had (or, more accurately, had *not*) been giving him lately—had broken out that morning as she was rushing to get ready for work. Its intensity took both of them by surprise. Though she had departed before he did, leaving him alone in their two-bedroom town house, he had found the atmosphere of the place so oppressive that, without even checking to make sure he had all his textbooks and papers, he had grabbed his briefcase and hurried out the door.

Slamming the car door closed behind him, Jerry felt his spirit lift at the sight of the Halloween decorations—crudely crayoned jack-o'-lanterns, grinning skulls, and black cats—taped to the windows of the kindergarten classrooms. The beauty of the morning was so piercing that, in spite of his lingering agitation, he felt a wave of simple gratitude wash over him, a sense of his own good fortune at being able to spend his days in such a place.

To be sure, there were times when he berated himself for leading a life that many of his friends from the old days would have regarded as a cop-out, a craven escape from the problems of "the real world." Occasionally, he still wondered whether he would have remained truer to his youthful principles by teaching in an inner city school. But Stoneham was also part of the "real world," he would tell himself, and the children of wealth required just as much attention, affection, and devoted teaching as the poor and underprivileged. At least he hadn't sold out by becoming a corporate lawyer, which seemed to be the profession of choice among the fathers he had met in this community.

His black mood burning off in the sharp autumn sunlight, Jerry turned the corner and approached the steps leading up to the main entranceway. Suddenly he stopped. *The gazebo. It was supposed to be completed this weekend.* Built as a memorial to a young colleague who had died the previous year of colon cancer, the gazebo was a handsome construction of light, unpainted wood, erected on an expanse of unutilized lawn that ran along the far side of the L-shaped school building. It would serve as a place for band concerts and school picnics, and he knew it would have pleased Marion immensely.

He recalled his last visit to her in the hospital—the straggles of gray hair sticking from her bumpy skull, the eerie translucence of her skin, the left eye filmed over with a bluish membrane. He hadn't been to see her in several weeks, and in that time, she had turned into—there was no other word for it—a monstrosity. Approaching her bed, he had tried keeping his expression as impassive as he could, but as he bent down to kiss her forehead, she had fixed him with her one good eye and croaked, "I look that bad, huh?"

Pausing on the pavement, he shook his head to rid it of the memory. Then he headed for the other side of the school building, focusing his attention on the brilliant foliage and the pristine beauty of the sky.

Danny was trying to get his sister and brother to hurry. Usually they moved faster when he told them to—in fact, sometimes they would speed up and beat *him* to the bus stop. (He refused to run for the bus. That was the last thing he wanted the older kids to see him doing, running for a stupid school bus.) But today everything was going wrong. The wind snatched away the signed permission slip that Amanda was carrying, and she had to run back toward their house before she caught up to it. Then Chris kept jumping in every little pile of leaves he saw. "C'mon, you guys! You're gonna make us late and Mom's gonna be mad!" Danny shouted.

Slogging through the leaves, Chris was thinking about the neat "Turtles" cartoon he had seen yesterday, and so he barely heard his brother. Then—not more than a few hundred feet from the house—he stumbled over something solid and fell, his hands out in front of him. They slid into something slimy and, as his eyes tried to make sense of what he saw lying there, partially hidden, another hard gust came along and blew the leaves away. He stared, his mouth open. Then he began to yell.

7

"Danny!" he cried. "Mommy!"

Danny turned around impatiently. "C'mon, Chris! Get up!"

But Amanda was running back up the road toward her younger brother, who was not moving and who looked funny, looked sick. When she reached him, she, too, stared down with widening eyes.

Amanda was in the third grade and liked dogs.

Amanda began to scream.

As soon as Jerry rounded the corner of the school building, he saw the handsome little structure, looking, as it stood in the sunlight, like a fairy-tale pavilion. Jerry grinned broadly as he imagined it occupied by the fifth grade Clarinet Choir, belting out an off-key rendition of "Oh What a Beautiful Morning" or playing the overture from *Star Wars*.

He was still thirty feet away from the gazebo when his brow furrowed with confusion. Through the spaces of the latticework running around all but one of its sides, he could see that the floor planks were covered with brown paint. It had been his understanding that the gazebo would remain unpainted.

His pace quickend slightly and he swung to the left so that he was approaching the gazebo from the front. From that vantage point, he could see clearly that the paint had been applied in irregular patches—that it had been spattered, not spread, across the floor. "Son of a *bitch!*" he said aloud, running now toward the structure.

Though defacing buildings with spray paint was a form of vandalism virtually unknown in Stoneham, there were plenty of bored teenagers around who occasionally amused themselves with a spree of mailbox-bashing or tire-slashing. And Halloween, Jerry knew, was a particularly lively time for such diversions.

Jerry, however, did not regard the defacing of Marion's memorial as a prank. To him, it represented an act of desecration.

Reaching the gazebo, he froze. He gaped. For a moment he simply could not make sense of what he was seeing. He stood there staring down at the floorboards of his dead friend's memorial for several long minutes. It was not until

8

he became aware of the iciness on his tongue and palate that he realized that, in his distress and alarm, his mouth had been hanging open like a child's.

Inside the house, Beth had not heard Chris's shout, but she had heard Amanda's scream, and her heart plummeted. Leaping from her chair, she sent coffee splashing over the table and puddling onto the pages of the *Stoneham Gazette*. Within seconds she had torn open the front door and dashed outside in her bare feet and bathrobe. Her children were not visible, and until she rounded the first curve, all she could think was that one of them had been hit by a car. *Oh, please God, oh please God, oh God oh God*, she prayed. And then she saw Amanda still screaming, Chris at her feet (but sitting up, Beth's mind registered), and Danny rushing toward them.

He got there first, and Beth could hear him say, quite clearly, "Oh, Jesus!" Then she had reached them. She dropped to her knees, hard, in front of her youngest. "Baby! What's wrong, what happened?"

He stared at her, speechless.

And then she looked down.

Right next to her, so close she was almost kneeling in it, lay the body of a dog. Though she would have liked to believe that it had been struck by a car, she saw clearly that it had been butchered. The throat had been opened with a neat slit, as had the belly. A coil of entrails lay heaped on the grass.

The dog's mouth was wedged open with a short stick. She glanced at the sharp, white teeth. Something—in her shock, she could not think what it was—had been done to the inside of the dog's mouth. She turned her gaze away quickly, her gorge rising. "Oh, God," she said aloud, and the words brought her back to herself and her children. Chris's face was terribly white, and Danny looked years younger than when she had sent him off only minutes before. Amanda was chewing on her fingers, hard.

"Come," Beth said quietly, standing, the pain shooting through her knees. "Come home."

She picked up Chris, whose body felt like dead weight in her arms. Amanda grabbed her leg, the way she used to when she was smaller, and held on tight all the way home,

9

making it difficult for Beth to walk. The wind felt icy and every now and then blew Beth's bathrobe open, exposing her short satin nightgown. She didn't care.

Twenty minutes passed before she could use the telephone. Her children were huddled together under a heavy quilt on the sofa in the den. She had quieted them with candy bars and the most convincing story she could think of to explain the dog's death.

She had told them that the dog was killed by a car going too fast. As for the stick in its mouth, well, dogs love to fetch sticks. That's probably how it had happened. The dog ran into the road for a stick and got hit by a car. By now she had repeated this story so often and with such growing conviction that even Danny was beginning to believe it.

Or so she thought. But as she stood up from the sofa, telling them to stay put, Danny asked her a question that stopped her dead.

"Mom," he said quietly, his voice sounding as small as a toddler's. "If the dog was hit by a car, where was the blood? Why wasn't there any blood?"

Jerry stared down at the floor of the gazebo. It was clear to him that what he had taken for brown paint was in fact dried blood. Lots of it. And the markings were, in fact, not random splatters but crudely made images and words, though he could make no sense of anything. He saw what looked like a five-pointed star and below it words in a strange language:

SEVIL NATAS
SELUR NATAS
!NATAS LIAH

Then he lifted his eyes and noticed for the first time the thing nailed to one of the support beams, just under the roof. For a moment he thought, absurdly, that it was a slice of lunch meat. Corned beef? Pastrami? It took him a full minute to register that he was staring at the severed tongue of an animal.

He clamped his mouth shut to quell his nausea. Then he spun on his heels and ran.

*   *   *

10

There was a telephone in the den and another in the kitchen, but Beth walked upstairs to her bedroom to make this call. The room looked cozy. The bedcovers were still rumpled, and the room was awash with sunlight. But Beth felt cold, cold.

Their town was laced with woods—when she drove home from a day in New York, it always felt as if she were in the real country—and so the sight of dead animals on the road, even deer sometimes, was not unusual. There was a special division of the local sanitation company that picked up animal bodies and did something (she had never before wondered what) with them.

But she didn't call them.

She called the police, reaching them just as Jerry Waller burst into the station, his face a white mask of fear.

Part One

Dogsbody

1

OUTSIDE, THE BRANCHES OF THE BIG MAPLE TREE RATTLED in the wind. Blowing leaves beat against the glass of the bedroom windows like large summer moths.

It was eight P.M. on Saturday, two nights before Halloween, and Anna Prince—sitting in a warm pool of light at her dressing table, a glass of Napa chardonnay in her hand—was feeling very happy.

She wore a black silk kimono, embroidered with a delicate spray of flowers—peonies, poppies, lotuses. Beneath it she wore nothing. She had just climbed out of a long, perfumed bath, and as she sat before her mirror, listening to the rush of the wind in the trees, she luxuriated in the sensation of having nothing at all to do except get dressed.

It had been a long time since she had felt so free and so good physically—since before the birth of her son Stephen, really, three months before. The last time she and her husband David had gone out together on a Saturday night— alone—was close to half a year ago, in May.

Tonight they were going out to dinner at an inn in Cold Spring Landing, forty miles north of Stoneham. She was excited, looking forward to the dinner. The *Times* had given the restaurant a rave review, there would be flowers and candles on the table instead of formula bottles and a box of baby wipes. And afterward . . . She slipped open the bottom drawer of her dressing table and removed the black lace panties she had purchased specially for the occasion. They were very sheer and very brief.

That was another thing they hadn't done in a long time—made love. For a while she hadn't felt like it, either before or after the baby, and Dr. Fischer—because of the difficulties she had experienced with the pregnancy—had cautioned against it. And David . . . David hadn't seemed interested, for some reason. Given her own aversion, she hadn't inquired too closely, accepting his apathy with gratitude.

Well, tonight she was going to wear something very sexy and feminine. Black because she looked good in black and because it was David's favorite color on her. And low-cut, to show off her creamy skin and the newly rounded contours of her breasts, whose size and fullness she had still not gotten used to.

At the moment, however, she was simply taking pleasure in the slow ritual of dressing. There was no need to rush. Stephen was safely in the care of the babysitter downstairs, and David was somewhere down there too, probably in his study making phone calls, as he so often was, even on weekend nights. Buying and selling options and currency. Doing deals. He knew people all over the world and called them every hour of the day, shifting effortlessly from English to German to French to Japanese.

She was proud of him, proud of his strength and resourcefulness. He had always been strong and commanding. Still, she had not expected, years ago, when she was a wide-eyed kid with hair down to her waist, taking her first-ever acid trip with him ("This is Owsley, baby, the best there is," she remembered him whispering, as he placed the blue tab on her tongue) that she would some day end up *here*—in a sprawling house, on six acres of rolling land, in rich, green Westchester County.

And now, after all these years, she had gotten another reward: a baby. For eighteen years David had refused to let her have a baby, refused even to discuss it, and she had been a good wife. She had accepted it. That was what he had said, laughing, the night he made her pregnant: "This is what you get for being such a good girl."

16

So in the end she had everything. She stood up from her dressing table and looked around at her bedroom. It was a beautiful room. The decorator, Charles Maurice, had done some of the fanciest houses in Scarsdale and Pound Ridge. Everything about it radiated elegance and taste: the antique canopy bed, the French country armoire, the handsomely framed, eighteenth-century botanicals.

No one else in her family had ended up in a place like this. No one who had known her growing up in her west Denver neighborhood, a tough section of the city gone irretrievably to seed by the late sixties, would have imagined her ending up here. Even she couldn't have predicted it. Her beginning had been rocky, all right. And she had had some bad years later too, after she had met David. But she wasn't going to think of them now—or of that other thing, that article in the *Times* today that had stirred up all the bad memories again. And scared her. Really scared her.

Until this moment, she had managed to put it out of her mind—with the help of lots of wine. Remembering was the signal that she needed some more.

Still barefoot, she crossed her broad bedroom and refilled her glass from the bottle sitting next to the Quimper pottery lamp on her night table. A few mouthfuls of wine remained in the bottle. "Waste not, want not," she said out loud. Tilting her head back, she poured the drink directly down her throat, like a kid chugging beer.

She grinned at herself in the cheval mirror that stood in a corner, near the four-poster bed. Much better, she thought. Undoing the sash that held her kimono around her, she let the shimmering robe fall open in front. Then she picked up a flacon of Opium from her bureau and stroked the perfume over her body: breasts, belly, the tops of her thighs.

Beside the green wine bottle on her night table sat an oblong, black velvet box. She picked it up and raised its hinged, satin-lined lid. Inside lay a lovely emerald and diamond necklace—a present from David, "to mark this special day." He had told her that when he came up to their bedroom to present it to her earlier that evening. Now she looked at it for a long moment before taking it gently in her fingers and lifting it to the lamplight, turning it to admire the glittering splendor of the gems.

A warm flow of tenderness, almost sexual in its intensity,

17

rippled through her. *Sweet David. He must be as excited about tonight as I am.*

David was sitting exactly as his wife had thought, in his study, a room nobody else ever entered, except the pair of Philippine cleaning women, who were permitted inside to vacuum, dust, and polish once a week. Though large and expensively furnished, the room had a perpetually somber atmosphere. The windows were narrow and, even on a bright day, the little light that slanted in seemed to be absorbed by the thousands of volumes stacked along the shelves of the dark, floor-to-ceiling bookcases.

Anyone examining these shelves would have been impressed by the variety of the titles ranged along them. Very few of them had anything to do with trading or markets. Unlike most successful businessmen, David Prince never confused business with life. Trading was only a means to an end. He took very little pleasure from it, except the satisfaction of doing it better than most people and hence becoming more powerful.

Situated in the corner of the study was another smaller bookcase, this one fronted with a pair of locked glass-paneled doors. The books it enclosed were all leather-bound and very old. Many of them had Latin titles. They had been passed down through David's family from generation to generation.

Spacious though it was, the room might have struck a different man as oppressive. But there was something about the enveloping darkness of the study that David found intensely soothing. Dressed for the evening in a smoke-gray Perry Ellis pinstripe, phone to his ear, he leaned back now in his large, leather-seated chair and listened closely to the agitated voice on the other end of the line, his green-shaded banker's lamp casting a yellow circle of light on the brightly polished surface of his desk.

The door to the study was closed. Though the sitter, Rachel Peary, was with the baby in the den, separated from his study by the length of the living room, he wanted to make sure she didn't overhear. He didn't want his voice to carry upstairs either, although even if it had, it wouldn't have mattered. David was careful in his speech, especially on the telephone or with those he didn't know and couldn't

18

vouch for. He knew that his father, who had been in the same business, was much better at sizing people up instinctively and instantly. He was so good that he had never lost a deal, never failed to land a prospect. But David was still learning.

Now, as he listened to the jittery voice on the other end of the line, he suddenly sat upright, struggling to control his impatience. He was trying to be reasonable. After all, he told himself, this was a new team and a young one, and though he had brought them along carefully to this point, though he had gone over every detail of this business a hundred times before, it was natural for them to be nervous.

And so, instead of being bullying or using threats, he decided on a different tack, letting his voice take on the warm, encouraging tone that he knew from experience could be highly persuasive.

"Listen, I understand how you feel. Believe me, I do. But nothing's going to go wrong. How's that song go?—don't worry, be happy." He paused for a moment, then laughed gently. "Exactly. Look, I've been through this kind of thing a hundred times before. It can get a little tense, no doubt about it. But—hey, that's part of the fun, right?"

He listened again, then relaxed back into his chair.

"Good. Very good. And I guarantee, I absolutely *swear* to you, that the payoff will be worth it. Just keep in mind—we've got the little bastard exactly where we want him."

Bidding his associate good-bye, he replaced the receiver in its cradle. As he did, he barked out a sharp laugh, as if he had just heard the cleverest joke in the world.

Ten minutes later no one could have guessed that David had just been absorbed in a tense conversation. When Anna came downstairs, a little light-headed from the wine and her building excitement, he was sitting placidly on the sofa, a glass of bourbon in hand, speaking quietly to the teenage sitter, Rachel. Dressed in Jordache jeans and a bulky Generra sweatshirt, Rachel stood before the sofa, looking intently at the face of the tiny infant who lay motionless in the crook of her right arm.

"Sweetheart," said David, rising at Anna's approach.

19

"Christ, you look beautiful." He set down his drink on the glass-topped coffee table, took her by the shoulders and kissed her lightly on the cheek.

"You really do look nice, Anna," Rachel said matter-of-factly.

David's eyes rolled upward in a "what's this world coming to?" look. "That's 'Mrs. Prince,' to you," he said good-humoredly.

"Sorry," said the girl, though her tone remained curiously flat. "I like your hair that way. Mrs. Prince."

Blond and hazel-eyed, with a flawless complexion, Rachel possessed the kind of natural prettiness that had as much to do with the freshness of her youth (she had turned sixteen only two weeks before) as with her regular but unremarkable features. She had been at the house helping out several afternoons in the past month. David had insisted that Anna get some rest those afternoons. But this was the first time the Princes would be leaving their baby alone for an entire evening in the care of another person.

Much to her dismay and astonishment, Anna felt herself reluctant to go. She stood within the protecting curve of David's arm, feeling the supple wool of his suit jacket against the bare skin of her shoulders. In the background, his latest toy, a stainless steel CD player, futuristic in the sleekness of its design, sent ripples of music into the room—a jazz pianist Anna didn't recognize, doodling a wistful improvisation in the air. The bone-white walls were hung with the somber prints she and David had begun to collect—Böcklins, Corinths, Schieles. They had managed to construct a world of beauty over the waste of their early years.

And now, though she had looked forward to this evening with the eagerness of a schoolgirl getting ready for her prom, the thought of going off into the night suddenly struck her as entirely unappealing. A strange anxiety had overtaken her. More postpartum weirdness, she thought. Or perhaps she was still suffering from the uneasiness stirred up by the article in the *Times*, a feeling that even a full bottle of chardonnay hadn't managed to submerge.

Or maybe the explanation was even simpler. Maybe she just didn't like the idea of leaving her three-month-old infant in the care of a sitter who was barely out of childhood herself.

Looking into Rachel's eyes, she held out her arms.

"You sure?" the girl asked. "I just fed him a bottle and he's already spat up a couple of times. He might make a mess of your dress."

Anna just stood there, arms outstretched, smiling, until Rachel relinquished the baby.

The warmth of her child against her body made Anna feel infinitely happier than any wine ever could. She lowered her head, her thick hair tenting the baby's face as she kissed his forehead, his nose, his chin. His breath smelled impossibly sweet.

She looked closely at her baby. He was going to have her own hair—silky whorls of auburn were already beginning to darken his scalp. But Anna hoped he would have David's light gray eyes. Now they were a deep, deep blue. His skin was very fair and flushed at the cheeks. Anna thought he would be beautiful. And he would be lucky. Anna deeply believed this. From the beginning, Fortune had smiled on her baby. He had a passionately devoted mother, a handsome, clever father, more stuffed bunnies, teddies, and puppies than most babies got in a year.

Stephen was making gentle, gurgling sounds, which Anna chose to interpret as contentment, knowing full well that they were probably nothing more than digestive noises. Cradling him in her right arm, she held her left hand over his body. Reaching up his own miniature hand, he clutched Anna's fourth finger, right below the wedding ring. She felt herself on the verge of tears, as she so often had been over the last few months.

She looked up at David, her mouth puckered into a frown.

David knew the look. "What's up?" he asked.

Anna shrugged.

"Anna," he said.

She gave him an imploring look. "Maybe this isn't such a good idea after all."

"What do you mean?" Rachel asked quickly, an odd note in her voice, impossible for Anna to read.

David shot Rachel a look that caused her to glance at her feet.

21

"What's going on?" David repeated.

He was angry. No one who didn't know him well would have realized that—his voice was quiet, his tone concerned. But Anna knew him. She felt that she had deeply affronted him. They had planned this evening for weeks. He had bought her the necklace, she had shopped for a special dress, and they had talked about their desire to be alone more. But the need to stay home had suddenly grown so great in her that she reached out in appeal, touched the fine wool sleeve of his gray suit. "Please, David, I—"

David looked hard into her face. Then, as if by an effort of will, the muscles around his taut mouth relaxed into a smile. He stretched out a hand and stroked the top of the baby's skull. "I think it'd be good to go out, Anna. I really do. For all of us." He bent down and kissed the top of her head. "But if you don't feel up to it, that's okay too."

Touched by David's gesture, Anna felt foolish, guilty. She shook her head to rid herself of her mood. "Never mind. I'm being—" She laughed shakily. "I guess it's just that I've never been away from Stephen for a whole evening. It feels strange. But it's crazy. Here, Rachel." She kissed the baby on the tip of the nose, nuzzled his cheek a little, then handed him over. The babysitter took Stephen back into her arms, though she avoided Anna's eyes, as if embarrassed by the scene she had just witnessed.

"We'll see you later," Anna said, unsnapping her black evening bag, removing a Kleenex and dabbing her eyes dry. "About one, I guess?"

Stephen went to the hall closet, came back with their coats, and helped his wife into her black balmacaan. They conveyed some last minute instructions to the sitter, then walked to the front door. David was holding it open for Anna when he said, "Just a sec," then stepped briskly back to the living room and exchanged a final word with Rachel, which Anna, standing by the doorway, holding her black coat tight at the neck, couldn't hear.

The night was cool for late October, and very windy. The spidery shadows of tree branches danced nervously on the Princes' broad, silver lawn. Their nearest neighbor had lit a candle in the scooped-out hollow of a jack-o'-lantern—across the road, a demonic grin and a pair of orange eyes quivered in the darkness. It was the perfect pre-Halloween night. The full moon burned whitely in the sky, obscured from time to time by scudding clouds that swept through the air like a congregation of witches on their way to a Sabbat.

Anna and David got into their black Lincoln Continental in silence.

They were well under way, the darkness enclosing them like a womb, before Anna finally gave voice to the worry that had been nagging at her all day. "David, did you see the article in the *Times* today?"

"The one about Simon?" he said with conspicuous unconcern. "Is that why you've been acting so weird?"

"Don't you think it's upsetting?"

"He's an old man, Anna. He's been in prison for the last twenty years. What the hell is there to be upset about?"

"I don't know. Sometimes, I still feel—"

"Hey, Anna, I thought we were supposed to have a good time tonight," David said. He had been tailgating a slow-moving minivan. All at once, with a quick nudge of the wheel, he moved their big Lincoln across the double yellow line to pass. Headlights blazed up ahead and a muffled horn honked wildly. Shooting ahead of the van, David pulled back into their lane without slowing down. Glancing over, Anna saw that they were doing sixty-five—far too fast for these hilly, winding roads. Her fists were hard balls in her lap.

A long moment passed before David reached across the space between them to take her nearest hand. Anna willed herself to relax. She hadn't meant to upset him, to spoil their evening.

David's tone conveyed infinite understanding. "I can certainly see why you don't like to think about that stuff, Anna. But we're talking almost twenty years."

Anna hesitated. "Did you hear about that dog?" she said softly. "The one they found on Woodland Drive?"

David sighed. "Rachel was just telling me about it when you came downstairs."

"So?"

"So? So *what?*" he said impatiently. "You think there aren't fucked-up teenagers in Stoneham, just like everyplace else? It doesn't mean a thing."

23

Staring out at the road streaming under their headlights, Anna sensed David's eyes on her briefly. She could feel his mounting annoyance, which might erupt at any moment into an unappeasable rage. And that was not what she wanted to happen. Particularly not tonight.

"I'm sorry, David," she said after a moment, moving closer to him and laying a hand on his leg. She forced a little laugh. "I'm sure you're right about Simon. This is just more hormonal craziness."

"That's better," he said, reaching down, raising her hand to his lips. "Now, come on. Let's have a good time."

The car slowed to a steady forty miles per hour and moved on through the darkness.

2

ANOTHER THRILLING SATURDAY NIGHT IN STONEHAM.

The thought made Jean Peary grimace. Five feet in front of her, on the screen of her ten-year-old Sony console, a trio of stylishly dressed matrons were exchanging crude double entendres to the accompaniment of raucous canned laughter. She watched for a while, a wan smile on her face, wondering idly whether a sitcom about the sex lives of three aging divorcees should be taken as a healthy sign of feminist progress—a step in the right direction from the days of "The Donna Reed Show" and "December Bride"— or as yet another symptom of the complete breakdown of Western civilization.

Whatever the case, the lives of these three vital, romantically active women—none of them younger than fifty—certainly didn't bear much resemblance to her own. After the third menopause joke in as many minutes, she gave a little snort of exasperation, then reached for the remote control unit lying next to her on the couch. She spent a few minutes flipping dispiritedly around the channels, pausing briefly to enjoy Gordon MacRae crooning "Oh What a Beautiful Morning" as he rode through a sun-splashed cornfield. *Oklahoma* was one of her favorite movies, but she had already seen it twice during the last couple of weeks—Why do they keep recycling the same films on these damned cable stations? she wondered for the thousandth time—and the thought of sitting through it again, all by herself on a Saturday night, seemed too depressing to bear. She aimed the remote unit at the TV like a laser gun, zapped the picture into blackness, and then, liquor glass in hand, headed into the kitchen.

Standing at the counter, she set herself up with some fresh ice and a healthy splash of Jack Daniel's. This would be her third drink of the evening. She carefully kept them small—doing so gave her a feeling of control, a reassuring sense that she was only a social drinker who didn't happen to have any society that night.

Unfortunately, it was becoming increasingly hard for Jean to maintain this comforting illusion, since she almost never had any society on a weekend night anymore, not even that of her teenage daughter. Nowadays, Rachel was almost always out on Saturday evenings, with a girlfriend, on a date—how Rachel managed to dig up the denim-jacketed long-hairs she preferred in a town filled with well-groomed preppies was a source of wonderment to Jean—or babysitting, as she was tonight, for that couple on Upper Brook Drive.

She, on the other hand, almost never went out on Friday or Saturday nights anymore. (During the week she couldn't care less about socializing, since she was generally wiped out from her job and happy to do nothing but fix supper, load the dishwasher afterward, and then sink onto the sofa with a detective novel or her trusty remote control.)

Jean Peary had just turned forty-eight, and though the idea of being only two years shy of fifty filled her with a mixture of disbelief and dread, she was not quite ready to give up on all the things the rest of the world apparently felt that a woman of her years should put behind her: Men. Romance. Fun. Sex. Three, four years before she had had a busy, even hectic, social life. She and her former husband, Bill, had been regulars at what sometimes felt like an endless round of cocktail parties, dinner parties, Sunday brunches. Even toward the tail end of their relationship, when their nonstop bickering must have made their hosts feel intensely uneasy, they had received constant invitations. The irony was that, in most respects, Jean's divorce

25

had made her feel freer, less constrained, than she'd felt in years—rejuvenated.

And now that I'm good company, now that I'm ready to laugh and enjoy myself, no one invites me anywhere.

In a way, she realized that her social isolation—almost, she sometimes felt, ostracism—shouldn't have surprised her. Stoneham, like so many exclusive suburbs, was a very insular community. Houses were spread far apart, separated in many cases by several acres of wooded property, and there was no such thing as dropping in on someone. Entertaining, which went on all the time, was formal: invitations were issued weeks in advance, calendars were crowded with plans. Jean remembered how hard it had been to juggle all their social obligations, to fit in all the get-togethers and affairs that they were asked to.

And now it was evidently impossible to fit in a forty-eight-year-old divorcée.

Though she resented her situation, Jean understood it. She had a friend, Irene, in a nearby town—a woman in the same position, with the same depressingly empty datebook—who had awakened her with a midnight phone call several Saturdays before. He voice slurred with drink, Irene had launched into a bitter complaint against several former friends who believed she was after their husbands. "Who would *want* their husbands, for Chrissake?" she had snorted. "I've been hearing all about their faults for years. They sound worse than my ex! I want to meet someone whose faults I get to discover for myself."

Without realizing it, Irene had put her finger on part of the problem. Stoneham was a family community and seemed to be devoid of single men over the age of seventeen. It was certainly not a place for bachelors. (She didn't count the twenty-year-olds home from college for holidays or semester break, though there were nights, like this one, when she half seriously wished she could.) Men her own age, newly divorced—who hardly ever wanted or got custody of their children—moved into the city or to some singles complex elsewhere in Westchester, depending on how much money the judges left them with. Their wives, anchored by their kids, stayed put. Jean didn't really believe that any of her female friends, many of whom she continued to see for an occasional lunch, thought she had designs

26

on their husbands. No, it was the formality of Stoneham that was mostly at fault. She was the unmatched woman, the fifth wheel, the person who messed up the seating arrangements at dinner parties.

This, at any rate, was the explanation she proposed to herself whenever she was feeling reasonably content with her lot. When she wasn't—when, as on this night, she was rubbed a little raw by her loneliness, by the empty evenings and the prospect of the big empty bed in her room upstairs—Jean believed she was not invited for a different reason. Then she felt she was not simply a social inconvenience, but a painful reminder of life's messy problems, of the trouble that can descend on an otherwise perfect day, when it is least expected. Stoneham was a community removed from most kinds of hardship—shielded by geography and wealth. People moved here to escape. But no Stoneham wife could be free of the fear of losing her husband.

"Shit," she said now, putting her glass down decisively and running her fingers hard through her graying hair. She eyed her watery bourbon distastefully. "A lot of good *you're* doing." Glancing up at the kitchen clock above the doorway, she was surprised to see that it was already nearing ten. She stretched, arching her back, and let out a sound somewhere between a sigh and a groan. "Might as well do something constructive."

Her first stop was the living room. All the table lamps were off, but the moonshine filtering in through the big bay window made the room bright enough for her to see. Jean had a fondness for the shabby comforts of old furniture—another thing that set her apart in her status-conscious community—and the shadowy hulks of her overstuffed sofa and easy chairs seemed like reassuring presences as she walked through the darkness to the bulky cabinet of her G.E. "audio entertainment center." It was hard to believe that anything so clunky could have ever been state-of-the-art. She could still remember how thrilled Bill had been on the day it had been delivered to their new home, twenty-five years before.

It took a moment for the receiver to warm up. When it did, she tuned in to a Charlie Parker tribute program on an FM station, turning up the volume loud enough to carry

27

throughout the entire first floor of the house. Then she walked back through the luminous darkness and into the laundry room, where she switched on the overhead light, emptied out the dryer, and began folding clothes.

Most of the things in the basket were Rachel's—sweats and socks, a few pairs of nylon panties. Ordinarily, Jean wouldn't have folded them. Rachel was a big girl, and Jean felt strongly that kids should take responsibility for their own things from an early age. Tonight, however, feeling maternal and missing her daughter, she sorted and folded and then carried the stack of clothes into Rachel's room.

It had changed dramatically over the past couple of years. Gone were the trinkets and knickknacks of childhood, the pewter animals and plastic good luck trolls, the seashell-encrusted "treasure box" and kaleidoscope collection—all of them stuffed unceremoniously into a cardboard carton and shoved to the back of Rachel's bedroom closet. In their place, scattered across the tops of the bureaus and bookcases, were the tokens of young womanhood: bangle bracelets and silver hoop earrings, mascara sticks and makeup cases. On the walls, the old posters of Michael J. Fox, Garfield the Cat, and winged unicorns soaring over a rainbow had been replaced by pictures of heavy metal rock singers, all leather and sweat and overstuffed crotches.

Jean knew from articles she had read in various women's magazines that Rachel's fascination with heavy metal music was unusual for a girl—that most fans of these aggressively macho bands were adolescent boys. But she regarded her daughter's infatuation as essentially harmless, particularly now that Rachel had invested some of her babysitting income in a Walkman, and Jean herself no longer had to be subjected to the noise.

True, Rachel had once left the lyric sheet for an album by a band called Venom lying around the living room, and Jean, examining it, had been taken aback by the sheer ugliness of its sentiments—by its dark preoccupation with sex, violence, suicide, and Satan. But she understood that her shocked reaction was precisely the point—that one of the main reasons teenagers listened to rock was to drive their parents crazy. She could clearly remember her own father's outraged response to Elvis (who seemed like a choirboy in comparison to the leatherclad freaks enshrined on Rachel's walls). In the end, she regarded heavy metal as just another adolescent fad, and her daughter's enthusiasm for it as a basically innocuous way of blowing off steam. She could certainly imagine worse.

Shoving aside a pile of costume jewelry to clear a space on the bureau top, Jean set the laundry down, then began to open drawers. She hadn't done anything like this for Rachel in years. The drawers were jammed—like most adolescents, her daughter had too many clothes—and at first Jean couldn't even figure out where Rachel kept her underwear. She found them, neatly folded, in the second drawer from the bottom, and began to lift the stack to insert the newly laundered panties underneath, as she had been taught by her own mother to do.

Something jabbed her finger.

Jean flinched, gave a little cry, and looked at her hand. Her left index finger had been sliced along the tip. She squeezed the wound gently, and a string of red drops beaded to the surface. "For heaven's sake," she murmured. The little cut hurt, but the pain was less severe than her irritation. Sucking on the finger, she reached into the drawer with her other hand and carefully lifted the underwear to see what had stabbed her.

The pleasant buzz of the bourbon had stayed with her throughout the evening. Now, all at once, she felt very sober.

At the bottom of the drawer lay a collection of objects so peculiar that, for a long moment, Jean simply stared down at them, her finger slipping from her mouth as her lips instinctively formed a silent question. What had stabbed her was a small, slender knife with a narrow blade. A dagger? she thought, shaking her head. *What the hell's she doing with a dagger?* She picked it up. It was silver—Jean could see that at a glance—and heavy too, despite its size. The handle was elaborately wrought with designs and printing of some sort. The words were too small to make out easily, but they did not appear to be English.

Two fat, partially burned-down candles, dark blue or black (Jean couldn't tell in the lamplight), sat on the dresser bottom. Beside them was a white cardboard gift box, the kind that might contain a bracelet or a pair of earrings. Jean reached into the drawer and lifted off the top. Inside, on a bed of cotton, lay a small glass vial filled with a brownish-red liquid.

Jean felt very cold. *What in God's name is going on?* Blood still ran from her fingertip, collecting around the rim of her nail. But she no longer noticed it.

Several strange objects made of feathers, beads, and what seemed to be chicken bones lay in the drawer. They looked very primitive, like something you'd see in a display case at the natural history museum. Picking them up one by one—there were three in all—she saw that they were tiny figurines or effigies, human in shape but distorted. They were curious things, and she held them for a while. But after only a few moments their weirdness seemed frightening, and she put them down with distaste.

One final item remained in the drawer: a sheet of tan, brittle paper—parchment?—folded into quarters. Hoping for a clue, Jean carried it to the desk and switched on the gooseneck lamp. The paper made a crinkling noise as she unfolded it. The message inside, crudely inscribed in what looked like brown ink, was written in a language Jean had never seen before:

Rex mantus canis devorare silut azgul sekhmed infans respirare. Nel nibur adz spiritus devorare namon mortuus lothrix rentnas. Belphegor descensus.

Though it was cozily warm in Rachel's bedroom, Jean noticed that her hands were trembling. Refolding the paper, she placed it next to the other objects on the top of the bureau.

A mirror hung on the wall above the bureau. Raising her eyes, Jean gazed at her reflection. Her face was so drawn that, for a moment, she thought she was looking at a stranger. She swallowed hard and tried a joke. "Other mothers find diaphragms. Or dope. But me . . ." But her voice trailed off.

Every book of advice for parents she had ever seen told her that she was invading her daughter's privacy, and, almost reflexively, she began to put the things back one by one and close the drawer. Then she heard an indignant voice and realized that it was her own. "What the hell are you doing?" She jerked the drawer open again and removed the objects. Carrying them into the living room, she cleared a space on the coffee table by shoving aside a stack of *Vanity Fair*s and *New Yorker*s, which slid in a heap to the floor. She was determined to get some answers as soon as her daughter walked through the door.

She needed to clear her head, to think things through. Returning to the kitchen, she filled the kettle with water, set it on the back burner, and loaded a Melitta filter with coffee. Waiting for the water to boil, she leaned against the counter and thought about her daughter. She wasn't sure what those damned objects meant, or what connection they had to Rachel's life, but she was certainly going to find out.

Unlike some of her friends, Jean was not a woman who cried easily. Now, so abruptly that she was jolted by the violence of her feelings, her windpipe clenched and her eyes swelled with tears as memories, grievances, and self-recriminations overwhelmed her. Among his other failings, Bill had never been a particularly attentive father, and during the last rancorous years of their marriage, even Jean hadn't had the emotional energy or strength of will to be the kind of mother she would have liked. She had been too busy fighting for her own survival. So the result was—Jean drew a deep, ragged breath, struggling for self-control—the result was that Rachel had slipped away during those years. There had been no open break between mother and daughter. Rachel had simply become someone Jean didn't know—a tolerant but distant housemate.

She had a sudden, unbidden recollection of Rachel at ten, her blond hair held back with a violet ribbon, giving her first solo performance on the flute after two years of lessons, in front of the elementary school orchestra and an auditorium packed with parents. Rachel wore a lemon-yellow dress and had been so excited she'd nearly floated to school. What she had played, Jean could not remember—something sweet and lilting, like bird song. She had played well and had been so brave, so full of high spirits, that, had there been no one else present in the auditorium, Jean would have wept.

She remembered another moment too. This one had occurred just before her divorce. She had returned from work one day to discover that Rachel had taken a big hank of her shining blond hair and dyed it dull black, then ratted it

31

and clipped it with some awful hair ornament that she never removed. Then there had been the ghastly, dead-white face Rachel had affected one whole winter, achieved with theatrical makeup.

And those boyfriends! Sullen, monosyllabic, they slouched in Jean's living room for a few painful minutes before bearing Rachel off to the movies. Jean had tolerated them too, as she had the punk hairstyle and bohemian makeup. For all their unkempt looks and social ineptness, they were, after all, Stoneham boys—the sons of lawyers and doctors, CPAs and advertising executives.

Perhaps, she thought now, Jean, like so many of her friends, had simply put too much of her faith in the magic of money and privilege, as though wealth were an amulet to ward away evil and secure Stoneham within a charmed circle.

She had believed that Rachel's music, her dress, her boys, were nothing but a phase, a predictable form of teen rebellion calculated to raise parental hackles. She had even secretly looked down upon mothers (some of them her friends) whose daughters too closely resembled them in dress and attitude, as if they were simply fresh-faced clones of the aging originals, homogenized products of the suburban cookie cutter. Jean had told herself again and again that if a kid didn't rebel as a teenager, she'd do it when she was thirty-three—run off to Europe with a twenty-year-old tennis bum or something and leave her two kids to be taken care of by their grandmother.

But now she wasn't sure of any of this. She carried her coffee into the living room and looked again at the things she had removed from Rachel's bureau. They seemed heavy with meaning, but meaning she could only guess at. Rachel would have to tell her. It was 11:05.

She had yearned for a little excitement in her life. She had hungered for something new and different

Well, here it is, she thought. You wanted it. You got it.

She sat down heavily on the sofa, a middle-aged mother waiting for her daughter to come home.

3

MARIANNE BYRNE SHOT AN IRRITATED GLANCE AT THE MAD-
dening flutter coming from the ceiling fixture above her
head. The dying fluorescent tube was driving her crazy, and
for a fleeting moment, she indulged in a pleasant fantasy of
putting it out of its misery with a blast from the Charter
Arms snubnose she kept strapped to her ankle.

She realized, of course, that a more reasonable course
of action would be to fetch a stepladder and replacement
tube from the custodian's storeroom and simply change the
light. But Officer Byrne wasn't feeling in an entirely reasonable mood this Saturday evening.

Part of the problem was simple weariness. She'd indulged
herself last night (though not as sinfully as she had half
hoped), and—as she'd learned from the good sisters who
had been responsible for her early education—you have to
pay for your pleasures. She had been up until almost three,
dancing and drinking at a club in White Plains with a funny,
curly-haired stereo salesman named Charlie—not exactly
tall, dark, and handsome, but (perhaps even better) single,
straight, and apparently stable. Though he lacked the muscular bulk Marianne preferred in her men, he was attractive
enough. In short, he was neither a slug nor a creep—which
already put him way ahead of most of the other guys she'd
encountered in the year since her breakup with Patrick.

Though she wasn't given to sleeping with strangers, particularly nowadays, she'd gone without sex for so long that
she'd even thought briefly about taking advantage of the
ribbed Trojan Enz she kept stored in her handbag for just
such contingencies. As a result, she had been both relieved
and crestfallen when Charlie had settled for a long, good-
night kiss in the parking lot and promised to phone her for
a date.

For some reason, the image of her eighth grade teacher,
a kindly-faced nun named Sister Margaret, suddenly drifted
into her mind. She wondered what Sister Margaret would
have to say about the little foil packets buried at the bottom

of her pocketbook. Or about the surge of disappointment Marianne had felt last night when it became clear that she wasn't going to have a chance to put them to some practical use.

Her glance fell on the reports lying on the desk, and she shook her head quickly, like a dozing person trying to snap herself awake. What a time to be daydreaming about sex, she thought.

Tilting her head back until it rested on her chair, she exhaled a long, soundless whistle of fatigue.

By the time she'd driven home last night and crawled into bed, it was almost time to get up. Her shift began at eight A.M. Mercifully, her morning patrol had been even more uneventful than usual. For once, she was grateful to be faced with nothing more challenging than a couple of parking meter violations at the railroad station lot. But around noon, just as Marianne was sliding back into her squad car after picking up lunch at the local deli, she'd received a call about a minor traffic accident on Route 28, the road that connected the hamlets of Stoneham and Collinsville and ran on north to Dutchess County.

A jet-black Mercedes, buffed to a mirror shine, had swerved off the road when its driver, a fiftyish matron with the unnaturally smooth complexion of a face-lift junkie, had tried to avoid soiling her tires on the messy remains of a flattened racoon. The woman was unhurt but hysterical— mostly, it seemed, over the minor injuries sustained by her car when it had scraped by a sapling along the shoulder. Marianne couldn't work up much sympathy for the overwrought driver. Though still a rookie, she'd already been at the scene of too many truly appalling traffic accidents. Still, she'd done her best to console the woman while they waited forever for the tow truck to arrive.

By the time she'd gotten back to the station house, her bean soup had jelled inside its styrofoam cup and her green salad resembled a clump of yesterday's lawn cuttings. She ended up dumping most of the meal in the big plastic trash barrel that hulked in a corner of the lunchroom.

Her only consolation was that her shift ended early in the day, at four P.M. In theory, at least. That things hadn't worked out that way was nobody's fault but her own.

She'd felt so lighthearted when her shift was up that,

34

instead of hightailing it out of the station house, she'd stopped to chew the fat with Tommy Reardon, the precinct's affable youth officer, who was hunched over his IBM Selectric, painstakingly tapping out a report. In spite of his twelve years as a cop, Tommy's typing style had never progressed beyond a primitive hunt-and-peck. Marianne had just perched herself on a corner of his desk when her chief, Dick Wayland, had strolled by and dropped a file folder on her lap, saying only, "Long as you're still around."

Marianne had stared at his receding back with a look poised somewhere between supplication and despair. But there was no point protesting. She gave Tommy a hopeless shrug, then trudged to the tiny report room, where she plopped herself down at the desk and began to review the file. And instantly became so deeply engrossed in it that the next time she looked up at the clock, more than an hour had passed.

Now, it was nearing seven, and she was still at it, still mulling over the details of the crime, considering the possibilities, trying to recall the particulars of similar cases she'd heard about from her father.

She knew she was going to call him in the city, but first she wanted to think things through herself, to draw her own conclusions. A matter of professional pride.

She closed her eyes, which felt as if they'd been dipped in sawdust, and massaged them gently with the heels of hands. Then, shoving her chair away from the desk, she headed for the Mr. Coffee machine that sat on a counter in the lunchroom.

Directly above the counter, a big plate-glass window stretched nearly to the ceiling. After filling her styrofoam cup, Marianne stood there for a moment, sipping the acrid coffee and gazing out into the gathering dusk.

It was going to be a beautiful October night. The branches of the tall old maples and oaks scattered on the lawn behind the station house twitched in the wind. Across the road, at the corner of Grace Street, the Episcopal Church and the town library were shuttered and silent. But there were homes on Grace Street too, and where the road curved up the hill, Marianne could see lights from the sprawling old houses—most of them built before the turn of the century—glimmering through the trees and bushes. It was a peaceful sight. Not a soul was out. There was nowhere to go in Stoneham on a Saturday night, except to one of the town's two restaurants—a chophouse and a seafood place—or to the tiny pizzeria, which stayed open until ten on weekends. Small-town sleepiness was precisely what the upscale families who moved to Stoneham were paying for.

They were also paying for security. Serious crime was virtually unknown in Stoneham. The only killing in recent memory had been a manslaughter case in 1954, fifteen years before Marianne's birth. The president of a flourishing young advertising firm had slammed his partner's skull into the sharp corner of an open metal door in the men's locker room of the Stoneham Country Club, after a quarrel over stock options that had begun on the links.

Otherwise—apart from the occasional domestic spat that degenerated into a beating—violence was almost as rare in Stoneham as middle-income housing.

The kids were the cops' biggest headache. Particularly on late weekend nights, they would speed around the twisty country roads, hitting the curves at sixty and sometimes missing, plowing into restraining rails or traffic signs or trees, or plunging into the streams that ran along the roadsides.

If they weren't totaling their daddies' Jags or BMWs, they were partying too hard and too loud, usually while their parents were away. They'd hit the liquor cabinets or pass around the drugs: grass and hash, uppers and downers, angel dust, cocaine—run-of-the-mill stuff (though never, as far as Marianne knew, crack). And before long some middle-aged neighbor, an acre away, would hear their racket drifting over the wide lawns and the trees and call the police.

Handling these kids could be tricky. Wayland had warned her of this the day she was hired, and it was one of the things that made her regret taking the job. Three months into her work she had had her first taste of how it would be.

Out on radar duty one evening, she had clocked a shiny new Saab doing fifty in a thirty mph zone. When she pulled the car over to the shoulder, the driver, a teenage boy with the most beautiful blond curls she had ever seen on a male, had leaned out his window and screamed incredulously: "Do you know who the fuck my father *is*?"

Marianne had considered letting him off with a stern warning until he'd begun shrieking at her, at which point she ordered him out of his car and asked to see his license. As it happened, he was barely sixteen and didn't have so much as a learner's permit. And when she beamed her flashlight into his car, she spotted a Ziploc freezer bag half full of marijuana lying on the passenger seat.

She'd escorted him back to the station, but after a few phone calls were made, she'd been taken aside by her chief, who commended her on her professionalism and then advised her to forget the whole incident. "Back off, Officer Byrne," Wayland had said when she'd begun protesting. "You did your job. Now drop it."

Turned out the kid's old man was some kind of hotshot Manhattan attorney. Stoneham was lousy with lawyers, and, as her chief went on to explain, those guys could tie up a case in the courts for years. There was no point in wasting the taxpayers' money. Besides, no one had been hurt. "You did your job," Wayland had repeated. "You alerted the parents. The ball's in their court now."

What kind of bullshit is this? Marianne had thought at the time. But she was too new to make waves. So she had swallowed her rage and did her best to erase the memory of the taunting look the kid had flashed her as he'd strolled out of the station house, his father's arm around his shoulder.

Now, standing at the window, Marianne swallowed a final bitter mouthful of coffee and gazed for a last moment at the perfect autumn night. As a young girl she had thought of the night as a great dark canopy, like a vast circus tent, spread high above the earth, and the stars as tiny holes poked into the fabric, through which the shining light of heaven could be glimpsed. For many people Stoneham was heaven on earth. But Marianne remembered that only yesterday, standing in this same spot, she had thought seriously about handing in her resignation. Just nine months into the job and she had already begun to think it would make her crazy—directing commuter traffic at the Main Street intersection during morning rush hour, lecturing ele-

37

mentary school classes about bicycle safety, cruising the postcard-pretty neighborhoods on dark-house patrol to check out the premises of vacationing yuppies.

It was the most routine kind of Mickey Mouse work, not even close to what she'd had in mind when she'd decided to become a cop. If it hadn't been for the promise she had made to her dad, she never would have come to Stoneham in the first place.

And then, just as her frustration had built to a peak, Dick Wayland had dropped those reports in her lap—reports that not only sickened her, but (she had to admit) thrilled her as well. At last, something significant had come her way, the kind of case she had been hoping for.

She squeezed the styrofoam cup until it caved, like a frat boy crushing an empty beer can. Then, chucking it underhand into the trash barrel, she turned and strolled back to the report room to take one last look at the documents before heading home.

She picked up the topmost report and, scowling at the eye-killing light, began to read.

Town of Northampton Police Department
Investigation Report
#641
Date and Time Reported to Police: 10/23. 0820.
Location of Incident: 23 Woodland Drive, Stoneham
Reporting Officer: N. Pasaglia

Witness 1 (Mrs. Beth Richardson, 43 Woodland Drive, Stoneham) reported the body of a dog in the road near her house. The body was discovered by Witness 2, Chris Richardson, 5. This R/O investigated and found a dead and mutilated dog in front of 23 Woodland Drive in a pile of leaves. The dog was lying on its side. The body of the dog was cold. The mouth was jammed open with a stick. The tongue had been cut off near the root. The mouth was filled with blood, but there was no apparent blood in the rest of the body. A large patch of hide had been skinned from the body. (See attached photograph A.) This R/O turned the dog on its back. The dog had been slit open from between the front legs to the rear legs. The genital area had been cut out. The intestines were nearby on the property at 23 Woodland Drive. Witness 1 said she had never seen the dog before. Owner of dog is unknown.

At 0935 this R/O was told by Chief of Police Dick Wayland to send the body to the County Medical Examiners' (at Grasslands) for examination by veterinary expert. (See Investigation Report #642. See also attached report from veterinary expert.)

This R/O returned to Woodland Drive at 1830 to interview residents at the 7 houses on Woodland. None of them could identify the dog, and no one saw anything.

Spread across the center of the desk were a half-dozen black-and-white glossies, enlarged to eight-by-ten inches, which she had removed from a manila clasp envelope inside the folder. Marianne picked them up, patted them into a stack, and began to look them over, one at a time.

The first, a full-body shot of the butchered dog, showed the animal as it had been discovered by the Richardson children. The big golden retriever was sprawled on its side, but a narrow black gash was visible under its jaw, and another could be seen running down the length of its belly. A section of its coat, about the size of a kerchief, had been peeled from the body, exposing a rectangle of raw, stringy flesh through which the pale rib cage protruded.

A few feet in front of the dog, in the lower left-hand corner of the photograph, a mound of entrails, like a knot of oversized worms, lay heaped on the lawn.

The animal had been turned onto its back for the next photograph. An officer's gloved hand was visible in the lower right corner, holding the dog's rear paws. In this picture the incisions gaped, ugly and vicious. The edges of the wounds, though, looked clean and straight, as if the cuts had been made by a cool and practiced hand wielding a razor-sharp implement.

Between the dog's hind legs, where the genitals should have been, was a neat circular hole. Even now, studying the picture for the dozenth time, Marianne found it hard to look at that part of the image.

The third photograph was a close-up of the dog's head. The stick propping the jaw open—a short length of dowel, whittled to a sharp point at either end—was clearly visible. But deeper than that, the mouth was such a mess that Marianne couldn't make out the nature or extent of the mutilation. Here and there a white tooth gleamed through the black clots of blood.

The next three pictures had been shot at the vandalized gazebo by Sam Ferris, the officer who had been dispatched to the Willow Brook Elementary School to investigate the crime.

Ferris had first photographed the little pavilion from a short distance. The congealed blood that covered the floor of the structure looked, in the black-and-white photo, like a bucketful of tar. Marianne had been shocked at the sheer quantity of blood. She hadn't known that a dog's body, even a large one, held so much.

She had had much the same response to the next photo. It was a close-up of the severed tongue, which dangled from a roofing nail that had been driven through its tip. The tongue, which terminated in a ragged mess of gristle, seemed impossibly long, and she wondered if the weight of the stump had caused it to stretch.

Ferris had then focused in on the cryptic markings, which, in his accompanying report, he had identified as "a foreign language (possibly Latin?)." Marianne had smiled thinly when she'd first read that bit of speculation. Ferris would never make a living as a cryptographer. The first time she'd looked at the photograph, she'd immediately recognized the "foreign language" as simple reverse spelling, a favorite code of occultists. Read in correct order, the message said:

SATAN LIVES
SATAN RULES
HAIL SATAN!

Ferris had been wrong about the other marking too. He'd described the symbol that appeared above the writing as a star "with an animal's face (possibly a wolf's?) inside it."

Marianne knew better, though. The star was a pentagram. And the image it enclosed wasn't the face of a wolf. It was the head of a goat.

The symbol of Baphomet, the goat-headed Satan.

Marianne dropped the stack of photographs back onto the desk and picked up the third and last report. Glancing at the wall clock, she was surprised to see that it was almost eight. She closed her eyes to rest them for a moment. In the distance, she could hear a phone ring—a soft, electronic trill—and the muffled voice of the desk sergeant, Mike Nash, answering the call.

Abruptly, Marianne became aware that she was no longer alone.

Something was looming behind her.

It was breathing heavily through its mouth, making wet, snuffling noises, which came nearer and nearer until she could feel its warm breath on the back of her neck. She tensed at the sensation, though the spark of fear that had flared in her for an instant had already faded away.

"Boo!" said a deep voice behind her.

Marianne smiled and shook her head. "Holson, you maggot."

"Happy Halloween," Mike Holson said, moving around to the front of the desk and half seating himself on a corner. "Spooked you pretty good, huh?"

Marianne leaned back in her chair and looked up at him, her thick black hair falling away from her face.

Holson had just arrived for his shift and was still dressed in his civvies. He was a good-looking man, with dark wavy hair, one of those neatly clipped moustaches favored by his generation of cops, and the broad-chested build of a Nautilus freak. If you let your vision go slack when you looked at him, you could see a trace of Tom Selleck. It was clear from the way he bore himself that, when he gazed in the bathroom mirror in the morning, *he* saw Tom Selleck. Though he'd been married for over a year to a pretty, blond nursery school teacher named Betty, he still worked hard to maintain his reputation as the station-house Romeo. And since the only other woman to be found in the Northampton precinct house was Evelyn Digges—the sixty-year-old secretary who outweighed Holson by a good forty pounds—Marianne was the sole object of his on-the-job attentions.

In fact, Marianne liked Mike Holson a good deal and vaguely regretted his unavailability. She'd been out with him a few times after work. He hadn't pushed her. She knew he would some day, but she also knew she could handle him. For now, he was a good drinking buddy. She enjoyed going out with him. He had been a cop for five years, and he was not dumb. He could teach her things, and he was willing to share what he knew.

Holson dug into the side pocket of his leather aviator jacket and came out with a small plastic bag containing a rubbery clump of iridescent candies. He held out the bag under Marianne's face.

"Gummi bear?"

Marianne grimaced and shook her head. "I don't see how you can eat that garbage."

"Like 'em," Holson said, hooking a forefinger into the bag and fishing out a few of the rainbow-colored creatures, which he dropped into his mouth. Glancing down at the desk, he lifted the topmost photo from the stack and stared at it for a long moment, shaking his head. "Fuckin' assholes," he said between chews.

Holson replaced the picture, then looked at Marianne intently. "Dick give this stuff to you?"

Marianne nodded.

"How come? You think because of your dad?"

Marianne shrugged. "I guess."

"You call him yet?"

"Uh-uh."

"For what it's worth, my own feeling is, shit like this happens. Couple of teenage jackoffs smoke a few joints, sit around listening to Twisted Whatever or maybe catch the latest 'Geraldo' special, get some bright ideas. Next thing you know, they're playing devil-worshiper with the neighbor's pet. Just have to see whether something else pops up."

"I guess."

He gave her an appraising look. "You look like you could use some shut-eye, Officer Byrne." Getting up from the desk, he gave her a brotherly pat on the shoulder. "Let me know what happens," he said. Then he was gone.

Marianne sat there for a few minutes, staring at nothing and tapping her pursed lips with the veterinarian's report, which she had absentmindedly rolled into a tube. She was thinking about what Holson had said. His explanation sounded plausible. It was certainly reassuring, and might even be true.

Marianne didn't buy it for a minute.

42

She gave a big, moaning yawn and stretched her back, arching her chest like a sprinter breaking through the tape at the finish line. One thing Holson was definitely right about. She was in desperate need of some shut-eye.

She uncurled the vet's report on the desk and scanned it quickly.

The vet's tone was brisk and detached, as if eviscerated dogs made up a normal part of his practice. The dog was a male golden retriever, approximately two years old. Belly and throat incisions had been made by a sharp, slender-bladed instrument, "perhaps a scalpel," and were "markedly at odds with the severance of the tongue," which was "clumsy," as if it had been done in haste. The vet—her eyes came back up to the letterhead to where Thomas J. Clayton's name was printed—theorized that "the mutilation of the body of the dog had been performed by a different person than had made the other wounds."

Judging from the quantity of blood in the mouth, Clayton believed that the throat had been slit and the blood partially drained through the jugular before the tongue had been removed. Then the draining had continued.

The penis and the testes had been professionally—that was the vet's word, "professionally"—excised. The trunk had been partly eviscerated. Evidence suggested that the small and large intestines had been forcibly pulled, not cut, out of the body cavity. The heart had been severed from its connections. And a rectangular section of hide, roughly nine-by-eleven inches, had been neatly flayed from the right side of the trunk.

The dog had been dead, Clayton surmised, six to eight hours before the body was discovered.

The report concluded with an interesting fact. "Blood analysis revealed trace amounts of ketamine hydrochloride, an anesthetic that is commonly administered prior to surgery on animals and that can produce catatonia."

Marianne had been momentarily puzzled the first time she'd read that line. Why had they used an anesthetic? Certainly not to spare the dog pain. That left only one explanation. The butchers, whoever they were, had wanted a docile animal, one that wouldn't bite.

Now, reading the sentence again, Marianne gave a little nod of satisfaction. She was glad ketamine had been used,

43

and not just because that meant the animal had suffered less. For one thing, it confirmed her belief that the perps weren't just sociopathic teenagers, the kind who got sadistic kicks from torturing animals. Creeps like that got off on hearing their victims howl and would never have deprived themselves of that sick pleasure by putting a dog to sleep before going to work on it.

Even more important, ketamine hydrochoride wasn't that easy to get. You couldn't just walk into a pharmacy and order it or ask your vet for it. Of course, it could have been stolen from an animal hospital. But if so, the person who stole it probably worked there. Which meant that he— or she—could be found.

Marianne let out a soft sigh of relief. Time, at last, to call it a day. She stuck the photos back in their envelope, replaced the reports in the file folder, and got to her feet. Between hunger and fatigue, she felt half-anesthetized herself, as if *she'd* just been given a shot of ketamine. Her legs felt as heavy as sandbags.

Fetching her down vest from her locker, she dropped the folder into the chief's "in" box, waved good-night to Tommy Reardon—who was fielding a phone call from a householder who'd just had his mailbox bashed—and walked outside to the precinct house parking lot, where her white '85 Honda stood waiting.

Twenty minutes later she slid the car into her assigned apartment space at the rear of a squat, red-brick building on the outskirts of Hoffmann's Falls, a historic but decidedly downscale river town thirty miles northwest of Stoneham.

Even though her first-floor apartment was tiny, it had a slightly vacant feel, as though some of its furnishings had been moved out and never replaced. Entering, she paused for an instant to toss her purse and down vest onto her old bentwood rocker, then headed straight for the kitchen.

The freezer contained nothing but a half-empty ice tray and a box of frozen French-bread pizza, but Marianne couldn't have been happier if she'd found the refrigerator shelves stocked with Thanksgiving leftovers. She tore open the box, tossed her dinner into the microwave, and zapped it, her stomach growling impatiently as the aroma of tomato sauce, melting cheese, and pepperoni began to fill the little room.

Then, grabbing a bottle of Rolling Rock from the top shelf of the fridge, she carried her supper into her room and placed it on the night table beside her bed. It took her less than a minute to change into a pair of men's-cut flannel pajamas and settle herself cross-legged on the mattress, her back propped against a couple of foam rubber pillows, the TV listings in hand, her dinner at her side.

For a full year Marianne had been unable to watch TV in bed alone without missing Patrick, one of whose favorite forms of Saturday night entertainment consisted of television, takeout food, and sex (not necessarily in that order). But tonight, sitting there with her simple meal, her remote control unit aimed at the cable box, she felt more content than she had for a long time.

After sampling most of the offerings on a score or so of channels, she finally settled on *Oklahoma,* a movie she had seen once, many years before, and remembered liking. Her plan was to polish off her dinner and drink, then snuggle down into the pillows and watch until she drifted off to sleep.

Much to her astonishment, she discovered that she had reached a point of fatigue beyond sleepiness. Her mind couldn't stop buzzing. She watched the movie until it ended, then clicked off the TV. But the silence and darkness didn't help. Finally, after trying out various positions for twenty minutes, she swung her legs off the bed and walked a few feet into the bathroom, where she removed a small bottle of Valium from the medicine chest. The tranquilizers had been prescribed by her family doctor two years before, in the bad months after her mother died. Marianne rarely availed herself of them; the pills in the bottle were part of the original prescription.

She shook a single tablet into her palm, popped it into her mouth and swallowed it with a swig of tap water. Then she returned to her bed.

This time she sank into a deep sleep almost immediately, and was soon lost in a strange and gaudy dream, featuring cowboys with clipped moustaches and a golden-fleeced creature—a goat? a lamb? a long-haired dog?—with large curling horns sprouting from its head.

She slept so profoundly that she did not respond at all when the phone rang a dozen times at one-thirty A.M. Nor did she awaken a half hour later, when it began to jangle again, with the same terrible insistency.

45

4

AT ONE-TEN IN THE MORNING THE PRINCES' BLACK LINCOLN
Continental slowly exited the Taconic Parkway and nosed
its way along Pine Ridge Road. Cocooned inside, with eyes
half closed and head cradled against her husband's shoulder, Anna Prince watched dreamily as the beams of the big
car's headlights burrowed a tunnel of brightness through
the enveloping night. The wind had blown off into the west,
sweeping the sky free of clouds. Along both sides of the
twisting, country road, the oaks and maples grew thick.
Tilting her head slightly, Anna could see the black tendrils
of the treetops silhouetted clearly against the ghostly silver
of the moonlit sky.

At the moment, she felt as blissful as a baby. Everything
about the evening had been perfect. The bud vases, each
with a full-blown white rose, that stood at the center of the
tables. The soft, pink-gold light cast by the wall sconces,
which made every woman's skin glow with the flawlessness
of youth. The succulent veal she had eaten. The incredible
wine. (What was it? Oh yes, a Montrachet, she remembered.) David's caressing voice. Everything had been perfect. Not once had she had been distracted by an anxious
thought, not even a fleeting one.

Never mind that she had eaten too much, never mind
that she was slightly drunk and hiccuping now and then.
Snuggled against her husband's body, she felt safe and serene. And unbelievably lucky. As she often found herself
doing lately, she began to recite the comforting litany of
her blessings. She was wealthy. She had a loving, handsome, and successful husband. She was the mother of a
healthy, beautiful child. She shook her head in disbelief.

"What?" David asked softly, in a tone that told her he
was smiling.

"Nothing." She nestled deeper against him. "I'm just
feeling . . . incredibly good."

He reached one hand down and stroked her left leg, moving his fingertips lightly over the place where, beneath the

silky fabric of her dress, her flesh was bare between her garter straps and stocking. "Me too." He paused for a moment. "You know, baby, I really meant it about what I said. I've missed you. I've missed you in bed. It's been months since we've had any time together."

"Mmmm," Anna murmured, smiling, but wondering fuzzily who was going to handle the two-thirty feeding. Maybe David was right, maybe they should hire someone to live in and take care of Stephen.

". . . I feel almost as if we're at the start of a whole new marriage," he was saying. "I've been thinking. Maybe we could go away for a while, just the two of us, fly to Paris or Italy . . ."

His voice droned on, soothing her into sleep. She woke a few minutes later when the car made a bumpy left onto Upper Brook Drive. There were only nine houses along the mile-long road. Theirs was number 37. As the Lincoln crunched up the gravelly road, a shaggy, gray raccoon hurried across the blaze of their headlights and vanished into the underbrush, a scrap of offal dangling from its jaws. David stopped at the end of their curving driveway. Anna sat up straight, making a small, purring sound of protest deep in her throat. She yawned loudly and said, "I'll send Rachel out."

"I'll come in with you," David said, switching off the headlights and the ignition. "Gotta use the john."

As he walked around to open her door, she shook her head to clear it. She would need to take something to stay awake. She wished she hadn't drunk so much.

David took her outstretched hand and helped her out of the car with a playful tug. As they started up the walkway, one of Anna's heels caught in a crack between the flagstones and she stumbled against his body, giggling like a sixth-grader. "Good thing you weren't driving, kid," he said, putting his arm around her and holding her steady.

Yellow light streamed out of the windows of their rambling old house, stenciling bright, cross-hatched rectangles on the lawn. "Look at that," David said with annoyance. "She turns the porch light off but she's got every other light in the goddamned place on and not a drape pulled."

"I think it looks pretty," Anna said, swaying a little as he let go of her to find his key. It took him a while, on the

47

dark porch. She looked up at the sky, savoring the sweet autumn night.

David opened the door, stood aside for Anna, then followed her into the house.

The spacious entrance hall was soft-lit and serene. Along the left-hand wall stood a simple rosewood table. On it were a creamy Deco vase, brimming with white dahlias, and a peach-shaded lamp, which cast a mellow glow on the dark-veined marble of the floor. Against the opposite wall the hardwood staircase, with its polished mahogany banister, ascended into shadow.

Anna glanced at the den to her right. Through the half-closed door she could hear the synthetic hilarity of a TV sitcom. "Rachel, we're home!" she called in that direction, then said to David, "God, I'm so thirsty. I'll be right back," and headed past the stairs and down the hall. The dining room was dark, as was the kitchen. She had just stepped into the kitchen and flipped the double switches on the wall to her right when she heard David exclaim from another room somewhere, "Jesus Christ! What the hell!"

The blank fluorescence from the overhead panels lit up the spotless white counters, the pale ceramic bowl piled with red apples, the copper cookware hanging above the stove, and the black-and-white checkerboard floor—where Rachel, completely naked, lay sprawled on her face in the grotesque semblance of a sunbather. A dark halo of blood surrounded her head. Near the scalp, her long blond hair was purple with it.

For several seconds Anna's shocked eyes could not take it in. She stood in the doorway, unable to move, unable to speak, terror clawing its way into her heart.

"Rachel!" David's voice shouted from a distance. "Where the hell are you?" Then, much closer, "Anna, something's—"

His voice set her free. Spinning, running blindly from the kitchen, she collided with him in the dining room and slammed into the wall. Staggered himself, he took her by the shoulders and felt her fingernails dig deep into his arms. Even in the darkness he could see how white her face was.

"The baby," she rasped, then was off again, crashing clumsily up the stairs, beginning to moan before she reached the top.

Stephen's tiny room seemed to shrink back from the overhead light, back from her frantic eyes and fluttering hands. The crib stood against one wall. Stephen's blue and white quilt hung half out of the crib, carelessly draped across the lowered restraining rail. Inside the crib, on the rumpled clown-printed sheet, lay his pacifier, his silver rattle, and three soft, tiny stuffed animals, which gazed up at the overhanging mobile with dead plastic eyes.

The baby was not there.

Anna fell to her hands and knees to look under the crib, she yanked open the door of the nearly empty closet, ransacked the antique painted toy chest, shoved aside the rocking chair, jerked each of the drawers out of the bureau, scattering tiny sleepers and sweaters and T-shirts around the room. Running to the far corner, she lifted the nearly life-sized stuffed pony and heaved it away from the wall.

Nothing.

She could hear David's footsteps pounding up the staircase as she ran back to the crib, tearing off the mattress, sending the stuffed toys and rattle and pacifier bouncing onto the floor.

Nothing.

Anna glanced at the doorway. Her husband leaned there, gasping loudly, a wild, uncomprehending look on his face.

Only then did she begin to scream.

5

THE JANGLE OF THE TELEPHONE EXPLODED IN THE STILLNESS of the house. Jean Peary, brooding on the living room sofa, nearly jumped off the cushion. At that time of night—and in her frame of mind—the sound was as startling as a scream.

It was 1:34 A.M. Three hours had passed with agonizing slowness since she had discovered the bizarre cache of objects in her daughter's bureau drawer. She had spent much of that time wedged into a corner of the big, overstuffed couch, staring blankly at the framed Van Gogh poster that hung on the opposite wall. Silence enfolded her. She had switched off the radio at midnight. In the mood she was in, the cool self-absorption of the jazz seemed unbearably melancholy. Outside the house the wind had died and the trees had ceased their clatter.

Jean Peary was not a woman given to brooding, but for the past several hours she had been able to do little else, caught in the clutch of a paralyzing distress, a dark, bitter emotion compounded of sorrow, dread—and anger. Anger at herself, at her daughter, and at a world too full of dangers and pitfalls for the young and vulnerable.

From time to time she would lean forward and snatch at the small parchment scrap that lay folded on the coffee table. Opening it, she would stare hard at the sinister-sounding gibberish and try to make sense of it. Was it a foreign language? A secret code? Perhaps, she thought hopefully, the message was completely innocuous. "Dear Diary, today Tommy Jones took me to Pop's Malt Shoppe for a strawberry milk shake and afterward tried to kiss me on the lips." The fantasy only made her more depressed. Grimacing disgustedly at the smudgy brown sheet, she had flicked it back onto the coffee table and retreated into her bleak, futile reveries.

Shortly after one she had hauled herself off the sofa and trudged into the kitchen for some more coffee. She wanted a clear head for her imminent confrontation with Rachel. The glass Melitta pot still held a cold cupful. Taking a mug from the cupboard, she poured in the coffee, then walked across the kitchen to the microwave.

As she set the timer and punched the start button, her eyes fell on the big wicker basket she had filled that afternoon with candy for trick-or-treaters. There were Three Musketeers, Mars bars, Milky Ways, and Kit Kats—all of them factory sealed.

When Rachel was younger, Jean had never thought twice about handing out—or letting her daughter consume—loose pieces of Halloween candy. She would buy small paper sacks printed with black cats and bright orange jack-o'-lanterns, fill them with goodies—candy corns, nonpareils, Milk Duds, and M&M's—then tie the bags closed with black ribbon. Nowadays, no sane parent would allow a child to eat anything that hadn't come packed in an unopened box or wrapper. Even in Stoneham, rumors abounded every post-Halloween week of youngsters who had bitten into apples booby-trapped with razor blades or who had been rushed to the hospital after eating a piece of poisoned chocolate.

The shrill electronic beep of the microwave jarred her from her thoughts. Removing the mug, she added a splash of milk to the bubbling coffee and headed back to the living room. On her way out of the kitchen she glanced up at the wall clock over the doorway: 1:16 A.M. Rachel had to be home any second. She was already later than Jean expected.

Exactly eighteen minutes later the phone rang in the family room. Fortunately, Jean had just set down her half-empty mug on the coffee table. If she hadn't, her white couch would have been spattered with brown, so violently did she start at the unexpected noise. It took her only a few seconds to dash from the sofa to the family room. She had lifted the receiver before the phone could ring twice. But that was still long enough for the fear to rise into her throat like bile.

"Yes?" she said. Considering her agitation, she was surprised at how controlled she sounded.

"Mrs. Peary?" The caller was a man, someone she didn't recognize. The tension in his voice was palpable.

"This is Jean Peary. Who is this, please?"

"David Prince, Mrs. Peary. Rachel was babysitting for us. I'm sorry to have to tell you this, Mrs. Peary, but there's been an accident here, and—"

"An accident?" she cried, cutting him off. The thudding of her heart made her voice quaver slightly. "Is Rachel hurt?"

"Yes. But I think she's okay."

"You *think* she's . . . Oh my God," Jean rasped.

"She was attacked. In our house."

"Attacked?" For a moment the room went out of focus. Jean blinked hard to clear her vision. "Attacked," she repeated—this time in a quiet, incredulous tone.

"Mrs. Peary, please. Listen to me. Someone broke into our house, Rachel was attacked, and she's unconscious. But her breathing sounds okay. The police are on their way. And an ambulance. Can you come over here?" In the background Jean could hear a high, keening sound, the kind of noise she associated with widow's crepe and graveyards. "Look," said Prince, "I've got to get off the phone. My

51

wife is in a bad way." He paused and drew in a ragged breath. "Our baby's gone."

"What!?"

"Kidnapped."

"Oh my God," Jean said again. "What's your address?"

"Thirty-seven Upper Brook Drive. Do you know where that is?"

Jean held her breath for a moment, listening. Somewhere in the distance, faint but audible, a siren's wail cut through the night.

"I'll find it," she said grimly.

6

PETE RYDELL, THE DESK SERGEANT ON DUTY WHEN DAVID Prince's call came in at 1:28 A.M., immediately got Stew Markowitz on the radio and sent him speeding from his patrol sector to Upper Brook Drive. Moments later Rydell rousted Lyle Kimball out of the Hudson View Diner, where he was just polishing off a cup of black coffee and a cinnamon Danish the size of a salad plate.

In his seven years with the Northampton P.D., Rydell had never needed to contact Chief Wayland at home, and he wasn't looking forward to the experience. Wayland could be a mean s.o.b. even after eight hours of sleep, but nothing put him in a nastier mood than a wakeful night. Word around the station house was that any dispatcher who disturbed the chief before daybreak had better have a major crisis on his hands.

Well, Rydell thought, crises didn't come any more major than this—at least not in Stoneham. He punched the chief's home number on the phone and waited.

Janet Wayland picked it up on the second ring. Her groggy "Hello" was tinged with alarm.

"Sorry to disturb you, Mrs. Wayland. It's Pete Rydell. I've got to talk to the chief." He could hear the shuffle of blankets and Wayland's sleep-thickened voice asking who it was as his wife passed him the phone.

"Yeah?" Wayland said.

52

"Chief, this is Rydell. I'm on the desk. We've got big trouble here, Chief." He paused for emphasis. "You still there?"

"Where the hell else would I be?" A deep, phlegmy rumble echoed over the phone as Wayland cleared his throat. "So?"

"Ready for this?" Rydell said. "We've got a missing baby out on Upper Brook Drive. It looks like a kidnapping, Chief. And an assault on the babysitter watching the kid."

A tense half minute passed in silence. Rydell could picture the chief propped up on one elbow, phone to his ear, his heavy-lidded eyes widening as the news burned the last shreds of fog from his brain.

"Jesus God," Wayland said at last. He was fully awake now, his voice sharp and commanding. "Who've you called?"

"I sent Kimball and Markowitz out—they should almost be there by now. And an ambulance is on the way."

"Good. We gotta have more people, though. Call Holson and Morino. Tell Morino to bring a print kit. And get Kimball and Markowitz back on the radio and tell 'em not to touch *anything*. Call the Prince house if you can't reach them." Wayland paused for a moment, then said, "If you can get hold of Byrne, tell her to haul her ass over there too."

"Byrne?"

"The baby's mother is gonna be off her nut. Byrne might come in handy."

Rydell hadn't thought of that. "Okay."

"How old's the girl?"

"The babysitter? Sixteen."

"And the baby?"

"I think just a few months. Real little. Wait a minute." Rydell checked the scrap of paper he had scrawled David Prince's message onto. "Three months old."

"Jesus," Wayland said again. "Okay, give me the address. I'm on my way."

The night air was sharp, cold enough to frost Wayland's breath as he squeezed behind the wheel of his navy-blue Dodge. He started the engine with a twist of the ignition key, stuck his portable dome light out the window and onto the roof, then backed the car out of his driveway. Through the windshield he could see the aluminum siding of his modest split level pulsate with the red glow from the rotating beacon on his car roof.

Heading along Howells Road, Wayland shook his head in disgust at the crappy tricks life could pull on you. Things had been going so smoothly for him lately. His daughter, who had dropped out of college to follow her musician boyfriend out west, was back home and enrolled at the local branch of the state university, where she was majoring in accounting. His eighty-three-year-old father, a headstrong widower who had refused to abandon his declining Bronx neighborhood, had finally agreed to move into a nice nursing home in Yonkers, removing a big worry from Wayland's mind. And in another two months the mortgage on his house would actually be paid off! The way real estate prices were booming in the area, Wayland figured he'd be sitting pretty when it came time to retire in a couple of years.

He had been counting on spending those years in relative peace and quiet, And now all this shit had landed in his lap. First a chopped-up dog. And now a missing baby. And both in one week!

As he swung onto Hawthorne Drive, turning the wheel with both hands, he winced at the pain in his shoulders. Lately, he wondered if he was developing arthritis. The cold seemed to make every joint in his body ache. Though he'd switched on the heater as soon as he'd started the engine, the car still felt like a mobile meat locker. Wayland took one hand off the wheel and pulled his coat collar close around his neck. Maybe he had goddamned Lyme disease. He was not a man who worried about his health, but something about a disease you got from ticks gave him the creeps.

Just two weeks before, he'd spent a sunny Sunday afternoon in his backyard, raking and bagging leaves. That night, soaking in his tub, he'd noticed a small black speck on his forearm, and thinking it was a spot of dirt, flicked it with a finger. When it stayed put, he'd looked closely and saw that it had legs. It had taken him a good ten minutes to work the little bastard out of his flesh with his wife's eyebrow tweezers.

54

Fucking deer ticks. Fucking mutilated dogs. And now this! What the fuck was going on? Northampton used to be some kind of paradise. "Idyllic" was the word his wife would use when she'd describe the area to her friends from the city after they'd moved here twenty years ago.

Now it was crawling with parasites. And something worse.

Wayland exhaled deeply, his breath rising before him like a ghost. There was no doubt about it. The whole world was going to hell.

7

BEFORE KNOCKING, WAYLAND STOOD FOR A MOMENT OUT-side the Princes' front door and looked around.

The sprawling colonial was located on a fairly isolated, lightly traveled road, giving it the kind of privacy that, in this part of America, only large quantities of money can buy. Coming up Upper Brook Drive, Wayland had passed only a few other homes along the half-mile stretch between the turnoff and number 37. One of them, a big Georgian manor, sat on a sloping hill across the road from the Princes' property. From that distance the manor seemed devoid of life. There were no lights on, not a single sign of curiosity over the fact that an ambulance and a string of police cars were parked in the Princes' long circular drive-way. Or that intermittently, but quite audibly, someone in-side the Princes' home—someone female—was wailing with grief.

Perhaps the sound couldn't carry that far. Dense clumps of trees dotted the wide lawns between the two houses, and even at the end of October they would absorb noise. Or maybe no one was at home at the other address.

In any event, it wasn't the kind of neighborhood that produced good witnesses.

As Wayland raised his gloved hand to knock, he noticed that, though every light switch inside the Prince house seemed to have been thrown, the porch lamp—a single-bulb affair in the shape of an old-fashioned carriage lantern—was dead. The fact struck Wayland as peculiar.

Holson answered his knock. "Chief."

Wayland nodded and stepped inside. The warmth was welcoming. But the sights and sounds—the crouching detective dusting for prints, the distraught young couple on the living room sofa, the tight-lipped paramedic hurrying past them, trauma box in hand—made it unmistakably clear to Wayland that he had arrived at the scene of a tragedy. "Fill me in."

Holson nodded his head in the direction of the couch. "Those are the parents. The Princes. David and Anna."

Wayland turned to get a better look into the living room.

It was large and tastefully decorated, full of sleek furniture and beige fabrics and antique Oriental rugs. Everything seemed to be in order, except for the overturned end table that Morino was busy brushing with powder, and the shards of a large terra cotta vase scattered across the hardwood floor.

The couple on the sofa seemed lost in grief. The woman was bent nearly double, her arms wrapped tightly across her stomach, as though she'd been socked in the belly. She was rocking slowly but steadily back and forth, emitting a soft whimpering sound that occasionally rose to an anguished cry.

Beside her sat her husband, staring emptily at the floor, one hand absently massaging the back of his wife's neck. Suddenly, David Prince seemed to become aware of Wayland's presence. He looked up at the chief, nodded grimly, then leaned down to whisper something soothing into his wife's ear.

"She's pretty upset," Holson said. "The baby was their only kid."

Wayland shot him a sideways look. "You think she'd feel better if they had a couple of others?"

Holson blinked a few times. "No, sir."

Pulling off his gloves, Wayland stuffed them into a pocket of his overcoat and turned away from the living room. "Where's the girl, the babysitter? And where's Markowitz?"

"Everyone else is in the kitchen back there. Except Lyle—he's upstairs taking pictures of the baby's room."

"So what'd you find out?"

"We got the story from the babysitter." Holson flipped open his notepad. "Rachel Peary, sixteen, lives here in town with her mother. The girl had put the kid to bed at around ten-thirty and was sitting in the den—"

"Where's that?"

Holson gestured with the pad, over Wayland's shoulder. "Back there. Across from the living room."

"Okay."

"The baby was asleep upstairs. The girl was watching TV—"

"What was she watching?"

Holson consulted his notes. " 'Saturday Night Live.' "

"Go on."

"At approximately midnight, the girl hears the doorbell ring and comes out here to ask who it is."

Wayland glanced around at the front door. It was a traditional solid-wood, six-panel door, painted a creamy white to match the color of the entranceway walls. There was no peephole in it.

Wayland looked back at Holson and nodded.

"She hears a guy say 'Federal Express,' so she opens the door—"

Wayland raised his eyebrows.

Holson shrugged. "She says she didn't know they don't make deliveries at night."

Wayland thought for a moment, his mouth puckered slightly as he chewed the inside of his cheek. "All right."

"When she opens the door, there's a guy standing on the porch, holding a big envelope."

"She get a good look at him then?"

Holson shook his head. "The foyer light was off. And the porch light is burned out."

"I noticed that."

"So this guy says he has a delivery for David Prince and the girl has to sign for it. Only he can't find his pen. He starts patting his pockets, like he's looking for one."

Wayland shook his head wearily, knowing what was coming.

"So the girl says wait a minute, there's one in her pocketbook. She turns away, and the next thing she knows, the guy's inside the house."

"What'd he look like?"

57

Holson gave a little shrug. "This hallway's real dark when the light is off. I checked. And the guy had a nylon pulled over the top of his face. Down to here." Holson drew a forefinger across his moustache.

"Smart. So then what?"

"The girl starts to scream, but the guy clamps a hand over her mouth. Tells her if she acts nice, she won't get hurt. She gives him a shove, but he grabs her by the shoulders and slams her back against the wall, real hard. Next thing she knows, she's flat on her back and the guy is sitting on her chest with a blade at her throat."

"Did he cut her?"

"Not then. He starts stroking her hair, telling her how pretty she is, the usual shit. The girl figures she's history. Then he says . . ." Holson flipped a page of his notepad and studied it for a moment. "He says, as best she remembers, 'You'd be fun, but I can't hang around. Where's the baby?' "

Wayland grunted.

"The girl tells him she won't show him. He presses harder with the knife. She says, okay. He lets her up." Holson paused, looking hard at the chief. "And then he says something interesting."

"And what was that?"

" 'Payback time.' "

Wayland's eyes narrowed. "Yeah, I'd call that interesting." He chewed the information over for a moment, then said, "Keep going."

"As soon as the girl's on her feet, she makes a beeline for the kitchen phone, figuring to push the 911 button on the autodialer. She makes it to the kitchen, but before she can get her hands on the phone, the guy tackles her from behind. Next thing she knows, she's coming to on the floor, naked, bleeding from the head, Prince kneeling beside her, calling her name."

"Was she raped?"

"They don't think so. If she was, he did it while she was out cold."

Wayland made a disgusted sound. "What's happening with her now?"

Holson stuck his pad into his back pocket. "The paramedics are just about to cart her off to northern Westchester. Her mother's in there too.''

"I want to talk to her for a minute before they take her away. I—'' Wayland stopped short, suddenly aware that Holson was looking past him. Swiveling his head, Wayland saw that David Prince had come up behind him and was standing a few feet away.

Wayland turned and held out his hand. ''Mr. Prince,'' he said solemnly. ''Richard Wayland, chief of police. I want you to know how sorry I am that this has happened. It goes without saying that we'll do everything in our power to get your child back safely.''

Prince had a hard, dry handshake, as Wayland would have expected from the look of the man. Tall, fit, and commanding, he was the kind of man who made the chief feel self-conscious about his own middle-aged paunch and bland civil servant's wardrobe. Even with his shirt collar open, tie askew, suit jacket rumpled and shoulders slumped slightly with grief, Prince created an impression of power and authority. He looked like the sort of executive who keeps an exercycle in his office and spends an hour a day on the squash court. Even now, in late October, his complexion was tanned. At the moment, however, his coloring looked sickly—more jaundiced than brown—and his face seemed taut with the effort to control his emotions. Though Wayland had trouble warming to hardchargers like Prince, the stricken look on his face made the chief's heart go out to the other man.

"I'm sure you'll do your best," Prince said. He glanced quickly at Holson, then, keeping his voice low, said, ''Chief Wayland, we've got a three-month-old infant in the hands of a psychopath. I know you understand the urgency of the situation. I'm assuming that kidnapping—and particularly baby-snatching—is not the kind of crime your department deals with every day.''

"What are you saying, Mr. Prince?''

"Just this. We want our baby back alive. Are you sure your department has the resources to deal with something like this?''

Wayland could sympathize with Prince's concern and even understand his need to exert some control over the situation. Still, he couldn't help bristling a bit at the sugges-

59

tion that he and his men weren't adequate to the job—partly because he secretly harbored some doubts on that score himself.

"Mr. Prince, there aren't any better cops in the county than my men."

"I don't mean to insult your abilities," Prince said gravely. "My wife and I just want our son back."

Wayland nodded. "Of course."

"What can we do to help?"

"To begin with, we'll need whatever information you can give us." Wayland motioned Holson to his side. "Officer Holson and I will be back in a moment. I just want to put a few questions to the babysitter first. I understand she's about to be taken to the hospital."

Prince closed his eyes and rubbed the back of his neck. "Right," he said with a sigh that seemed to originate somewhere deep in the chambers of his heart. "We'll wait for you in the living room." Turning, he walked back to the couch, where his wife sat whimpering, cocooned by grief.

Wayland asked Holson to show him the way to the kitchen.

Like the other rooms they passed through, the kitchen had an oddly formal quality, as though it had been designed for display, not for any purpose as mundane as cooking. Everything about it—the sleek white countertops and ceramic-tiled walls, the stainless steel fixtures and glass-paneled cabinets—was a proclamation of money and good taste. Not a cabinet door was ajar, not a dirty dish or unwashed utensil was in evidence. Nothing was out of place.

Nothing, that is, except for the small group of people clustered at the far end of the room.

Stewart Markowitz was there, with an open notepad in one hand and a ballpoint in the other. He was talking heatedly to a paramedic—a powerfully built black man with insignias stitched to the sleeves of his windbreaker and a beeper clipped to his belt. Though Wayland couldn't make out the words, it was clear that the two men were engaged in some kind of dispute.

Beside them, on a kitchen chair, sat a middle-aged woman in a bulky sweatshirt, down vest, and jeans. She seemed totally oblivious to the two men as she reached down and stroked the hand of the pale figure lying motionless on the stretcher at her feet. On the other side of the stretcher knelt a second paramedic, who was adjusting a broad strap across the blanketed midsection of the recumbent figure.

As Wayland crossed the kitchen, the kneeling paramedic rose to his feet and, looking at his partner, said "Quit arguing with the man. We got our instructions. Let's go."

His partner nodded and, without saying another word, turned away from Markowitz.

Spotting Wayland, Markowitz pointed his chin at the paramedics. "These gentlemen"—he spoke the word with heavy irony—"aren't being real cooperative, Chief."

Wayland stepped over to the nearer of the two paramedics—the one Markowitz had been wrangling with—took him by the elbow and led him a short distance away from the stretcher.

"I'd like to ask the girl a few questions," Wayland said after identifying himself.

"No way is this girl doing any more talking," the paramedic said, shaking his head emphatically. "No way."

"Look, Mister—" Wayland peered at the name tag on the pocket of his jacket. ". . . Mr. Campbell. It's very important that we talk to her now. She's the only witness."

"I understand that. But this girl's got a head wound. No telling how serious. Time counts."

"We're wasting time right now," Wayland said. He looked down at the girl. She had a thick gauze bandage taped to her forehead. Her puffy left cheek was blotched, but the rest of her face was as pale as the bandage. Her eyes were closed. A gout of blood had crusted between her swollen nose and split upper lip, and a thin line of red ran across the center of her throat, where the skin had been sliced by something very sharp. Wayland could see that the cut was superficial.

"Is her skull fractured?" Wayland asked, keeping his voice low.

Campbell shifted his weight from one leg to the other. "Probably not," he conceded after a moment. "But it's hard to say without X-rays. Could be a hairline."

"I can do this in a few minutes."

His face sour, Campbell shrugged. "It's up to her," he said, jerking his thumb toward the middle-aged woman who

61

sat holding her daughter's left hand in both of hers. Wayland looked at her closely. Her complexion was nearly as white as her daughter's, but she had a strong, handsome face, though at the moment it was pinched with anxiety.

Wayland walked over and stood beside her chair. "Mrs. Peary?" he asked.

"Yes," she answered without looking up.

"Richard Wayland. I'm chief of the Northampton Police Department. I'm sorry about all this."

"Thank you," Jean said tonelessly.

"You know there's been a baby abducted from here."

Jean's head bobbed. "Yes," she said in a hoarse whisper.

"I'd like to talk to your daughter for just a few moments."

Jean looked up at Wayland. "She's already told your men everything she knows. Can't this wait until later?"

"No, it can't. Time matters in a kidnapping, Mrs. Peary. Especially with an infant. They don't do well away from their mothers. And there's another thing. Kidnappers find out that babies are a lot more trouble than they thought. So anything can happen. And it can happen quickly."

Jean took a deep breath, blew it out tiredly, then turned to her daughter. "Rachel," she said softly, giving her daughter's hand a gentle squeeze.

The girl looked up at her mother, wincing slightly, as though it hurt just to open her eyes.

"Honey, do you feel up to talking to this policeman? Just for a minute?"

Rachel's gaze shifted to Wayland. Her hazel eyes were rimmed with red. She gave a slight, barely perceptible nod.

Wayland crouched by the girl's head, groaning inwardly at the strain on his knees. Behind him, Holson leaned forward, pen and notepad at the ready.

"Rachel, I'm Chief Wayland. I know this is hard for you, and I appreciate how brave you're being. I'll keep this as short as possible. Rachel, we need to know as much about the kidnapper as you can remember. When you first opened the door, could you tell anything about him? About his looks or age or anything?"

"Not really," Rachel answered, so faintly that Wayland had to cock his head so that his ear was closer to her mouth. "The bulb in the porch lamp had burned out, I guess, and the foyer light was off. So I could just see a shape."

"Was he wearing any kind of uniform?"

"He had on a jacket. And some kind of a cap."

"What kind? Did it look like Officer Holson's here?"

Rachel glanced over Wayland's shoulder. "No. More like a trucker's cap."

"How about when he entered the house? Did you get a better look at him then?"

"Not his face. He had this mask on, like a nylon stocking. Not over his whole face, just down to his mouth. He looked so creepy," she whimpered.

"Yes? Was there anything particular you noticed about the part of his face that wasn't covered? His mouth or his chin?"

Rachel thought for a moment. "He didn't have a moustache or anything. I don't know. He just looked like a guy."

"A white guy? A black guy?"

"White."

"Was he tall or short? Fat or thin?" Wayland asked.

"He was around six feet, maybe slightly less. And I think he would weigh like, I don't know, maybe 160 pounds. He was strong, but he wasn't heavy."

Wayland could hear Holson's pen scratching away above him. "Rachel," he said. "I realize this is painful, but we have to know everything we can about this man. Did he touch you?"

"You mean sexually?"

"Yes."

She drew in a ragged breath. "No. He was *saying* creepy things to me, like how much fun he could have with me if he had time. But he didn't do anything. So after a while I thought, well, maybe this guy's just some creep and once he's scared me he'll leave. I began to hope maybe it was just some sick joke or a bet some kid had with a friend—"

"Some *kid?*" Holson interrupted sharply. "This was a kid?"

"Well, I don't mean a kid kid. I mean some young guy, eighteen or nineteen or something."

"What made you think that?" asked Wayland.

"I don't know." She frowned. "Yeah, I do. He had like a very young body. Broad shoulders, narrow hips. He just looked young, you can just *tell* about a guy, even from the back. And he *sounded* pretty young."

"I see. Go on."

"Well, anyway, then I said, 'Look, have you had enough? You've had your fun, now will you leave?' And then he said, 'Not quite. I'm gonna go soon. But you have to take my hand and show me where the baby is.' 'The baby?' I said. 'What do you want with Stephen?' and he goes, 'Is that the little bastard's name?'

"I told him he couldn't have Stephen, that I wouldn't show him where he was, and he just laughed and said, 'Shit, I'll find him with or without you. What are you going to do about it?' And I knew he was right. I was so *scared*. I probably would have done anything." Her voice cracked slightly, and she paused, clearing her throat. "But anyway, I didn't get a chance to show what a coward I was. I pushed him and began to run toward the kitchen. It was like a reflex or something. I think maybe I had some idea that if I got to the phone, there'd be an emergency button. I could hear him behind me, like one of those dreams when you can't get away. The next thing I knew, he grabbed me from behind. I couldn't breathe or move. I was lying there on my face on the floor, trying to catch my breath. I thought I was dying. It felt like my ribs had punctured my heart or something. Then I heard him get up and walk away and I couldn't even move. A few seconds later, he came back and I started to lift my head to see. Then something hit me." Her eyes were squeezed tight, and her voice was small and unsteady. "And then there was nothing."

"So you didn't see the baby removed from the house?"

"No."

"And you don't know what he hit your head with?"

"No."

"Chief Wayland, *please*," Jean Peary said in a tone that was half reprimand, half plea. "Hasn't she—"

"Just a few more questions. Please, Mrs. Peary," Wayland said. Then, turning back to the girl, he asked, "Rachel, did you see a car or van or any kind of vehicle out on the driveway when you first opened the door."

"No," she said miserably. "I didn't look."

"And you don't know whether he had an accomplice?"

Rachel, weeping now, mouthed soundlessly, "No."

"Enough," Jean entreated.

Wayland rubbed a hand over his mouth and, sighing, got slowly to his feet.

"Can I take my patient to the hospital now?" Campbell asked.

"Yeah. I'll walk outside with you. Rachel, Mrs. Peary, thank you again. You've been a big help already."

As the two paramedics began to wheel the stretcher toward the doorway, Wayland glanced at Holson, who stepped over to the girl's mother. "If I could just get your address and phone number, Mrs. Peary?"

Wayland followed the stretcher out to the ambulance. As he passed the living room, he spotted a gray-haired man dressed in a cable-stitch sweater, tan trousers, and loafers, seated on the living room couch, speaking quietly to Anna Prince. Her doctor, Wayland guessed. He hoped she hadn't been given a sedative.

Outside, the air was as cold and sweet as a draught of iced cider. After Rachel was loaded in the ambulance and Campbell had swung the rear doors shut on her and the other attendant, Wayland said, "Listen, I want you to tell whoever examines her to check if she's been sexually assaulted."

"She said she wasn't."

"That was while she was awake. Some of these creeps get off on seeing women struggle. Others like to have them quiet."

"I'll see to it." Campbell climbed into the driver's seat and stuck his head out the window to back carefully out of his space. As the ambulance pulled out of the driveway, Wayland inhaled deeply and started back into the house. Just then Jean Peary came rushing down the front steps and nearly collided with him.

"Have they left already? I just stopped to give those poor people my condolences. I was going to ride with her."

"She seemed all right, Mrs. Peary," he reassured her. "Would you like one of my officers to drive you to the hospital?"

Jean smiled wanly and shook her head. "I have my car here."

Wayland felt profoundly tired. "Thanks for letting us talk to your daughter. We're going to need all the help we can get."

Jean gave a short, mirthless laugh. "You're not the only one, Chief Wayland," she said. Then, walking briskly to her aging Volvo station wagon, she got inside and drove off after the ambulance.

8

BY THEN, TWO MORE OF WAYLAND'S MEN HAD ARRIVED: Sergeant Ernie Cosgrove—a bull-necked forty-year-old with a military crew cut and eyes as round and blue as the Gerber baby's—and Lieutenant Raymond Miles, the only black on the Stoneham force. Tall and debonair, with a piercing gaze and a pencil moustache, he looked enough like the actor Billy Dee Williams to have been nicknamed "Lieutenant Lando" by some of the younger patrolmen, who had been raised on a steady diet of *Star Wars* movies.

Inside the house, Wayland put his men to work: Markowitz and Morino lifting prints, Kimball examining the carpet in the baby's nursery inch by inch, Miles checking for clues in the hallway and kitchen. Though Wayland assumed that any tire marks or footprints left by the kidnapper would have long since been obliterated by all the comings and goings, he sent Holson and Cosgrove outside with a pair of heavy-duty flashlights to see if they could turn up anything suspicious.

Then, removing his overcoat and draping it across the polished banister in the hallway, he went to join the Princes in the living room.

David Prince was quietly conferring with the doctor in the center of the room. Anna Prince had uncurled herself and was sitting more or less upright on the sofa. She looked devastated—her eyes bloodshot and vacant, her chestnut hair a tangled web, her face as white as a death's head, except for the sooty streaks of mascara that had dribbled down her cheeks.

Spotting Wayland, David Prince whispered something to

66

the gray-haired doctor, who nodded and moved to a quiet corner of the room, where he slipped on a pair of half-lens reading glasses and began searching for something inside his black leather bag. Prince picked up an armchair with a carved wood frame and leather seat, carried it across the room and placed it in front of the sofa. Then he sat down beside his wife, while Wayland lowered himself onto the chair.

Leaning toward Anna Prince, Wayland quietly identified himself.

The sound of his voice seemed to call her back from someplace faraway. Her eyes slowly came into focus and, for the first time, she became aware of Wayland's presence. She gave a barely perceptible nod. Her hands were clasped so tightly on her lap that the pressure of her arms caused her breasts to swell over the top of her low-cut black dress. Wayland chided himself for noticing the size and shapeliness of her breasts, a wildly inappropriate observation under the circumstances. Still, it seemed equally inappropriate to him—a man with old-fashioned notions of propriety—that a married woman and mother should be dressed in such a provocative manner.

"Mrs. Prince, I know this is a bad time to bother you," Wayland said softly. "But every minute counts in a situation like this. I need to find out from you and your husband if you can think of anyone who might have reason to do this terrible thing."

Though the question had been addressed to Anna Prince, the answer came from her husband. "No one," he said emphatically. "I suppose it's remotely possible that there's someone who feels they got screwed in a business deal, but—"

"No!" Anna Prince's cry startled her husband into silence. Wayland was startled too, and stared at the woman, who sat there glowering at her husband, her body so taut that Wayland could see a vein throbbing at the base of her neck.

"No," she repeated bitterly. "Don't lie! You know who did it! You know!" With every word, her voice rose in pitch and volume, until she was shrieking at her husband, flecks of spittle gathering at the corners of her mouth. "It was Simon!" she screamed. "He said he'd get back at us!"

Her face, like her voice, was racked with rage and hatred. But staring at the anguished woman, Wayland saw something else in her face too.

Anna Prince was scared to death.

"Anna, for God's sake," David said quietly. He placed a comforting hand on her shoulder, as if to quiet her trembling, but with a sudden, vicious motion, she reached up and knocked it away. David looked stricken, but something seemed to flicker in his eyes—a cold angry glint that flared up and faded so swiftly that Wayland thought he might have imagined it.

"It's true!" Anna hissed. "Why won't you face it?" Her fists were clenched into tight balls, her face contorted.

"Anna," David said softly, shaking his head. "This is crazy—"

Wayland interrupted. "Who is this Simon?"

Anna turned and glared directly at Wayland. Her wide eyes glittered with tears. "He's an awful man!" she cried. "Dangerous and evil." Her voice shook, her lower lip trembled. "He murders people! And now he's taken our baby!" Anna Prince gave a hopeless, bellowing moan, her body crumpled and, burying her face in her hands, she surrendered again to a raw, animal grief.

David shot a desperate look at the doctor, who had been watching the scene from a discreet distance. Now, the older man stepped quickly to the sofa, a hypodermic needle in one hand and a damp wad of cotton in the other. Wayland saw there was no point in protesting—the sorrowing woman was in no shape to talk.

Seating himself beside Anna, the doctor whispered soothingly into her ear—"Just a gentle sedative, it'll make you feel better"—stroked the alcohol-soaked cotton over her upper arm and slid the needle into her flesh. Then, supported on either side by the two men—David holding her around the waist and the doctor cradling her right arm—Anna was helped from the couch and led toward the stairway. As David passed Wayland's chair, he looked down and said mournfully, "I'll be back in few minutes."

After they had left the room, Wayland stood up, sighing. Extreme physical tiredness always made him feel like the Tin Woodman in *The Wizard of Oz*—joints rusted stiff and

68

insides as hollow as an empty oil drum. He was dying for a smoke. But he was six weeks into his latest attempt to kick his nicotine habit, and when he reached his left hand into his pants pocket, all he felt was a plastic container of Tic Tacs. He pulled it out, popped it open, and spilled a half dozen of the green pellets into his mouth. They didn't do much to kill his craving for tobacco, but he had to admit that his wife seemed a lot happier about kissing him lately.

Directly in front of Wayland, on the wall behind the sofa, hung a somber framed print of a strange, craggy isle, with towering cypress trees and dark holes, like tunnel openings, cut into the sides of its sheer, soaring cliffs. The sky was gray and lowering, and on the black waters surrounding the isle, a small boat piloted by a white-hooded figure seemed to glide toward the shore, where a huge, hulking creature— to Wayland it looked like a dragon with a dog's face— crouched on the rocks.

Wayland—whose taste in art ran to Leroy Nieman sports scenes and Frederic Remington cowboys—studied the picture thoughtfully, his mouth puckered into a frown as he sucked on his mints. The picture struck him as intensely depressing—certainly nothing *he'd* want to look at every day. But it exerted a weirdly hypnotic fascination. He was so engrossed in it that he turned with a start when someone came up behind him and tapped him on the shoulder.

"Sorry," said David Prince. "We just put Anna down. Didn't mean to sneak up on you."

"That's okay." Wayland nodded toward the engraving. "Interesting picture."

David glanced around. "My wife and I have started to collect a few things." He paused for a moment, and his haggard gaze turned inward. "Funny. All this stuff that seemed so important. I'd give it all up in a second if only—" His voice quavered. He clamped his lips tight and swallowed hard. It took him a few seconds to recover his composure. Then he looked straight at Wayland and said, "Come on. Let's go into my study. I'll tell you all about Simon— the whole ugly story."

Settled into a leather armchair, Wayland glanced around the shadowy room, while Prince, seated at his massive desk, poured himself a bourbon. In the yellow glow of the desk lamp, the amber liquid shone as if the tumbler were lit from within.

Like the studies of many wealthy men, the room seemed less like a workplace than a refuge—shut off and insulated, the high, hardwood bookcases placed around the walls not to hold Prince's library, but to form a barrier against the outside world. Wayland could see where some men might feel comfortable in such surroundings. But to him the room had the atmosphere of an expensively appointed bunker. He felt as if he had gone underground.

Prince had removed his suit jacket and hung it over the back of his desk chair. Now, with his shirtsleeves rolled up and tie undone, he took a swig of his bourbon and sighed gratefully. "Sure you won't have one, Chief Wayland?"

"No thanks."

Prince nodded and drank again. Leaning back in his chair, away from the puddling light of the desk lamp, he gazed at the ceiling. But even with his features half hidden in shadow, Wayland could see the pain inscribed on his face. After a long moment Prince cleared his throat. "This is a very difficult subject for me. I've never told anyone about it, not even my closest friends." He laughed uneasily. "It's not the kind of background that would impress the neighbors, particularly not in a place like Stoneham."

"Mr. Prince," Wayland said. "If you're worried that this story will somehow spread around, I can guarantee that—"

Prince held up a hand and waved it rapidly. "No, no, no. I'm not asking for reassurance." He smiled thinly. "I'm just trying to find the best way to begin."

Sitting forward, he polished off his drink. "It all seems so long ago. Very unreal. Like someone else's life." He took a deep breath. "Hard to believe that it's mine."

David kept the story brief. At times it seemed difficult for him to continue, or at any rate to find the right words. He would stop and stare into space or frown at the desktop for long moments. His voice was often faltering—suprisingly so for a man who radiated such complete self-assurance.

Wayland soon understood why. David Prince came from the kind of family it wouldn't be easy to talk about. His mother had abandoned him and her husband when David was five, and David's father, a successful businessman, was

70

hardly ever home. David had not done well in either public or private New Mexico schools. Lonely, alienated, he had begun to cut school regularly at twelve and drink by the time he was fourteen. Then, in 1967, when he was sixteen, he left his home for good and found himself, like many runaways at the time, living in San Francisco, on the streets and in the crash pads of the Haight.

"It was the so-called Summer of Love. Flowers in your hair and all that bullshit. Mostly it was serious drugs and various forms of V.D. Thank God for the Free Clinic."

It was around this time that he met Anna Stewart, another runaway who had drifted to Haight-Ashbury with dreams of peace, love, and flower power. And it was shortly after the two of them began living together that they were introduced to the man named Simon—Simon Proctor.

"He was a very charismatic individual," David explained. "A big, broad-shouldered man, somewhere in his forties at the time, with a mane of flowing black hair, a booming voice, and a smile that made you feel like his oldest friend. He seemed to know everything, to have studied everything, from classical literature to clinical psychology to Oriental religion. He was like the father you always wanted to have—wise, protective, someone who knows all the answers."

Proctor was teaching a course in meditation techniques at something called the Center for Creative Development when David and Anna met him. He owned some property in the mountains outside Taos, a fifty-acre ranch called La Cruz and, in early 1968, he and a group of his followers, including David and Anna, moved there to start a commune.

"The living conditions were very primitive," David said. "No electricity or indoor plumbing. We pumped water from a well, bathed in a pond, crapped into holes dug in the ground. But to us, it seemed like paradise. We went around half naked." He laughed. "Sometimes all naked. Raised vegetables, baked bread. Some of us made handicrafts—baskets, blankets, wall hangings—and peddled them to the tourists in Taos. There was lots of laughing, lots of singing. Lots of sex. Sometimes, it felt like being a part of a big, loving family. At other times, it seemed as if we were part of a whole new race, maybe the first members of the *human*

71

race. As if we had started all over again from scratch. Only this time, we'd do it right.

"And Simon was at the center of it all, offering us comfort and guidance and wise words. Telling us Iroquois creation myths and quoting from the *Bhagavad Gita*. Playing Big Father." His tone had suddenly turned bitter. "Playing God."

The group was into drugs from the beginning—mostly grass, hash, and LSD. But gradually they turned to harder stuff: cocaine, speed. "That was the snake in the garden. After a while the drugs began to feed everyone's paranoia. And Simon's power trip just went spinning out of control."

For a long time the group members tried to ignore what was happening. "You know how it is. The way kids turn a blind eye to their parents' worst excesses." But it soon became clear that Simon was growing genuinely crazy, beginning to think of himself as some kind of prophet or messiah. By 1971 David had seen all the drug overdoses and wasted people he ever wanted to see. And he had heard all the rants about good and evil, Heaven and Hell, darkness and light, he ever wanted to hear from Simon's lips.

David paused in his recitation. "There was something else," he said quietly after a while. "Simon wanted Anna. Not just for sex. The sex was very free anyway. Everyone was available to everyone else. But Simon wanted Anna as his 'consort.' That was the word he used. So I took her and split. Simon knew what we were planning—he seemed to know everything. Sometimes, it felt as if he could read your mind. He warned us that if we left him, he'd find us wherever we went and get us." David shrugged. "He was pretty far gone by then.

"And that's basically the story. We got out. I created a whole new life for us. I'd lived so long at La Cruz that I'd begun to feel it was the whole world. Once we escaped, I realized it had been like living in a lunatic asylum. Eventually it just seemed like a bizarre dream, something that hadn't really happened."

He stopped talking. His face was still and his eyes unfocused, as if he were looking at something a long way off.

"Mr. Prince," Wayland prodded. "Your wife said Simon Proctor was a murderer."

"That happened after we left. Simon killed a young guy

named McKluskey. Apparently there was some kind of power struggle." David reached for his bottle of Old Grand-Dad and poured himself another tumblerful. "It was pretty nasty. From what I read in the papers, there was some kind of mutilation involved."

"Mutilation?"

"They found McKluskey with his tongue cut out."

Wayland raised his eyebrows. "I see." Then, after a moment: "Your wife said he murdered people. Plural."

"Not that I know of. He was only charged with one murder."

"And what happened?"

"He was convicted and locked away for twenty years." David took a pull from the tumbler, swished the drink around his mouth and swallowed. "He got out yesterday. Anna read about it in the paper. That's why he was the first person to come to mind." Holding the tumbler to the light, he stared into it as if it were a crystal ball that might reveal the whereabouts of his missing child. "But there's no way Simon could have done this."

"What makes you say that?"

"Well, for one thing, he was two thousand miles away. For another, he's an old man by now. Sixty at least. And after twenty years in the pen, that's got to be an *old* sixty. Besides, whatever else he might be capable of, I just can't see him doing something like his." He tilted his head back and emptied the tumbler, then set it down softly on his desk. "As well as any normal person could, I understood him. For a long time, we were very close."

Listening to the details of Prince's hippie past, Wayland had to suppress his disapproval. God knows, he mused, thinking of his daughter, lots of people are screwed up when they're young. The important thing was that Prince had straightened up and made something substantial of his life. He was living proof of the possibilities of self-rehabilitation—something Wayland deeply believed in. And whatever misdemeanors Prince may have committed in the past—drug use, sexual promiscuity, whatever—well, he was more than paying for them now.

They remained in the study for nearly an hour. The gray-haired doctor came back downstairs during that time, in-

73

formed David that Anna was sleeping peacefully and that he would call later that day. Frank Morino took David's fingerprints, and Mike Holson made instant coffee. Everyone had some but David, who helped himself to another bourbon and still showed no signs of having drunk anything.

Wayland spoke to him about the trap-and-trace they were going to place on the Princes' phone. Cosgrove was sent back to the station house to start setting up the tap with the phone company. It was possible, Wayland explained, that a ransom note might arrive in the mail. But if the kidnapper phoned, it was crucial that David remain calm and keep the caller talking as long as possible.

Then Wayland asked David to go over the details of his evening out with Anna, beginning with their departure and ending with their discovery of the empty crib. Mike Holson pulled out the pad into which he had copied Rachel's testimony, flipped to a fresh page, and scribbled notes as David spoke.

Prince was almost finished with the story when Lyle Kimball appeared at the doorway to the study with a plastic sandwich bag in his hand.

Stepping to the desk, he set the bag down carefully in the yellow circle of light. The three men huddled around the desk. Inside the bag was a small chunk of dried mud, roughly an inch long and semicircular in shape, as though it had come out of a curvilinear mold.

"Where'd you find it?" Wayland asked.

"The nursery. There was all kinds of stuff—pillows, blankets, baby clothes—tossed around the floor. This was lying on the carpet under a stuffed animal, right next to the crib. There was another, smaller piece lying there too, but"—his tone became apologetic—"it crumbled when I was scooping it into the Baggie."

"What do you make of it?" Wayland asked, glancing up at Holson.

"Looks to me like it might have been wedged into the bottom of a work boot—the kind with those deep ridges in the sole."

Wayland nodded, then noticed that Prince had lowered himself back into his chair and was sitting there, lost in thought, tugging at his lower lip.

"Mr. Prince?"

David raised his eyes to Wayland. "I was just remembering something. There's this kid . . ."

"Yes?"

"What the hell was his name?" Prince tapped a finger against his lips. "Greg," he said after a moment. "He just might . . ." Prince was nodding now, and his eyes had taken on a hard, angry look. "He was just fucked-up enough to try something like this. And he's real pissed at me."

The story emerged quickly. The summer before last, right before Anna got pregnant, he had hired a young man named Greg to mow his lawn and keep up the garden a bit. The Princes' regular gardener had given up his business and retired, and both he and Anna thought it would be neighborly to provide summer employment for some local teenager.

Stopping to pick up a few provisions one Saturday morning at the local A & P, David had spotted a mimeographed sheet tacked to the supermarket bulletin board. "Lawnbusters!" it said. "Call Greg." The bottom of the sheet had been cut into a row of small rectangular tabs, each inscribed with a phone number. Amused by the flyer, David had torn off one of the tabs and phoned the following day.

Greg turned out to be a good-looking, muscular kid about seventeen years old. David couldn't remember much more about him than that. He didn't think this Greg was from Stoneham, but maybe he was from Oakdale or Ridgewood, one of those towns to the immediate south or east. And he couldn't recall his last name. He had always paid him in cash.

Greg's work was adequate for a few weeks. Then things began to deteriorate—small and then larger patches of lawn weren't mowed, edges weren't trimmed, clumps of weeds poked up through the grass. There were days when he didn't show up at all, other days when he seemed to be totally out of it. "Probably stoned," David said.

"Then I came home early one afternoon. I remember, it was early in August. And there's Greg. It's three-thirty, the lawn hasn't been touched, and what's he doing? He's in my *house*. In fact, he's in my goddamned *bedroom*, staring through the glass door at my wife. You know, he often copped peeks at her as she'd go in and out on errands. She

75

was aware of it, but she's a beautiful woman, and guys have always given her looks. But this was obviously going too far."

Swiveling his chair away from the desk, Prince got to his feet and began to pace back and forth. "We have a private sun deck off our bedroom, and she was out there, lying on her stomach, with the top of her bikini undone. She had on a big straw hat. And there he was, standing at the glass door, practically drooling all over himself."

"What did you do?" Wayland asked.

Prince stopped dead and stared at Wayland. "I canned him, of course. The incredible thing was, he didn't seem to think there was anything wrong with what he'd done. He kept repeating mindlessly, 'I was just looking. What's the big fucking deal?' Then he said that she *knew* he was there, that she *wanted* him to watch her. I could have killed him." David's voice sounded raw. "But the little creep wasn't worth my time or energy. So I kicked him the hell out. But he was burning when he left—furious at being fired, furious because I wouldn't pay him the money I owed him for the previous week's work."

"No? Why not?"

"Why not?" He barked out a laugh. "Because he was a fucking pervert, that's why not. And anyway, he'd done a completely shitty job. I remember he was so mad, he was spitting. Kept saying he was gonna come back and get the money I owed him. I told him I'd have him arrested if he set one foot on my property again."

"Mike," Wayland said, turning to Holson. "Let's hear the babysitter's description of the perp." Prince lowered his head and listened attentively. Wayland listened too. "Does that sound like him?" Wayland asked after Holson was finished.

"In terms of his age and physique, definitely. But there's something else too."

"What's that?"

David leaned forward on the desk and pointed to the half ring of dried mud in the Baggie. "Never," he said, "not even on the hottest day, did I ever see this kid wearing anything but a white T-shirt, jeans, and high-top leather work boots."

Wayland and Kimball exchanged looks. Then Wayland,

nodding, said to David, "I think we better talk to this Greg."

"If that kid had anything to do with this," David said hoarsely, more to himself than to Wayland, "he'll wish I *had* killed him that day."

The police left soon afterward, at 4:15 A.M., with several photographs of the Prince baby and a dozen or so plastic evidence bags in hand. David agreed to travel down later that day to Grasslands, where the county police were located, to meet with a sketch artist who would draw a picture of Greg from David's description. Wayland had nobody on his staff who could do that kind of thing.

At the front door Wayland shook hands with David, expressed his sympathy again, and repeated—with more assurance than he felt—that things would turn out all right. Then he got into his car and drove away.

Thinking over the events of the evening as his car sped down the dark country roads, he suddenly realized that, although he had asked Pete Rydell to contact Marianne Byrne, she had never shown up. He wondered about that for a moment, then decided she had probably gone out for the evening after getting off her shift.

The idea of dancing or dining or even sitting in a movie theater—of doing anything, in fact, except sinking into a soft bed—seemed so profoundly unappealing to Wayland that he marveled at the memory of his own younger days, when he and Janet would sometimes stay out until dawn. As he swung his car onto Howells Drive, his tiredness pressed down on him like an enormous weight—as if that hulking creature in the picture on the Princes' wall were squatting on his shoulders.

He hadn't completely forgotten what it was like to be young. But at the moment, he couldn't recall ever feeling quite so old.

9

THE BABY HAD FINALLY FALLEN ASLEEP.

"Son of a bitch. I didn't know they could scream so loud. Here. You hold it for a while."

"He's all wet."

"Fuck it. Just let it sleep."

"Do you know when to feed it?"

"Yeah. I've got all the instructions."

"He's no good to us dead."

"Don't worry. It'll be fine. Alive and kicking."

The red-faced baby squirmed, and a long, sighing breath escaped his puffy lips.

"Music to my ears," said the first.

They both laughed softly.

10

"SHHH, BABY. IT'LL BE OVER SOON."

Seated on a molded plastic chair in the curtained-off cubicle of the emergency room, Jean Peary stroked her daughter's hand and crooned comforting words to her. Rachel lay facedown on the examination table, squeezing her mother's hand spasmodically and making small, whimpering sounds. Out of the corner of her eye Jean could see the deft, delicate hand-motions of the resident—a young blond woman who might have been Rachel's older sister—as she stitched the ugly gash in Rachel's head.

"Almost done," whispered the doctor.

Jean had taken one look at the procedure and then averted her eyes. She was not a particularly squeamish person. But she was already woozy from tension and fatigue, and her single glimpse of the operation—of the curved surgical needle penetrating her daughter's skin, of the pale filament tugging at the ragged edges of the

78

wound—had made her feel momentarily queasy. Now, she sat beside the table and focused on her daughter's sheet-covered form.

Jean heard a soft metallic snip. "There," said the doctor, straightening up and reaching for the gauze pads and tape on the little metal tray beside her. Jean waited until the bandage had been applied to her daughter's scalp, then stood up and gazed at Rachel's bruised and swollen profile. She reached down and lightly touched the girl's cheek with her fingertips. The girl winced as if Jean had pinched her.

"Sorry," Jean said with a pained smile.

"Will I have a scar?" Rachel asked the doctor in a tremulous voice.

"Nothing that anyone will notice. When your hair grows back in a few weeks, the sutures will be invisible."

Rachel gave a deep, fluttering sigh of relief.

Tossing her green, plastic gloves into the trash can, the young doctor explained that she wanted Rachel to remain there overnight. "The X-rays don't show any signs of fracture. But she was hit pretty hard. I think it'd be a good idea for us to keep her here for observation."

"Do you think you can sleep here, hon?" Jean asked.

"No. I *hate* hospitals."

Rachel hadn't been inside a hospital since birth—not even as a visitor, as far as Jean knew. The comment made her realize just how young, how much of a child, her daughter still was. She thanked God again that Rachel was alive, that the maniac who had stolen the Princes' baby had let her own baby live. "Can you give her something to help her sleep, Doctor?" she asked.

"She won't need it. People with bad concussions don't have trouble sleeping. That's the whole point of keeping her here—to wake her up a few times during the night and make sure she's okay."

And in fact, Rachel drifted into sleep almost as soon as she was wheeled to her room and helped onto the high, railed hospital bed. Jean sat in the darkness for a few minutes, listening to her daughter's deep, rhythmic breathing. Then she wandered blearily back down to the emergency room desk to finish filling out the insurance papers.

One of the ambulance drivers—not Campbell, but his sallow-skinned partner—was just leaving. The nurse, to whom he had evidently told the entire story, shook her head and clucked her tongue as she took the papers from Jean. "I can't believe it. In *Stoneham!*" Her tone was a perfect mixture of disbelief and outrage. But there was something else in the sideways glance she flashed at Jean, something hard, almost gloating, as if she regarded Jean not simply as a suffering mother, but as the member of a pampered, privileged class.

It was as if she were thinking: *Welcome to the real world.*

After the white fluorescent glare of the hospital, Route 28 seemed black as a mine shaft. Arriving at 18 McClellan Place, Jean pulled her Volvo into the garage, whose automatic door rumbled shut behind her. The garage light would stay on for a little over two minutes—more than enough time for her to get out of the car and stroll slowly to the door that opened into the basement. Tonight, however, tired as she was, she hurried.

Closing the basement door behind her, turning on the lights in every room she walked through—even though she could have found her way upstairs to her bedroom blind-folded—she wished for the first time since her childhood that she had a dog. A big, fierce, noisy dog.

All at once she remembered the dog someone had found on Woodland Drive. Ellen Roberts in the Wine and Cheese Shop had told her about it earlier that day—*yesterday,* she corrected herself. And it struck her as remarkable that within a few days two such terrible things had happened in a town where nothing ugly ever happened.

Though her breath tasted sour and her face felt greasy, as if smeared with a light coat of Vaseline, she didn't have the energy to brush her teeth or wash. She let her clothes lie where she dropped them on the bedroom carpet, dragged on her flannel nightgown, and collapsed into bed, pulling the down comforter up to her chin.

She had pulled it too high, however, and her right foot stuck out into the cold. The sensation brought with it a powerful recollection from childhood. Lying there in the dark, she remembered how, as a very young girl, she had always been careful to keep her extremities under the blanket, believing that if a hand or some toes stuck out, then the shapeless monstrosity that crouched at night in the shadowy corner of her bedroom would spring out of the darkness and drag her down into Hell.

Now, Jean was hit with the same paralyzing fear. Slowly, agonizingly, she retracted her foot until it was safely under the cover. Her heart was thundering and it took a few moments for it to resume its normal beat. But even as her brain misted over with sleep, she was overcome with the conviction that it was too late—that the horror lurking in the blackness had already sprung.

She slept fitfully, waking once, her heart racing, after a nightmare in which she and her ex-husband Bill were fighting over an object—a shabby but strangely lifelike rag doll—wrenching it back and forth between them. It began to tear in her dream—she could hear it rip clearly—and when she looked down to see whether she would get the largest half, she saw that it had turned into Rachel, and she began to scream over her child's bloody, ruined body.

At eight-thirty she dragged herself out of bed. In the mirror, she looked even worse than she had the night before. An ashen face with bloodshot eyes and furrowed cheeks gazed back at her. She took a long, hot shower and gulped down three full cups of coffee.

Then, eager to see her daughter but dreading the coming confrontation, she left for the hospital.

She was going to have to ask Rachel about the things she had found in the drawer. She had thought she could wait—perhaps for a week, until Rachel had recuperated a bit from her trauma.

Overnight she had changed her mind; she was not sure why.

Feeling halfway decent, Jean presented herself at the hospital. The doctor who discharged Rachel told her to make sure her daughter got lots of rest. A young, sunken-chested man with a pasty complexion and livid pouches under his eyes, he looked as if he could use a good long vacation himself.

Rachel seemed fragile and weak, grimacing as Jean helped her into the Volvo. The sky had cleared, and Jean put on her sunglasses. Once they were on the road, Rachel told her mother that she had been visited first thing that morning by Detective McCarthy, who had taken her finger-prints and questioned her again at length.

"Could you remember anything else, honey?"

"No. Just a few more obscene things that creepy guy said to me."

It was Jean's turn to grimace. "I'm so sorry you had to go through that. I guess we should be grateful he didn't do anything worse to you." Jean reached over and gently squeezed her daughter's hand. "Rachel, there's one thing that's very important for you to keep in mind."

Rachel raised her right hand to her brow, shielding her eyes from the sun. The white plastic ID band hung down from her wrist like a bangle. "What's that?"

"You shouldn't feel responsible in any way for this."

Rachel lowered her hand and looked at her mother. "What do you mean?"

"Well, it's just that I don't want you to blame yourself for what happened." Jean cleared her throat. "To the baby. It wasn't your fault."

Rachel was quiet for a long moment. "I know," she said finally. "Look, if you don't mind, I don't want to talk about it." She slumped down in the seat, her eyes clamped tight against the late October glare.

The two of them were silent the rest of the way home.

Inside Rachel's bedroom, Jean helped her daughter undress out of the jeans and sweatshirt she had brought to the hospital. Jean had not seen Rachel naked in years. She was beautiful, with a narrow waist and gently swelling hips, long, slender legs, and breasts with the smooth, rounded shapeliness of teacups. Her skin, except for the bruises scattered here and there, was honey-colored. Jean felt nauseated when she thought of that maniac stripping her daughter's clothes off while she lay helpless.

Wearing only white lace bikini panties, Rachel climbed into bed and instantly closed her eyes, sighing as she laid her head down. Jean sat on the bed and pulled the flower-strewn sheet and soft, faded comforter up to her daughter's chin, just as she had every night until Rachel was ten. The room was cool. It would not get sun until the afternoon. Bending to plant a kiss on Rachel's smooth forehead, Jean

82

felt her eyes dampen with tears. "I'm so glad you're okay, sweetheart. I think I would have died if—"

Rachel's eyes fluttered opened. "I know, I know," she said in a weak voice. "Mom. I really need to sleep. Could you . . . ?" And when Jean rose from the bed, her daughter rolled to one side, pressed her head into the pillow, and breathed, "Thanks . . ."

For the rest of the day Jean struggled to find ways to distract herself. She spent nearly an hour on the phone with her friend Irene, spilling out the story of the previous night's horrors. Jean did nearly all the talking, while Irene responded with shocked or sympathetic exclamations. Though Jean was tempted to unburden herself completely, she couldn't bring herself to tell her friend about the sinister cache she had found in Rachel's drawer. Even so, she felt slightly better when she finally hung up.

Later she went outside to rake leaves for a while, then came back into the house and tried, unsuccessfully, to nap. At midday she made an effort to eat something—a simple meal of crackers, Vermont cheddar, and a flawless Granny Smith. But the apple tasted as flavorless as Styrofoam, the crackers and cheese like cardboard and wax.

She wandered aimlessly through the house and looked in occasionally on Rachel. The girl hadn't moved. She lay on her side and breathed easily out of her battered, slightly parted lips.

As the day dragged on, Jean's anxiety intensified like a rising fever. She felt sick with the need for an answer. Like a patient awaiting the results of a biopsy, she prayed that the truth would not be as awful as she feared. But good or bad, she needed to know.

At five o'clock Jean decided that it was time to rouse Rachel and give her something to eat. Rachel liked onion and green pepper omelets. She would make one for each of them and wake the girl when the meal was ready.

Then, after dinner, she and Rachel would have their talk.

Jean went to work on the omelets, whisking the eggs, chopping a pepper and onion. Standing at the counter, she gazed out the window at the backyard. The day was already darkening. The lawn lay muffled in shadow. Though she had spent nearly two hours raking, the grass was still peppered with fallen leaves. In the grainy light of dusk, they looked as drab and unsightly as liver spots.

Jean tossed together a salad, split and toasted a couple of English muffins, fried the omelets. Then she walked to Rachel's bedroom and swung open the door.

The hallway light cut a wedge of brightness in the murk of Rachel's room. Jean was surprised to see Rachel lying awake, staring up at the ceiling. "Have you been awake long, honey?"

"Not long."

Jean switched on the table lamp next to her daughter's bed. Rachel looked better. Color had returned to her face, and when she rose to her feet, assisted by Jean, she seemed far less wobbly than she had that morning.

They sat at the small, butcher-block table in the kitchen. Rachel seemed starved. She devoured her entire omelet, both English muffins, and fully half of the Sara Lee German chocolate cake Jean had defrosted.

Jean was delighted to see her daughter eat so avidly. But she couldn't help thinking that Rachel was using her hunger as a way of avoiding conversation. The girl kept her eyes riveted on her food and didn't say a word.

Thinking back over their recent life, Jean realized how infrequently she and Rachel had dinner together. Sometimes Jean didn't get home from work until seven-thirty or eight, by which time Rachel had already consumed a microwave meal. And even when Jean was home by six, Rachel often had plans—study dates in the town library, babysitting, a test to prepare for. They'd eat hastily, if they ate together at all, exchanging only a few trivial remarks.

Then Rachel would deposit her dishes with a clatter in the kitchen sink and disappear. Jean was too exhausted during the week to regret it. Now she regretted it. Rachel and she had become strangers. And Rachel didn't seem to care.

Jean plucked the paper napkin from her lap, crumpled it into a ball and dropped it onto her empty plate. "Rachel, there's something I need to talk to you about," she said, pushing her chair away from the table and rising. "I'll be right back."

Rachel looked mildly surprised. "Okay."

Jean slipped quickly into her own bedroom. Opening the

84

drawer of her night table, she carefully removed a faded blue bandana, its corners folded together and knotted. Wrapped inside were the objects she had taken from Rachel's room. *Was it only last night?* It felt like another lifetime.

Returning to the kitchen, she pushed aside Rachel's dishes and, without a word, deposited the little bundle on the place mat in front of Rachel. Jean sat down, then reached across the table and undid the corners of the bandana, keeping an eye on her daughter's face.

Rachel's reaction was a long time coming. Finally, she looked up, her face expressionless. "Where did you get these?"

"I got them from your room. From your bureau."

"How could you—how dare you go snooping around my room, searching through my drawers?" Rachel said angrily. "I can't believe—"

Jean cut her short. "I wasn't snooping. I was putting away some of your underwear, and that little dagger or whatever it is sliced my finger." She waved the bandaged finger in the air. "And naturally I looked to see what had cut me. I certainly wasn't *searching* through your drawers. I never even looked in the others. Should I have? Would I have found more strange stuff?"

"That's none of your business, is it?"

Rachel spoke with such coolness, such nonchalance, that Jean drew in a sharp breath. "I want to know what these things are, Rachel. This paper, for instance—what language is this? And what does it say? And this vial . . ." She picked it up and shook it slightly. The brownish-red fluid sloshed thickly. "What is this stuff? And that knife—where did you—"

"I can't believe you're doing this!" Rachel exploded, half rising from her chair. "First you go snooping around my things, and then you—I just got out of the hospital, remember? I was attacked last night by some madman, *remember?*"

"Rachel, I feel very bad about having to do this right now, I really do." She reached out to lay a gentle hand on her daughter's arm, but Rachel snatched it away. Jean's lips tightened and she went on. "I am sorry, believe me. But there's been too much silence between us for too

85

long. I'm mostly responsible for that, I admit it. But there are things we need to talk about, and talk about now. Sweetie . . . Rachel," she urged, her voice rising. "Please help me. I don't know what this stuff is, what it *means!*"

"You'll just have to live with that."

"What?"

"I can't help you." Rachel sat down again, her arms drawn tight across her chest, and gazed coolly at her mother.

Jean stared at her daughter's scornful face for several moments. "Can't help me or won't help me?"

Rachel shrugged.

"And why is that?" Jean demanded, beginning to feel an icy fury build up inside her.

Rachel shrugged again. "Look, what I do with my life is my own business. I don't pry into *your* life, right? This is my stuff and you shouldn't have looked for it, and you shouldn't be asking me about it. That's all. People like you . . ."

"People like me!"

". . . don't want your little girls to grow up. You think—"

"Is that what you think this is all about, Rachel? That I don't want you to grow up? That's ludicrous, I won't even discuss it. Now you can just start to give me some answers—"

"No."

They stared at each other. Rachel's face was composed and lovely. Jean could feel the muscles of her own face, tense and rigid.

"All right then, Rachel. I'll tell you what's going to happen. You're grounded. You go to school and then you come home. You're not going to anyone's house, you're not talking on the telephone. You're not going to a party or out on a date. You're certainly not going to spend time with those characters you've been seeing lately, like that boy, what's his name—Kip?—the one with the earrings and bracelets. For all I know, he's the one responsible for introducing you to this craziness. You're not going to have any freedom at all until you tell me the truth!"

Rachel stood up, her composure gone. "You can't do that to me—"

"Oh, can't I? You watch how fast I do it. I'm your mother and—"

86

"I hate you!" Rachel screamed, leaning over the table, spitting out the words. "I hate you! You'd be happy if I were *dead!*"

"Rachel, Rachel," Jean pleaded, genuinely alarmed. What was her daughter talking about? "Wait a minute, let's sit down quietly—"

Rachel's face had turned red with fury. "I *won't*. I'm not going to talk to you. I *hate* you and I don't care if I *never* talk to you again!"

Dazed, Jean watched her rush out of the room and heard her slippered feet thud up the stairs. For several moments she sat immobilized, her mind vaguely registering the muffled sound of drawers sliding and slamming. *She's looking through her dresser, what else is in there?* She could not think clearly. What should she do? How had things gone so badly awry? Who was her daughter, and when had she become this total stranger?

She felt mortally sick. It was not Rachel's words. She knew adolescents were capable of saying anything. But the cold loathing in Rachel's eyes and in the tone of her voice—the last time she had felt herself to be the object of so much contempt had been during the last months of her marriage. And then it hadn't mattered so much. She simply hadn't cared. She had been ready to walk away from Bill anyway.

She gazed dully at the things in the bandanna. They looked primitive and uncanny, like a shaman's fetish-objects used in some dark ritual of witchcraft or foretelling. She stared at them as if they might provide an answer.

They told her nothing.

Rising slowly from the table, she reached for the things. Abruptly, the combined shocks of the last twenty-four hours hit her hard, in the very center of her body. Her insides twisted and roiled, like a living serpent. Clutching her stomach against the pain, she rushed to the bathroom and was violently sick.

When she emerged fifteen minutes later, pale and shaking, she went straight to Rachel's room. Pushing open the door, she stepped inside. And froze.

The room looked as if it had been ransacked. Every drawer in the dresser hung open. The light in the walk-in closet was on. Clothes were scattered across the unmade bed and floor.

Rachel was gone.

11

THE MORNING OF MONDAY, OCTOBER 31, WAS CLOUDLESS and cold, one of those bright autumn days when the sun, for all its brilliance, seems to give off as little heat as a refrigerator bulb. By the early afternoon the quiet country lanes and gloomy pathways of the little community would be alive with small bands of giggling, garish figures—pint-sized vampires and Gypsies, superheroes and ghosts.

Normally, the housewives of Stoneham would have spent the day worrying about nothing more serious than putting the finishing touches on a pirate outfit or figuring out a way to keep a five-year-old ballerina warm without covering up her costume. But this was not a normal Halloween, and for the residents of Stoneham—with a few notable exceptions—the looming rituals of All Hallow's Eve were the last thing on their minds.

That morning, the front page of the *Stoneham Gazette*—the biweekly paper whose reporters had never had to deal with anything more dramatic than the occasional drunk-driving incident—was given over entirely to the snatching of the Prince child. LOCAL BABY KIDNAPPED! screamed the sixty-point banner headline. A grainy, black-and-white photo of little Stephen occupied the center of the page, above a caption reading "Have You Seen This Baby?"

The story itself was accurate in the essentials but sparse in detail. Of all the principals, only Wayland had agreed to be interviewed. The *Gazette* ran a photo of the harried-looking chief and another of the sprawling Prince house, its sweeping front lawn cordoned off by police sawhorses. David Prince himself declined to speak or to be photographed. His grief-stricken wife, according to the accompanying article, was "in seclusion."

Copies of the paper were at the railroad station by six A.M. Ranged along the platform, the somber commuters—dark-suited squadrons of men, leavened by a handful of female executives in somewhat brighter plumage—kept their *Wall Street Journal*s folded under their arms and pored over the *Gazette*. They shook their heads and murmured as they read, feeling more vulnerable than they were either accustomed to or comfortable with.

Inside the cars, they broke the usual early-morning commuter silence to make grim conversation with their seatmates. Expressions of sympathy for the Princes mingled with outrage at the crime itself. Outside the windows of the speeding train, the thickets of trees that framed the tracks and swelled the hillsides—trees that told at a glance the difference between life in Westchester County and the hard, gray life of the city—blazed with color. One man, gazing at the radiant foliage, muttered aloud what many were thinking: "Christ, you'd think for what it costs to live here, you'd be safe."

Marianne Byrne arrived at the station house fifteen minutes early, still as irritated with herself as she had been the previous afternoon, when she'd learned of the Prince kidnapping from Frank Morino, who had eventually reached her after his unsuccessful attempts on Saturday night. Here she'd been waiting six months for something interesting to happen—and when it finally did, she'd been zonked out on sleeping pills!

Inside the women's locker room—which Marianne, as the sole female member of the Stoneham force, had all to herself—she changed quickly into her uniform. Standing at the wall mirror, a small, white elastic band clamped between her teeth, she brushed her black hair tight against her scalp and secured it into a ponytail with the band. Then she picked up her police cap and set it on her head—not gently, with a hand on each side, the way most women put on hats, but with a quick downward flip, the visor gripped between the thumb and forefinger of her right hand. It was the way she had watched her father do it all throughout her childhood.

She stepped into the corridor and headed straight for Wayland's office. The chief was already at his desk. Summoning her inside with a wave of his hand, he began by reproaching her mildly for being inaccessible Saturday night.

"Out partying?"

"Not exactly," Marianne sighed, refusing Wayland's

offer of a seat. She remained standing across from his desk, resting her right hand on the butt of her holstered .357 Ruger. "Believe me, I feel bad enough as it is."

Wayland nodded, then filled her in on what they were doing and what they had to go on. She had already heard most of it from Tony.

"Not much, is it?" she said.

"No." Tension and fatigue were engraved on Wayland's face; his complexion was ashen and haggard. But even without looking at him, Marianne could tell that he was under enormous strain. She had smelled the cigarette smoke as soon as she'd stepped into his office. Before him on the desk lay an old, black plastic ashtray, imprinted with the word "Campari" and already cluttered—though it was just eight A.M.—with the stubbed-out butts of several Marlboros.

"What can I do?" asked Marianne.

Wayland spun around in his chair to look out his wide window at Wycherly Avenue. Two steady streams of cars flowed down the street in either direction, converging at the turnoff to the train station. Following Wayland's gaze, Marianne could see Greg Nugent posted at the intersection, one hand raised, the other making quick waving motions, directing the oncoming commuters like an orchestra conductor signaling for more verve from the woodwinds.

"Make yourself visible," Wayland said. "Walk back and forth along Wycherly and up Randolph, as far as the Unitarian church. Stick your head in a few shops." He swiveled back around and looked straight at Marianne. "This whole town's going to have a bad case of the jitters. Seeing a few cops on the street will do people some good."

Marianne felt her face flush with anger. Another Mickey Mouse assignment! She tightened her lips to keep from venting her frustration. But her feelings must have showed. Wayland's voice hardened the way it did when anyone questioned his authority.

"I know you're hot for some action, Officer Byrne," he said harshly. "But right now I've got all the people on this case I need."

For a moment, as Marianne stared down at Wayland's scowling face, all she could see was one of those hard-ass old-timers whom she'd had to contend with from the instant she decided to join the force, the kind who'd never get used to seeing a woman in uniform. But as she looked more closely, she saw something else—a tired and worried middle-aged man, just a few years away from retirement, who'd just had a pile of trouble dumped into his lap. Her face muscles relaxed and she gave a conciliatory shrug.

"Sure, Chief," she said quietly. "If that's what you want."

Wayland nodded. "Good," he said, his voice softening to its normal tone. He rubbed his jaw with his hand, gazing thoughtfully at Marianne. "There is one thing you might do," he said after a moment. "Dig around a little into this weirdo Proctor, the guru or whatever. The one who freaked and offed the guy on the commune. Start with the Taos P.D. Not that I think he's involved in the kidnapping. But since his name came up, we might as well cover all the bases. That Mrs. Prince"—he pawed through some papers on his desk until he found her name—"Anna. She was pretty hysterical on the subject."

"Can you blame her?"

Wayland conceded the point with a slight lift of his eyebrows. "That's something else you might do," he said. "Pay her a visit."

"You want me to question her again?"

Wayland shook his head. "Nah. If she has anything interesting to say, listen. But don't push it. She's in pretty bad shape. I just thought she'd appreciate a visit."

"A sisterly shoulder to cry on?"

"Whatever," said Wayland, either oblivious or indifferent to the trace of sarcasm in Marianne's tone. He began shuffling through the stack of files on his desk in a way that made it clear to Marianne that she was being dismissed. She turned and headed for the door.

Before she reached it, however, Wayland called out her name.

She turned and saw him holding a fat file folder in the air—the reports on the butchered dog. "By the way," he said, "what'd you make of this? Speak to your dad yet?"

"No. But I think he's gonna agree with me. . . ."

"Yeah? So what's your thinking?"

She returned, resting her hands on the back of the chair that faced his desk. "First of all, I think at least two people were involved. Clayton says the carving was very smooth, very professional, except for the tongue, which was done very clumsily. And then there's the fact that ketamine was used."

"So?"

His tone sounded impatient, and she hurried on. "Whoever did it wasn't doing it just for jollies. I don't think we're dealing with a sadist. And then there's the missing organs. Where'd they go? And the words painted on the floor of the gazebo. They weren't Latin—"

"I know. I saw what they said."

"And then there's the drawing, the animal head. That wasn't a dog. It was Baphomet."

"Baffa-who?"

"Baphomet. It's an occult symbol, a devil with the head of a goat. It goes back to the Middle Ages. Witches were supposed to copulate with it—him—during their sabbaths." She took a deep breath. What she was telling him sounded ridiculous in the bright morning light. She could see it in his eyes. It even sounded silly to her, to the part of her that was rational and skeptical.

But there was another part of her too, the part that had been shaped by the church and by the nuns who had educated her for a dozen years. To that part, it didn't sound silly at all.

For an instant she thought of Sam, her father's partner and closest friend, and the way he had died. Quickly, she banished the thought.

"What I'm saying is, I think we're dealing with some kind of cult activity. It often begins this way, with this type of animal sacrifice. And sometimes," she added ominously, "it gets worse."

"What are you telling me, Byrne? That we've got a bunch of devil-worshipers in Stoneham?"

"It definitely fits the pattern." She frowned. "Except for one thing. That rectangle of skin removed from the dog's side . . . I've never come across anything like that before. Never heard my father mention it." She shook her head. "I don't know what it means, but—"

Wayland slid open the center drawer of his desk, reached in for a fresh pack of Marlboros, then closed the drawer with a savage shove—hard enough to rattle the PBA coffee mug that he used as a pen holder. He knocked out a cigarette and stuck it in a corner of his mouth. Marianne felt bad for him. She knew—everybody in headquarters knew—how much he had wanted to quit smoking.

Wayland put a match to the cigarette, then looked up at Marianne, squinting through the smoke. "No offense, Byrne. But I hope you realize what a complete load of bullshit this is. You want to know what *I* think? I think the dog was sliced up by a couple of adolescent creeps, probably not even from Stoneham. Back when I was your age, we used to have a name for them—juvenile delinquents. Only then it wasn't crack and heavy metal. It was reefers and Elvis Presley. But it's the same difference, same fucked-up teenagers. So Halloween's here and they figure they'll spook a few people, maybe prove what big bad dudes they are." He shook his head. "This isn't serious stuff—"

"Not *serious?*" she asked incredulously.

He gave her a look. He hadn't liked her tone. "Hell, Byrne, I *like* dogs. I mean, it's not something that's part of any kind of big pattern." He blew some smoke her way. "Not serious in comparison to this other crime we've got on our hands now."

"Which is probably connected."

"*What!?*" Marianne's remark caught Wayland in the middle of a deep drag on his Marlboro. His mouth fell open and a thick puff of smoke wafted out.

"I said it's probably connected." She hadn't believed this, hadn't even known she was going to say it, until that moment. But as soon as she said it, she was sure it was true.

"The hell you say." He was sitting up straight now, and he looked flushed and angry. "Jesus, Byrne, I thought you were smart. What is this, one of those 'Unexplained Mysteries of the Universe' things? Someone breaks a mirror in Nebraska and two days later a DC-10 goes down at the Omaha airport, and you see a connection? Shit. Keep dumb-assed ideas like that to yourself." He stabbed his cigarette out.

On the wall behind Wayland's desk hung a framed Norman Rockwell print, showing a little boy and a burly policeman perched on adjoining stools at a neighborhood luncheonette. Lying on the tiled floor behind the little boy was the classic trademark of the runaway schoolboy—a bandana-wrapped bundle stuck onto a wooden pole. The policeman was buying the little boy an ice cream sundae, clearly in an effort to dissuade him from his plan. Marianne always thought the picture revealed a lot about her boss—not just about his taste in art but about a soft, even sentimental, side of his personality, that he generally tried to keep hidden.

Right now, he was doing a particularly good job of concealing it. "Let me tell you something about being a cop," he went on, aiming an index finger at her like a gun. "Don't guess. Don't jump to conclusions. When a cop starts guessing, people get hurt. Beginning with other cops." He picked up the handpiece of his phone and nodded toward the door. "Now give Evelyn back that file and go ask the Stoneham ladies and merchants how they're doing."

Ten minutes later Marianne left the station, glad to escape. She was still smarting from Wayland's tongue-lashing. It hadn't helped that Roy Auslander and Tommy Reardon, hovering near the watercooler outside Wayland's door, were trying hard to pretend that they hadn't been listening. Or that Evelyn Digges, taking the file back, had whispered maternally, "He hasn't had much sleep the last couple of nights, dear."

She felt foolish—and angry, mostly at herself. What she had said about the Prince baby was stupid. Wayland was right about that. She had spouted off too fast.

Outside, the sunlight was sharp enough to hurt her eyes. She slipped on her aviator sunglasses and headed for the center of town. The cold air smelled of damp leaves and wood smoke. Inhaling it deeply, Marianne began to feel better.

She walked up and down Wycherly Avenue, and partway along Randolph Street. Every fall the downtown merchants of Stoneham let the local schoolchildren decorate their shop windows with Halloween scenes, painted directly onto the glass in bright daubs of tempera. Marianne never got tired of looking at these brash, vivid pictures. A chorus line of skeletons kicking up their heels in a graveyard. A headless horseman astride a rearing, coal-black stallion. A leering, spike-tailed devil brandishing a pitchfork. Here and there were portraits of the more popular, up-to-date demons—

Freddy Krueger, Leatherface, and Jason, the hockey-masked slasher of *Friday the 13th*. Few of the pictures would have won any prizes in an art competition. But all of them were festive and amusing.

In Stoneham that morning their playfulness seemed jarringly out of place.

By nine A.M. the main streets of town were already crowded with people, most of them women. It was as if, having seen their husbands off to work and their children safely loaded onto school buses, the wives had found it too disturbing to stay home alone. They gathered in small clusters—in the parking lot of the A & P, outside the dry cleaners, in front of the new Korean greengrocer's, on the pillared porch of The Country Collector—to share their worry and dismay, the tips of their noses turning red in the cold. Occasionally one of them would ask Marianne whether anything was new in the case. But most of them didn't even see her stroll by. As she passed, Marianne could hear their hushed, nervous whispers.

". . . Right out of his crib! Can you believe it! . . ."

". . . I've *always* let my children wander freely . . . well, you know, within reason. But now . . ."

". . . I heard about it from a friend who lives on Upper Brook Drive. The police were all over there yesterday, going over the lawns and the road. I couldn't sleep all night after she told me . . ."

". . . So Mary said, 'Let's move to Connecticut.' But I said to her, why assume Connecticut is any safer? My God, until yesterday . . ."

From time to time Marianne would overhear an outlandish bit of gossip—that David Prince was a drug distributor who had double-crossed the Medellín cartel. That his baby had been kidnapped by a jealous ex-lover. That he had received a ransom demand for one million dollars.

Marianne grimaced at each of these rumors, though she understood the psychology behind them—understood that, for all the wealth and sophistication of its inhabitants, Stoneham was no different from any other small town. And right now, it was a small town in the tight grip of fear.

By 10:45 Marianne was cold. She was hungry too. In her rush to get out of her apartment that morning, she had

95

yanked open the refrigerator and grabbed the first thing that had come to hand—a single slice of Kraft American cheese, hard as wax around the edges. (Marianne was notoriously forgetful about rewrapping food properly before putting it away; it had been one of Patrick's pet peeves about her.) Now, with her stomach gurgling loudly enough to be audible through her jacket, she decided to duck into the deli for some coffee and a Danish—apricot, if they had it.

She cut through the parking lot from Randolph to Wycherly and entered the Stoneham Deli through the rear. The Petrocellis' coffee smelled good and the pastry tray contained one last apricot Danish. Just the sight of it raised Marianne's spirits a notch.

She had taken a seat at one of the deli's three booths and was contentedly munching away when she felt a heavy hand on her right shoulder and heard a deep voice behind her say, "This what we pay you cops for?"

Looking around, she saw Mike Holson looming over her.

Marianne motioned across the table with her half-devoured Danish. "Have a seat, Holson. I'm just fueling up. It's *cold* out there."

Unzipping his jacket, Holson slid into the seat. "Don't mean to disturb your mid-morning snack. I was passing by and saw you sitting in here. Thought you might want to talk. I heard about Wayland."

Marianne took another nibble of her Danish. "What'd you hear?"

"Not much. Just that the chief got a little pissed at you."

Marianne grinned. "Yeah. I got chewed out. I guess I shouldn't have opened my big mouth." She shrugged. "No big deal."

"The chief can get a little cranky when the pressure piles up. And this is a shitload."

"That's for sure," Marianne said, and popped the last bit of Danish into her mouth.

From the moment he'd sat down, Holson had been idly twirling something between the thumb and index finger of his right hand. Now, sipping from her styrofoam cup, Marianne glanced down to see what he was playing with.

Instantly, she felt her entire body go rigid with shock. Her vision darkened and her hands began to tremble so violently that her coffee splashed onto the Formica table-top. She squeezed her eyes shut and struggled for control.

"Marianne?" said Holson. "You okay?"

"That thing in your hand," she said in a strangled voice. "Put it away."

Holson glanced down at what he was holding. It was a rubbery, rainbow-colored earthworm. "This? It's just a Gummi worm. I eat shit like this all the time. You know that."

"Get rid of it," Marianne rasped, clutching the edge of the table. Her heart was racing and she honestly thought she might faint.

"Sure. Okay."

She kept her eyes clamped tight, listening to the rustle of nylon as he stuck the thing into the pocket of his windbreaker.

"It's gone," he said after a moment.

Breathing deeply and rhythmically, like a Lamaze pupil in labor, Marianne opened her eyes. Muttering an apology, she rose from the booth on shaky legs and made her way out of the deli, Holson following close behind.

"What the hell was that all about?" he asked as soon as they were in the parking lot.

Marianne leaned against a delivery van and gulped down deep draughts of cold air. As her panic subsided, it was replaced by a profound sense of embarrassment. She felt like an utter fool.

"I have a problem with those things," she said after a moment.

"Gummi worms?"

"*Worms*, you jerk. I'm phobic."

"Jeez. Someone toss a nightcrawler into your cradle when you were a baby or something?"

Marianne smiled wanly. She looked deeply into Holson's face and saw genuine concern.

So, though she never liked to speak of it to anyone, and though she had felt an urgent need to conceal it from her fellow cops, she told him the story of her phobia.

It had begun spontaneously when she was about six, and neither her father nor her mother had ever been able to say where it had come from. One day it was just there. The sight of a worm—wiggling out of the soil after a rainstorm,

97

for instance, and eventually even on television—threw her into a panic. Her family doctor had told her the name of her condition: vermiphobia.

She had learned to conceal her responses a little better as an adult, but the phobic reaction—the fear, the constricted breathing, the nausea and shakiness—was actually worse. There was nothing to be done about it. She had tried everything: hypnotism, desensitization, therapy of various kinds, biofeedback, meditation. Nothing worked.

A glimpse of an earthworm could send her reeling off the edge of sanity. She hated herself for it. She berated herself for being weak. But there was nothing she could do about it.

"Ever read *1984* in high school?" she asked Holson, who shook his head. "You ought to. Anyway, there are these torturers, and they have a perfect method—a different torture for each prisoner, playing on that person's worst fear. This one guy, I've forgotten his name, his thing is rats. So they threaten to attach this rat cage to his face. It completely breaks him. He's ready to do anything they want, betray his lover, anything." She took a deep breath and shrugged. "That's me, except my thing is worms. It's weird, because I'm not freaked out by anything else, not spiders, not cockroaches, not even snakes." She shook her head. "It's got me licked. For now, anyway. I keep trying to fight it."

Holson stepped beside her and put an arm around her shoulders, giving her a warm, brotherly hug. "You'll do it," he said.

Marianne slipped an arm around his back and returned his embrace, then quickly broke away.

"Mike! You've got to promise me one thing. You won't tell anyone about this, right? I mean, the other guys. I'd never live it down."

"That's for sure," he said, with a wry laugh. "You'd probably find a rubber worm floating in your coffee cup or dropped down the back of your shirt."

Marianne grimaced. "Don't even joke about this, Mike. Just promise, okay?" She peered into his serious face. He nodded. "Thanks," she said, and patted his arm. "Look, I've got to get back to the station to make some phone calls. You coming?"

Holson shoved the sleeve of his jacket up over his wrist and gazed at his watch. He shook his head. "I've got to get back to my sector."

Bidding Holson good-bye, Marianne turned and walked back toward the station house. She was still feeling fragile and slightly shamefaced, but there was nothing she could do, except hope that Holson would be true to his word.

She thought about what he had said, shuddering at the idea of raising a coffee cup to her mouth and discovering an earthworm, even a fake one, floating on the surface. She didn't know how she'd react to something like that. She had heard of extreme phobic episodes in which people had actually died of fear. She could just see herself, the intrepid young police woman, dying of a practical joke.

Somehow, the notion didn't seem very funny.

12

RACHEL PEARY AWOKE IN THE CLIMATE-CONTROLLED MURK of the motel room. For an instant, eyes still half shut with sleep, she wondered at the strangeness of her surroundings.

Suddenly, memories of the previous night flooded her consciousness—memories of her flight from home, of the fast trip up the Taconic Parkway in her lover's steel-gray Jaguar, and then of the sex they had had, the sex that had lasted for hours. Remembering that, she felt a dizzying rush, as if the mattress had tilted violently on the bedsprings. Her eyes popped fully open.

Though it was sunny outside, the room she was in was almost as dark as it had been the night before. Heavy double drapes blocked out the light of day. What she could see after a moment were dim, vague shapes against the walls—two bulky armchairs, a table, a long, low bureau, a large-screen TV.

And then her lover next to her. Peering at him, she could just make out that his eyes were still closed. Her own traveled over his body possessively. She wanted desperately to touch him, half reached out her hand to do so, but stopped.

Maybe he would want to sleep, maybe he needed to sleep. Because of tonight.

She didn't know what time it was, but it didn't matter. She was too excited to sleep. And what was exciting her right now was his naked body. She would enjoy him with her eyes in the quiet darkness, all alone.

The room was close and warm. He had flung back the sheet and blanket, which now lay tangled around his right leg. He lay on his side, facing her, one arm flung up over his head. Her eyes traveled down the line formed by his broad shoulders, his narrow waist and hips, his long, muscular thighs. Her eyes sought his groin. With a swift, small intake of breath, she saw that his penis was hard. As it had been last night, whenever she had needed him, again and again.

Her hand, hungry as her eyes, crept tentatively toward him.

"Do you want it again?" His low-pitched, seductive voice startled her. She had been so sure he was asleep! Stifling her cry with his hand, he rolled onto her, his mouth near her ear. His body moved slowly against hers. "Do you want it—do you?" She could not speak. His hand was still over her mouth, hard, hurting a little. She realized suddenly that his hand smelled like her; she remembered his fingers and what they could do to her, and she felt she was going to faint. When his hand came away from her lips, she moaned.

And then he was inside her, smiling as he thrust.

He made love to her slowly. At one point he pulled out of her abruptly—a little cry of protest escaped her as he did—then nudged her onto her stomach and entered her again from behind. Shoving his hand under her body, onto her mound, he worked his fingers between the tufted lips and massaged the buttery nub of her clitoris. She was very wet now, and very open. He continued to touch her as he slipped in and out.

He held back his own climax until she had reached hers. When her convulsions finally subsided, she discovered that she was weeping. The right side of her face was pressed deep into the pillow, which was damp with her sweat and her tears.

Raising her head slightly, she whispered "I love you"

100

again and again, reaching behind her to clutch his buttocks, to pull him deeper inside her. When he came, he cried out like a child.

Afterward they lay on their backs, side by side. He idly stroked her left hand as they talked. He was much more experienced sexually than she was—that had been part of his initial appeal for her. She had only had two boys, and the first one hadn't counted—she had only slept with him once, at a Fourth of July party in Stoneham, to get rid of her virginity. But the person at her side had never made her feel clumsy or ignorant in bed, as so many others might have. She raised his hand quickly and kissed it.

She hadn't been with him very long, yet he seemed to know her even better than she knew herself. Sometimes he shocked her with what he did. He took her places she was afraid to go. Shrinking back, feeling very young, she often had to be dragged into doing things. He was always right, though. And afterward, when the pleasure flooded her (as he had promised her it would), she was so grateful she would have done anything for him.

Neither of her previous lovers could have given her one-thousandth of what he gave her, not if they'd devoted their whole lives to it.

And yet there were times when he was like any boy of eighteen or nineteen. It was part of the way he had of never forgetting what she needed. He would be tender or boyishly obsessive about her. He would hold her hand, twine her long blond hair around his fingers—once he had even brushed her hair! He would tell her he loved her whenever she asked, get jealous if anybody else looked at her. And he wanted her all the time. He never seemed to get enough of her.

What she got from him, she thought—besides the pleasure as heady and addictive as any drug—was freedom. He set her free from everything that had tied her down and made her unhappy. He gave her power too—power to control her life. And he made her feel like a woman, not like a sixteen-year-old just months away from hair ribbons and a mouthful of braces.

But there was something else too, something just as

important, and she whispered it aloud now. "You make me feel so safe—whenever I'm with you I feel so safe."

He squeezed her fingers. "You are safe."

Rachel turned her head to look at him. "I don't ever want to go back." His dark eyes met hers, and she faltered, "But I will, if you think—"

"I *know*, Rachel, I don't *think*. I thought we had this all settled last night, before we drove up. You have to go back. You have to live with your mom, you have to apologize—listen to me—and you have to make her think everything is okay. We don't want her suspicious. And it's too soon for you to come live with me."

"But when, *when?*" she said urgently.

His eyes were suddenly cold. "You don't get to ask questions like that, remember?" As he spoke, his hand moved roughly down her belly and began to play with her, in the wetness between her legs. Her own anger was roused, and she made a move to push him away. But even as she did, the pleasure caught her and her thighs opened involuntarily. "There's nothing you wouldn't do, is there, baby?" he asked softly. "Not when I do this."

"No . . . no," she whispered forlornly.

His fingers stopped stroking her. "Good. So after our little celebration tonight is over, you go home. Put Mama's fears to rest—"

"She doesn't care what I do!" Rachel exclaimed. "She's hardly ever home anymore, and when she is, she doesn't pay any attention to me—"

"But she's paying attention now, isn't she?" He sat up abruptly, his back to her. His tone had turned harsh and accusatory. "Since she found those things in your drawer. Not very bright to leave them lying around."

"They weren't lying around—they were in my drawer!"

"But mothers look in drawers, don't they?" He turned to look at her appraisingly. "I wonder why you did it? Should I be wondering about that, Rachel?"

She could hear him breathing lightly, waiting. It was hard for her to catch her breath for a few moments. The thudding of her heart sounded in her ears as though she were hearing it through a stethoscope. His silence was awful to her.

Finally she burst out, "I don't know what you're talking about! It was an accident! She hasn't looked in my dresser in years. She doesn't even come in my room!" Rachel licked her lips and pulled the sheet up over her breasts. "And anyway, didn't I . . . didn't I do everything right on Saturday night?"

After a while he answered, "Yeah. Saturday night you were perfect. Everything went just the way we planned."

"And my head still hurts," she whined. "I still don't see why I had to be hit so hard—"

He laughed. "Well, it had to look good, right? For your own protection. You know that." He stroked her soft cheek gently. "But I'm sorry it hurt so much," he said.

He was no longer angry at her. Relieved, she sat up and threw her arms around his broad, muscular back. "Never mind," she whispered, face half buried in the curve of his neck. "It was worth it."

He embraced her and she snuggled, childlike, against him. "It will be worth it—you'll see. You get to carry him up."

"I do? *Really?*"

He laughed again. "Well, it seemed fitting. Babysitter reunited with baby, briefly." He laughed again—a clipped, cruel bark. "And then we'll have our party."

13

AT PRECISELY 5:08 P.M., WITH THE SETTING OF THE SUN, Halloween arrived in the East. Like millions of their countrymen, the good citizens of Stoneham made ready their baskets and bowls full of candy—their sacred offerings of Hershey Kisses, Mars Bars, and Snickers—and prepared to pay homage to the unholy.

Tugging worriedly at her lower lip, Jean Peary sat at her kitchen table, frozen into inaction—as she had been all day—by a paralyzing combination of anger, fear, and guilt. When the door buzzer sounded, her heart leapt with hope. She hurried to the front door, praying that when she pulled it open, Rachel would be standing there, hands thrust deep in her jacket pockets, an apologetic grin on her face.

So vivid was this wish in Jean's mind that she actually caught her breath in surprise at the sight that did confront her—a four-foot Dracula with a corpse-white complexion and luminous fangs, who held open a plastic shopping bag decorated with pumpkins and, at the sight of the startled woman in the doorway, squealed triumphantly, "Trick or Treat!"

Thirteen miles to the north, Marianne Byrne sighed with defeat as she flipped the last page of the heavy volume that lay across her lap—J. R. Huyssard's *Dictionary of Demonology*. She had spent the last hour scanning its pages for some clue to the mystery that had vexed her for the past few days—the significance of the section of hide that had been flayed from the butchered retriever. But she had found nothing that might explain it.

She closed the book and tossed it onto the sofa cushion beside her. Then, reaching for the phone on the side table, she pulled it onto her lap and punched in her father's number.

At exactly that moment, Police Chief Dick Wayland wearily removed his winter coat from the rack in the corner of his office. Between one thing and another—the failure of his men to make any progress whatsoever on the Prince case, the insistent clamorings of the reporters who had bivouacked in the station-house lobby and whose number now included representatives of the city's major newspapers—it had been the single worst day of his professional life.

As he slipped on his overcoat, he was aware of something else that was worrying him, some anxiety gnawing away at the ragged edge of consciousness. Suddenly he realized what it was—that throwaway comment Byrne had made about a connection between the mutilated dog and the missing baby.

He stood there for a moment, absently picking at a hangnail on his right forefinger. Then, with a disgusted wave of his hand, as if he were gesturing angrily to a mule-headed disputant, he turned on his heel and headed for home.

Staring dully at the ceiling of her bedroom, Anna Prince lay motionless under her down comforter. She had always

104

thought that the expression "to cry yourself out" had been nothing but a figure of speech. Now she knew that it described an actual physical state. She simply could not produce any more tears.

Just ten minutes earlier, her husband had called to see how she was doing, and hearing the hollow despair in her voice, had urged her to take a pill and get some sleep, promising that he would be home soon. Incapable of anything but blank obedience, she had raised herself, invalidlike, on an elbow and swallowed down the sedative.

Now, feeling its first effects steal through her, she lay there and thought of her baby. She pictured his sweet face, the chestnut silkiness of his hair, the way his tiny hands clenched and unclenched with pleasure as he suckled at her breast. A sob rose into her sore and swollen throat, and she bit her cracked lip to keep from crying out. Her eyelids began to feel weighted, and she gave herself over to the suffusing numbness.

As she did, a different image, an old man's face surrounded by a wild nimbus of hair, began to form itself in her mind. But before it could come fully into focus, the darkness overtook her and she sank gratefully into the fathomless depths of sleep.

14

THE SPRAWLING OLD HOUSE DEEP IN DUTCHESS COUNTY stood on a thickly wooded hilltop overlooking the Hudson River. It had been built in 1842 as a summer retreat for the neurasthenic wife and two, whey-faced daughters of a Wall Street financier. With its sweeping view of the Hudson, the house, even in its present condition, was imposing. On moonlit nights the river shone in the distance, a shimmering vein of silver embedded in the blackness of the encircling hills.

Once, it had been beautiful and graceful—the very picture of a grand country residence. But for years it had been unoccupied. Its sixteen rooms, including servants' quarters, were ruinously expensive to heat. And during that time its decline had gone unchecked.

The roof had sprung a dozen leaks, and the fine oak floors had buckled in places from water damage. Bands of bored teenagers had used the windows for target practice, until not a single pane remained. Under the flaking ceilings of the empty rooms, spiders hovered in the shadows. Powdery cobwebs dripped from every doorway, and the baseboards were banked up with piles of dust and rodent droppings. To local real estate agents, the house had acquired an almost legendary reputation as a white elephant.

It had come as something of a shock, therefore, when, just a year earlier, it had been purchased by a new owner, who had done much to restore the interior of the place. The spiderwebs and mouse droppings were gone, the windows reglazed, the floorboards repaired and refinished. The kitchen had been equipped with new appliances and the bathrooms with sleek, modern fixtures. The second-floor bedrooms had been thoroughly cleaned and refurbished. Downstairs, the library and the drawing room had been extensively renovated, the wall between them having been removed to create one large chamber—an area for dining and dancing, for worship, and for public copulation.

To reach the house, you followed a steep, snaking path up the hillside. If, on that icy Halloween night, a stranger to the area, lost and seeking directions, had ignored the "No Trespassing" signs posted on the mossy stone columns that flanked the entrance to the pathway and driven through the woods to the house—earth crunching beneath his tires, dead leaves skittering in front of his headlights like living creatures darting out of harm's way—he would have seen nothing suspicious. Unless it was the dark windows, and the presence of a sizable number of cars parked on the grass to the right of the house. From under the pillared porch roof a yellow light shone, glinting off the brass, wolf's-head knocker on the front door. But other than this single light—nothing.

Approaching the house, the stranger might have caught some muted noises coming from somewhere inside: a muffled laugh, perhaps, or a curious, pulsing music—more a rhythmic throb than a melody. Something like a chant. Hearing it, he might have concluded—correctly—that some sort of Halloween celebration was going on, and that, being uninvited, he ought to seek his directions elsewhere.

If wise, he would have crept back to his car and returned to the highway as speedily as possible, taking care not to alert anyone inside to his presence. And in truth, it would have been a most unpropitious moment for a stranger to knock on the door.

For midnight was approaching. And deep in the secret heart of the isolated old house, the ceremony was under way.

Around an altar table draped in blood-red satin huddled a circle of votaries, twelve in number, six males, six females. The thirteenth member of the group—the high priest himself—stood at the head of the table, facing the rest. All of the participants were naked, though the priest was partially cloaked in a heavy scarlet cape, trimmed in rabbit fur, its back embroidered with the image of a pig.

The walls and ceiling of the chamber were painted black, with thick ebony drapes drawn across every window. The main source of illumination was a large, wrought-iron chandelier suspended directly above the altar table. Each of its eight sockets, formed to resemble the lips of a mouth or vagina, held a thick, phallus-shaped black candle. A half-dozen iron sconces, also containing black candles, hung at intervals along the walls.

The light in the room was dim. The inky walls seemed to absorb the yellow candle glow and give back only long, flickering shadows. In the gloom of the chamber the naked flesh of the worshipers had a spectral cast.

The walls of the chamber were decorated with a grotesque collection of objects: grimacing masks of African and Far Eastern origin, with leering mouths, jutting tongues, and sharp, snaggled tusks. The chasuble of a Roman Catholic bishop displayed like a tapestry, but caked with mud and dung. An inverted crucifix upon which hung the waxen effigy of a toad. And, arranged in a grouping on the wall directly behind the altar table, a set of rare and costly engravings, dating from the fourteenth century and extravagant in their blasphemy.

One depicted a crucifixion. A man with a dog's head hung on the cross, grinning lewdly at the copulating worshipers at his feet. His swollen tongue lolled and the cloth

107

around his loins bulged with his erection. Another showed a young woman with the aspect of the Virgin. Skirts hoisted to her waist and buttocks outthrust, she was being entered from behind by a bat-winged angel with a monkey's face. In the third, a goat-headed demon defecated into a chalice, lifted to his buttocks by a kneeling hag dressed in the habit of a nun. The last was an obscene parody of a Pietà, portraying the Holy Mother and her son in a carnal embrace.

Grim music suffused the dark chapel. One of the worshipers had prepared a special tape for the occasion. The songs were an eclectic mix—Schubert's "Erl King," "The End" by the Doors, Klimm's dirgelike adaptation of Poe's "The Conqueror Worm." But the feelings they evoked were the same. Desolation. Nihilism. The ecstasies and terrors of the lost.

At the moment, the poisoned strains of The Cure's "Pornography" pounded in the background. The churning music stirred the celebrants, already aroused by the drugged libation dispensed by their priest. The atmosphere of the room was thick with the odor of incense, an odd tangle of cedar and jasmine. Something else was in the air too. The piercing aroma of fresh urine. And another, subtler smell—the smell of sex, binding the group together, hinting of the pleasures to come.

Later, after the offering had been made.

Their faces concealed behind stylized animal masks—of monkeys and lizards, ravens and dogs—the young men and women (some of them no more than adolescents) were free to gaze at one another's bodies. Without exception, they all had beautiful bodies, even the slightly older ones—bodies sculpted by shining machines in health clubs and home gymnasiums. Earlier, before the ceremony had commenced, they had greased each other's bodies with scented oils.

Their leader—who sometimes joined in their erotic rituals, sometimes stood apart, watching intently and orchestrating their intricate couplings with exultant commands—had praised them for their vanity and self-absorption. He had shown them that their bodies were holy, their appetites sacred. He had taught them that the mass of humankind had been misled by its priests, that the God of sacrifice and sensual renunciation was an enslaving hoax, and that

108

divinity was not manifested in the heart but in the living fire that burned between young legs.

Now, the twelve votaries slowly passed a large silver bowl around the circle. Each urinated into it in turn, the women squatting deeply, feet wide apart, drawing pleasure from the men's keen attention.

By the time the reeking bowl reached the last person in line—Rachel Peary's lover—he was so sexually aroused that he had trouble urinating for a few moments. In spite of the solemnity of the occasion, one of the women beside him, her features concealed beneath a leopard mask, tittered softly. Finally, his water came in a gush.

Carefully, so as not to spill a drop from the nearly brimming bowl, he passed it to the priest, who quickly added his own libation, then lowered the bowl onto the altar table. A dark streak of red floated on the foul, yellow surface. One of the worshipers—the girl in the leopard mask—was menstruating heavily.

The moment of the offering had arrived.

Rachel's lover, wearing the mask of a grinning hyena, led the others in a solemn invocation—an invocation whose words, had Rachel's mother overheard them, would have rung with a dread familiarity in her ears.

"Rex mantus canis silut azgul sekmed infans respirare," the votaries chanted, their twelve voices twined into a chorus of triumph and hate. *"Nel nibur adz spiritus devorare onnam mortuus lothix rentnas. Belphegor descensus!"*

Meanwhile, their priest made his final preparations.

He was forty years older than most of the men and women in the room, but it was only the coarseness of his skin and the deep lines scored into his face that betrayed his age. His dark, tightly curled hair showed no trace of gray, and his body, though large, was all muscle.

On either side of his shaven chest, an eye-shaped figure had been tattooed around the nipple. Earlier, before the ceremony had begun, two of his females had painted his nipples with a flame-red cosmetic. The effect was as if a fiery demon were glaring out from the very heart of the man.

He was in better physical condition—could lift more weight and run greater distances—than most men half his age. His strength and stamina he owed to the taxpayers of

New Mexico. In exchange for his good behavior at the state penitentiary near Albuquerque, he had been permitted almost unlimited access to the prison gym and exercise yard.

He had used prison the way an ascetic might use a desert retreat—to harden himself for the rigors of his worship. For two decades he had hoarded his powers, sharing his visions with no one except the single follower in whose loyalty he had absolute faith. But in all that time he had never ceased dreaming of the glories to come.

Now, at last, fulfillment was at hand.

The hungry god that Simon Proctor served was about to be appeased.

As the invocation ended, the high priest removed a circular wafer from the folds of his scarlet cloak, spat a mucousy glob in its center, then crumbled the host into the stinking bowl. He nodded once to Rachel's lover, who strode to the double doors leading out into the entry hall and flung them open.

There, in the doorway, stood Rachel herself, naked like the others and cradling under her cuplike breasts a naked infant. A boy. The three-month-old child of Anna and David Prince.

Rachel hesitated for a moment. Then, beckoned forward by the high priest, she entered the chapel.

She walked slowly toward the altar, moving in time to the music, long blond hair swinging slightly with every step. Alone among the young worshipers, she wore a human mask—the face of a gentle madonna, a blissful smile playing about the corners of the lips. Rachel's oiled nakedness made a mockery of the beatific mask. With the stolen infant in her arms, she looked like a grotesque travesty of the Holy Mother.

Her lover walked beside her. When they reached the foot of the altar table, she passed the infant over to him. Her hands quavered slightly as she let the baby go.

Stephen Prince's tiny brow furrowed as he looked at the hyena's face looming above him. Rachel's lover extended the child to Simon Proctor, crying out, "Accept our gift, Hierophant!"

"Accept our gift!" echoed the others, in joyful, feverish unison.

As the high priest received the infant and lowered him onto the satin altar cloth, the votaries raised their voices in a triumphant shout. Stephen's head jerked uneasily toward the noise.

Reaching beneath the crimson altar cloth, Rachel's lover removed an elaborately carved ebony box and held it across the table. The high priest raised his hands as though bestowing a benediction, instantly stilling his clamorous followers.

His voice boomed out, deep and compelling.

"Dark Father, Lord of the Pit. We offer you our fealty. The reign of the slave-god Christ is at an end! The Great Beast has shown the way. 'Do what thou wilt shall be the only law!' "

" 'Do what thou wilt shall be the only law!' " the others chanted in response.

Dipping his fingers into the silver bowl, Simon Proctor made a reversed sign of the cross on the baby's forehead and chest with the urine. "In the name of the Goat," he intoned, "I baptize you with the holy water of humankind."

At the splash of urine on his skin, Stephen Prince began to cry loudly, his legs pumping over his belly, his arms jerking feebly in the air.

Quickly, Rachel's lover raised the lid of the ebony box. A strange, fabric object lay folded inside. Simon Proctor reached into the box and removed the thing it contained.

It was a pouch, stitched together from two rectangles of contrasting material. The back was shiny black satin, decorated with a crude pentagram, stitched in red thread.

The front of the pouch was made of an entirely different material—a rough, matted rectangle of fur, golden-brown in color. The fur of an animal. The fur of a golden retriever.

A length of black ribbon had been threaded around the mouth of the pouch, forming a drawstring. Now, Simon Proctor held the pouch suspended over the head of Stephen Prince.

"Master of the Night! Soul Devourer!" Proctor's voice swelled, echoing off the black walls of the chapel. "We offer you this gift—the living soul, the undefiled breath, of

111

innocence. In return, bestow upon us the powers of thy abyss.''

Reaching down with his left hand, the high priest pinched the baby hard on the inside of its thigh. The baby began to shriek. The priest waited a moment, then pinched again, in the same spot. The baby's cries mushroomed into an outraged hysterical scream.

With one swift motion, Simon Proctor fitted the sack over the infant's head and pulled the drawstring tight. The music had ended. Except for the muffled wails of the baby, the chapel was hushed.

"Yes," whispered the priest, staring intently at his victim. "Yes."

Behind her mask, Rachel's eyes were closed. But nobody saw.

The baby's feet twitched wildly. Its tiny, splayed fingers rubbed frantically at the smothering hide.

Eventually, all movement stopped.

When it was over, the priest quickly slipped the sack from the corpse's head, tightening the drawstring with a single jerk. Someone lifted the infant's body—as limp as a rag doll's—by one foot and, with a vicious, underhand toss, heaved it into a shadowy corner of the room.

One of the women let out a sharp, whooping laugh.

Eyes gleaming, Simon Proctor held the sack aloft. "Satan!" he exulted.

His followers returned the jubilant shout; Rachel too, though her voice trembled badly.

Raising the pouch to his lips, Proctor spread its mouth apart with a violent yank and inhaled sharply, like an emphysemic taking oxygen from a tank. Then he flung the empty sack aside and bellowed, "In your service, Nightlord, I drink in the soul of the innocent!"

His cry was the signal for the orgy to commence.

Like animals taking down prey, the men brought down the women. Except that this prey found unspeakable pleasure in violation. The room became a tangle of writhing bodies.

Rachel's lover entered her hard, without any of the words or prolonged stroking she had come to expect. His entry was so sudden, so brutal, that she cried out in astonishment and pain.

A second later it was precisely what she wanted. Her nails raked across his chest before he caught her wrists and held them stretched high above her head.

In the crisis of his orgasm, his grip loosened. Deliberately she reached up to remove the grinning hyena's mask, to see the face of the man she would have done anything for—had already done everything for.

The mask came off. Leering down at her was the face of her demon lover, Simon Proctor's only begotten son—David Prince.

Part Two

The Dark

15

IT WAS ONLY 11:45 IN THE MORNING, BUT EVEN WITH ALL the blinds raised and the drapes pulled back, the house was filled with nothing but gloom.

Standing at the living room window, Jack Byrne glared out at the wet, gray world beyond the glass and, for the hundredth time in the two years since his wife's death, thought about selling his house and moving to a sunnier clime. Out to Arizona, maybe, where the sky is a shade of blue never seen in Flushing, Queens, and the occasional clouds look as clean as sterile cotton, not like some massive, sopping dishrag spread over the sky.

He didn't know if it was his age or the ozone layer, but with every passing year the climate in the Northeast seemed to grow more unbearable. Four days earlier, November had arrived with a blast of foul weather, and the storm hadn't eased up since. Outside, cold sheets of rain gusted up and down the street. Hell, sometimes they even blew sideways. He had put off all the errands that needed doing, things that still didn't come naturally to him, even now. The grocery shopping, the six-block walk to the bank to deposit some checks, the trip to the post office to pick up a roll of stamps.

All the vital, everyday chores Peggy had handled through-

117

out their married life. Chores he had never had to think about. Now they were all his to deal with. Slowly, he was getting used to them.

The loneliness was another matter.

He knew he should quit stalling—throw on his trench coat, grab his old, black umbrella, and just get the damned errands over with. He had always believed in taking care of business. But the thought of going out into the cold, lashing rain made him scowl.

The bank and post office could wait. As for lunch, well, he could always make a dash around the corner to the Bamboo Wok. Maybe the rain would have let up by then. It had been a while since he had treated himself to some Hunan-style beef. And dining in the company of other people—even strangers—would do him good. He was tired of eating alone at the Formica-topped kitchen table with a book propped open before him, while "E-Z Listening" music drifted from the portable radio he had set up on the counter.

He never used the dining room anymore, not since Peggy's death. Even when his daughter visited, they ate together in the tiny kitchen. The dining room was too formal, too full of Peggy's presence. It had been her favorite room, the one she was proudest of, with the handsome Ethan Allen dining room set purchased on their twenty-fifth wedding anniversary, and the cabinet filled with her beloved collection of ceramic Hummel figurines.

Nowadays, the only time Jack went into the dining room was to consult one of his books. His collection had grown so large that he needed more space to accommodate it, so he had installed a row of floor-to-ceiling shelves along one of the walls. By now the shelves were packed with hundreds of volumes, volumes with titles like *The Black Arts*, *Anatomy of Witchcraft*, *Satan's Underground*, *Necronomicon*, and *The Devil's Mass*.

For the last few days, as the rain drummed against the roof, he had spent most of his time leafing through dozens of these works. When he wasn't reading, he was brooding, brooding about the things his daughter had told him.

Marianne. Thinking about her now as he stared out at the endless downpour, he knew that his fantasies about

118

clean western skies were just idle daydreams. He'd never move that far away from her. She was all he had left.

She had called him nearly a week ago, on Halloween night. It had been an awkward time to talk to her. He'd had to keep interrupting their conversation to hurry to the front door and pass out M&M snack packs to the neighborhood trick-or-treaters.

Still, he understood her sense of urgency, her fired-up enthusiasm. It was what he used to feel when he was on the trail of something—a long time ago, before he'd lost his heart for the whole dirty business, before Sam's murder.

He had already known something about the nastiness up in Stoneham, even before Marianne phoned. He'd been following the newspaper accounts of the baby-snatching with close interest. When Marianne called, he had been curious to get the inside dope from her.

But as the details emerged, his curiosity gave way to concern.

"I don't know," she had said hesitantly as if thinking aloud. "Maybe the dog and the kidnapping aren't connected. But I just have a hunch about it." A bitter note had crept into her voice. "Not that I'd say that to Wayland again, not without proof. What do you think, Dad? About that missing patch of fur? Think that means anything?"

He had mulled the question over for a moment before answering. "Maybe," he finally acknowledged.

"But what? I've been searching through some of the standard references. I can't find anything about it."

Jack had thought for a moment, then sighed deeply. "It seems to me that I once came across something . . . I don't know, Marianne, let me do some checking." As he spoke, he pulled his Marlboros from his shirt pocket, shook a cigarette free, and lit it with a Bic portable. The orange flame flared in the black panes of the bedroom window. Sitting on the edge of his mattress, Jack stared at his own reflection in the glass a few feet away. Square, craggy face. Thinning gray hair. A close-trimmed gray beard that had begun to sprout in the terrible days following Peggy's death, when even shaving seemed like more than he could manage, and which, much to his surprise, he had come to like. The bulky upper torso of a two-hundred-pounder whose muscle has started to go soft.

119

"Wayland acts like I'm some kind of hysterical female," Marianne was complaining over the wire. "He thinks it's just some screwed-up kids who've been listening to too much heavy metal."

He could hear the muted anger in his daughter's voice. He didn't like to hear her so upset. But he considered Dick Wayland's opinion impartially.

"I know you don't want to hear it, Marianne. But he could be right, you know. There sure seems to be a lot of that crap going around lately. Hell, I get calls about it from all over the country these days. And Wayland's an experienced cop. He's been around the block a few times."

But even as he said this, he was thinking—Yeah, he's had experience, all right. Being a cop in a place where a perpetrator is someone who doesn't bring his pooper-scooper along when he walks the springer spaniel.

Jack took a deep drag and said, "You might be onto something, sweetheart. But you want my advice? Cool it for a while. Let me do some digging around. In the meantime, try not to piss off the boss. Even if you think he *is* a schmuck."

They hadn't talked much longer. She had mentioned that she intended to see Anna Prince again to ask about Simon Proctor. At the end of their conversation, he had warned her to be careful.

Laughing, she had accused him of being a "worrywart." Marianne didn't look much like Peggy—his wife was a lovely woman in his eyes but nowhere near the looker Marianne had turned into. But her laughter was the same. He liked to hear it; there was nothing he liked better. Still, hearing it always filled him with a fresh sense of loss.

Their conversation had ended with the usual exchange. Jack had fondly scolded Marianne for not calling more often, and Marianne, after assuring her dad that she loved him, had sworn that she would.

Afterward, Proctor's name kept nagging at him. He didn't know why. The name wouldn't have stuck with him just because the man was a murderer. In the course of his career, Jack had heard about, and worked on, more killings than he cared to or could possibly remember. So there was something else there. But what?

The day after Marianne's call, he had driven into Manhattan. He wanted to do some digging at the New York Public Library Newspaper Annex.

He'd parked his car by a construction site off Ninth Avenue, locked up, and headed north. One of his retirement gifts from his buddies—far more practical than a gold pocket watch—was a laminated PBA card, which he kept conspicuously displayed on the dashboard of his Chevy. It allowed him to park in any tow-away zone in the city and still find his car there when he returned.

It had been a while since Jack had visited that section of town, and he was struck by its weirdly schizophrenic quality. Part of it had become pure yuppie West Side Manhattan—expensive clothing boutiques, wood-paneled cafés advertising blackened redfish and angel hair pasta with pesto.

The other part was still as seedy as ever, strictly skid row. Crossing Tenth Avenue in the rain, he'd been accosted by a filth-caked derelict who looked and smelled as if he'd just been exhumed from potter's field. Jack had thrust a few coins into the man's grimy hand, then continued up the block to the library. Climbing the stairs to the entranceway, he had turned to look back at the derelict, who was busily rummaging through a garbage can on the corner of Forty-third and Tenth. Jack turned away just as the man fished out a half-eaten chicken leg and began gnawing on it.

Inside the cavernous library, there was more of the same crazy contrast. At one of the microfilm machines, a prim, middle-aged gentleman with the look of a literature professor was jotting down notes with a Mont Blanc fountain pen as he examined the screen. A few seats away a bag person—man or woman, it was impossible to say—was snoozing noisily with his—her?—head down on the table.

Jack filled out a request form and handed it to the teenage attendant, who was perched on a stool behind the counter, engrossed in a Stephen King novel. Shooting Jack a look of pure resentment—as if he had just been made the victim of an outrageous demand—the young man grabbed the slip out of Jack's outstretched hand and stalked off into the stacks. A few minutes later he returned with an armful of small cardboard boxes, each containing a roll of microfilm.

121

It took Jack about twenty minutes of searching, but he finally found what he was looking for. The *Los Angeles Times* had run an article on May 24, 1971, and the Albuquerque papers had done a whole series. Apparently there had been some local fear that Proctor might be another Charles Manson. Those initial fears had proved groundless. But Jack finally understood why he'd remembered the man's name.

Simon Proctor had indeed been involved in Satanism.

TAOS. May 24—Taos police said today that evidence of mutilated animals had been found at La Cruz, the ranch outside Taos where Simon Proctor is accused of slaying Daniel McKluskey, 26, of Phoenix, Arizona. The evidence, which includes the decomposed remains of several goats and at least one dog, lends support to unconfirmed rumors of devil worship at the commune.

Police sources claim that some of the animals were missing their tongues and had been mutilated in the genital area. Satanic symbols, including inverted crosses and the number 666, were reportedly painted in blood on the walls of the group's sleeping quarters.

Originally there were over fifty members of the commune, many of them teenage runaways, a police source said. At present, fewer than a dozen followers of Mr. Proctor remain at the ranch.

"All we've found," Detective José Osario told the *Albuquerque Daily Record,* "is the animals and evidence of extensive illegal drugs. From what we've heard, there was some pretty wild stuff going on out there—rituals, orgies, what have you. There were kids from all over the country following this guy Proctor. But the situation has been contained and the so-called commune is splitting up."

One member of the La Cruz group, Lisa Birnally, 24, of Chicago, claimed that Proctor had been arrested unfairly. "Dan wanted power. He was always after Simon. He told lies. He tried to turn us against Simon. It's like God and Lucifer, right? How many people can sit on the throne?"

Mr. Proctor is accused of stabbing Mr. McKluskey to death during an argument. According to unconfirmed reports, McKluskey's corpse had also been mutilated and its tongue excised. The county coroner could not be reached for verification.

Mr. McKluskey was one of the original members of the commune, which was established in 1968.

Proctor is being held in the Alamosa County Jail near Taos, awaiting arraignment.

Jack read the article over again. Then he dug into his pants pocket, fished out a quarter, and fed it into the coin slot at the top of the microfilm machine. Immediately, the machine whirred to life, and seconds later a moist, shiny photocopy slid out of its port and plopped into Jack's waiting hand.

That had been three days ago. Since then he had heard nothing more from Marianne and had been unable to reach her on the phone. He figured she was probably leading a busy social life when she wasn't on duty. He wondered if she'd been dating anybody decent for a change. Jack hadn't particularly cared for that guy Patrick she'd been shacking up with for a while. In fact, he'd felt deeply relieved when Marianne called to say they'd broken up, though he was sorry to hear her so depressed about it.

Still, she seemed to have put it all behind her. All this unpleasantness up in Stoneham obviously gave her something else to think about besides her own problems. That was one good thing about it, anyway.

Jack turned away from the living room window and headed for the kitchen. It was not quite noon, but his stomach was already growling.

Along the way he paused to pluck the topmost volume from a foot-high stack sitting on the living room coffee table.

He walked to the refrigerator and yanked open the door. The barren interior yawned before him. The top shelf was completely bare, except for a jar of kosher dills and an open milk carton imprinted with the smiling face of a missing schoolgirl. A few sorry slices of week-old deli food, loosely wrapped in plastic, were stuck inside the door shelf. Jack lifted them out and examined them. The roast beef looked as dry as jerky, and the Swiss cheese was going green around the edges. Peggy would probably have trimmed off the moldy parts of the cheese and made the rest into a sandwich. She hated to waste food. He stared at the meat and cheese for a moment, then put his foot to the pedal of the garbage can and dumped both packages inside.

Eventually he settled on a can of Campbell tomato-and-rice soup with a handful of Ritz crackers, which he carried to the little dinette table. Settling into his chair, he spread a napkin on his lap, picked up his spoon, and opened the book to the index.

He had found the volume a year or so before while browsing in the Magick Eye book shop on Fourth Street. Titled *Demonolatry,* it was a treatise on medieval devil and witch cults, with a particular focus on sacrificial ceremonies involving newborns.

Jack wasn't sure exactly what he was looking for. He knew that most recent reports of baby sacrifice were absolute bullshit, the lurid inventions of calculating publicity hounds, people who would do anything for a guest shot on "Geraldo." Or of desperate young women with deeply disturbed imaginations and a pathetic need for attention.

But he also knew something else—that baby sacrifice was an unspeakable reality practiced throughout the centuries by hardcore Satanists. And he recalled, though only vaguely, having come across a reference to a particular ceremony that had struck him at the time as exceptionally ghastly, even in the context of Satanic ritual.

This man Proctor sounded like a hardcase all right, and if he was deeply into Satanism, then maybe . . .

It just didn't make sense. First of all, Proctor was an old guy—at least ten years older, Jack thought, than he was. Second, he had been imprisoned in New Mexico. Was it possible that on the very day of his release—or even the day after—he had managed to travel two thousand miles east and steal someone's baby? And for what? To get revenge on a couple who had abandoned his cult twenty years before? And how would he have even known about the Princes' baby anyway? No. It just didn't hold water.

Still, it was strange that no ransom note had been received.

Maybe the child was stolen because someone else hated

Prince bitterly. The kid, Greg, who mowed his lawn? To Jack's mind, that explanation seemed unlikely too. Still, the answer might be found in Prince's past, in some injury or insult he had inflicted on someone, perhaps unknowingly.

He blew on a spoonful of soup and sipped.

"Not bad," he said aloud. His voice sounded almost startlingly loud in the quiet of the dark, empty house. He realized how long it had been since he'd had a real conversation with another human being. Probably not since that last call from Marianne. He would try phoning her again tonight. He wanted to tell her about what he had managed to turn up, not that it was very much so far. He was also beginning to get a little worried about where she might be, why he hadn't been able to reach her.

In fact, the whole idea of her getting mixed up in this business was beginning to make him very unhappy. It wasn't that he feared for her physical safety. She was, after all, a rookie cop, and Jack felt sure that, in any situation involving violence, Marianne would be kept in the background.

What was bothering him was something else—the danger to her spirit. His daughter had been raised with old-fashioned religious values. She had been taught about sin and evil, to be sure, but she had also been infused with a deep faith in the essential goodness of humankind, with the belief that light was a greater power than darkness.

He hated to think of that belief dying in her.

Jack sighed and nibbled at a cracker. But what could he do? Marianne was a big girl now. And even more to the point, she was a cop. Hard to stay innocent under those conditions. He adored his daughter. He would have loved to shelter her from the unimaginable things he had seen and suffered. But how the hell to do it—well, he'd be damned if he knew.

16

SITTING CROSS-LEGGED LIKE A MAN—RIGHT ANKLE RESTING on the opposite knee—Marianne leaned back in the green-and-beige-striped love seat and surveyed the Princes' living room, wryly comparing its subdued elegance to the thrift-shop informality of her own quarters. No doubt about it, she thought. Money might not buy you happiness, but it sure helps you enjoy your misery in comfortable surroundings.

Shoving herself to her feet, she made a circuit of the room, pausing every now and then to admire a porcelain vase or to study one of the somber prints arranged in asymmetrical groupings across the bone-white walls. In one hand she held her police cap loosely by the rim, and as she walked, she beat it absently against her leg as if it were a tambourine.

Marianne examined a small, vaguely Egyptian-looking statue of a naked woman with a raven's head and decided that if she had enough money to afford fancy furniture and art, she would definitely pick things that were a little cheerier. She was impressed by the obvious costliness of the furnishings; the living room looked as perfect as a layout in *House Beautiful* magazine. But like a formal photograph, there was also something artificial about it. Something dead.

Or maybe, she thought, she was simply responding to the air of desolation that filled the house like the aftermath of a fire.

Maybe the house hadn't seemed quite so dead when a new life had breathed within it.

She had been waiting now for nearly ten minutes. A gray-haired, dark-skinned woman wearing a cheap cotton dress and an old cardigan sweater had answered the door when she arrived—evidently one of the Philippine cleaning ladies the police report mentioned. It had been hard to communicate with her, since Marianne didn't speak a word of Spanish and the woman's English seemed limited to the word "Yes?" Marianne had spent a few moments repeating the

126

name "Mrs. Prince" and using her hands to convey the concept of "talk," while the cleaning lady stared at her quizzically. When the woman finally nodded and headed for the stairway, Marianne thought she had managed to get her message across.

But now, as she shoved up her jacket sleeve and glanced at her watch, she was beginning to wonder.

She had almost made up her mind to mount the stairs and find Anna Prince's bedroom herself when she heard some movement from the hallway—a faltering shuffle, as though an invalid were slowly descending the stairs.

A moment later Anna Prince stood in the living room entranceway.

She was wearing an oversize gray sweater and loose pants of the same soft fabric. The outfit looked like the world's most expensive jogging suit. Her feet were bare and her cherry-red toenails seemed incongruously cheerful. No makeup brightened her pale, stricken face, and her auburn hair was a long, wild tangle.

Marianne stepped forward and, holding out her hand, introduced herself in a soft, consoling voice. She found it impossible to speak in any other tone to this ravaged-looking woman. Anna took her hand and led her to the nearest sofa. It was a small couch, and Anna positioned herself very close to her visitor.

Marianne felt uncomfortable. She was here on official business, and anyway, she didn't much like strangers pressing at her. But she sensed that Anna Prince was one of those women who like to touch and be touched constantly. Or perhaps it was just a natural part of grieving, a human need for solace in the aftermath of loss. Marianne remembered how much she needed to be held by Patrick even a year after her mother's death.

In any case, she was close enough to Anna Prince to smell the scotch on her breath. It was ten in the morning.

"Mrs. Prince—"

"Anna," the woman whispered. "Call me Anna." She looked at Marianne with the desperate hopefulness of a cancer patient praying for a miracle.

Marianne hesitated for a moment, then smiled gently. "Anna," she said. "How are you feeling?"

Anna Prince closed her eyes and sagged back against the

127

sofa. "You don't have any news for me, do you," she said dully. She massaged her forehead with the heel of one hand, as though she were trying to ease a migraine. "Of course you don't."

Marianne took a deep breath. "I'm sorry, Mrs. Prince. Anna. Without a ransom demand, there just isn't that much to go on. So far, the fingerprints haven't led anywhere. There are only a few unmatched partials. And this kid Greg—well, we've got a good likeness of him, but so far we haven't turned up anyone who—"

Anna seemed to grow agitated. "That boy had nothing to do with this." She was twisting her wedding ring round and round on her finger. "I've already told the police who's behind it."

"You mean Simon Proctor."

Anna nodded. "But no one will believe me."

"Anna," Marianne said gently, "I have to tell you that, to the best of our knowledge, Simon Proctor is still in New Mexico."

"It makes no difference. Simon's behind it." There was neither anger nor obstinacy in her voice, only an infinite sadness.

Marianne glanced down at the floor for a moment, then looked back up at Anna, who seemed mesmerized by her ring.

"Why are you so sure?" Marianne asked, forcing herself to voice Wayland's skepticism. "I mean, I know that you and your husband lived in that commune near Taos, and that Proctor got angry when you left. Obviously he was a dangerously disturbed individual. I've read the news stories on him. I'm sure you know about that guard he assaulted in prison. But it's been twelve years since that incident happened. Everyone down there—the police, the prison officials—say he's harmless now, a harmless old man."

"Let me tell you something about Simon," Anna said, her voice dropping to a whisper. "Dan McKluskey wasn't the only person he killed. There was someone else too. A sixteen-year-old girl who showed up at the commune one day and then . . . disappeared."

"Who was she?"

Anna shrugged vaguely. "Some runaway."

"Are you saying Simon killed her?"

Anna kept her gaze fixed on Marianne.

"How do you know? Did you witness it?"

"We knew. We all knew."

Marianne didn't know whether she believed Anna Prince or not. But she felt herself growing angry all the same. "And everybody just let him do this stuff? Why?"

"We worshiped him," Anna said simply.

Marianne took a deep breath. How much of this story was true? She remembered what Wayland had told her—that Anna Prince was teetering at the edge and could dive off the deep end any minute. It didn't help matters that she was hitting the bottle so heavily. Maybe all this stuff about Proctor was just some kind of paranoid weirdness.

On the other hand, there were definitely some spooky things in the woman's past. And it was the business of spooks to come back and haunt you.

"Anna," said Marianne, "I want to help you. But I need information. You're going to have to tell me everything you know about Simon Proctor."

Anna made no response. Her blood-red eyes were vacant, her complexion chalky white against the auburn tangles of her hair. "There is no help," she said finally. With a little moan of effort, she rose unsteadily to her feet. "I have to lie down," she muttered, and began making her way toward the staircase.

Marianne rose too. "Should I wait?"

Swaying slightly, Anna reached for the newel post to steady herself. "Please, Officer Byrne," she said. "I can't talk anymore right now. I just don't have the strength for it. Do you think you could come back in a few days? Maybe I'll feel a little stronger by then."

Marianne sighed. "Sure," she said after a moment. She reached down and plucked her cap off the sofa cushion. Then, straightening up, she said, "Mrs. Prince, do you think I might speak to your husband?" Wayland had told her that David Prince often worked at home.

"David? He's not home. He stays away. There's too much pain here."

Wayland would have a number in the city where Prince could be reached. Marianne let it go and joined Anna at the foot of the stairs. "I'll come by again in a couple of days." Reaching out a hand, she laid it on top of Anna's.

"If there's any news about Stephen before then, I'll let you know right—"

"You won't get any news about my baby," Anna interrupted. "He's gone."

It was what Marianne feared too. But she said gently, "Mrs. Prince, you shouldn't give up hope. It hasn't been that long. You could still hear from the kidnappers, or—"

"No. He's gone. The night he was taken, I knew I'd never see him again. I'm being punished."

"Punished? Why?"

"For what I've seen. For what I've done. For what I didn't do. Who knows?" She squeezed her eyes tight as though fighting back tears. But when she opened them again, they were dry. "I just know my baby's dead."

Standing on the porch, watching the rust-red leaves float from the treetops to litter the broad lawn below, Marianne reflected on Anna Prince's despair. It seemed strange that the mother of a kidnapped child would lose hope so quickly.

Marianne didn't know what to think. Wayland hadn't believed Proctor was involved. And as she knew from the talks she'd already had with them, the cops out in New Mexico agreed with Wayland.

What did Marianne have to counter that skepticism? A feeling, that was all. An intuition. An intuition that Anna Prince was telling the truth.

Marianne flipped on her cap and fitted it snugly over her thick black hair. As she did, she turned her head slightly and caught sight of the porch lamp to the right of the front door. Immediately she recalled something that had struck her as peculiar in the police report on the kidnapping— something that had slipped her mind until that moment. The part about the porch light. How the bulb had been burned out on the night of the kidnapping.

How convenient for the kidnapper, Marianne had thought at the time.

Now, peering closely at the light bulb, she saw something that made her frown. At the end of the stem, where the bulb was screwed into the socket, part of the metal base was visible.

Reaching into her jacket pocket, Marianne pulled out her

leather gloves and slipped the right one onto her hand. Carefully, she undid the metal slide on the lantern and popped open the panel that permitted access to the bulb. Reaching inside, she delicately gripped the end of the bulb with the tips of two fingers and gave it a single clockwise twist.

Her eyes narrowed at what she saw.

In the brightness of the late morning sunlight, the dead bulb beamed dully to life.

17

JEAN PEARY CRUNCHED OFF A CORNER OF HER BUTTERED toast and smiled across the kitchen table at her daughter. From time to time the sun outside the east-facing window disappeared behind a cloud, dimming the brightness in the room. It was eleven-fifteen in the morning, Saturday, November 7.

Forty-five minutes earlier Jean had stepped into Rachel's room and, moving softly to her bedside, had reached down and smoothed the fine blond hair off her daughter's forehead. Rachel had awakened with a little purr of protest, then rolled onto her back and mumbled "good morning" without opening her eyes. Now they were eating breakfast together—something they hadn't done for several years—and making small talk about the Benetton outlet that had just opened in town and about Rachel's social studies teacher, Mr. Cullum, a thirty-year-old Kevin Costner lookalike whose sexual orientation was a matter of widespread speculation among the student body.

"Think he's gay?" Jean said, reaching for the coffeepot.

Rachel finished chewing her mouthful of bagel. "Annie Schiff says she once ran into him in the city with another guy. They were on their way to the opera."

"Well, I guess that proves it," Jean said wryly.

It had been four days since Rachel's return. She had shown up, apologetic and subdued, on Tuesday afternoon. Her two-day disappearance had been the blackest time of Jean's life, infinitely worse than anything she'd suffered during her divorce. The breakup of her marriage had left Jean feeling deeply shaken and vulnerable, as if a wrecking

131

ball had smashed into her house while she was still inside. But her life with Bill had become a prison, and its demolition, once the initial shock had subsided and the dust had settled, had brought with it a feeling of release. She hadn't come through unscathed. But she was still on her feet.

When Rachel had stormed off into the night, however, it was as if the bottom had suddenly dropped out too, and Jean had felt herself hurtling into a black and bottomless despair.

And then her daughter had come home. Standing in the tiny front hallway, they had embraced, wept in each other's arms, and murmured mutual words of apology and forgiveness.

Now it was time to rebuild.

Outside the kitchen window the sky brightened as suddenly as if God had flipped a switch. A sparkle of sunlight glimmered on the surface of Jean's black coffee. "Here's an idea," Jean said, sipping. "How about a movie this afternoon? Louise was raving about the new Woody Allen. And then we can go out for dinner. Maybe that Spanish place in Hartsdale you like so much, the one with the great fajitas?"

Rachel lowered her eyes. "Sure. If you want to." There was no enthusiasm in her voice.

Jean put down her coffee cup and leaned forward on the table. "What is it, hon?"

Rachel sat there, head down, lips drawn tight, and shook her head. A single tear, heavy as a raindrop, fell to the table.

"Baby," whispered Jean. Rising, she pulled her chair around to Rachel's side, then drew her daughter against her body, reaching up to stroke Rachel's soft, damp cheek. "Don't cry."

"I feel bad about the baby," Rachel said hoarsely.

Jean kissed the top of her daughter's head and felt her own throat constrict with sorrow. But she forced her voice to brighten. "It's still early," she said. "I bet they'll get him back. The police seem to think so. I spoke to Chief Wayland just yesterday. He called to see how you were feeling. He's very hopeful. His men are making real progress, he said." This last statement was, if not a lie, then at least a serious exaggeration. What Wayland had really said was that his men were following a few new leads.

Rachel said nothing for a long moment, then worked herself free of her mother's embrace and sat up stiffly, blotting her eyes with a balled-up napkin.

A twinge of rejection pinched at Jean's heart, and she struggled to subdue it. Giving her daughter a little rub between the shoulder blades, she rose to clear the table.

"Rachel," she said gently, removing her daughter's juice glass and plate. "Do you think it would help if you talked to someone?"

Rachel shot her mother a sideways look. "You mean like a shrink or something?"

Jean nodded. "Someone you can talk to without feeling judged. It might be good for you."

Rachel cleared her throat and shook her head. "I'll be okay." Her juice glass had left a small, watery ring on the table. She reached out a fingertip and began doodling aimlessly in the moisture. "Mom," she said quietly after a moment. "I'm really sorry for all the trouble. For running away like that. And all that other stuff."

Jean took a deep breath. She hadn't worked up the courage to raise the issue since Rachel's return. "Can I ask you something about that 'other stuff'? One last question and then I promise never to bring it up again?"

"Sure," Rachel sighed, after the briefest hesitation.

"Why were you fooling around with those things in the first place? Those things in your drawer."

Rachel kept her head down. Her long hair curtained her face from Jean's gaze. "I don't know," she said softly. Then she gave a little snort, a noise that sounded shockingly cynical to Jean's maternal ears. "Teenage rebellion, right?"

"How did you get involved with it? Through your friends?"

"Not friends, really. Just a bunch of kids I started hanging with at school. No one you know. Thought they were cool."

"Who thought they were cool? You or them?"

Rachel shrugged. "Both, I guess." She looked up at her mother with a sheepish grin. "I was dumb, I admit it."

"But what would you do with those things?" Jean persisted. It was her turn to look sheepish. "I guess I lied about having just one more question."

Rachel smiled, then turned serious. "It was no big deal. We'd just go to someone's house after school, sit around in the basement, listen to some tapes and say a lot of stuff. Prayers and chants, that kind of thing. We got this book, *The Satanic Bible*. One of the guys found it in an occult bookstore in the city, along with all these weird amulets and things. That's where the stuff you found came from." Rachel drew in a deep, quivering breath. "It was like, I don't know, a secret club or something. It made us feel special. I guess it was something to do, a place to go after school and hang out. I mean, you were hardly ever home. Nobody's parents were."

Jean winced. "Tell me this. Was anybody doing drugs?"

"Never," Rachel said emphatically.

Jean didn't know whether Rachel was telling the truth. Still, she hadn't found syringes or pills or packets of white powder in Rachel's drawers. She chose to believe her.

"Rachel. Don't get angry or upset with me, but there's one more thing I have to know. Did these friends of yours have anything to do with that dog, the one that was found mutilated on Woodland Drive?"

Rachel made a "give-me-a-break" face. "These kids would puke if they had to dissect a frog in biology lab," she scoffed.

It wasn't until that moment, when she felt her shoulder muscles uncramp, that Jean fully realized how tense the past few minutes had been. She pushed up the sleeves of her sweatshirt and began loading the dishwasher.

The conversation returned to local gossip. No stranger coming onto the scene would have guessed that only moments before this suburban mom and her pretty daughter had been engaged in a conversation about a disemboweled dog and after-school Satanism.

A few minutes later Rachel got up, stretched, and announced that she was going to take a shower. At the kitchen doorway, however, she paused and looked back at her mother. "Mom," she said, fidgeting with the sash of her bathrobe. "I have one question for *you* now."

"Shoot," Jean said.

"What did you do with that stuff you found in my drawer?"

Jean loaded a cup carefully in the upper rack. "I threw it away." She risked a look at her daughter.

"Oh." For a moment Rachel's expression was blank. Then she smiled. "Good."

After Rachel was gone, Jean leaned back against the counter, arms folded. Seconds later she heard the shower start up with a muffled rush.

She felt that they were making progress, slowly but steadily. Desperate to mend the rift between them, Jean had to keep reminding herself that their injured life would take a while to heal. Rachel appeared genuinely remorseful and anxious to repair their relationship. That was the important thing.

Still, her daughter seemed painfully distant. Not angry or resentful. Jean couldn't really detect any bitterness in Rachel. No, it was as if she simply weren't *there*.

Shaking her head, Jean removed the last remnants of their breakfast from the table and stuck everything back in the fridge. "What the hell did you expect?" she demanded aloud. Had she really expected Rachel to come crawling back into her lap like Mommy's little girl after everything that had happened?

No, she thought, wryly. But it sure would have felt nice.

They needed time, that was all, she kept telling herself. Ordinary evenings, chatting over supper and watching TV. Lazy weekend breakfasts. Leisurely Sunday afternoons. Eventually they would get close again. Eventually Rachel would learn to trust her mother, to treat her like a friend, to talk openly and honestly.

For that matter, Jean hadn't been entirely honest with Rachel either. She had lied when she told Rachel that she had thrown away the little effigies, the vial of liquid, the dagger—all those creepy, repulsive things. She wasn't sure why she had lied.

She wasn't sure why she had kept them either.

18

PINE RIDGE CEMETERY STOOD ON A LITTLE HILLTOP TWO miles northeast of Stoneham, midway between the town center and the Willow Brook Elementary School. Every morning, and again in the afternoon, hundreds of children would suck in their collective breath and hold it for several seconds while their big orange school buses rattled past the graveyard. Bad luck to inhale the tainted atmosphere given off by the dead.

A connoisseur of antique tombstones, the kind who tours through the Puritan graveyards of New England, rice paper and rubbing crayon at the ready, would not have found much of interest at Pine Ridge. Though many of the headstones looked ancient and weatherworn—plain white tablets, many so badly eroded that their inscriptions were barely legible—the oldest dated back only to the late 1800s. The rest were of more recent vintage: handsome gray memorials, as dignified and unadorned as a banker's three-piece suit. Here and there a red-granite cenotaph rose like a stone phallus from a fenced-off family plot, and in a far corner of the graveyard stood a little mausoleum, housing, behind its padlocked steel door, the mortal remains of one of Stoneham's most venerable clans.

Though Pine Ridge might have disappointed a collector of tombstone rubbings, it was a strikingly pretty and peaceful spot, even in an area rich in country quiet. Sheltered by trees and elevated from the roadway, it had the air of a small, pleasantly unoccupied park. Few burials took place there anymore, for only fifty or so of Stoneham's oldest families owned plots in the little graveyard. In any given year, no more than a dozen new inhabitants would be installed among the bones of their relations.

To the followers of Simon Proctor, therefore, it seemed a wonderful coincidence (if not further confirmation of their high priest's special powers) that, on the afternoon of Thursday, November 10—precisely when they needed one—Pine Ridge Cemetery received a fresh corpse.

*　*　*

Her name was Melissa Campbell, and she had died suddenly, though not wholly unexpectedly, of cardiomyopathy, a congenital heart-muscle disease whose potentially fatal consequences had been averted for the thirteen brief years of her life by daily medication.

Two days earlier, for reasons still unknown to her doctors, the medicine failed to work. Outside in the backyard, kicking a soccer ball back and forth with her ten-year-old sister, Melissa had suddenly felt her heart flutter wildly. A moment later she lay convulsing on the ground. Neither parent was at home. By the time her little sister's screams had brought the housekeeper running, Melissa was gone.

On the morning of her funeral, the priest delivered an eloquent eulogy, taking the verse "For ye know not the hour" as his text. Though the day had an Indian summer mildness, both parents shivered at the gravesite. Before he led his weeping wife away, Mr. Campbell took one last look around, plucking a shred of consolation from the beauty of the little hilltop on which his daughter would rest in peace until the resurrection.

Or so, at least, he believed.

A heavy cloud cover blocked the moonlight that very night, as though the darkness Proctor worshiped were responding with another gift.

At a few minutes past two A.M., an hour when Stoneham seemed as dead as a ghost town, a dark Toyota sedan moved slowly along Route 107, cutting its headlights as it swung left onto the narrow, paved road that wound up the hillside into the cemetery.

A few yards up the hill the car pulled to a quiet stop. Seconds later a pair of figures emerged from either side— two young men, clad in black Levi's and dark turtleneck sweaters. Each wore a black wool cap pulled low over his neatly clipped blond hair. Around their necks they wore loosely draped bandanas, which could be drawn up to their noses in an instant to help conceal the brightness of their faces. And to filter out the smells.

They stood for a moment in the darkness, letting their eyes grow fully accustomed to the night. Then, leaving the front doors and trunk lid open, they moved quickly up the hill until they reached the crest, where they paused, crouching, tools in hand. Two shovels. One flashlight. One twelve-inch pry bar.

The caretaker's house stood at the far end of the graveyard. Like virtually every other residence in Stoneham at that hour, it seemed as lifeless as the little mausoleum.

The young men scanned the darkness for a moment. Then the one clutching the pry bar pointed it toward the left.

Even in the murk of the moonless light, the shape of the backhoe was unmistakable—a hulking, angular mass like the silhouette of a monstrous insect.

As stealthily as commandos, the two young men stole across the graveyard, snaking their way between tombstones. A few yards from the backhoe the grass gave way to bare ground. The young man holding the flashlight switched it on for the briefest of moments, just long enough to register the patch of raw earth with a bouquet of roses laid upon it.

One of them stooped to move the flowers, then, without a word, they pulled their bandanas up over their mouths and began to dig.

They were muscular young men, their upper bodies hardened by daily workouts. The loosely packed earth, dredged up and replaced less than twenty-four hours before, gave way easily beneath their spades.

They worked steadily, pausing periodically to listen attentively to the sounds of the night. Once or twice a car whooshed past on the roadway below. Otherwise—nothing.

Fifty-five minutes later their shovel blades scraped wood. Kneeling on the coffin lid in the dark trench, they paused for a moment, yanking off their woolen caps to let the night air cool their sweat. Then, while one beamed the flashlight on the coffin, the other worked his pry bar beneath the upper panel and, leaning his full weight down on the tool, levered open the top half of the lid.

A sickly sweet stench wafted up from the casket, palpable even through their bandanas. Melissa had been buried in her favorite outfit, an emerald-green velvet dress with a high-necked lace collar. In the beam of the flashlight her face seemed as smooth and yellow as wax. She looked wholly unreal, like a museum mannequin in a Victorian costume exhibit.

Shoving the pry bar through his belt, the young man scuttled to the far end of the casket, stooped, grabbed the corpse beneath its armpits and pulled, grunting with the effort. As her lower body emerged, his friend seized it beneath the knees and helped to lift it from the casket.

In life, the girl had possessed a ballerina's grace. Dead, she was as lumpish as a large sack of feed. Hauling her out of the pit left the young men so winded that they had to pull off their bandanas to suck in enough air.

But they had no time to waste. Snatching up their spades, they shoved the blades into the mounded dirt. And froze at what they heard.

The snapping of a twig. Someone was moving in the graveyard.

They had been tutored for this contingency and were prepared to leave the caretaker's corpse in place of Melissa's. Reaching slowly around to their hip pockets, each withdrew a linoleum knife, sliding out the blade with a shove of the thumb. Crouching, they scanned the darkness.

Suddenly, one of them emitted a soft, nasal snort of amusement, nudged his partner and pointed.

Ten yards away, a small, whitish shape seemed to bob in a blackness even denser than the night. As the young men stared, the black mass resolved itself into the figure of a white-tailed deer, stepping insouciantly across several graves to get at a low-hanging evergreen branch.

The young men replaced their weapons and returned to their work.

Forty minutes later they were tamping down the soil on the pillaged grave.

With the help of his friend, the taller of the two teenagers heaved the corpse over his shoulder and started down the hillside. His companion retrieved the shovels and flashlight and followed after. Abruptly, he pulled to a stop, muttering a soft, barely audible, "Shit!"

Swiveling, he trotted back a few steps, switched on his flashlight and rapidly searched the ground until he spotted what he was hunting for. He stooped to pick it up from the grass where he had carefully placed it two hours before.

The bouquet of roses.

He positioned it at the head of the grave, where Melissa's

mother, her gloved hand trembling with grief, had laid it the previous morning.

Then he turned and hurried down to the car.

It wasn't until they were a mile from the graveyard, their plunder safely stowed inside the trunk, that they slapped palms in triumph.

"Hope the new boy appreciates this. What's his name again?"

"Rutherford. Tim Rutherford."

"Lucky fuck. Little Miss Muffet's a piece."

"Fuck of a lot nicer than the one I had to do."

"Gotta take what's available."

The driver sniffed. "Smell that?"

"Yeah. Better crack open some windows."

Reaching down, the driver fingered the buttons on his armrest. The side windows slid down with a whine.

Damp predawn air rushed through the interior, washing out the faint perfume of death.

19

EVERY DAY THAT WEEK, JEAN LEFT WORK PROMPTLY AT five, even when that meant turning one of her appointments over to another agent. Edgar Davison, the diminutive, white-haired office manager, wasn't happy with Jean's new routine and took her aside first thing Thursday morning to caution her, in gentle, grandfatherly tones, that she was jeopardizing her opportunity to be named regional sales agent of the year. But Jean just smiled and said she'd take the chance.

What about the potential loss of income? Davison asked more pointedly.

"I appreciate your concern, Edgar," Jean said, hoping he wouldn't hear the sarcasm she was struggling to control. "I'm sure I'll muddle through."

It was not that Jean was free of money worries. She had accepted child support but no alimony from Bill. Still, a commission or two, even on a chunk of Stoneham's extravagant real estate, seemed like a small price to pay for the extra time with Rachel.

Later that Thursday morning, Jean had received a forceful reminder of just how precious her time with Rachel was. Sitting at her desk, leafing through her appointment book, she had glanced up at the big plate-glass window that faced Main Street. Like every other business in town, Abercrombie Realty had taken down its Halloween decorations on the first day of November and replaced them with cutout turkeys and cardboard pilgrims.

Jean was gazing at the Thanksgiving decor, wondering idly when the new tradition of pushing major holidays ahead by a month had started, when she saw it through the window. A stately procession of cars and limousines, led by a big black hearse, moving slowly along Main Street and turning right toward Route 107.

Melissa Campbell's funeral. Jean had learned of the tragedy the day before. She knew the Campbells slightly and had a clear image of their daughter, a pretty, slender child, just blooming into adolesence.

Jean's heart went out to the girl's mother, but at the same time, she experienced a guilty pang of gratitude. She had come close to losing her own daughter. But she'd been given—both of them had been given—a second chance. And she had no intention of letting it slip through her fingers.

She stared at a cardboard cornucopia taped to the window and thought, This year, I really do have something to be thankful for.

On Friday evening Jean arrived home at five-thirty and found her daughter bent over the kitchen stove, big red mitts on her hands, removing a casserole from the oven. Straightening up, Rachel held the baking dish before her like an offering. The glutinous contents bubbled and steamed.

"Macaroni and cheese," she said shyly. "I thought I'd cook for us tonight."

Instantly, Jean felt her eyes well up with tears. As Rachel set the dish down on the stove top, Jean stepped forward and embraced her. Rachel, her hands still encased in the oversized mitts, hugged her mother back awkwardly, then quickly broke away.

141

"It's not very fancy," she said, with an apologetic laugh. "I got the recipe off the macaroni box."

Jean quickly set the table, and they sat down to eat. Rachel had managed both to overcook the casserole and drown it in cheese. The noodles had the texture of pudding, and the taste of grated Parmesan was overwhelming.

Jean thought it was the most delicious meal she'd ever eaten.

She was spooning another helping onto her plate when Rachel said, "By the way, is it okay with you if I go out on a date tomorrow night?"

Jean, taken aback, made a conscious effort to keep her voice even. "A date?"

"Yeah. You know. With a guy."

Jean squinted at Rachel. "Are you saying that you already *have* a date or that you're just *thinking* of going out?"

Rachel glanced down at her plate. "I already have one."

Jean took a deep breath. "Rachel," she said gently. "Are you sure you feel up to socializing again? I mean, so soon?"

"Mom," Rachel said with a hint of exasperation. "You didn't expect me to stay home every weekend the rest of my life."

. . . *with you* were the unspoken words that sounded in Jean's head. "Of course not," she said. "I just thought"— she shrugged—"last Saturday night was so much fun."

Rachel nodded. "We'll do it again."

Jean looked doubtful. "Who is this boy?" she asked. Then, hearing the suspicion in her voice, she quickly softened her tone. "I mean, is this someone I know?" Already she was conjuring up images of black leather jackets and blue jeans gaping at the knees.

"No. He's not from Stoneham. He lives in Ridgewood. I met him last month at a party at Katie Brill's house. Before . . . the accident. He called me up yesterday from out of the blue to see if I wanted to go to a movie. I said yes."

Jean gazed hard at her daughter. "He's not one of that group you were hanging around with after school, I hope."

Rachel looked indignant. "Of course not!"

Jean sighed after a moment. "Well, if it'll make you

142

happy." She slid another forkful of macaroni into her mouth, chewed, and swallowed.

But the food had lost some of its savor.

There were many things about the younger generation's social customs that Jean found highly questionable, even slightly grotesque. But she had to give Rachel and her friends credit for doing away with one inane tradition. Unlike the girls of her own generation, they did not make a ritual out of keeping their dates waiting.

By 7:45 on Saturday night, Rachel was already downstairs, dressed casually but quite demurely in tan corduroy slacks and a white cable-knit sweater. With her hair pulled back into a ponytail, she looked fresh-faced and pretty. The scar on her forehead was already starting to fade into invisibility.

Ah, the recuperative powers of the young, Jean thought.

Precisely fifteen minutes later the doorbell buzzed.

Rachel hurried to answer the door, while Jean remained seated on the living room sofa, steeling herself for several uncomfortable minutes of small talk with another of her daughter's monosyllabic dates. As soon as the young man stepped into the room, however, Jean's apprehensions began to dissolve.

He was as far removed from her anxious fantasies as possible. His blond hair was carefully groomed, he wore a herringbone sport jacket and neatly pressed wool slacks, and his bearing, as he stepped across the floor with Rachel at his side, was impressively poised.

If anything, he looked slightly too preppy for Jean's personal taste. I can't believe you're complaining! she chided herself silently.

Beaming, Jean held out her hand. The young man reached down to shake it.

"Mother, I'd like you to meet my date," Rachel said happily, laying a hand lightly on his shoulder.

Jean continued to smile up at him. "I'm very pleased to meet you . . ." Her voice trailed off into uncertainty.

"Tim," said the young man quickly. "Tim Rutherford."

20

A DOZEN FAT BLACK CANDLES SCENTED WITH MUSK BURNED
in the bridal chamber, but their reek did little to conceal the
stink of corruption that filled the airless room. The room
contained a single piece of furniture—a king-size four-
poster that towered in the center of the black-tiled floor.
Black satin drapery hung down from the canopy, completely enclosing the bed. But the fetor emanating from the
mattress seeped freely through the fabric.

The same satin material had been used to fashion the
curtains that blocked the bedroom windows. The walls
were lined with floor-to-ceiling mirrors, which reflected to
infinity the only contents of the room—the brass candelabra, the black-shrouded bed.

Nothing stirred or breathed in the dark, smoky chamber.
Certainly not the bed's hidden occupant, the waiting bride.

Through the ebony floor the faintest of dronings, as of
voices joined in prayer, filtered up from the chapel below,
then seemed to float into silence, as though the votaries
were filing out of the chapel. Gradually the chanting grew
stronger again, and the staircase creaked as the congregation, still praying, mounted to the second floor.

Suddenly, the heavy door of the bridal chamber swung
open and the little party of worshipers filed into the room,
led by their black-robed priest and his duteous son.

The twelve worshipers arranged themselves in facing
lines, males and females on opposite sides. The animal
masks were gone. Instead they wore small, velvet eye
masks, the girls' black, the boys' white.

They smiled at each other's nakedness. One of the girls
reached down and fingered herself briefly, then lifted her
moisture to her lips, leering at the stiffening males.

The priest stood at the head of the line. His own erection
was sheathed in an enormous black leather phallus. Secured to his loins with leather straps, it jutted straight out
from his crotch, donkeysize and bristling with spikes.

He held his palms open flat before him, as though supporting a hymnal. But his hands were empty, and the prayer he murmured as he gazed down at the emptiness came from nowhere but the black core of his soul.

Abruptly, he looked up at his followers and boomed, "Let the novitiate come forth."

The worshipers turned their gaze toward the door. Tim Rutherford stood there. He too wore a mask, but of crimson moiré. He stepped into the chamber.

Naked like the others, he walked with a slightly unsteady gait. Through the eyeholes of his mask, his pupils gleamed with an unnatural, drugged brightness.

As he passed down the aisle formed by the facing rows, the young women and the men alike reached out their hands to fondle and stroke him.

Seconds later he stood before the black-robed priest.

"Welcome, my child, to the communion of your race," said the dark figure. "You have found thus young, your nature and your destiny."

"Welcome!" intoned the twelve worshipers.

"Tonight, you will be wedded to the darkness and taste the sweetness of night's womb. Death's bride shall be your lover." He nodded to the worshipers. "Let the solemnities begin."

With that, three of the girls quickly stepped forward and knelt on the tiled floor, two at Tim Rutherford's feet, one behind. Laughingly, they applied their lips and tongues to his body. The somber room was hushed. The only sounds to be heard were the boy's rapid breathing and the wet, contented, sucking noises produced by the ministering girls.

Proctor watched Tim Rutherford's face closely, smiling as the boy's excitement mounted. Suddenly, he held out his hands and cried, "Bridesmaids!"

Two young women, their greased flesh warm in the candle glow, stepped to the bed and drew aside the curtains, releasing a foul miasma into the room.

Flat on its back in the center of the big mattress lay Melissa Campbell's cadaver. Two pillows had been shoved behind her head, so that she seemed to be sitting up in bed. Her eyes appeared to gape with a crazy brightness. But this was only a crude illusion. Her shuttered lids had been painted white, and black dots daubed in the center. Garish red lipstick smeared over her lips made her mouth look both clownish and obscene.

The waxen corpse was completely naked. Her legs had been shoved up and bent at the knees. Soles flat on the bed, thighs thrust wide apart. Her stiff hands were positioned between her legs, as though separating the lightly downed lips for inspection.

Someone had stuck fishhooks through her nipples. A length of nylon line was knotted through the eye of each hook, then sewn tightly to the fabric of the canopy, yanking her nipples taut in a grotesque parody of sexual arousal.

The three young women rose and led Tim Rutherford to the foot of the bed. Climbing onto the mattress, he shuffled forward on his knees, positioning himself between the legs of the slender corpse.

The worshipers surrounded the bed. Rachel moved around the little circle to stand beside David, but he was too intent on the ritual to notice her.

"Embrace the night," the celebrants chanted. "Satan's bride! Fuck her!"

Leaning down, the boy struggled to work himself into the body. He paused for a moment to get a better grip on the mattress with his knees.

"She's a virgin!" one of the watching girls tittered.

"Two virgins," another said.

"So pretty," whispered a third, stroking the corpse's thick hair.

The first reached a hand beneath Tim Rutherford's buttocks and massaged.

A wave of faintness washed over Rachel. She took a step away from the reeking bed to catch her breath. As she did, she noticed one of the boys standing slightly apart from the group, head bowed. In the murk of the chamber, and through the grogginess of her own drugged perception, it took her a moment to recognize the masked boy.

Frowning, she moved back into the circle.

A dozen hands caressed Tim Rutherford's sweat-drenched body, and a purring chorus whispered into his ears.

The mattress creaked and groaned. One of the pillows slid out from beneath the corpse's neck, but the stiff body remained upright.

Moments later Tim Rutherford reached his climax. His

146

come-cry was a keening wail that a listener might have mistaken for pain.

Afterward, Simon himself helped Tim Rutherford climb down from the bed. The boy was wobbly on his feet. Placing his strong arm around him, Simon beckoned to the two bridesmaids, then led the three young people to a separate bedchamber to complete the ceremony of induction.

The rest of the congregation, deeply aroused, returned downstairs to continue their Sabbat in the orgy room. As the masked young men and women disposed themselves in various combinations on the mattresses spread over the floor, David pulled Rachel aside.

He slid his hand down the flatness of her belly and cupped it between her legs, letting one finger rest lightly between the damp cleft. She took his face in both her hands, and they kissed hungrily for a moment before he pulled away.

"I'd better drive you home," he said softly.

"No!"

"It's already close to one. Your mother's probably up waiting. Wouldn't do to get you home too late, not on your first date." With a little nod, he gestured overhead, laughing softly. "I don't think Tim will be inclined to leave for a while."

Rachel pouted. But she saw there was no use in protesting. David took her by the hand, and the two of them made their way out of the dimly lit room, maneuvering around the undulating bodies.

Inside the car, snuggled against David's chest, his right arm encircling her shoulders, Rachel felt profoundly secure, like a child who, being driven back late at night after a Sunday jaunt, dozes off contentedly in the rear seat, knowing that when they arrive home, Daddy will carry her upstairs to bed.

She could feel David's heart beating against her cheek. She was drifting off to its steady rhythm when her lover said, "I think our new member will work out nicely."

"Mmmm." Rachel forced her eyes partway open. "By the way, I noticed something."

"Yes?"

"Kevin Peterson. He's been acting kind of weird."

147

"What do you mean?"

"I don't know. Like he's not really into things. He was kind of keeping himself apart tonight."

David was silent. "Interesting," he said quietly, as if to himself. He bent down and kissed the top of her head. "Good girl. I'll keep my eyes open. It might be nothing. But you never know. I've seen it happen before."

"What's that?"

"Apostasy."

Rachel felt too drowsy to ask David what the word meant. Besides, she didn't want him to think she was dumb.

They drove on in silence, Rachel's head still pillowed on his chest. After a while she gave a deep sigh. "Your father's an amazing man," she said dreamily.

"I would do anything for him," David said. The solemnity of his tone made her raise her head and glance up at him. In the orange glow cast by the panel lights, his skin had a lurid cast.

"I would do anything for *you*," she said playfully. She lifted his right hand to her lips and kissed his palm.

He hugged her more tightly to his body. "Actually, there *is* something I want you to do," he said.

"Tell me."

"I want you to start keeping track of your periods."

Rachel stiffened slightly.

"How come?"

"You've been chosen for a great honor," David said.

She waited for him to continue. But he said nothing more about it.

She was still wondering what distinction was in store for her when David dropped her off at the end of her driveway and then sped away into the night.

21

A TRUMPETING SNEEZE EXPLODED OUT OF MARIANNE, PRO-
pelling her into a half-sitting-up position. Wiping her nose
with the sodden remains of a Kleenex, she sank back onto
her pillows with a self-pitying groan.

She remembered reading somewhere—probably in that
issue of *Cosmo* she'd been leafing through at the hairdress-
er's—that the sneeze reflex was physiologically similar to
the spasmodic release of an orgasm. Figures, she thought
miserably as she pulled her comforter up to her chin. Other
people get to have sex on Saturday night. I get to stay
home and blow my nose.

She'd been under the weather for most of the week, ever
since Tuesday. That afternoon, the traffic light on Wycherly
had gone on the fritz, and she'd been obliged to stand out
in the rain for two hours, directing commuters—snug in their
warm, cozy cars—through Stoneham's central intersection.

She should have asked Wayland to assign someone else
to the job. She'd already been feeling crappy when she
came into work that morning. But Marianne was always
reluctant to make excuses for herself. Not that she hadn't
seen some of her more hypochondriacal colleagues, like
Roy Auslander, beg off of work because of a low-grade flu.
But being a woman, Marianne felt she had to be twice as
much of a man as anyone else in the department.

Now she was paying the price—a raw and swollen throat,
a head that felt stuffed with Styrofoam packing, and just
enough of a fever to knock her off her feet.

Time for an aspirin fix, she thought, reaching for the
bottle of Bayer and the water glass on her night table.

There was something else making her feel lousy too.
Charlie Mowder, the stereo salesmen she'd met at that club
in White Plains a few weeks earlier, had finally gotten
around to calling her. What he'd proposed had sounded
like fun: dinner at a Tex-Mex place on the Upper West
Side in Manhattan, then dancing down in SoHo. And then,
who knew?

Instead she was spending another lonely Saturday night with nothing beside her in bed but a half-empty Kleenex box and a growing pile of soggy tissues.

Another sneeze built up inside her, then erupted with a wet blast. She didn't care what *Cosmo* said. Somehow, the feeling just wasn't the same.

She reached for her book on the night table, *Wuthering Heights*. She'd caught the movie on cable a few weeks before and had fallen wildly in love with Olivier's fierce, brooding Heathcliff. The very next day, driving home from work, she'd stopped off at the mall and picked up a paperback copy. She was thoroughly enjoying it too. She opened it to her place, marked off with a folded corner.

For some reason—maybe because of her cold, maybe because Catherine and Heathcliff's undying passion made her own situation seem too depressing tonight—she couldn't seem to concentrate. Marianne tossed the book aside and reached over the edge of the bed for the legal pad lying on the floor. Its yellow pages were scrawled with names, dates, times, places, and addresses, all connected with a crazy network of dashes, dotted lines, and arrows—a flow chart of her obsession.

The top page detailed everything the Northampton police had been able to learn about the butchered dog. There wasn't a hell of a lot. Its owner had turned out to be a seventy-two-year-old widower named Wilson, a retired construction worker who lived off Route 28 in Collinsville, some eight miles north of Stoneham. He had called the local police the day after "Ranger" disappeared, but it had been nearly a week before anyone in the precinct connected it to the case of animal mutilation reported down in Stoneham.

The old man couldn't explain how his dog had ended up in Stoneham. He was in the habit of letting Ranger roam around the neighborhood after feeding him in the morning. One day the dog simply hadn't come back.

The rest of the page listed the names and addresses of every veterinarian in northern Westchester. A check of all twenty-three had led nowhere. None was missing any ketamine hydrochloride. None of them could name a single employee who had ever behaved suspiciously around animals.

The vets themselves seemed above suspicion. Stew Markowitz, who had been assigned the task of interviewing them, told Marianne that the idea of one of these prosperous, mild-mannered men being involved with dog mutilation was impossible to conceive. "I could see Mr. Rogers doing it before one of these guys" was how he had put it.

Marianne yanked another Kleenex from the box, wiped her runny nose, then flipped to the second page. It was covered, top to bottom, with all the leads the police had pursued in the Prince investigation. Pursued directly to dead ends.

The Prince baby had been missing now for exactly two weeks, and Wayland's men weren't any closer to a solution than they had been on the night of the kidnapping. There wasn't a cop in the precinct who didn't feel the sting of that failure.

But Wayland kept telling them, as much to boost his own morale as theirs, that the Prince case was different from most abductions. Without a ransom demand, the police simply had nothing to go on. No motive. No fingerprints or physical evidence of any kind.

They'd had no luck in finding the yardman, Greg. Investigators had scoured the nearby towns, checking out the high schools, local gyms, video arcades, and gas stations, anywhere a teenage boy might conceivably spend time. No one recognized the composite sketch the police had put together from David Prince's description.

Following a suggestion by Lyle Kimball, they had contacted every pediatrician in Westchester County. The theory was, if the Prince baby had been black-marketed to a childless couple, desperate for a healthy white infant, they might bring him to a doctor's office for a checkup or vaccine.

Even Lyle knew it was a long shot. And so they were only mildly disappointed, but not at all surprised, when none of the pediatricians could recognize Stephen Prince's photograph or description.

Pressed, the child's father, David, had come up with the names of three individuals who bore grudges against him. All were men he'd "tangled with," as he put it, over business deals. Interviewed by the police, none of the three even bothered to fake any sympathy for Prince. One of them, an investment banker at a big Wall Street firm, threat-

151

ened to sue for an enormous sum if his name appeared in print anywhere in connection with the case. They were enemies, all right.

All three had foolproof alibis.

There had been the usual flood of crank mail to the parents. Marianne was still amazed at the sheer number of creeps that came swarming out of the woodwork whenever a family tragedy occurred. Some of the letters were just gibberish. But others were so full of sick, sadistic taunts that even old-timers like Wayland and Reardon, who'd seen plenty of hate mail before, were left shaking their heads in disgust.

As always in a highly publicized case, the police had also been inundated with anonymous phone tips—sightings of the missing baby, names and addresses of possible suspects. Many of the callers clearly had an axe to grind—embittered divorcées trying to stick it to their exes, sour old men accusing their neighbors out of spite. But the rest seemed sincerely motivated by good intentions.

The police had followed through on every tip, no matter how thin or farfetched. Nothing had panned out. As far as leads went, that was about it. Holson summed up the situation best. They knew jack shit.

There *was* one new bit of information Marianne had learned just a few days ago, though she was the only one who attached any significance to it. She turned to the third page of her legal pad. Written across the top in big block letters was the name SIMON PROCTOR. After it, Marianne had added a string of question marks.

The ex-cult leader had jumped parole. Simon Proctor had vanished.

Marianne had received the call on Thursday. It still irked her that it had taken the Taos police almost a week to phone her. Proctor had failed to show up November fourth for his first appointment with his parole officer. Nor could he be found at the fleabag boardinghouse in Santa Fe he had given as his permanent address. He hadn't been seen there since he rented a room on Saturday evening, the twenty-ninth.

The sergeant who called her seemed unconcerned. "He's probably shacked up with a hooker," he'd told Marianne. "Happens when a guy's been in the joint as long as Proctor. They go a little crazy for cu—'' He caught himself, suddenly mindful of Officer Byrne's gender. "They go a little woman-crazy. He'll probably show up in a few days."

Marianne had decided not to share this piece of news with Wayland, whose mood had deteriorated dramatically over the last two weeks. The atmosphere of tension and frustration in his office seemed as tangible as the cloud of cigarette smoke that surrounded him these days. She didn't want to risk another confrontation. Not until she had something more substantial to bring him than a hunch.

Wheezing out a sigh, Marianne dropped her legal pad back onto the floor and glanced up at the big red digits on her bedside clock. It was nearing eleven-thirty P.M. After a whole day in bed, much of it spent dozing, she didn't feel especially sleepy.

She thought fleetingly of calling her father. They hadn't managed to make contact all week. But he was probably asleep, she told herself. Ever since her mother died, he'd started getting up early Sunday mornings for mass. She herself hadn't been to church for God knew how long. She couldn't even remember the last time she'd been to confession.

A sudden image, vivid as Technicolor, popped into her mind—Laurence Olivier, dark-eyed and impossibly virile, locked in a steamy embrace with a swooning Merle Oberon.

Oh, well, Marianne thought. I haven't done very much lately that requires confession. Unfortunately.

"Shit," she muttered aloud, pulling aside her comforter and swinging her legs out of bed. Her throat felt as if it had been worked on with a cheese grater. Maybe a cup of tea with honey and lemon would soothe the pain.

A little wobbly on her feet, she made her way into the kitchen, wearing her heaviest wool socks and her long-sleeved, high-necked, plaid flannel nightgown. Patrick had always hated it. He'd even had a nickname for it—the "lust-killer."

Well, Patrick wasn't around anymore. She needed *something* to keep her warm.

Back in bed, steaming mug in hand, she propped herself up with some pillows and zapped on the TV. "Saturday Night Live" was just beginning, guest-hosted by Mel Gibson. He wasn't Heathcliff on the moors, but he would do.

153

As the heartthrob wound up his monologue, Marianne remembered the last time she had spent a solitary Saturday night watching TV. That had been two weeks before, the very night of the kidnap—

Wait a minute, she thought. She froze, like a kid caught in a game of "Statue," hand raised, mug suspended a few inches from her lips.

Something had just occurred to her. She clearly recalled flipping through the stations that Saturday night in search of something decent to watch. She'd thought of "Saturday Night Live," but when she'd punched up the station, the show had been preempted for a Halloween double feature.

What made the memory stick in her mind was the title of the first movie—some Grade-Z horror flick called *The Worm Eaters.* Marianne had hit the channel changer even before the announcer had finished intoning the final syllable.

And yet, Rachel Peary, the girl who had been babysitting for the Princes on the night of the abduction, had testified several times that she'd been watching "Saturday Night Live" when the kidnapper knocked on the door. Marianne was sure of that. She had gone over the babysitter's testimony again and again.

Setting her mug down on the night table, she heaved herself out of bed and padded out into the living room.

Three weeks worth of old newspapers sat heaped in a corner, waiting to be bundled up for recycling. Marianne's standard procedure for disposing of old papers was to wait until they had piled so high that the addition of a single sheet of newsprint would send the whole stack toppling.

She rummaged through the pile until she found what she was looking for—the TV section of the Sunday edition from the week in question. She opened it to Saturday, October 29.

"I'll be damned," she said aloud, though the word came out sounding like "dabbed." She was right. The listing read "Halloween Midnight Movies." Then, in parentheses. "Regular Programming Preempted."

She carried the TV section back to bed. *What can this mean?* Here was another inconsistency. First there'd been the business with the Princes' porch bulb—presently located in the fingerprint lab at Grasslands, where Marianne had dispatched it after removing it on Monday morning. She was still awaiting the results.

154

Now this.

A burst of laughter greeted her as she walked back into her bedroom, but she was too distracted to pay attention to the skit flickering on the screen. Crawling back under the covers, she lay there for a while, gazing at the television without seeing it. Eventually she turned it off.

In the darkness, she ran through the babysitter's story again and again, until her thoughts blurred, broke apart, and dissolved into the jumble of a dream.

She slept until eleven the next morning, when she was awakened by the trill of her phone. It was her father. She was glad to hear his voice, even though he began (as always) by chiding her for not calling more often. He himself had tried reaching her on a number of occasions, always without success.

Once she'd offered her ritual apology, they chatted easily for a while, filling each other in on the events of the past week. After a whole day in bed, Marianne felt a lot better, but her voice was still husky from her cold. Her dad admonished her to give herself another day under the blankets and dose herself up with vitamin C—his unvarying medical advice for everything from a minor headcold to a severe case of the flu.

After five minutes or so of casual chitchat, she got around to asking the question she'd been holding back since she picked up the phone. Had he come up with anything more related to the Prince case?

"Nothing you don't already know. How about you? Hear anything new?"

"Proctor's disappeared from Santa Fe. The police don't know where he is."

There was a brief silence at the other end of the line while her father processed the news. "Well, that could mean anything."

"Yes, but—"

"Now look, Marianne," her father interrupted. "Don't start leaping to conclusions. All we know about Proctor is that he and that commune of his were screwing around with Satanic practices—cutting up stray animals, spray-painting pentagrams on the adobe, that sort of thing. That doesn't

155

tell us much. Back then, a lot of these druggie groups started spicing up their sex with kinky rituals."

"I know, I know," Marianne said. "But maybe . . ."

"Maybe what?"

"Maybe there's something to what Anna Prince says after all."

Jack Byrne didn't even try to keep the exasperation out of his voice. "How the hell could the man get out of a New Mexican prison and snatch a baby in New York the same day? It doesn't make sense."

"Not unless . . ." Marianne let the sentence trail off.

"Unless what?"

She shook her head. "Nothing. Just thinking out loud." She put her hand over the mouthpiece, turned her head away and sneezed. "Did you turn up anything yet about the dog?" she asked.

"You mean about that skinned-off square of hide? Not yet. I haven't forgotten, though."

They talked for a while longer. Jack asked his daughter if she'd be driving down for Thanksgiving dinner, and Marianne promised she would. He reminded her again to stay warm and drink lots of orange juice.

He was about to hang up but couldn't resist a last word of fatherly advice. "Marianne, I know how gung-ho you get when something grabs your interest. But do me a favor. Don't get too caught up with this stuff. Let the others handle it."

"You mean the men."

"I mean the cops who have some experience with potentially dangerous matters. I know what I'm talking about."

She didn't want to be angry with him. "Don't worry, Dad," she said gently. Then she gave him a long-distance kiss and said good-bye.

Replacing the receiver, she leaned over the bed, scooped up her yellow pad and flipped to a fresh page. She uncapped her felt-tip pen and listed the questions that had been swirling inside her head before she'd fallen asleep. All the questions focused on the same subject, and when Marianne was done, she printed the subject's name across the top of the page.

The heading read: RACHEL PEARY.

156

22

FROM HIS DESK IN THE SECOND-FLOOR CLASSROOM, JERRY Waller could look out the windows at the little lawn that nestled in the crook of the L-shaped school building. Just beyond, he could see the climbing nets, tire swings, slides, and monkeybars of the schoolyard playground, currently overrun with a small army of children, making the most of their lunchtime recess.

Turning back to the artwork in front of him, Jerry chewed off another mouthful of his favorite sandwich—a whole-wheat pita stuffed with Monterey Jack cheese, bean sprouts, green pepper, and avocado, a concoction his wife called "Waller's Woodstock Special."

Jerry was glad it wasn't his turn to do recess duty. The day—Monday, November 14—had a wintry edge, and Jerry had awakened with the first stirrings of a cold. Besides, he wanted time to study the little stack of pencil sketches that Donna Frosch, the school's art teacher, had passed along to him that morning.

Suddenly, a child's shriek, very real in its terror, detached itself from the muted din of play-screams, squeals, and shouts emanating from the schoolyard. Jerry half rose from his chair, squinting through the windows.

Just below, a couple of boys—probably sixth-graders, judging from their size, though no one Jerry recognized from his own class—were dragging a smaller one by the elbows. The little one was kicking and screaming as his two tormentors hauled him toward the gazebo that stood in the center of the lawn.

Jerry was just about to yank open a window when Sally Whittemore, the third grade teacher on schoolyard duty, came hurrying up and pulled the little one away. He clung to her waist, sobbing, while Sally scolded the two shame-faced sixth-graders. Jerry couldn't make out her words, but from the tone of her voice—and the look on her face—it was clear that she was letting them have it, but good.

157

Sinking back into his chair, Jerry propped his chin in his hands and gazed glumly down at the gazebo.

There were no traces of the outrage that had been perpetrated there. The bloodstained planks had been sanded clean, the big nail hole patched in the supporting beam. The taped-up warning signs posted by the police—CRIME SCENE. DO NOT ENTER—had been removed a week earlier.

But Jerry feared that the gazebo would never be the same. The younger children gave it a wide berth, while the older ones saw it as a place to prove their courage, demonstrating their bravery by climbing inside and remaining there for a few minutes.

Jerry was heartsick at the cruel practical joke that life had played on his dead friend. At a single awful stroke, Marion's memorial—the charming little structure erected as a tribute to her joyous, loving spirit—had been converted into the schoolyard equivalent of an amusement park spookhouse.

That, of course, wasn't the only fallout from the events of the past few weeks. Indeed, there wasn't any clearer evidence of the lingering contamination than the artwork spread out on the desktop before him.

For their weekly assignment, Donna Frosch had asked the sixth-graders to do pencil sketches on Thanksgiving themes, and some of the results were pretty hair-raising. One sketch in particular—a beautifully rendered drawing by Lauren Wilson, the best artist in Jerry's class—was grotesque enough to cause him real concern. It depicted a group of axe-wielding pilgrims, evil-eyed and grinning, committing mayhem on a squawking turkey.

Donna Frosch, whose sardonic wit often veered into very black humor, had commented, as she dropped Lauren's creation onto Jerry's desk, that it looked like a publicity still for some turkeyland version of *Friday the 13th*.

Between the baby-snatching and the butchered dog, the children of Stoneham had suffered a double-barreled trauma in recent weeks, and they were reacting with a rash of anxiety symptoms, ranging from stomachaches to dizziness to bed-wetting. A child psychiatrist had been hired to help the school nurse cope with the epidemic of psychosomatic ailments. Some of the kids, like Danny Richardson—the boy whose little brother, Chris, had stumbled onto the remains of the butchered dog—seemed to be handling the crisis pretty well. At least during school hours.

At night it was a different story. Jerry had heard from Danny's mother that her son was suffering from terrible nightmares. All three of her children were currently seeing a private psychiatrist.

Jerry could certainly empathize. He'd had a few bad nights himself since that unspeakable morning when he'd come upon the foulness in the gazebo.

For Jerry, the only silver lining was that his wife was lavishing more tenderness and attention on him than she had for a long time. He was sorry that it taken a crisis to bring them closer. But he wasn't about to look a gift horse in the mouth.

Jerry's bearded cheeks ballooned out as he exhaled a long sigh. Crumpling his lunch bag into a ball, he lofted it with a practiced underhand toss halfway across the room. It banked off the wall into the corner wastepaper basket.

"Nice shot," said a quiet male voice behind him.

Jerry swiveled around in his seat. Standing in the doorway was a tall, athletically built teenager. Jerry stared at him for a moment, then broke into a grin.

"Kevin!" he exclaimed, rising from his desk.

"Mr. Waller." The boy stepped into the room, right hand extended.

They shook hands warmly, while Jerry looked the boy up and down. "You've bulked up."

"Yeah, well, I've been doing some lifting."

"Got a minute?"

"I can't stay long. I've got to take Robby to the orthodontist. I had to cut my afternoon classes, but, you know, my mother's at work and all, and I'm the only one who can do it." He shrugged. "Thought I'd stop up here and say hello."

"Great to see you," said Jerry, reseating himself behind his desk. "Grab a chair."

Kevin pulled up a turquoise, molded-plastic school chair—the kind with the little desktop attached to the seat—and squeezed himself into it.

Jerry laughed. "It doesn't fit you very well anymore, Kevin."

"Feels good, though," the teenager said softly, glancing around the room. "I still think about this place sometimes.

Nothing's changed at all." A note of pure melancholy—so intense that Jerry's eyebrows furrowed with concern—came into the teenager's voice. "Not in here, anyway."

Five years before, Kevin Peterson had been Jerry's student at a time when the boy's world was falling apart. After twenty years of marriage to his college sweetheart, Kevin's father—a handsome corporate lawyer in his early forties—had simply ditched his wife and two kids for a new life with a twenty-eight-year-old blonde.

The story was a bona fide cliché, one of those situations so familiar in the modern world that they seem almost trite, except to the human beings whose lives are devastated by them. Especially the little human beings.

As it happened, Kevin's younger brother, Robby—currently a student in Sally Whittemore's fourth-grade class—was almost *too* little at the time to suffer the full force of the trauma. The brunt was borne by Kevin, who had worshiped his tall, commanding father.

Jerry had done everything he could to help Kevin deal with the crisis. His heart went out to the shy, skinny boy, who sat in the classroom day after day, gazing out the windows with a stricken, faraway look. Childless himself, he had been happy to serve as a surrogate father, reaching out to Kevin, taking him under his wing, staying late after school to have long, earnest talks with the boy. And Kevin had warmed to Jerry's attentions, slowly reemerging into the sunny, boisterous world of sixth-grade boyhood.

When Kevin had graduated into junior high school at the end of that year, he seemed as carefree as any of his classmates. For a while he had stayed in contact with Jerry, calling him occasionally at home, coming by for after-school visits. Gradually they fell out of touch. Life went on. It had been over a year since they had spoken, though Jerry still stopped Robby Peterson in the hallway every now and then and told him to say hi to his brother.

For Jerry, the whole episode had been a source of pride, a kind of validation. He felt that if he accomplished nothing else in life, he had, at the very least, helped restore one wounded child to normalcy and happiness.

Now, looking over at the troubled young man, he wasn't so sure.

Thin, wintry sunlight leaked in through the windows.

Kevin gazed through the glass at the lawn. In the light, his hazel eyes were as clear as a baby's. But his face was clouded with cares.

"I read about you in the newspaper," he said, nodding toward the gazebo. "How you were the one who discovered that stuff out there."

"Yeah. I was just thinking about that when you came by." Jerry picked up a few of the pencil sketches, then dropped them back onto the desk. "Nasty business. It's really done a number on a lot of little heads. Not to mention my own."

Kevin flashed his old teacher such an odd, stricken look that Jerry was suddenly jolted with a thought.

"You don't happen to know anything about that stuff, do you, Kevin?" Jerry asked quietly.

"No, no," the boy replied quickly—a little too quickly, Jerry thought. He stared hard at Kevin, who slumped in the undersized school chair, gnawing on his lower lip.

"What's wrong, Kevin?"

The teenager gave a mirthless little laugh. "What's wrong?" He crossed his arms, glanced at the ceiling, then down at the floor. "How about everything," he said, shaking his head.

Jerry peered at Kevin's downturned face. "Like what?"

"Like what?"

The boy had a disconcerting habit of repeating Jerry's questions in an utterly hopeless tone, as if the answers were too vast or exhausting to go into.

"You were doing so well the last time I saw you," Jerry said.

"I was never doing well," Kevin shot back, glancing up at Jerry with a hard, almost accusatory look. Then his expression softened, rearranging itself into something profoundly unhappy, something almost like despair. "And now things are really fucked up."

Jerry was taken aback. He sat there silently for a moment, hands clasped before him on the desktop, thinking hard. Finally he said, "This doesn't have anything to do with drugs, does it?"

Kevin looked up, surprised. "Drugs?"

"Yeah. Drugs. I hope you're smart enough not to mess around with them, Kevin."

161

Kevin shot him a withering look, as if to say, Look who's talking, Mr. Sixties.

Jerry didn't blink. "They can screw up your life, Kevin. I've seen it happen to a lot of people."

Kevin sighed. "The drugs aren't important." He paused, as if considering the advisability of pursuing the conversation. Then he said, "It's these people."

"People?" Jerry said. He seemed to have caught Kevin's parroting habit.

"Some people I got involved with. Like a family, sort of. For a while, it was cool. But things have gotten weird. Very weird."

"Where do these people live?"

"North a ways. You know the old Vanderdam place?"

Jerry shook his head. "Uh-uh."

"Well, anyway, that's where—" He hesitated for the briefest of moments. "It's near there."

"Well, if you don't want to be friends with these people anymore, why don't you just end the relationship?"

Kevin stared straight into Jerry's eyes with a look of such absolute skepticism that Jerry had the strangest sensation, as if their roles had suddenly been reversed and it was he, the teacher, who was the true innocent.

"It's not that easy," Kevin answered simply.

Working himself free of the chair, Kevin got to his feet. "I shouldn't even be talking about this."

"Kevin," Jerry said, genuinely hurt. "You can talk to me about anything." He too rose, and walked around the desk to stand beside the teenager.

"I've got to go," Kevin said. He grabbed Jerry's right hand and shook it with surprising warmth, and something else too—a kind of urgency. "You were the only one that ever really tried to help me, Mr. Waller. But this time I just have to work things out by myself."

He turned and hurried from the room.

"If there's anything I can do . . ." Jerry called out after him. But even as he said it, he was filled with a sense of dread—a feeling that had grown increasingly intense over the past two weeks—that something was deeply amiss in Stoneham. And there wasn't a damn thing he could do about it.

23

Leaning on his fists, Jack Byrne stood hunched over his desk in the wood-paneled basement he had converted into a home office shortly after Peggy's death. The room still contained evidence of its original function, including a Ping-Pong table and a fully stocked bar complete with four swiveling stools and a gold-veined mirror that stretched across the length of the wall behind it.

But these furnishings now seemed completely out of place amid the filing cabinets, bookcases, and storage shelves crammed with specimens of occult paraphernalia. A corkboard pinned over with new clippings, note cards, and police photos hung above the big wooden desk. Shoved against the adjacent wall were a half-dozen cardboard cartons piled high with mimeographed pamphlets.

Jack scowled with impatience as he proofread the pages lying between his hands on the desktop. He was a lousy typist—it had taken him a full forty-five minutes to peck out the letter on his thirty-year-old manual Underwood—and he was eager to head off to the city.

The request he was answering—from the chief of police in Greenvale, Illinois, a former small town transformed by urban sprawl into a suburb of Chicago—was a routine matter, at least as far as Jack was concerned. The principal of the local high school had discovered black candles, silver neck chains with goathead amulets, and other occult objects in the lockers of several senior boys. A reporter from the *Greenvale Herald* had gotten wind of the story and splashed it across the paper's front page, setting off a full-blown Satanism scare in the community. The police switchboard had been jammed for a week with calls from panicked parents, terrified that their teenagers might be involved in devil-worship and desperate for information.

As he always did in such cases, Jack had struck a reassuring tone in his letter, cautioning the chief not to make more of the incident than the evidence warranted. Though an interest in Satanism should never be taken lightly, he had written, most adolescents who dabbled in the occult were simply crying out for attention. Black candles and sterling silver goatheads were no reason to start calling in the exorcists. "Family counseling would do a lot more good," Jack had advised. Obviously, some occult-related activities were cause for more serious concern—graveyard tampering, for example, or ritualistic animal mutilation.

Most of what the Greenvale cops needed to know was covered in the eight-page, mimeographed pamphlet Jack was sending along. The pamphlet contained a brief description of the better known Satanic cults, a glossary of terms like "coven" and "Baphomet," descriptions of common occult appurtenances—chalices, black hoods, and the like—and drawings of Satanic symbols such as the pentagram and the "cross of confusion." It concluded with a section called "Why Today's Teens Are Attracted to Satanism."

Jack had originally put the material together for a talk he'd been invited to give down at police headquarters a couple of years before. As much as anything else, his ex-colleagues had been curious to know what he'd been up to since his retirement.

Nowadays, he mailed the pamphlets out by the dozen. He had become enough of an expert on Satanism and the occult to be solicited by police departments and youth service organizations across the country.

He could have made it into a lucrative business if he had wanted. Some of his buddies told him so, and he believed it himself. He could have bought himself a fancy suit and charged a fat consulting fee for jetting around the country, conducting Satanism seminars. He could have done the talk-show circuit, maybe snagged a guest shot on "Oprah." Others had.

Instead, he was scraping along on his pension, still buying his clothes off the peg at Penney's, riding the rattletrap subways.

What the hell, Jack thought. He never gave a shit about clothes, anyway. He wasn't doing it for the bucks or to get his picture in *People* magazine. He was doing it because something monstrous was alive out there, something that had risen up and destroyed his partner and friend.

He was doing it for Sam, God rest his soul.

Jack lifted the letter off his desk. It contained a scattering of typos, but nothing he couldn't live with. Clipping the letter to one of his pamphlets, he stuffed them both into a big manila envelope.

Three minutes later, wearing his snap-brim hat and top-coat, he was out the front door and striding along the sidewalk. At the corner of Main and Kissena he slid the envelope down into the mailbox chute, then walked a block and descended into the rumbling bowels of the subway.

A copy of the *Daily News* lay folded on the seat beside him, and he picked it up, intending to check out the latest football scores. But he was too distracted to read. As the train clattered through the darkness, his mind kept returning to the problem of the missing hide on the mutilated dog up in Stoneham. It was ironic, he thought. Here he was, the big expert on Satanism, and he couldn't come up with an answer to his own daughter's question. What made the situation even more frustrating was his gnawing sense that he had once come across a reference to something similar in his reading.

Maybe Marianne was right. Maybe he should invest in a home computer, store his research on a disk, cross-reference it, have it all available at the push of a button.

Jack snorted at the image of himself seated at a computer. He still hadn't figured out how to use all the keys on his Underwood.

Fifty minutes later he climbed out of the smelly maw of the subway at Twenty-third Street on Manhattan's East Side. A mound of greasy rags, overlaid with old newspapers and stinking of piss, lay heaped on the sidewalk at the top of the stairs. As Jack stepped around it, the rag pile grunted and stirred.

Jack made a disgusted face and continued on his way. The whole damned city is going straight to hell, he thought. Used to be a time when you could walk the streets without tripping over bums. A fierce gust of gritty wind stung his face. It made his conscience sting too. He knew what Peggy would have said. He could hear her voice inside his head, chiding him.

They're homeless people, Jack. Human beings. Not "bums."

Turning the corner onto Nineteenth Street, he saw the

165

grimy display window of L. Remuzzi and Son across the street and halfway down the block. NEW AND USED BOOKS read the faded gold letters on the window. It was the seventh bookstore Jack had visited that week.

A little bell attached to the door lintel jangled as he entered the store. The air was suffused with the familiar smell of mildewed paper and dust, emanating from the towering rows of wooden bookcases that filled the cavernous space.

Jack stood there for a moment, letting his eyes grow accustomed to the gloom. Anthony Remuzzi, the fifty-year-old son of the original owner, wasn't visible. The store seemed devoid of customers too. The only other person in the place, as far as Jack could see, was a squat old woman with a shade of hair, a kind of chemical orange, never seen in nature. Dressed in a faded, flowered muumuu, she was perched on a stool behind the paper-strewn desk at the front of the store, nibbling on a corn muffin that rained a continuous stream of yellow crumbs onto the book that lay open in her lap. She wore round, wire-framed glasses with lenses as thick as Coke-bottle bottoms. An electric space heater glowed at her feet.

Jack walked up and stood in front of the desk. It took a few moments for the old woman to notice him. With her shapeless bulk and liver-spotted face, she looked like a giant toad. The resemblance was reinforced by the thickness of her lenses, which magnified her eyes to amphibious proportions.

"What can I do for you?" she demanded. Her voice was a croak.

"Tony around?" asked Jack. He stared straight into her eyes, mostly to avoid looking at the spongy yellow crumbs that clung to the moist corners of her lips.

"He ain't here. Daughter's getting married down in Florida. He'll be back next Monday." She returned to her reading.

Jack blew out a sigh. "When you see him, tell him Jack Byrne dropped by."

The old woman looked up, blinking. "Byrne. You the Satan guy?"

"That's right."

"Tony left some books for you to look at," she said in her hoarse, croaking voice. "Picked 'em up at an auction

166

up in Massachusetts last week." She looked at him with enormous, mud-colored eyes. "Tell me this. You believe in the devil?"

Jack had a peculiar sensation, as if he were being put to some kind of test. "Lady," he said after a brief pause, "I was a cop in this town for almost thirty years. I've seen too much not to."

Her eyes fixed his for another long moment. Then, apparently satisfied, she heaved herself off the stool and waddled down the center aisle, Jack following close behind.

At the back of the store was a padlocked door. The old lady groped in her pocket for a key ring, unlocked the door, and reached inside for the light switch. A single yellow bulb lit up the dusty storeroom, cluttered with boxes, books, and stacks of old magazines. One large carton stood by itself in the center of the wooden floor. The old woman pointed at it with a stubby finger. "There," she said. Without another word, she turned and shuffled from the room.

Crouching, Jack unfolded the interlocking flaps of the carton and began removing the books one by one.

It was an impressive collection—scarce, mostly nineteenth century books that had clearly belonged to someone with a serious interest in the occult. Robert Brown's *Demonology and Witchcraft*, William Perkins's *A Discourse on the Damned Art of Witchcraft*, Nathaniel Crouch's *The Kingdom of Darkness*, Thomas Wright's *Narratives of Sorcery and Magic*, and the *Daemonomania* of Jean Bodin.

They were in beautiful shape too. The first twelve volumes Jack removed from the carton were books he already owned, though his copies were in far shabbier condition.

It wasn't until he got closer to the bottom of the box that he finally lifted out a fat, leather-bound volume whose title was unfamiliar to him: *De Ritualis Satanis, or the Devil's Cultus, Being a Treatise on the Unholie Practices of the Children of Lucifer*. The book was liberally illustrated with woodcuts of supernatural subjects—triple-tongued demons devouring the souls of the damned, devils with dragon heads tempting sleeping women with lascivious dreams, goat-headed fiends presenting their buttocks to be kissed by their followers. Jack let his eyes linger briefly over each illustration as he flipped through the pages.

Halfway through the book, he came upon a particularly

167

unsettling image. It depicted a sacrifice of some sort. Jack paused over the picture, trying to make sense of its details. Slowly, he arose from his crouching position and held the book closer to the light.

The picture showed a group of naked men and women, their faces twisted with obscene delight. They were gathered around a priest, whose devil's tail stuck out from the back of his cassock. One of the worshipers held out a flailing baby, while the priest fitted something—a sack or bag of some sort—over the infant's head.

The scene was set in a clearing in the woods. The encircling treetops blazed like sinister birthday candles. In the foreground of the picture lay a four-footed creature of some kind, maybe a calf or a goat or a large dog. The animal had been butchered—throat cut, wormy entrails visible through a gaping wound in its belly. And it had been mutilated in another way too. Missing from its side, quite distinctly, was a large, square patch of hide.

Jack felt a surge of excitement as he turned to the accompanying text.

The passage described the rituals of a fourteenth-century devil cult, supposedly active in pockets of Central Europe, that worshiped the demon Belphegor, the horned god of the biblical Moabites, mentioned in Numbers 25:3. According to occult legend, Belphegor was a night fiend, a bat-winged creature who soared through the darkness, seeking slumbering infants to feed on. The demon was believed to suck out their life's breath as they slept. Probably how the Moabites explained crib death, Jack thought.

The central ritual of the medieval European Belphegor cult was a ceremony known as soul-stealing, which the book proceeded to describe:

When these members of the devil are met together, they light a foule and horrid fire. Their dark priest is president of the assemblie, and the worshipers approach him to adore him. They offer him the flesh of corpses or infants' navel cords, and kiss him upon the buttocks in sign of homage. Having committed these and similar execrable abominations, they proceed to other infamies, polluting themselves by their filthy copulation with devils that are incubi and succubi. They

168

do all these things in a manner altogether foreign to the use of other men.

At the height of their orgies is performed their blasphemous sacrament called the stealing of the soule, by meanes of which the breath of new life is offered in homage to their dark master. Infants of either sexe are employed for this foule purpose, sometimes the very offspring of the devil worshipers themselves. Where none is available, infants are stolen from the houses of the innocent. A foule sack being fashioned from the hide of a beast, either a wolf or dog, ass or goat, the dark priest causes the infant to be smothered by placing its head in the sack and capturing its dying breaths.

Believing that the breaths of the youngest infants forme the greatest gift to their dark lord and master, some of these inhuman fiends contrive to breede newborns for this very purpose, ripping them untimely out of their mothers wombes to capture their first breath of life in the sack. It is said that when Belphegor's priest holds the sack to his lips and causes the pure breath to fill his body, he sheds many of his years. Some priests of Belphegor have performed this magic many times and one of them is said to have lived 216 years, having robbed the living breath of more than half a hundred newborn souls. Now his own soul suffers the everlasting torments of the damned, all praise be to God.

Now Jack remembered why the mystery of the missing patch of hide had teased his memory. Several years before, he had come across a fleeting reference to the Belphegor cult in an occult encyclopedia but had put it out of his mind.

He stood there for a moment, breathing the stale air of the storeroom. He thought about the mutilated retriever up in Stoneham and about the kidnapped Prince baby. He thought about his daugther's suspicions.

As he clapped the book shut and headed for the front desk, he felt something stir deep inside his chest, like a serpent awakening from its night torpor in the blaze of a new day. It had been a long time since he had experienced that sensation, but he recognized it at once.

What he felt was the stirring of fear.

24

THE FIRST WINTER STORM OF THE SEASON HAD SWEPT INTO New York State, driven by an icy wind out of Canada. Forty miles to the north of Stoneham, in the impenetrable darkness of the deep country, frozen gusts whirled around the big nineteenth-century house, piling snow onto the rooftop and sills. The night was frigid, twenty degrees colder than the temperature in New York City.

But inside the old Vanderdam house, the atmosphere was nearly tropical. Simon Proctor preferred it that way. He liked his disciples naked and languorous.

Simon Proctor loved young bodies—especially the bodies of the girls, with their high breasts, tight buttocks, and flat bellies. He relished the warm delicacy between their thighs, its salt taste and pungent odor.

But he liked the bodies of the young men too—their supple muscles and heavy genitals, so easily aroused. He could talk a young man into an erection in half a minute, bring him to orgasm—without touching him—in two or three.

Simon knew that raw carnality was like a hothouse orchid, flourishing in the thick, sultry air.

Only one area in the house remained unheated. This was the damp, high-ceilinged cellar, rock-walled and coal-pit dark. A steep, wooden staircase led down into the blackness of the cellar, with a single light switch at the head of the steps. But the light revealed very little. There was almost nothing to reveal, only a cracked cement floor, ceiling beams receding into shadow, and—shoved against one wall—a large, white enamel freezer chest, installed at Simon Proctor's bidding.

The freezer made a constant hum. Though roomy enough to accommodate a side of beef, its interior was vacant, except for a small bundle, tightly wrapped in a black plastic trash bag. Lifting the heavy freezer lid, an outsider to Simon Proctor's little family might have taken the bundle for a Thanksgiving turkey, awaiting its holiday preparations. Examining its contours more closely, he would have

170

been forced to revise his first impression, though his face would almost certainly have reflected his puzzlement.

Not knowing the nature of Simon Proctor, or the fate of little Stephen Prince, he would have wondered why a doll was being stored inside a freezer.

In the dark chapel on the floor above, the disciples of Simon Proctor could not hear the hum of the freezer, of course, even though they were standing in absolute silence. The only sound in the room was a soft scrabbling noise coming from the shadows in the northeast corner. An old-fashioned bird cage hanging from a wrought-iron floor stand had been placed in the corner. Inside, a pair of red-eyed, brown rats were contending over a scrap of raw meat.

The rat cage was not the only unholiness newly added to the chapel. At that very moment a far more conspicuous addition held the congregrants transfixed.

This was a large wooden crucifix that had been suspended by a chain from the ceiling at the far end of the room. A life-sized wax Christ, face contorted in agony, gazed heavenward from the cross.

The figure's thorn-crowned head had been topped with a flowing mane of thick, honey-colored hair. The hair might have been a wig, except for its exceptionally lifelike quality. And for the ragged flap of scalp that stuck out from beneath it.

Tacked across the chest of the crucified figure was something that appeared, in the dim candle glow, to be a young girl's brassiere. Only by stepping close and squinting could an observer see that the fleshy band was a strip of human skin, flayed from a girl's upper torso, small breasts still attached. Two fish hooks sagged from the nipples.

A plump, notched triangle of lightly-haired flesh was nailed to the loincloth of the carved figure, directly over the crotch.

These profanations were the handiwork of Simon Proctor himself, who had excised the raw materials with a skull-pommeled dagger.

The rest of Melissa Campbell's mutilated corpse had been buried deep in the woods behind the house.

A strain of organ music, so soft that it was nearly subliminal, seeped into the room. Slowly, the somber music deepened, swelled. As the roiling chords crescendoed, Simon

171

Proctor appeared in the doorway. He paused for a moment, head bowed as if in prayer, then stepped into the chapel, followed by his son.

The high priest stationed himself at the head of the altar table, his son at his side. His followers gathered around. The table was draped in a black satin sheet. A pillow, sheathed in the same shimmering fabric, had been placed at the far end of the table.

Raising his hands in a gesture of benediction, Simon looked around at his acolytes. In the flickering light of the black candles, the two eyes that glared from his oiled breast seemed to shine with a feverish life.

"Belphegor Satanis," the dark priest suddenly cried. "Thee we invoke. God eht fo eman eht ni."

A chorus of fervent voices echoed the chant, though one voice remained silent. But in the frenzy of the moment, even the people pressed against Kevin Peterson couldn't tell that he had only mouthed the words.

Simon nodded over his shoulder at the blasphemy behind him. "Behold the lamb of God," he sneered, "adorned with the marks of his effeminacy. See how he hastens to cast off the living flesh. Not for him—or his followers—the pleasures of the body. His gaze points skyward, into pallid air.

"But the Shadow Lord shows us the way. The kingdom lies downward. Here"—he hammered his chest with a fist—"and here." Sliding his hand down the length of his belly, he cupped himself between the legs. "Our flesh is the kingdom. The body's strength, the lusts of the heart— these are our birthright and fulfillment. Let the meek seek salvation in the air. Let them wait for their bliss until their corpses lie rotten. The masters of life will have their delight here on earth, in the power and glory and sweetness of the body. Here we will dwell and claim our pleasures, here in the kingdom of flesh!

"Tonight," he continued after a moment's pause, "we give thanks to the Dark One who teaches us the true way. A new life will arise in his honor, bred and bestowed as his gift."

He fixed his son with a fierce stare. "Bring in the breeder."

Answering with a quick nod, David turned and strode

172

from the room. Moments later he reentered, cradling Rachel like a groom bearing his bride across the threshold. Rachel's head lolled drunkenly, her blond hair cascading over David's bare arm.

Bending, David set her on the altar table, her buttocks propped on the pillow.

Moving around to the front of the table, Simon placed a hand on each of her thighs and shoved them apart. Reaching down with his right hand, he slid his long index finger slowly in and out.

"The vessel flows," he said, smiling. "Come, let each one of you taste."

The small circle of worshipers moved slowly around the table, each one in turn, male and female, stooping to lap between the drugged girl's open thighs. Rachel sighed and squirmed. Nimble hands anointed her with oils—her belly, breasts, nipples.

When the last of the worshipers stood up, wiping his smeared moustache with the back of a hand, Simon, rampant, grabbed the girl's legs and shoved himself inside her. He thrust furiously, head thrown back, neck cords bulging. Moments later he quivered silently, then slowly drew himself out.

He took a step backward. Instantly, David moved to the table, grabbed Rachel at the hips and flipped her onto her belly. Pulling her toward him, he entered her from behind, wrapping a thick strand of her hair around his hand and yanking it hard, like a cowboy on a bronco.

Proctor stepped to the front of the table, bending to peer into the girl's contorted face. "Yes," he whispered at her strangled cries. David came with a bellow, while the others broke into a tumult, their flailing limbs casting crazy shadow puppets on the walls of the candlelit room.

Simon glared around at the frenzied scene, his eyes bright with triumph.

Only then did he notice that Kevin Peterson was gone.

25

NO MORE!

The words had roared so thunderously inside Kevin's head that, for a terrifying moment, he thought that he had screamed them out loud.

But no. The dozen naked and sweating bodies crowded around the altar table had remained frozen in place, oblivious to everything but the spectacle before them—their sixty-year-old leader furiously shoving himself into and out of the spread-eagled young girl.

At that moment the sickness that had been building inside Kevin for weeks had welled up like the backflow from a drainpipe. Clamping his lips tight to cut off the howl of protest that threatened to erupt from his throat, he had stepped backward out of the room—away from the candlelit obscenities, the ghastly music, the stink of sex and death—and fled, barefoot, down the long hallway.

Though the air in the house was stifling, Kevin felt icy with fear, a pure animal terror, deeper than thought. At that moment he was incapable of formulating a thought, except for one—to get away, to scrabble out of the black pit he had fallen into and try, as best he could, to make things right again.

At the far end of the corridor was a little room, once a servant's bedroom, where the coven members dumped their clothing when they arrived. This night, Kevin had tossed his clothes in a small pile in a corner, apart from the other garments.

He snatched them off the floor and was dressed in a moment.

Throwing on his fleece-lined leather bomber jacket, he grabbed his lace-up hiking boots and hurried back in the direction he had come from.

To reach the front door, he had to pass by the chapel. There was no other way out of the house. The back door and bedroom windows were always locked. And only Simon kept the keys.

At the doorway of the chapel Kevin froze, back pressed against the wall, listening to the sounds from inside. He could hear nothing but the surging of the piped-in organ music. Drawing a deep breath, he made a sprinting leap across the open doorway.

As he did, a terrible shout exploded from inside the chapel.

Kevin was startled so badly that he nearly lost control of his bladder. He stood paralyzed on the opposite side of the doorway, stifling the whimper that had risen into his throat. It took him a moment to realize that he had not been spotted after all—that the shout was a chorus of demonic jubilation, the howl that always heralded the start of the Sabbat orgy.

He was at the front door in an instant, stooping to shove his feet into his boots.

An image flashed into Kevin's mind, Simon pumping between the legs of Rachel Peary. What had he called her? "The breeder." Simon was going to create a new life, for some ungodly purpose.

Kevin shook his head and thought, Not if I can help it.

Suddenly he went rigid. The Prince baby. He knew where its corpse was stored. He would bring it with him. Kevin didn't know what Simon had in mind for the murdered infant. But he'd seen what had been done to the corpse of the Campbell girl. If he could prevent a similar outrage from being perpetrated on the Prince child—well, perhaps that would serve as a first, small atonement.

Besides, the police would *have* to believe him if he showed up with evidence like that.

The door to the basement was located a few steps down the hallway. Kevin pulled his stockinged feet out of his boots and hurried over to it.

He paused at the head of the stairs and listened, one ear cocked toward the chapel. From inside the chapel he could hear lewd cries and raucous shouts mixed in with the music. The orgy was in progress. Kevin knew the exhilarating chaos of the orgy—the absolute sense of self-loss, of merging into an undifferentiated mass of lips and tongues and fingers and genitals.

They would be too busy to miss him.

175

He groped at the inner wall until he found the light switch and flipped it on.

The narrow wooden stairs creaked as he descended from the shadows. A long, jagged splinter snagged his sock and pierced the heel of his right foot. He bit his lower lip and continued down into the ghastly fluorescent brightness at the foot of the steps.

Swinging open the lid of the freezer, he reached into the frozen mist for the black, plastic-wrapped object that lay on the bottom and lifted it out with both hands. It was surprisingly heavy and horribly rigid. A baby sculpted from a block of ice. He tried not to picture what was inside the black plastic trash bag.

He hurried back up the staircase. At the top of the landing he poked his head through the doorway and peered in both directions, up and down the dismal corridor.

Nothing.

Swiftly, his heart jackhammering in his chest, he stepped to the front of the hallway, stuck his feet into his boots, and opened the door. Heavy snowflakes lashed his face as he plunged through the storm toward the line of cars parked in the yard.

He had been careful to leave his car a short distance away from the others, and though it was blanketed with snow like all of them, he found it easily, even in the blackness of the moonless country night.

Pulling open the door on the passenger side, he carefully placed the frozen bundle on the front seat. Hurriedly, using his forearm as a wiper, he swept the snow off the front and rear windshields.

Inside the car his breath rose out of him like a dying man's departing soul. Yanking off his right glove, he reached into his jacket pocket and pulled out his keys. The inside of the car was frigid and his fingers went numb in an instant.

He fumbled the keys, dropping them onto the floor below the steering wheel. He bent to retrieve them, forehead pressed against the icy wheel, groping around at his feet. Straightening, he scratched around the steering column until the key slid into the lock. He was trembling now, and not only from the cold. He pumped the pedal a few times, praying that the car would start, and turned the key.

The motor churned and came to life with a roar.

176

Kevin's heart leapt. He swiveled in his seat to look out the rear window while he backed up. Already the windshield was beginning to blot over with fresh snow.

A shadow rose up from the backseat directly behind him.

A powerful hand reached out, clamped itself around the back of the boy's neck, and squeezed ferociously on either side, cutting off Kevin's scream.

As he slipped into unconsciousness, Kevin thought he heard a voice. "Pleasant dreams," said Simon Proctor.

26

KEVIN PETERSON AWOKE TO THE SPLASH OF WARM LIQUID on his face and a sharp, briny stench in his nose.

His eyes shot open. Directly above him, straddling his face, loomed Simon, holding himself between his legs. Gasping and spitting, Kevin tried to move away from the gushing stream. But, flat on his back on the chapel floor, hands tightly secured beneath him, he could only roll his head from side to side.

The yellow stream tapered off. Shaking himself, Simon took a step back from the prostrate boy.

"The traitor is awake," he said icily. "Raise him."

A strong hand reached down, clutched Kevin by the hair, and yanked him upright, forcing him onto his knees. Kevin felt as if his scalp were being torn from his skull. He howled, and tears filled his eyes.

He gazed through his tears at the circle of naked people around him. Kevin himself was still fully dressed, though his leather jacket had been removed.

All of their faces were contorted with hatred and contempt. He could not see Rachel among them.

"So, Kevin," Proctor said. "You have chosen the path of betrayal. The gifts you were offered, of power, protection, the ecstasies of the flesh, were somehow insufficient. You have turned against your family." He made a sweeping gesture that encompassed the rest of the group. "You have turned against your worship. You have turned against your master." Simon's voice had risen steadily and now trem-

177

bled with barely contained rage. He bent low and stuck his face close to Kevin's.

"Betrayal leaves a bitter taste, Kevin," Proctor said fiercely. "Do you know what betrayal tastes like?"

Straightening up suddenly, Simon stepped around Kevin and strode off into the shadows behind him. Kevin tried to look over his shoulder but the hand that clutched his hair—David Prince's, he realized—yanked his head forward. Kevin screamed.

He looked imploringly at the faces around him. One of the girls, a seventeen-year-old named Pamela, took a step forward, crouched before him and spat into his face. The others tittered as she stood up and stuck her buttocks into his face before moving back into the circle.

Michael, a powerfully built six-footer—and the oldest member of the group, next to Simon and David—approached Kevin. Slowly, he drew back his fist. Kevin flinched, eyes clamped tight in anticipation of the blow, but David barked out, "No!"

Kevin opened his eyes.

"No marks," David said to Michael.

Michael hovered over Kevin for a moment, "Motherfucker," he snarled, then swiveled on his heel and returned to the group.

Now Kevin became aware of a sound, a soft metallic rattle, somewhere behind him. Then he heard a high-pitched, animal squeal. His blood turned to ice.

A moment later Simon stood before him. In one hand he clutched a squirming rat.

"Do you know what betrayal tastes like?" he repeated. He nodded at his son.

Kevin clamped his lips tight. Reaching down with his free hand, David pinched Kevin's nose hard. When the boy gasped for air, David grabbed his jaw and forced his mouth wide open.

"Taste," said Simon.

Kevin made a horrified gurgle as he stared up at the rat. Its pink tail flicked wildly a few inches above his head.

Then, like a man uncapping a beer bottle, Simon reached up with his opposite hand and tore the head off the rat with a single savage twist. He held the twitching carcass neck-down over the weeping boy's mouth and squeezed.

178

27

IN HER DREAM, ANNA PRINCE WAS BACK IN THE DESERT, racing toward a jagged range of mountains that stretched across the horizon like a dragon's spine and never seemed to grow nearer, no matter how fast she ran. Something fearful was gaining on her. Though her sobbing breath boomed in her ears, she could hear her pursuer's footsteps close behind her.

A terrible burden weighed her down. Clutched against her chest, her baby, Stephen, stared up at her blankly, his dark eyes unblinking in the fierce southwestern sun. In the oven-hot air, her child felt impossibly heavy. Anna stumbled on, her bare soles blistering as she fled across the endless, bone-white sand.

Up ahead, a spiky brown plant thrust itself out of the desert. As she ran past it, the sharp-pointed leaves turned into long fingers that curled around her ankle and began to drag her downward. She opened her mouth to scream, raising her child high above her head as her body was pulled underground. Something loomed over her—the silhouette of a man backlit by the sun. Shadow hands reached down and snatched away her baby, and a booming voice began to speak in mocking tones. But by then the ground had closed around her ears and she could not understand the words, nor make her own cries heard through the heavy sand that spilled into her mouth.

She awoke with a start, mouth parched, heart racing, gulping air in loud, tortured breaths. Her long hair was slick with sweat. She lay motionless on her back, wondering how long she'd been asleep. The light in her bedroom was almost gone. Outside the window, the branches shivered and white flakes swirled, blown from the rooftop by the rattling wind, the tail end of the winter storm that had hit the area over the weekend, three days earlier.

What time was it? She rolled onto her side and gazed at the clock on the bed table. Four-thirty. She could not remember when she had dragged herself upstairs to rest. She

179

remembered that her lunch—the soft-boiled egg and toast Luz had fixed—had sickened her, and she'd had to leave the table.

Or was that yesterday? She could not remember.

She struggled to a sitting position and reached for the pills Dr. Fischer had given her. If she took enough of them, they wiped out everything.

The trouble was, they were making her dreams worse. Every day her nightmares grew more frightful. The one she'd just awakened from had been the scariest yet. She closed her eyes and thought about her dreams. It was strange that she never really saw the shadow who pursued her. She was sure it was Simon. But his features were always hidden from her sight. Terrifying as her nightmares were, she would have liked, just once, to look her dark tormentor in the face.

She would not take the pill. She would wait up for her husband and ask him why he was never there for her anymore when she needed him so badly. Throwing off the comforter, she swung her legs off the bed and perched on the edge of the mattress, rubbing her sleep-numbed arms to get the circulation going. Even through her flannel shirt and heavy wool cardigan her arms felt like sticks. She was growing thinner every day, alone in the lifeless house. Surely David would not leave her alone much longer.

But it was almost nine-thirty before he entered the house. She could hear him whistling as he unlocked the front door. He looked startled to see her in the living room. His surprise shifted to concern as he walked toward her, nodding at the half-filled glass clutched in her right hand.

"Vodka?" he asked.

"Perrier. I've stopped drinking. I've decided to stop taking those goddamned pills too."

He hovered over her for a moment, looking down. "Good," he said, and bent to kiss the top of her head. "You've washed your hair. Smells nice." Standing straight, he glanced around the living room. "Why the hell do you keep it so dark in here all the time? It can't be good for your mood."

He turned and began to circulate around the living room, reaching under lamp shades and twisting on the lights. The room lit up in a cream-colored glow. Anna watched him as he moved, struck at how fit and handsome he looked. It was strange, she thought, that he seemed so physically unaffected by their tragedy. She herself looked like a phantom, so hollow and sickly that she'd begun avoiding mirrors. Her own reflection frightened her.

"Where have you been for the last few weeks, David?" she suddenly burst out in a half-pleading, half-reproachful tone. "Every time I wake up, you're gone. You're never here for dinner anymore."

David stood in the center of the floor and stared at her. "Anna, I still have a business to run," he said softly. "And I've been doing what I can to keep on top of the investigation. I've been on the phone with Wayland every day. Besides"—he shot a glance around the room—"this house is like a tomb. And you've been locked in the bedroom most of the time anyway. What difference does it make if I'm here or not?"

She conceded the point with a weary shrug, then fixed him with a look of desperate hopefulness. "There's no news, then?"

"None." He was standing by the liquor cabinet, pouring himself a bourbon. He took a swig. "They're still searching for that yardboy."

"You know that's a fucking waste of time, David," she said in a trembling voice. The glass in her hand trembled too, spilling a few drops of water onto the sofa cushion. "You know who they should be looking for."

"Please, Anna. Don't start that shit again."

"Simon!" she screamed.

"Bullshit! Christ, Anna, you say things like that and people'll think you really are crazy."

"He did it, David."

"That's a lot of crap. He's in New Mexico."

"No. He's not."

He looked at her appraisingly. "What are you talking about?"

"That policewoman told me—Byrne. She called me this morning. Simon's been missing since he got out of prison."

They stared at each other for a long moment before David demanded, "And where does Officer Byrne think Simon is?" His tone rang with sarcasm.

"They don't know," Anna answered miserably.

David polished off his drink with a long swallow, then set the glass down on the cabinet top. "Simon's got nothing to do with this."

"Why are so sure?" She looked up at him quizzically. "Don't you love our baby?"

David took a quick step forward, his face so taut with anger that Anna flinched. "Don't ever say anything like that to me again," he said in a voice quiet with rage. He loomed over the sofa, glaring down at her. Finally, his fists unclenched and his expression softened. "You know how much I loved that child," he said quietly.

Anna raised her eyebrows. *"Loved?"*

"Don't play word games with me, Anna. Stephen means as much to me as he does to you. Whose idea *was* it to have a baby now, anyway?"

Anna opened her mouth to say something, then shut it abruptly. Her gaze seemed to turn inward. "Funny," she said, as if to herself.

"What?" he asked harshly.

"I never thought about that before."

"About what?"

"How, after all those years of not wanting a child, you suddenly decided I should get pregnant. Just about a year before Simon's release."

"What are you getting at?" he said icily.

Her own voice cracked as she gazed up at him through her welling tears. "I don't know! I have such terrible thoughts. You and Simon were so close to each other, almost like twins." Abruptly, she raised her empty water glass high above her head and hurled it across the room. It shattered against the opposite wall, showering shards of glass onto the furniture and across the white-carpeted floor.

Pushing herself off the sofa, Anna came at David, screeching. "Where is he?" she shrieked again and again. Her balled fists flailed at his chest. "I want my baby back!"

David grabbed her wrists, trapping both of them in one powerful hand. She looked up into his dark, unfathomable eyes, and all at once she was terrified.

"Listen to me," he whispered hoarsely. "I don't know what you're thinking. But if you don't stop, you'll end up locked away. Institutionalized, Anna. I'll see to it myself."

His mouth curled into a sneer. "You were nothing once. You'll be nothing again."

She gasped. Then, as if a plug had suddenly been pulled inside her heart, her fury drained out of her and she collapsed against his chest. "David," she sobbed. "What are you saying?"

He released her wrists and stood there rigidly as she wept. Finally, he seemed to will himself to soften. As Anna continued to cry convulsively, he placed an arm around her heaving shoulders and stroked her hair with his other hand.

"I'm sorry for what I said, Anna. You know I didn't mean it. This whole thing has been a nightmare for me too. I just show it differently."

She was still sobbing, her shock and wretchedness barely assuaged, in spite of David's comforting tone and soothing hands. She looked up into his face. "David," she whimpered. "I want Stephen back. I don't think I can go on much longer."

He held her by the shoulders at arm's length and smiled reassuringly. "Have faith, baby. It's what's kept me going." Bending forward, he kissed her softly on the forehead. "C'mon, baby, don't cry," his lulling voice went on. "I won't leave you by yourself anymore. I'll take care of you." Placing one arm around her waist, he drew her close against his side. "Come with Daddy, come on," he whispered, leading her out of the living room. "Let's go upstairs and get you one of those nice pills."

28

THE TEMPERATURE ON WEDNESDAY NEVER ROSE ABOVE freezing, and the sky was a sharp, flawless blue. Under the brilliant sun the snow-blanketed land sparkled. By the time the big orange school buses had unloaded their passengers, there were only a few hours of daylight left, and the children of Stoneham, chattering and laughing as they tumbled into the dazzling afternoon, were determined to make the most of them.

Ten-year-old Melanie Bernstein was so excited by the

time she reached her front stoop that she burst into the house, dropped her books, and with a shouted hi to her mother, dashed down the basement steps and into the garage. Her Flexible Flyer leaned in a corner. She picked it up in both hands and looked at it lovingly. It was so much better than the big plastic saucers and inflatable snow tubes most of the other kids used. Her dad had bought it for her last winter, but a series of earaches and coughs had prevented her from getting much use out of it. She felt as if she'd been waiting forever for this day to arrive.

Outside, she hauled the sled toward the big hill behind her house, the red-painted runners inscribing parallel ribbons in the deep snow. The Bernstein property abutted a few acres of land set apart by the town as a sanctuary for local wildlife. Beyond that, invisible through the snow-carpeted woods, ran Route 28.

Melanie positioned the sled at the crest of the hill, laid herself belly down on the slatted deck, then pushed off down the bare slope that descended to a small, level clearing surrounded by a thicket of evergreens.

She "wheeee"-ed with delight as the sled bulleted downhill, snow-spray stinging her cheeks, already apple-red from the cold. She kept her eyes fixed on the rushing ground in front of her as her daddy had taught her to do. The air was so crisp and clear that every detail stood out in sharp relief.

She had almost reached the bottom of the hill when she spotted, dead ahead, a strange-looking lump poking out of the snow. She shoved the steering bar hard to avoid it. The sled veered sharply and overturned, spilling her into the snow.

She got to her knees, wiping the icy wetness from her eyes with the back of one wool-gloved hand, searching the ground for the thing she had nearly run over. Her sled lay on its side, half wedged into a snowdrift. A few feet away lay the thing.

Melanie crawled toward it on hands and knees, pausing a few feet away. It *is* a doll! she thought. Why did someone throw her doll away in the woods? The doll was mostly buried in the snow, just its stiff legs, one curled hand, and part of its head showing.

As she stared at the discarded doll, Melanie began to notice several strange details. First, its color was all wrong,

184

not the shiny flesh tone of her own dolls, but an awful white. And the hands and feet had tiny nails that looked amazingly real. The hair looked real too, and delicate eyelashes fringed the doll's tightly closed eyes. Its face looked very sad, its tiny mouth puckered open, as if frozen forever in a painful cry. Melanie pulled off one snow-crusted glove and reached out a finger to feel the doll's face. The moment she touched it, she scuttled backward with a cry.

It was then that she became aware of the thing overhead. She stared upward, mouth agape, drinking in cold. It took her a long moment to identify what she was seeing, and even then she could not make any sense of it.

Stuck up among the branches of a big pine tree was a teenage boy, dressed in boots and jeans and a plaid flannel shirt and a leather jacket. His head was twisted at a funny angle and his tongue was sticking out of his mouth, all horrible and black. There was something yanked tight around his neck—a rope, Melanie realized, that disappeared upward among the dark green branches. Sticking out of the boy's shirt pocket was a folded piece of white paper.

Melanie pushed herself to her feet and backpedaled through the snow, stumbling over her sled and twisting her leg as she fell. She was whimpering loudly now, and her insides were gripped by a terror even colder than the snow. Shoving herself to her feet, she half crawled, half scrambled uphill toward her house.

By the time she reached her backyard, her screams were so shrill and so constant that her mother could hear them even with the phone still cupped snugly to her ear.

29

STANDING BY THE BIG PLATE-GLASS WINDOW IN THE STATION-house lunchroom, Marianne took a sip of her steaming black coffee and stared out at the snow-trimmed houses along Grace Street, postcard pretty in the sharp winter sunlight. With her senses still dulled by her cold, she could taste little of the coffee but a scalding bitterness that matched the blackness in her heart. It was 9:45 A.M., Thursday, November 24, Thanksgiving morning, the morning after the discovery of the bodies of the Prince infant and his confessed kidnapper and murderer, Kevin Peterson.

Seated around the table behind her, Sam Ferris and Roy Auslander were filling Mile Nash in on the details. The small room was gray with cigarette smoke.

"Did the scumbag leave a note?" Nash asked.

Auslander took a deep drag on his cigarette. "Yeah," he said, exhaling. "Whole fucking letter. All neatly typed and folded inside his shirt pocket."

"What'd it say?"

"Crazy shit. The fuckhead decides he needs some extra cash, who knows why. Probably drugs. So he decides to snatch the kid. Said he got the idea from a cop show on TV." He gave a humorless snort.

"Why'd he pick the Prince kid?"

"Luck of the draw. Spotted the mother and the kid in the supermarket the week before."

"What about all the 'payback' crap he told the babysitter?"

"Pure bullshit, just to throw us off the scent."

"Christ," Nash muttered. Then, after a few seconds' pause: "So?"

"So, he pulls off the kidnapping but then gets the shits, panics, doesn't know how to set up a ransom drop. The kid is more trouble than he counted on."

"Where was he hiding him?"

"Basement storeroom. Gagged. Mother's hardly ever around, kid brother never goes down there. We questioned them both. Anyway, he wakes up one day and the baby's dead. Suffocated. That does it. Scumbag snaps, decides to end it all. End of story."

"Amazing." Even without turning to look, Marianne knew that Nash was shaking his balding head slowly in disgust. She'd seen the gesture a hundred times. "You'd think with all the fucking money these kids have . . ." He left the thought unfinished. "I was really hoping—"

"What?" Auslander's gravelly voice cut in.

"That we'd get the kid back alive." Marianne started as a fist slammed down hard on the table, making the ashtrays rattle. Nash had two little boys of his own. "Fuck it," he growled.

All of them had been clinging to the same hope, in spite of the knowledge that, with every day that passed without a ransom note, the likelihood of recovering the child grew slimmer. Like the others, Marianne had been steeling herself for this eventuality since the day of the abduction.

So she was unprepared for the extent of her misery. It went beyond a sense of terrible failure and touched something deep, almost primal, inside her, something whose very existence came as a surprise. Marianne didn't regard herself as a particularly maternal woman. In her daydreams of the future, she could imagine a home and children, but only as vague abstractions.

Now, thinking about the Prince baby, murdered at only three months, as if he had been put on earth for no other purpose than to suffer this horror, tears stung her eyes and began to slide down her cheeks. Keeping her back to the table, she drew a hankie from her hip pocket, dabbed quickly at her eyes and face, then blew her nose. "Damn cold," she muttered, loud enough for the men to hear.

"Shoulda stayed in bed, Marianne," Sam said. "You still sound lousy."

"Couldn't," Marianne answered hoarsely. "I'm having Thanksgiving dinner with my dad down in Queens."

"Happy Thanksgiving," Nash said glumly.

"Yeah, well, at least it'll be a good one for the chief," Roy Auslander said. When Nash shot him a disapproving look he added quickly, "Hey, I don't mean because of the baby. But at least we can close the files on this motherfucker. Wayland's been worrying himself sick over it. Must've lost twenty pounds these last few weeks."

At that moment the booming voice of the desk sergeant, Pete Rydell, came rumbling down the corridor. "Yo, Byrne!" he called. "Pick up on three!"

Lobbing her empty cup into the trash barrel, Marianne hurried down the hall toward an empty desk, grateful to escape. She dropped herself into the swivel chair, grabbed the handset of the phone and punched the button for line three. "Byrne here."

"Yeah, Byrne, this is Santucci at Grasslands. Got a message you called yesterday. What can I do for you?"

She was still so preoccupied with thoughts of the baby that it took her a moment to remember. "That light bulb I

187

sent over to you to be printed. When are we going to get the results?'' It wouldn't make any difference now, Marianne supposed. Still, she didn't like to leave any loose ends untied.

"Light bulb?'' Santucci sounded surprised. "Hold on a minute.''

While she waited, Marianne picked up a Bic Stic lying on the desktop and began scratching absently on a legal pad. At first the doodle seemed like a random design. It wasn't until she'd been sketching for a minute that the image evolved into a dark-haired woman's face with a single beadlike tear, as shapely as a pearl, suspended from each eye.

At the other of the line she could hear Santucci's muffled voice as he conferred with someone else. Then he was back loud and clear. "Byrne? We sent that back by messenger a week ago—Thursday the seventeenth. It was included with a bunch of other results—Breathalyzer tests on two DWI cases, latents in that Kisco house burglary, some other stuff. We got a signature, let's see . . .'' Marianne could hear the rustle of paper. "It was signed for by Mike . . . Hoffman, looks like.''

"Holson?'' she asked, surprised.

"Could be.''

Marianne sat there for a moment after hanging up, wondering what the hell had happened to the fingerprint results. Why hadn't Holson passed them along to her? Shoving herself out of the chair, she strode to the front desk. Holson was due back from patrol in about an hour, Rydell informed her. Marianne headed back to the report room to take care of some paperwork and distract herself from her churning emotions—her heartsickness at the outcome of the Prince kidnapping, her simmering annoyance at Holson.

The effort was only partly successful. She managed to dispose of the paperwork all right, but by the time Holson showed up, she had worked herself into a lather. She began chewing him out as soon as he appeared in the doorway, still wearing his winter jacket and mirrored aviator glasses.

"Hey, hey,'' he protested, hands up in a gesture of mock surrender. "I didn't see the goddamn thing. Chill out, Marianne. You're not the only one in a shitty mood around here.'' As he spoke, he pulled off his sunglasses and massaged his eye sockets with the heel of one hand. Marianne felt slightly chastened. Holson looked pretty ragged, as if he'd only had a few hours of sleep.

"Sorry," she said. "But why the hell haven't I seen that report?"

"Probably got stuck in with some others. Look, I'll help you find it."

And he did, after a search that took them almost up to lunchtime. Marianne was just about to call it quits and phone Santucci to request another copy when Holson spotted the folder at the back of a file drawer. She snatched it out of his hands and they read it together, Holson leaning over her shoulder.

The technicians at Grasslands had come up with three sets of latents on the Princes' porch bulb. One set had been matched to the Princes' Filipino cleaning woman, Luz Mariposa.

That makes sense, Marianne thought. Anna Prince didn't strike her as the type of woman who would deign to change a light bulb. That would be a chore she would leave to the hired help.

David Prince's fingerprints were also on the bulb, and Marianne frowned at that. Assuming that the bulb *had* been installed by the cleaning lady, why would he have handled it too? Still, that wasn't so inexplicable. Light bulbs sometimes work loose and need to be tightened every now and then.

She flipped to the next page. And caught her breath.

The third set of prints had been identified as those of Rachel Peary.

Marianne simply stared at the name for a few seconds. "Jesus!" she finally whispered.

"What?"

"Look," she said, poking the page with a finger. "Don't you get it?" Glancing up over her shoulder, she realized that she'd never told Holson—or anyone else, for that matter—what she had discovered about the porch bulb. She quickly filled him in. "There wasn't anything wrong with that bulb. It wasn't burned out like the babysitter said. Someone unscrewed it. Half the base was showing. And the way I read this report, there's the very real possibility . . ." Her voice drifted off as she bit her lower lip in thought.

189

"Yeah?"

"That Rachel Peary was the one who unscrewed it."

His eyes narrowed with perplexity. "Why the hell would she do that?"

"To make the porch dark," Marianne said simply.

Holson's eyes slowly grew larger. "What are you getting at, Marianne? Are you saying that she was in on the snatching with that motherfucker Peterson? That she was his accomplice?"

"I don't know." Marianne was shaking her head. "But something weird's going on, Mike. There was another hole in her story. I don't think she was watching TV that night."

She had just begun to tell him about the inconsistency she had discovered when a gruff voice behind them said, "What're you two huddling over?"

Marianne and Holson swiveled their heads at the same time.

There stood Wayland, pulling off his leather gloves. Beneath his unbuttoned overcoat he was casually dressed in brown slacks and a blue plaid shirt open at the collar.

Roy Auslander had been right about one thing. Four weeks of unrelieved stress had wrung some of the flab off Wayland. But if he was grateful that the Prince case had finally been solved, there was no visible sign of it on his face, only an infinite weariness.

"How's it going, Chief?" Holson asked. "I thought you were taking the day off."

Wayland nodded. "We're driving down to Janet's sister's house on the Island. Just thought I'd drop by to see how things are going. What's that?" He gestured toward the papers in Marianne's hands.

Marianne hesitated, grimly aware that the report was more than just a new and potentially important piece of evidence. It was a king-size can of worms. But Wayland had asked her a direct question, and she wasn't about to dodge it.

"They're test results from Grasslands," she said. "I sent the porch bulb from the Prince house down there for printing."

Marianne could see the muscle in Wayland's right cheek twitch as he tightened his jaw. "And?" he asked in a voice flat and hard as a skimming stone.

Marianne looked directly into Wayland's eyes. Their expression was as stony as his voice. "Chief," she said softly. "Are you absolutely satisfied that this case is closed?"

Wayland expelled a noise that sounded like a wordless curse. He stood there for a long moment, shaking his head and saying nothing. Finally he began to speak, in a tone devoid of everything but a terrible sadness. "Officer Byrne, I appreciate your dedication and zeal. I really do. But I don't want to hear any more conspiracy theories. Now. Tomorrow. Ever. We've got a dead infant, murdered by an emotionally disturbed adolescent, who has also taken his own life. We've got parents who are horribly upset, as you can imagine. It's a rotten situation all around. What I'd like to do, what I'd like all of us to do, is try to put this thing behind us and get back to normal."

Throughout Wayland's speech—one of the longest she'd ever heard him make—Marianne had stood there, feeling her face grow flushed with anger. Now, she opened her mouth to protest. But before she could get out a word, Wayland held up his hand like a traffic cop signaling stop.

"If there's something you need to report, put it in writing," he said. "I don't want to worry about anything today except whether to eat white meat or dark." He reached out and gave Marianne's arm a paternal pat, then shook Holson's hand, wishing both of them a good Thanksgiving. "If you see your father today, tell him hello from me," he said to Marianne. Then he turned and disappeared down the corridor.

Marianne felt as if she might exhale a blast of steam. She stood there, lips clamped tight, until the boiling inside her chest subsided. Then she glanced around at Holson, who gave a helpless shrug, as if to say, What can you do?

Marianne muttered something under her breath.

"What'd you say?" asked Holson.

"I said he doesn't give a shit about the truth."

Holston stepped around so that he was standing directly in front of her. "Listen, Marianne, you can't blame the chief. We've just been spinning our wheels for the last four weeks. He knew we were going to find zip. Now he feels things are under control again."

"Maybe. But I'm not going to try to convince him anymore. I'm going to do this on my own."

Holson reached out and put his hands on her shoulders. "Hey, you're not alone. I think you're onto something."

Marianne smiled at him gratefully.

"So what's your next move?" Holson asked.

Marianne looked thoughtful. "Maybe I'll pay a visit to the babysitter, Rachel."

"Makes sense," said Holson. He looked at his watch. "Jeez. I'm late. We've got to drive way the hell out to New Jersey." He gave her shoulders a squeeze. "Let me know what happens. I'll help any way I can."

Standing on tiptoe, Marianne kissed him on the cheek. "Thanks, Mike."

Holson stared at her for a few seconds. Then, reaching around with one hand, he pulled her toward him, kissed her firmly on the lips, and released her. "Happy Thanksgiving," he said, flashing his most rakish smile, then strolled away before Marianne could respond.

Twenty minutes later, dressed in her civvies, Marianne headed out into the glare of the parking lot. She was still feeling agitated, though only partly from Wayland's rebuff. She could still feel the touch of Holson's lips on her own.

Driving down the Saw Mill River Parkway, she began to unwind. She looked forward to seeing her father. She hadn't spent time with him in over a month and missed his company. And she was curious about the new discovery he'd made. He hadn't told her anything about it. "It'll be easier to show it to you," he'd said during their last phone conversation. She wondered what the big mystery was.

All he'd said was that it was something he'd found in a book.

30

"GREAT DINNER, DAD," MARIANNE SAID, LAYING HER FORK down on the dessert plate beside her half-eaten wedge of store-bought pumpkin pie. She reached across the table and squeezed her father's hand. The compliment was only partly a lie. The turkey had been roasted to the point of dehydration, the sweet potatoes were at least twenty minutes underbaked, the green beans soggy with Campbell's mushroom soup. Even the canned cranberry sauce, a tube of purple gelatin sliced into fat, wobbly disks, had a harsh, synthetic flavor.

In spite of everything, Marianne had enjoyed the dinner. She was touched at the pains her dad had taken to give the afternoon a holiday feel. Except for the pie, he had prepared the whole meal himself. He had even set the dining room table with the family's best china and silverplate. It was the first time since her mother's death that Marianne and her dad had eaten in the dining room.

Sitting there now, gazing over at the glass-fronted corner cabinet containing her mother's prized collection of bisque figurines, Marianne felt a sudden pang. It was not only her mother she missed, but the Thanksgiving afternoons of her own faraway childhood, when the dining room would ring with the laughter and talk of a dozen assembled relatives—grandparents, uncles, aunts, and cousins, all of them now either scattered or deceased. The feeling was compounded by yesterday's tragedy, a subject that she and her father had studiously avoided throughout the meal.

Now, giving his daughter's fingers a fond, answering squeeze, Jack leaned back in his chair and said, "Sorry things fell out the way they did. With the kidnapping. I was afraid this is how it would end."

Marianne nodded glumly. "We all were."

"The papers had a field day with it. It made the front page of today's *Post*."

"The press has been swarming around like roaches," Marianne said.

"I suppose this wraps it all up."

"As far as Wayland's concerned."

"And you?"

Marianne picked up her fork and began poking holes in her leftover pie. "I don't know," she said softly. Then, looking up at her father, she said, "There was something you wanted to show me. Something in a book?"

Sucking in his cheeks, Jack stared at his daughter, as if debating about the wisdom of sharing his discovery. Finally he shoved himself away from the table and left the room, returning moments later with a big, leather-bound volume in one hand. He set it down in front of Marianne, who tried to make out the faded gold printing on the ribbed spine. The book looked ancient to her.

"When I first came across this, I thought it might be relevant. But now that the kidnapping is solved . . ." Jack left the sentence unfinished.

Marianne opened the book to the page marked off with a scrap of paper and began to read as Jack watched her face intently from his place at the head of the table.

Marianne blinked and her lips parted. "This is it!" she whispered. Jack could see that nothing existed for her at that moment but the pages in front of her widening eyes. He knew the feeling.

Leaning forward, he put a hand gently on her forearm. "Marianne, it's important not to leap to conclusions."

"But this is the answer," she exclaimed, looking up at him with bright, excited eyes. "This explains it all. The dog. The baby. It all comes together!"

"Marianne, nothing has 'come together.' Yes, there seems to be a similarity between that picture and the mutilation of the golden retriever. But what about this Peterson boy? He left a detailed confession. Perfectly plausible. Is there anything to suggest that he was involved with the occult?"

"Not that we know of," Marianne admitted.

Jack nodded toward the open book in his daughter's lap. "That's a very obscure variety of Satanism you're reading about, Marianne. Hell, even I'd forgotten about it. How would a kid like Peterson know about it?"

"Maybe he didn't. Maybe someone else did. Someone with just as much knowledge of the occult as you. Maybe more. Someone with enough time on his hands to make a very serious study of it."

"You mean Proctor," Jack said with a sigh.

For an answer, Marianne simply stared back at her father.

"Marianne, all this is pure speculation. There's not one iota of proof to link the dog to the baby's death. There certainly isn't anything to connect Proctor to all this. In fact, Peterson's suicide seems to point the other way."

Marianne held up the book. "Why did you want me to see this?"

"That was before yesterday," he said. But his voice lacked conviction.

Both of them sat silently for a few moments before Jack exhaled a deep sigh. "If you're convinced there's more here than meets the eye," he said quietly, "then the thing to do is to tell Wayland. Take the book with you. Show it to him."

Marianne gave a clipped, bitter laugh. "Wayland doesn't want to hear it."

Jack rose from his chair and reached for Marianne's dessert plate. "Maybe he'll listen to me."

Darkness had fallen. At the very moment that Jack Byrne and his daughter were clearing the dishes from the dining room table, another young woman about Marianne's age, a red-haired hooker who went by the name of Trish, was huddling in the doorway of a boarded-up luncheonette on Eighth Avenue and Forty-fourth Street in Manhattan, doing her best to light her thirty-first Virginia Slim of the day. There was a sharp wind slicing down the dirty boulevard, and Trish was having trouble shielding her lighter.

After a few tries, she succeeded. With the guttering cigarette dangling from her lips, she stepped out of the shadows and began to stroll up the sidewalk, stepping around mounds of soot-coated slush, dog shit, and the occasional derelict dozing by a trash can or fire plug.

Under the blinking marquee of a porno palace, she stopped, shoving her jacket sleeve up to reveal her flipper. By bowing slightly, she could lift it high enough to reach her mouth. Grasping the cigarette with the little nub that poked from the flipper end, she plucked it from her lips and blew a fume of smoke into the night air.

Her right arm didn't really look like a flipper, though that was what her pimp called it. She still remembered the first time VeeJay had taken a close look at it, back at his apartment after he'd come on to her at the Port Authority bus terminal. She'd just stepped off the Greyhound from Columbus. It was mid-July, and she was dressed in tight jeans and a tank top.

"What you call that?" he asked, gazing raptly at the stunted appendage that terminated in a bony knob. A pink, fleshy bulge that looked like a baby's thumb protruded from the end.

She knew the medical term. Her shithead of a father, the hotshot businessman, had told her when she was twelve years old, and she'd never forgotten it. She had even looked it up once in a dictionary at the high school library. That was just before she'd run away.

"Phocomelia," she'd said.

"Fuck a *what?*" VeeJay had said.

Two weeks later she'd begun to whore for VeeJay. Lying next to her in bed, both of them naked and drenched in the city swelter, he had stroked her shriveled limb and explained what a gold mine it was. Sure, some johns would be turned off by it. But there were plenty of freaks who would pay a premium to feel that sweet flipper on their cocks. VeeJay had lifted the knobby end and kissed it as sweetly as an English lord would his lady's hand.

Trish took another drag and checked the wristwatch on her normal arm. It was only seven-fifteen, still early. Nevertheless, she didn't have much hope of scoring, not on Thanksgiving night. On the other hand, as VeeJay had pointed out when he'd sent her onto the street, guys who get off on hand jobs from cripples don't necessarily spend holidays at home carving the Thanksgiving turkey.

A dark-colored Toyota cruised slowly past the porno theater. Maybe VeeJay was right. It was the third time she'd seen the car drive by. Moments later it turned the corner again and pulled to a stop directly in front of her. The door on the passenger side swung open. Tossing her cigarette into the gutter, Trish stepped to the car, slid onto the seat, and slammed the door closed beside her.

As the Toyota turned west on Forty-fourth, Trish glanced over at the driver. He was a big man. Though his features were mostly hidden in shadow, she could see his strong profile and the powerful bulge of his shoulders, arms, and chest. It was hard to say how old he was. As the car passed into and out of the streetlamp glow, she caught glimpses of a face deeply creased with wrinkles and crow's feet. But he had a full head of dark, curly hair.

Sidling closer, she twisted around and laid her pale, sticklike limb on his upper thigh, close to the bulge of his crotch. She began to stroke him with the little knob.

"Have a nice Thanksgiving?" she asked.

"It's not a holiday I celebrate," the man answered, keeping his eyes fixed on the street. His voice was as deep and rich as a radio announcer's.

"So what'll it be?" Trish asked, reaching down with her good hand and taking hold of the metal tab of his zipper.

Powerful fingers clamped down on her hand and removed it from his crotch. "Not now."

"That hurt," she complained.

The man said nothing.

"Where're we going?" Trish asked, suddenly aware that the car was heading toward the northbound lanes of the Henry Hudson Parkway.

"My place," he said. There was an amused undertone in his voice, as though he were enjoying an inside joke.

"That'll cost you extra."

"Oh, I'll do right by you," he said, glancing over at her for the first time and smiling. Removing his right hand from the steering wheel, he reached across her body and delicately stroked her deformity. "You're just what I've been looking for."

SHE HAD NEVER BEEN INSIDE A BIGGER HOUSE. OR A DARKER one.

Standing just inside the threshold, the tall man hovering behind her, she tried to peer into the blackness. Ahead of her a hallway seemed to stretch forever into the dark.

Years ago, during a trip to Rye Playland amusement park with VeeJay, he had taken her into the funhouse. She remembered how scared she'd felt at the start of the ride, VeeJay's hand clutched tightly in her own while she stared straight into the spooky black tunnel. It was the way she used to feel as a child, huddled under the blankets at night, hearing the rustle of monsters as they crept from her bedroom closet.

Now, she felt the same sensation creep over her.

She had no idea where the tall man had taken her. They had driven northward for what seemed hours, the high-rises of Manhattan dwindling into suburbia, the suburbs thinning out into country. When she'd asked him where they were going, he had only repeated, "My place."

She didn't like being carried so far from the familiar streets to an unspecified destination. Now that they had arrived, she liked it even less.

"Any lights in this place?" she asked, trying to keep the nervousness out of her voice. She knew that it was important to project an attitude of coolness and control. "Or don't they have electricity up here in the sticks?"

Behind her she heard a hollow scrape. Match light flared over her shoulder, then bloomed into a deeper glow. The tall man stepped in front of her, a silver candlestick in one hand. Behind him, his looming shadow wavered on the dark-papered wall.

"Come," he said. Turning, he headed down the corridor.

He proceeded halfway down the hallway, then stopped before a heavy, paneled door on the left. Opening it with a shove, he disappeared inside.

Trish, following a few steps behind, hesitated at the

198

threshold, peering around the doorjamb into the murky room. At first she could see very little. The tall man, his features masked in shadow, circulated around the room. Wielding his candlestick like a wand, he tipped its flaming end to the wicks of a dozen other candles, ranged around the room in silver candelabra. The flickering glow brought a bewildering array of objects into view. Trish squinted into the gloom, trying to make them out. The tall man turned and beckoned her inside with a little wave of the hand.

Swallowing back her anxiety, Trish stepped into the room. The air was unpleasantly hot, and dense with a mixture of smells she couldn't sort out. Incense? Sweat? She wrinkled her nose at the unmistakable whiff of urine. She couldn't see any windows, and stared at the objects surrounding her. The place was so strange that it took her a moment to register what she was looking at.

The room was some sort of chapel.

A big table draped with a black satin sheet occupied one end of the room. The walls were hung with religious pictures whose content she could not decipher in the gloom. Suspended from the ceiling above the table was an enormous crucifix. Trish stared at the crucified figure. Insanely, it seemed to be clad in a woman's bathing suit—some sort of flesh-colored bikini. She peered intently at the garment, her mind unable to conceive the truth. When it finally broke in on her, she felt her heart go numb with dread. She spun on her heel, not realizing that the tall man had stepped behind her.

Grabbing her good arm, he twisted it sharply up behind her back, forcing her down on her knees. She knew that it was useless to scream, that there was no one nearby to hear. But she could not keep from crying out in pain and terror.

Above her the tall man's voice began to boom. " 'And when the men of that place had knowledge of him,' " he intoned, " 'they sent out into all that country round about, and brought unto him all that were diseased; and besought him that they might only touch the hem of his garment; and as many as touched were made perfectly whole.' " He barked a savage laugh. "Behold the good of his promise," he said in a voice heavy with contempt. "God of the cripples! Freak-lord!" Bending his face close to hers, her arm

199

still locked in his grip, he whispered, "Do you seek remedy, freak?"

"Please," Trish whispered through her tears. Though she struggled to keep her voice steady, it trembled. "Don't."

"Here is your only deliverance, through the grace of the Lord Belphegor, who covets your soul."

Behind her the tall man groped inside his pocket, removed something. She could hear a rustle, like the sound of a plastic bag being worked open.

She began to shake her head wildly from side to side, but the tall man yanked up on her arm, freezing her for an instant with pain. In that instant, he slipped the plastic bag over her head and pulled it tight around her face. She opened her mouth to scream. The airtight membrane clogged her mouth and nostrils.

Frantically, she tried to grab at the smothering hood with her free arm. Above her the tall man burst into uproarious laughter.

The stunted limb flapped weakly against the plastic like a broken wing before subsiding into stillness.

32

SATURDAY WAS MARIANNE'S DAY OFF. SHE SLEPT UNTIL nine, then switched on her bed lamp and opened the musty volume her father had given her, propping the heavy book on her stomach. It was almost ten-thirty before she left her apartment and unlocked the door of her Honda. Twenty-five minutes later she arrived in Stoneham, pulling into the driveway of 18 McClellan Place shortly before eleven.

Good timing, Marianne thought, checking her watch. It was unlikely that the mother would still be asleep. But it was still early enough to catch the daughter at home. She hoped.

The Peary house was a sturdy, clapboard Cape, lemon-yellow with dark green shutters. In the neighborhood Marianne had grown up in, it would have stood out as a showplace. By Stoneham standards it certainly ranked higher than a humble cottage. But not by much.

An air of slight neglect hung about the house. The roof gutter was hanging loose, and whole sections of yellow siding were blistered and peeling. On the little patch of lawn that ran alongside the driveway, a few plastic garden pots, drab green and empty of whatever plants they had originally held, poked up through the crusty snow. The rundown feeling was intensified by the weather. Another storm was on the way, and the sky was dark and lowering. In the gray morning light the whole world seemed coated with a thin layer of grime.

Marianne remembered that Mrs. Peary was divorced. It must be tough, she reflected, for a middle-aged woman to keep up a house while holding down a full-time job. Especially when she also had to ride herd on a teenager. It occurred to Marianne that Kevin Peterson had also come from a broken home. She wondered how common that was among Stoneham high-schoolers, and made a mental note to check with Tommy Reardon, the precinct youth officer.

Marianne put her finger on the door button. A distant buzzer sounded inside the house. Almost at once she heard the muffled tread of approaching feet. She took a step back as the storm door swung toward her.

"Yes?"

Marianne looked up at the woman holding open the glass-fronted door. She liked her face. It was frank and good-humored, framed by a helmet of thick, brown hair that had begun fading to gray. The steel-gray streaks had been left unretouched for all the world to see. In a town where the average woman wouldn't dream of driving to the supermarket without makeup, perfectly coiffed hair, and casuals by Ralph Lauren, such unaffectedness impressed Marianne as a sign of character.

"Mrs. Peary?" Marianne said, reaching into her shoulder bag for her black-leather badge case. "Marianne Byrne. I'm with the Northampton police." She flipped the case closed and slipped it back inside her bag. "I wonder if I could speak to your daughter."

Deep grooves materialized between Mrs. Peary's eyebrows. "She's not at home. Is there something I can help you with?"

Marianne made a disappointed face. "Not really. I needed to ask her a few things."

201

A sharp gust of wind made Mrs. Peary shiver. "Why don't you come inside and wait," she said. "Rachel should be home in a little while. She just had to run a quick errand in town."

Thanking her, Marianne stepped into the house and followed the older woman through a small foyer into the kitchen. Marianne could see that she had interrupted Mrs. Peary's breakfast. A crumb-speckled plate and half-filled coffee cup sat on the table. Beside them lay an uncapped fountain pen and the morning's *New York Times,* folded open to the crossword puzzle. "Sorry for disturbing you."

"I was just finishing my coffee. Care for a cup?"

"Sounds good," Marianne said, slinging her shoulder bag over the back of the chair and removing her parka. Seating herself, she tilted her head to glance at the half-completed crossword puzzle. "Never was any good at these things," she said.

"You get better with practice," Jean said, placing a cup and saucer in front of Marianne. "I started doing them when Rachel was a newborn and I was trapped inside the house all day. By this point, I'm so good that I do them in ink."

She stepped over to the stove to fetch the coffeepot, giving Marianne a better chance to observe her. Marianne had often been struck by the way people and their houses mirrored each other. Mrs. Peary was a perfect example. Dressed in baggy, brown corduroys and a plaid flannel shirt topped with a man-sized, navy cardigan, she possessed the same sturdy, informal, down-to-earth quality as her home. There was something reassuringly solid about the woman, an aura of quiet strength. Looking at her, Marianne felt a twinge of longing for her own lost mother.

Jean filled Marianne's cup, then seated herself across the table.

"Rachel just walked over to the library to pick up some books for a research paper. It's due Monday, so naturally she waited until today to begin working on it." She gave an exasperated headshake. But there was an unmistakable note of contentment in her voice, as though she were grateful to have nothing more dire to worry about than typical teenage procrastination.

They began talking about the events of the past few

202

days—the discovery of the kidnapped baby, Kevin Peterson's suicide, the reaction of David and Anna Prince.

"That poor woman," Jean murmured. "I can't even imagine what she must be feeling." She gazed into her coffee cup, cradled in both hands. "I tried calling her yesterday. Her husband answered the phone. He sounded just awful. Said his wife was doing very badly—refuses to talk to anyone, won't eat, cries constantly. I'm just grateful he doesn't seem to hold a grudge against Rachel. She has enough guilt to deal with as it is."

"How do you mean?"

"She doesn't talk about it. But I can tell she still feels responsible on some level."

"Responsible?"

Jean nodded. "In a general way. After all, she was the one who was watching the child that night. She was the one who opened the door."

Marianne set down her coffee cup. "I understand Chief Wayland came to see Rachel a few days ago. After the two bodies were discovered."

"That's right."

"And she confirmed the Peterson boy's identity."

"Well, based on the description Chief Wayland gave her, she said that he sounded very much like the kidnapper."

"Yet she hadn't recognized him that night—not even his voice. Didn't she *know* Kevin Peterson? They both went to the same school."

Mrs. Peary regarded her silently for a moment. "But he was a senior, Officer Byrne," she said. "Rachel's just a junior. Their paths wouldn't have crossed. She told me she only remembered passing him a few times in the hallway."

Jean frowned. "Do I detect—is there some question that Peterson *was* the kidnapper?"

"Officially the case is closed." Marianne said, aware that she was sidestepping.

Jean smiled thinly. "Then what are you doing here?"

"As I said, I'd like to ask your daughter a few more questions. Just to clarify a few details."

"Such as?" Mrs. Peary's manner had suddenly turned wary. Turning in her seat, she looked at the wall clock above the counter. "It's possible Rachel might take longer than I thought," she said. The warmth had evaporated from her voice. "Maybe you'd better—"

Before the sentence was completed, they heard the storm door slam. "I'm back!" a girl's voice shouted from the front hallway.

"We're in the kitchen, hon!" Jean called out. "There's someone here, a police officer, to see you."

A moment later Rachel Peary stood in the doorway, her baby-smooth cheeks flushed with the cold. Dropping a stack of hardcover books onto the counter, she pulled off her red ski mitts, plucked her earmuffs from her head, and fluffed her fine, blond hair with a few, vigorous head shakes. "Boy, it's *cold* out there," she said, unzipping her brown leather jacket.

"I keep telling you, that jacket isn't warm enough for winter," Jean scolded. "You're going to get pneumonia." She nodded toward Marianne. "This is Officer Byrne."

Marianne stood up, holding out her hand. "Rachel. Nice to meet you."

Rachel shook hands and smiled easily.

"Do you mind if I ask you a few questions?" Marianne asked.

"More questions!" Rachel exclaimed in a tone of mock exhaustion. Then, still smiling, she said, "I guess it would be okay." Pulling around one of the kitchen chairs, she straddled it like a biker, folding her arms along the top rail. "I already told the police chief that I didn't know Kevin Peterson."

"This isn't about Kevin Peterson. It's about the night of the kidnapping."

Jean lowered her coffee cup and looked at Marianne intently. "Again?"

"Mrs. Peary, I just need to doublecheck a few . . ." Marianne paused, choosing her words carefully. "A few anomalies."

Jean looked skeptical but offered no comment. Marianne turned back to the daughter. "Rachel," she said gently, "do you remember what program you were watching on TV when the kidnapper came to the door that night?"

"Program?" Rachel gave a shrug of indifference. "Not really. Why?"

"You told the investigators at the time that you were

204

watching 'Saturday Night Live.' Is that what you remember?"

"Did I say that?" Rachel said in the same offhanded tone. "I usually watch it on Saturday night when I'm not out. I can't really remember."

Marianne leaned closer to the girl. "So are you saying that you may *not* have been watching it?"

"I know the TV was on. That's all I really remember."

Marianne was determined to pin the girl down. But she had just begun to ask a follow-up question when Jean interrupted. "Officer Byrne, my daughter received a very nasty blow on the head that night. She was unconscious for a considerable period of time. The wound required over a dozen stitches. Not to mention the emotional trauma she suffered. Is it surprising that she might have been confused about such a minor detail under the circumstances?"

As far as Marianne was concerned, the matter was no "minor detail." But she decided against arguing. "I suppose not," she said quietly after a brief pause. Then she turned back to Rachel.

"Just one more question," she said, fixing the girl with a hard stare. "Can you explain how your fingerprints came to be on the porch bulb of the Princes' house?"

"Sure," Rachel said without hesitation. "Just as they were leaving, Mr. Prince noticed that the porch bulb was burned out. He got one out of the hall closet and asked me to replace it. He and his wife already had their coats on and all, and he didn't want to stop and do it."

Rachel continued to smile serenely. Her mother appeared relieved. Marianne was struck by the look on Mrs. Peary's face.

"The funny thing is," Rachel continued, "the new bulb didn't work either. I figured it was defective."

"It wasn't defective," Marianne said. "It just wasn't screwed in all the way."

Rachel lifted her eyebrows. "I guess I didn't do such a good job."

"Guess not," Marianne said dryly.

"Is that it?" Rachel asked after a moment. " 'Cause if there are no more questions, I'd better get to work on my paper." She screwed up her face with displeasure. It was, thought Marianne, the first time in her presence that Rachel had acted like an ordinary adolescent.

Marianne stood up, thanked Rachel for her time and Mrs. Peary for the coffee. Jean escorted her to the front door. Pausing at the threshold, Jean started to say something, then tightened her lips and gave a small, almost imperceptible head shake, as if she'd thought better of it. The two women shook hands and bid each other good-bye.

Driving back home, Marianne replayed the events of the visit over and over in her mind. What had Mrs. Peary been about to say to her? And why had she looked so relieved at Rachel's explanations? Was she troubled with doubts about her daughter? Is that why she had suddenly become so defensive?

Rachel's replies had certainly been plausible, if not wholly satisfactory. It was the girl's behavior that bothered Marianne most.

She knew it was crazy, but she couldn't help feeling that the pretty adolescent with the unblinking gaze and unruffled manner had been ready with her answers—as if they'd been rehearsed.

33

BY SIX-TWENTY ON WEDNESDAY, THE MOONLESS NIGHT WAS already as dark as it would get. Moments before, the train from Manhattan had rolled into the Stoneham station. A crowd of commuters, most of them men, had poured down the platform stairs to the sprawling lot, hurrying through the frigid darkness to their Audis and Saabs and BMWs. Within minutes, after quick drives through the winding country roads, they would pull up at their warmly lit houses, where their children awaited with news of the day, their wives with a drink and a welcoming kiss.

But at 37 Upper Brook Drive, darkness prevailed. From the road running past the wide front lawn, no light could be seen inside the house. In the darkness, the big white colonial seemed deserted, ghostly. Not even the porch lamp was on.

There were, in fact, several lights burning within, but only an observer viewing the house from the rear could have seen them. Upstairs, a light glowed dimly through a second-floor window. Though the window was unobstructed by drape or shade or slatted blind, there was no danger of anyone's peering in, since the back of the house faced nothing but several densely wooded acres.

Across the center of the big canopy bed in the second-story room sprawled the lady of the house, Anna Prince. Naked beneath her disheveled kimono, she lay facedown on the mattress, legs bare and slightly parted, head twisted to one side, eyes shut tight, one white arm flung out over the crumpled sheet, the other limp at her side. A spoonful of saliva had pooled on the sheet, directly below one corner of her half-open mouth.

Another lamp—also visible only from the back—burned downstairs in her husband's study. The study door, almost always locked, stood open to the darkness and silence of the rest of the house. David Prince, at ease in his club chair, sipped from his glass of Gentleman Jack, savoring the suffusing warmth of the whiskey. He was savoring the sweetness of the evening, too—the pleasure of being on his own again. For the first time in years he was in complete control of his life, having rid himself of this final complication. And he owed his gift, like so much else in his life, to his magnificent father, whose plan he had followed to the letter.

He glanced at his wristwatch. He had a dinner appointment—some business meeting he had carefully concocted—at eight-thirty in the city. In another fifteen minutes or so he would carefully rinse out and dry his glass.

Then he would go upstairs to check whether Anna was dead yet.

Thinking of her made him smile. After Luz and Alba, the cleaning ladies, had left for the day—he had made sure that they had seen him hard at work all afternoon in his study—he had gone upstairs. As he'd expected, she was already half drunk. On her night table, next to several bottles of tranquilizers, stood a liter of Absolut, three-quarters drained. She was propped against two pillows, her kimono undone. Reaching down, David had removed the glass from her fingers, then slipped his hand inside the kimono and

207

began massaging her right breast. She had tried to beat him away, but he had taken her easily. She was laughably weak.

It had been a long time since he had felt any real desire for her. To his delight and astonishment, he discovered that the idea of fucking a woman minutes before he intended to kill her aroused him to a frenzy of excitement.

So Simon had been right about that too.

Afterward she had lain their blubbering. It was the baby, always the damned baby.

Persuading her to take the pills had been trickier than he expected. He remembered how easy it used to be, in the early days of their relationship, to feed her drugs—speed and acid and mescaline. What a willing and eager learner she had been.

This time he'd had to call upon all his powers of persuasion. Cradling her in his arms, he had murmured soothing words. No more nightmares, he had promised. The sweetest sleep she would ever know. And Stephen would be waiting for her! What good was life without Stephen, anyway?

Nodding and sobbing, she had agreed to swallow a few of the tranquilizers. He had cupped them in his palm, feeding them to her like a child offering food pellets to a lamb at the petting zoo. After swallowing down half a dozen or so, she had suddenly shoved his hand away. When that had happened, he'd wanted to smash her puffy, slack-lipped face to pulp, and managed to restrain himself only by remembering that any visible mark of violence would fuck up the whole plan.

So, forcing himself to remain calm, he had hugged her to his body, smoothed back her hair, stroked her cheeks, whispered seductively. How delicious it would be just to sleep, sleep. Eventually she had swallowed more. More than enough to do the job.

When it was done, he had showered quickly and shaved the shadow from his cheeks, then come downstairs to reward himself with a drink.

Now, David drained the final swig of bourbon from his glass and rechecked his Rolex. Time to go. He strolled into the kitchen to clean his glass and replace it in the cabinet. Then he climbed the stairs again.

Anna was lying in the position he'd left her in. Using a

handkerchief, he picked up the bottle of Xanax from her bed table and scattered the few remaining tablets onto the mattress and floor. He dropped the empty bottle close to her outstretched hand.

Then, placing three of his fingers against the side of her neck, he felt for her pulse. It was very faint and irregular, almost undetectable. He timed it by his watch. She'd be dead in a few moments.

Her profile, partly hidden by a coil of auburn hair, looked lovely, her parted lips invitingly moist. Death, as he had promised, was smoothing the care from her features.

A sudden bolt of desire, as shocking as an electrical charge, surged through his loins. He wanted to have her again, to fuck her from behind as she lay there on her stomach.

But no. A glance at his watch confirmed it. There wasn't time. He'd save himself for Rachel. Bending over the body, he contented himself with a final kiss on her corpse-cold cheek.

Ten minutes later he was sitting behind the wheel of his Jaguar, speeding down the dark, sinuous highway and humming along to a classic rock station on his Blaupunkt.

34

AS SOON AS MARIANNE STEPPED INTO THE STATION HOUSE early Monday morning, December 5, three days after Anna Prince's funeral, she saw him: a broad-shouldered man in a hooded ski parka, leaning his forearms on the front desk and asking to speak to Chief Wayland. Marianne, approaching from behind, had a quick impression of a husky physique, a headful of thick, salt-and-pepper curls in serious need of trimming, and a voice tinged with urgency.

Nodding hello to Greg Nugent, who was manning the desk, Marianne swung open the little gate that separated the public space from the work area and walked over to her pigeonhole to check for messages. She glanced around to look at the stranger. His thick beard was in keeping with

209

his burly appearance. He was the kind of man that the term "bearlike" was invented for.

"Chief Wayland won't be in until nine, Mr. Waller," Greg Nugent was saying.

"Shit," muttered the bearded man, glancing up at the big wall clock. "I've got to be in class in fifteen minutes."

The phone bleeped. "Excuse me," Greg said, turning away to answer it. "Northampton police."

Marianne suddenly realized who the bearded man was. Jerry Waller. The teacher who had discovered the dog's tongue in the elementary school gazebo.

Walking back to the front desk, she leaned over the counter. "Mr. Waller?" she said. "I'm Officer Byrne. Can I help you with something?"

Waller's eyebrows unknit themselves. "Thank you. Yes. Is there somewhere we can talk?"

Marianne stepped to the little gate, unlatched it and held it open for Waller. Then she led him back to one of the small, featureless offices at the rear of the station, used by whatever patrolmen were on duty that day. It was empty. Marianne had been the first to arrive for the morning shift.

Seating herself behind the desk, she pointed to the molded plastic chair beside it. Waller dropped himself into the chair with a grunt.

In the flat, fluorescent glare of the overhead fixture, Marianne saw that she had misjudged the big, bearded man in one respect. Her first impression had been of health, ruddiness, vigor. Waller looked strong, all right. But his face was drawn and pasty, as if he were recovering from a bout of the flu.

Leaning back in his seat, Waller unzipped his coat and looked at her intently. "Excuse me for staring," he said, "but you're the best-looking cop I've ever seen."

Marianne acknowledged the compliment with a half smile. "What brings you down here this morning, Mr. Waller?"

The bearded man's expression became grave. "Kevin Peterson," he said quietly.

Marianne leaned forward on the desk. "Yes?"

Waller blinked a few times and swallowed, as though he were on the brink of tears. "I'm just sick over it."

Marianne waited for him to continue.

"I would have come in earlier, but my wife and I were away for Thanksgiving. Up in Vermont, visiting friends. We stayed a couple of extra days. So I didn't even hear about it until last Tuesday when I came into school and some of my colleagues told me about it. It just blew me away. I haven't slept for a week, thinking about Kevin. Jesus." Digging into his pants pocket, he pulled out a crumpled hankie and swabbed his damp eyes. "Sorry," he said.

"Did you know Kevin well?" Marianne asked gently.

Waller nodded. "I was his teacher. More than his teacher. A surrogate father, really. At least for a while."

"When was the last time you saw him?"

"About a week before he killed himself," Waller said hoarsely. "That's what I'm here to talk about."

"Please go on," she urged.

Taking a deep breath, Waller gave her a rundown of Kevin's family history—Thomas Peterson's desertion, the nasty divorce, the boy's desperate need of a father.

"He was a troubled kid, no doubt about it," Waller said. "But baby-snatching?" He shook his head emphatically. "No way."

"But he left a suicide note with a full confession."

"I know all about the note," he said, conveying his skepticism with a sideways twist of the lips. "I went to pay a condolence call on Barbara Peterson. Kevin's mom. She told me all about it." He shook his head. "I still don't buy it. It just didn't sound like Kevin. Not the Kevin I knew. And I knew him as well as anybody."

Marianne regarded Waller speculatively. It was clear that the man had been deeply attached to the Peterson boy. His feelings were etched in every line of his care-worn face. Were his emotions simply blinding him to the truth? Marianne had seen the phenomenon many times before—the murderer's mother, insisting to the press, "Not my boy! He's a good boy! He couldn't be guilty!"

A passage of scripture, one of many planted in her brain during her parochial school days, popped unbidden into Marianne's thoughts. *The heart is deceitful above all things, and desperately wicked. Who can know it?*

"Did Kevin come to see you for a particular reason?" she asked.

Jerry ran a hand through his graying curls. "There was

211

something weird going on in his life. That was the exact word he used—'weird.' Something really bothering him. Looking back on it now, I see he was trying to send an S.O.S. I just wasn't smart enough to pick up on it." He paused to draw in a quivering breath. "That's what's tearing me up inside. I keep thinking I could have done something to save him."

Marianne experienced a deep pang of sympathy. She knew exactly what Waller was feeling. An image of Anna Prince, slumped on the sofa cushion, hollow-eyed and deathly pale, flashed into her mind. Marianne had not been able to do anything to save that anguished woman either.

She pulled her attention back to the bearded schoolteacher. "Mr. Waller—"

"Jerry."

"Jerry. Can you remember any details of your last conversation with Kevin?"

"He said he was involved with some kind of family."

Marianne's eyes narrowed. "Family?"

"Either an actual family or people who were like a family. It was a little hard to tell."

"And you have no idea who these people were?"

He shook his head.

"Other high school students?" Marianne asked.

"I just don't know. I wish I did."

"And what were these people doing?"

"I don't know that either. Obviously something that had begun making him intensely uncomfortable. As soon as he began talking about it, though, he clammed up, as if he were sorry he'd brought it up at all. Sorry or . . ."

"Or what?"

"Scared." Waller paused, softly chewing on his lower lip. "One thing . . ."

"Yes?"

He eyed her intently. "I had the impression that these people might have had something to do with that dog. The one whose tongue I found hanging in the gazebo."

Marianne stiffened. "What gave you that impression?"

"He mentioned my discovering it. There was just something in his voice." He gave a weary shrug. "I don't know. Maybe I'm imagining it. That stuff with the dog has been making me a little crazy."

212

Marianne jotted something on her legal pad before looking up again. "Did Kevin mention any names to you at all, Jerry?"

"Not of the people involved. He did say something about where they were from."

"Yes?" she asked quickly.

He made an apologetic face. "That's the hell of it. I can't remember exactly. It was a Dutch name. I keep wanting to say VandeCamp but I think that's because of the baked beans. But it's something like that. Vande-something."

She wrote it down. "Is this a town?"

"I don't think so. I think it was a house or an estate. One of those old places known by a family name."

"But you have no idea where?"

"I'm sorry." He glanced at his watch. "Damn, I've got to get out of here." Rising, he reached out to shake Marianne's hand, then held on to it for a moment, clutched inside his own. The look in his eyes was beseeching. "I know I haven't given you a hell of a lot to go on. But you've got to take my word for it. There's something going on in this town. Something nasty. You can't just let this case drop."

"Believe me," said Marianne, meeting his gaze with matching intensity, "I don't intend to."

35

STANDING BETWEEN THE BEECHWOOD DRESSER AND THE stereo rack, Marianne surveyed Kevin Peterson's bedroom briefly before turning to face the woman in the doorway. "It's very tidy," Marianne said.

Barbara Peterson exhaled a cloud of smoke. An angular blonde in her early fifties, Mrs. Peterson had probably been a stunner in her day. Now, plastic surgery had given her face a lacquered veneer, dyed to a deep, nutty brown by the miracle of modern tanning technology. She was wearing a tight red jumpsuit designed to prove that her $1200 yearly dues at the Stoneham health club had not been spent in vain. Incongruously—in a town where smokers were sub-

213

jected to the kind of dirty looks formerly reserved for scofflaws and adultresses—she sucked continuously on filter-tipped Capris and carried a small, crystal ashtray wherever she moved. Her smile, which displayed the most even set of teeth orthodontic science could provide, looked like something she had mastered in finishing school.

At the moment she was favoring Marianne with her brightest smile.

"Believe me, it didn't look this good before the housekeeper straightened it up," she said breezily. "Kevin left it in a terrible mess." Her voice took on a low, mock-confidential tone. "You know how teenagers are, especially teenage boys."

Marianne stared at the woman. Judging from her manner, a stranger would have assumed that her son had gone off on a weekend ski vacation. Marianne couldn't tell if Mrs. Peterson's weirdly inappropriate behavior was a symptom of massive denial or seriously arrested development. But as the woman babbled on, she began to suspect the latter.

"So you think you might find something about these mysterious friends of Kevin's? I wish I could help you. Kevin never said a word about them to me. Of course, he tended to be secretive about lots of things. But he didn't seem unhappy. Maybe a little moody at times. But as I told Jerry Waller, what adolescent isn't? Christ, I remember how high-strung *I* was as a teenager. I don't know how my parents put up with me sometimes." She gave a phony laugh and took a deep drag on her cigarette. "Of course, Kevin and I haven't spent a lot of time together lately. I'm away from the house so much of the time, what with one thing and another. The Gay Divorcée," she trilled in her phony, theatrical way.

Marianne nodded, trying her best to look sympathetic. For the life of her, she couldn't think of a thing to say. But as she stood there gazing at the chattering woman, she saw something flicker deep in Barbara Peterson's eyes. The woman's brittle smile began to crumble. She fell silent for a moment, then spoke two words in a husky, faltering voice: "My baby."

Tears welled in her eyes and slid down her creaseless face. She raised her cigarette to her mouth, but her hand trembled so badly that glowing cinders showered onto the bosom of her jumpsuit. Brushing them away, she opened her mouth to say something. Marianne waited, but nothing emerged. Turning abruptly, Mrs. Peterson disappeared from sight.

Marianne remained frozen in place for a moment, staring at the empty space Kevin's mother had occupied. Then she walked across the room and shut the door.

Through the wall she heard the muffled pound of rock music start up from the adjoining room. Marianne listened closely. She recognized the song, which seemed to be playing whenever she switched on the radio these days—"Welcome to the Jungle" by Guns N' Roses. Must be the kid brother's room, Marianne realized, grimacing. The boy was only a fourth-grader at Willow Brook.

Maybe Mrs. Peterson should take the child and move to a different part of the country, Marianne reflected—someplace in the Midwest or New England, where schoolboys were still preoccupied with fishing and softball, not junkies, bitches, and blowjobs.

If there *is* such a place anymore, Marianne thought.

Tossing her cap onto Kevin's bed, she took a slow look around, doing a complete, counterclockwise rotation. At a glance the room could have been the living quarters of any well-to-do teenage boy—bed, dresser, desk, bookshelves, stereo, Apple computer, twelve-inch color TV hooked to a VCR. On a poster above the headboard, Michael Jordan, limbs splayed, soared toward the rim in full, antigravitational glory.

But as she continued to scan the room, she began to sense something strange—a quality she couldn't put her finger on at first, something she could feel but not quite define.

Marianne was still close enough to her own teenage years to have vivid memories of what it felt like to inhabit her bedroom back home. Like the rooms of all her friends, it had been much more than a place to sleep and store her clothes. It had been a refuge, a sanctuary—a private, almost womblike, world. Every knickknack on her shelves, every photograph stuck into the frame of her dressing mirror, had been alive with the most personal meanings, memories, fantasies, and dreams.

By contrast, Kevin Peterson's room was weirdly impersonal, like a hotel room. No, the room was like a stage set, every prop in place, from the stereo to the sports poster. It was a room where Kevin could play a part, act out the role of the typical suburban teen, while his real existence was going on elsewhere—in the unknown place Marianne knew only as Vande-blank.

Well, Marianne thought, if there *are* any clues to his other life, they sure as hell won't be lying around in the open. Barbara Peterson had given her permission to search wherever she wanted. She stepped to the beechwood bureau and began opening drawers.

She rummaged through each one. Other than some foil packets of condoms in the top drawer, she found nothing besides clothing—underwear, socks, sweaters, and shirts. She refolded every item she pulled out, leaving the drawers neater than she'd found them.

The bookcase was filled with paperbacks. Crouching, Marianne examined the spines closely, looking for any of the standard titles on Satanism or the occult. But though the shelves contained a generous selection of horror fiction, including the complete works of Stephen King, Clive Barker, and Dean Koontz, Marianne found nothing suspicious—no *Satanic Bible* or *Necronomicon* or *Crystal Tablet of Set*.

A few of the books on the bottom shelf stuck out in a peculiar way. Pulling them out, Marianne reached her hand into the space and came out with a gray, tin box, the kind used to store three-by-five index cards. She felt a pang of excitement that evaporated the instant she flipped up the lid. Inside was a small cache of marijuana—nothing to write home about. She stuck the three rolled joints in her breast pocket anyway. She'd send them to Grasslands for testing, to see whether they were pure or laced with anything stronger.

Kevin's tape collection, neatly lined up in a teakwood cassette rack, was equally unrevealing. There were albums by weirdly named groups Marianne had never heard of before—Cowboy Junkies, They Might Be Giants, Psychedelic Furs. But nothing by the "black metal" bands favored by teen Satanists—Judas Priest, Black Sabbath, Blue Oyster Cult, Slaughter. If Kevin Peterson *had* been involved with some sort of devil worship, there was certainly nothing in his musical tastes to indicate it.

216

Standing beside Kevin's bed was a neat stack of magazines nearly two feet high and topped with a recent issue of *Rolling Stone,* showing a bug-eyed Bart Simpson waving cheerfully from the cover. Perching on a corner of the bed, Marianne began going through the pile, tossing each issue onto the mattress after she'd looked it over. Besides *Rolling Stone,* the stack contained copies of *Sports Illustrated, Spin,* and *Playboy.*

As she neared the bottom of the pile, she came upon a nine-by-twelve manila clasp envelope. Undoing the metal clips, she opened the flap and out slid a dozen Polaroids of naked girls. The models were quite young—not older than sixteen or seventeen, Marianne judged—and surprisingly sweet-faced and pretty. They were standing or sitting with their legs wide apart, spreading the lips of their genitals with their fingers while they smiled coyly into the camera. Several of the girls had been shaved.

A few of the photos might have been the work of professionals, but others were poorly lighted and amateurish, the girls in them perhaps local kids. But maybe not, Marianne thought, after studying the backgrounds carefully. The rooms were small, dingy, and sparsely furnished, like cheap motel rooms.

Allowing her professional detachment to lapse into a look of extreme distaste, she put back the pictures and stuck the envelope underneath her cap, so that she wouldn't forget to take it with her to the station house.

Sighing, she checked her watch. She had been in the boy's bedroom for nearly an hour. So far all she had discovered was that Kevin Peterson smoked an occasional joint, listened to rock music, and jerked off. In other words, he appeared to be your average, all-American teenage boy. Just as his mom had said.

Marianne knew that cultists sometimes kept secret diaries of their ritual practices. Her dad's pamphlet described these "shadow books" as one of the danger signs worried parents should watch out for. If Kevin Peterson had kept such a journal, Marianne reflected, he probably would have wanted it near at hand—maybe squirreled away in his desk?

That'd be convenient, she thought, shoving herself off the mattress. She knew it was a lot to hope for. Still, she might find *something* useful—an address book, letters from friends, a telephone number scrawled on a scrap of paper.

No such luck. The desk drawers contained nothing more interesting than the sad evidence of Kevin's academic decline. He had flunked a trigonometry test on October 2 and another on October 17. The second one carried a stern warning from his teacher printed in big red letters across the top margin.

There was some older work filed away in the big bottom drawer—mostly term papers written when Kevin was a sophomore and junior. He had been a much better student then—he'd actually gotten an A+ on a history paper. She found several old report cards. All his grades had plummeted during the end of his junior year.

She did come across one interesting item, which shed some unsuspected light on the boy—a spiral-bound pad filled with pencil sketches. Kevin had been a talented artist. Though the images were not much to Marianne's taste— the subjects tended to run to comic book fantasies involving muscle-bound barbarians rescuing half-naked slave girls from the clutches of slimy, tentacled monsters—their execution was surprisingly polished. Marianne flipped through the pages, then tossed the pad onto the bed beside the porn-filled envelope. She wanted to show the drawings to a police psychologist. Perhaps they would offer some clues to the boy's emotional life.

Standing hunched over the desk had put a crick in Marianne's lower back. Slowly, she arched herself backward, hands on hips, grunting softly as her lumbar muscles unclenched themselves. Straightening up, she stretched her arms over head and gazed around. There was only one place left to look. The bedroom closet.

She pulled open the door and recoiled at the locker room smell. The closet was a complete mess—the one area of the room that the housemaid hadn't put in order. The floor was littered with shoes, including several pairs of Reeboks stuffed with dirty athletic socks. An unlaundered sweatsuit, the pants emblazoned with a Nike logo, was drapped over the crossbar, as though Kevin had simply tossed it there after a jog around the high school track. A mound of soiled jockey shorts lay heaped on a lower shelf. Marianne wrinkled her nose in distaste.

The crossbar was crammed with an assortment of shirts, pants, sport jackets, and blazers. Most of the garments had been shoved, helter-skelter, onto their hangers. However atypical Kevin Peterson may have been in many respects, he'd clearly had the housekeeping habits of a normal teenager.

Crouching, Marianne unclipped the miniature flashlight from her utility belt and beamed it at the closet floor.

Scattered among the sneakers and shoes were the standard accouterments of male adolescence—basketball, aluminum bat, tennis racket, guitar case, a pair of twenty-five-pound barbells. A cardboard grocery carton overflowing with old comic books, record albums, and a few items that Marianne couldn't quite make out had been shoved into a corner.

Marianne aimed the flashlight at her wrist. It was late— nearly four o'clock. Sighing, she crawled partway into the closet and dragged the carton out onto the gray carpet. Seating herself cross-legged in front of it, back to the door, she began to sift through the contents, sneezing now and then as a puff of dust wafted up into her nose.

"Mom says you're a cop."

Marianne started, heart thumping. She twisted her head. Behind her stood a small boy with a spiky blond haircut that seemed to have been modeled on Bart Simpson's.

"I didn't hear you come in," Marianne said, smiling. "You're very quiet."

He nodded. "When I stay at my grandparents', they never even hear me come downstairs late at night."

"Why do you come downstairs?"

"To sneak stuff from the fridge."

Marianne worked herself around on her behind to face him. "You must be Robbie."

"Yup. You really a cop?"

"Sure am. My name's Officer Byrne. Marianne."

"My mom says I'm not supposed to bother you 'cause you're looking for something important."

"That's right."

He smiled, revealing a retaining wire over his top row of teeth. "Well, you won't find anything in that box. Kevin never even touched that stuff. It's just a lot of his old junk. You should look in his secret place."

Marianne's eyes narrowed. "Secret place?"

219

"Sure. I peeked in one day and saw him put something there. What'll you give me to show you?"

Marianne was taken aback. "How about a guided tour of the police station?" she said after a moment.

The boy screwed up his face like a used car salesman considering a counteroffer. He's probably holding out for cash, Marianne thought. But after a few seconds Robbie shrugged and said, "I guess that'd be okay."

Walking to the beechwood bureau, he began pulling at the bottom drawer. "This is heavy."

"Here, let me help you," Marianne said, getting to her feet and coming to stand beside him. Stooping, she jerked at the drawer until she had pulled it out to its farthest extent.

"I've already looked in here," she said.

"Not *in* the drawer," he said. "Underneath it."

Marianne gave the drawer another tug, catching it by its bottom as it slid out of its space. She set it down on the floor.

"There," said Robbie, pointing.

Marianne aimed her flashlight into the darkness. The dresser had no bottom. There, on the carpeted floor, sat a small, rectangular wooden box or chest. A pentagram had been engraved on its lid, apparently with a wood-burning iron.

"Jeez," Robbie breathed over her shoulder.

"Robbie, said Marianne, taking him by the shoulders and turning him toward the door. "You've been great. A tremendous help. But I need to look at this alone." She patted him on the behind. "Tell your mommy to call me at the police station in a day or two and we'll set up the tour."

She waited until he was out of sight, then stepped to the door and locked it with a twist of the handle button.

Seating herself on the edge of the bed, she placed the box on her lap and lifted the lid slowly, as if the little chest were one of those novelty items booby-trapped with spring-loaded snakes.

The box, lined with black velvet, contained five items, which Marianne stared at for a long moment, feeling her heart begin to gallop.

Reaching into her pants pocket, she drew out a handkerchief and used it to lift each of the items, one at a time.

The first was an amulet on a chain—the head of a snarling dog or wolf, lips rippled to reveal knifelike canines. The charm looked like real gold. Marianne hefted it in her palm. It was heavy.

Next, she removed a pair of interlocking, little effigies made of ivory and feathers—one male, with an oversized phallus, the other female, with a kind of cavity between her legs, into which the phallus was inserted. Marianne carefully pulled them apart and then reconnected the figures as though fitting together the pieces of an obscene puzzle. She felt a dryness in her throat as she stuck them together. They seemed to assert a strange power, tiny as they were.

A small glass vial, about an inch and a half long and slenderer than her little finger, contained a thick, brown-red liquid. It looked like blood to her, perhaps treated with an anticoagulant to keep it fluid.

The final items inside the box were two sheets of heavy paper, each folded into quarters. Marianne picked up the first and opened it. It was some sort of chant or prayer or ritual formula, written in a language unknown to her. But one word stood out as clearly as if it had been printed in Day-Glo ink.

Rex mantus canis devorare silut azgul sekhmed infans respirare.
Nel nibur adz spiritus devorare namon mortuus lothrix rentnas.
Belphegor descensus.

Marianne looked at the word again. Belphegor—the Moabite night demon, plunderer of the living breath of new-born babes. A rush of emotion, part triumph, part terror, hit Marianne so powerfully that the paper trembled slightly in her hand.

She placed it carefully on the mattress beside her, then lifted out the second sheet. Unfolding it, she saw that it was a pencil sketch in Kevin's distinctive style. He had titled his drawing too. THE KING, he had printed in mock-Gothic letters across the top of the page.

Beneath these words bulked a tall man, as heavily mus-cled as the comic book barbarians in Kevin's sketch pad. But this one wore nothing but a cape and some sort of

221

sheath over his stiff penis. The outfit might have been amusing. It was not. The picture was menacing and obscene. The head in the drawing was of course not very large, not more than about an inch high. But the hard and ruthless face, framed by a corona of dark, curly hair, stared from the page with a frightening malevolence.

Marianne studied the drawing, a frown creasing her forehead. The face looked familiar. Where had she seen it? In one of the other sketches in Kevin's pad?

Then she drew in a sharp breath. She knew. She had had the Taos police department send her some photographs of their missing parolee.

Simon Proctor's face stared up at her from Kevin Peterson's drawing.

36

SOARING FROM THE CLOCK RADIO, THE CHRISTMAS CHORALE rose to a ravishing height, the voices so angelic that Jean set her lipstick down on the dresser top and closed her eyes to concentrate. Seconds later the music faded to silence. Jean continued to stand there, eyes shut, listening for the name of the recording.

"That was Samuel Scheidt's *In Dulci Jubilo,*" came the chipper voice of the morning deejay. "Performed by the Vienna Boys Choir, Marinus Voorberg conducting. You're listening to WNPN, New York's most popular classical station. The time is now, lemme check the old Swatch here, um, exactly ten-seventeen, give or take a minute or two."

"Here's a little change of pace," chirped his cohost, a young woman as perky as a Disney World tour guide. "Well, not that much of a change, maybe. I always thought old Alfred kinda looked like Santa Claus."

Both of them burst into chuckles.

Couple of clowns, Jean thought as the playfully ominous strains of Gounod's "Funeral March of a Marionette"—the signature song of the old Alfred Hitchcock TV show—started up from the radio. *Everything has to be "lite" entertainment these days, even classical music.* She picked up

222

her lipstick again and leaned closer to the wall mirror. I'm dreaming of a lite Christmas, she thought dryly.

Though it was a weekday morning, Friday, December 16, Jean was not going in to the office. She still had some Christmas shopping to do and was determined to avoid the weekend crush. The previous afternoon, after steeling herself for an argument, she'd informed Edgar Davison that she would be taking Friday off. Much to her relief, he had limited his protests to a few token grumbles. Christmas was a slow season for the real estate business, and, though Edgar possessed all the holiday spirit of Scrooge, he could afford to be munificent.

As a result, she and Rachel had been able to eat a leisurely breakfast together that morning. Or rather, Jean had eaten while Rachel sat across the table from her, taking half-hearted nibbles from the edges of her raisin toast. Once, when Jean had glanced up from her paper, she'd caught Rachel staring queasily at the bread, as if the raisins were actually houseflies that had gotten trapped in the dough. When Jean had suggested that she remain home from school, the girl had nodded and slumped off to her room.

Probably a touch of the flu, Jean thought now as she finished applying her lipstick. When she heard Rachel's footsteps thumping down the hallway and the bathroom door slam, Jean hurried from her bedroom. Through the locked door she could hear her daughter retching. A few seconds later the toilet flushed.

"You okay, hon?" she called through the door as the rushing noise subsided.

"I guess," came the muffled voice.

"You throw up again?" Jean asked worriedly. Rachel had vomited after yesterday's breakfast too.

"Yeah. I think maybe I'm still sick." Jean could hear the creak of the medicine chest hinges, then the sound of Rachel gargling with mouthwash.

A moment later the bathroom door opened and Rachel stepped out, hugging her terry-cloth bathrobe close to her body. She looked as anemic as a vampire's bride.

"Poor baby," Jean said, reaching out a hand to rub her daughter between the shoulder blades as the girl trudged by on the way back to her bedroom. "I want you to rest

223

today, sweetie. If you're not better by tomorrow, I'm going to make an appointment with the doctor."

Half an hour later Rachel sat crosswise on the living room sofa, back propped against the side cushion, comforter pulled up to her chest. Resting open on her legs was a fat history textbook.

Jean, dressed in her overcoat and toting her handbag, came up and stood beside the sofa. "Feeling better?"

Rachel shrugged. "A little."

"Well, I see you're able to read, anyway. That's a good sign."

Rachel nodded without looking up. "My history midterm's on Tuesday."

"Let's hope you're all well by then." Bending, Jean planted a kiss on her daughter's forehead, told her to stay warm, and headed for the front hallway. "I'll be back in a few hours." She opened the door and stepped out into the brilliant winter sunshine.

Heading down the Saw Mill toward White Plains, Christmas carols flowing from the car radio, Jean wondered what kind of weird bug her daughter had caught. Rachel didn't have a fever. Her forehead, when Jean had stooped to kiss it, had felt perfectly cool. And Rachel didn't seem to feel especially bad once the day was under way. Yesterday, her appetite and coloring had been back to normal by evening.

Whatever bug she'd caught seemed to restrict its attacks to breakfast time. It was almost like morning sickness.

The thought was so jarring that Jean's hands jerked on the steering wheel and the car swerved to the right. A car horn blared beside her. As Jean pulled back into her lane, her heart thudding, she glanced to her right and saw the driver—a burly man, bald as an egg except for some dark tufts at his temples—mouthing something at her. It did not look like a compliment.

Jean took a moment to steady herself and gather her thoughts. She switched off the radio. The holiday music suddenly seemed as distracting as a mosquito's buzz.

As far as she knew, Tim Rutherford was the only boy Rachel had been dating. They'd been going out every Saturday night for slightly more than a month. Surely they hadn't started sleeping together right away! Jean hoped her daughter was still a virgin, though she couldn't say for sure.

224

Certainly, she thought, Rachel wasn't the type of girl who would hop into bed with a boy on their first date.

Of course you don't think so, jeered a little voice inside her head. *But then again, you wouldn't have thought she was the type to stash occult paraphernalia in a bureau drawer either.*

Jean did some quick calculations. For Rachel to be pregnant, she would have had to conceive instantly. Was that likely?

The thought was reassuring. Until the taunting little voice piped up again, mimicking the classic lament of the pregnant adolescent— *But we only slept together once!*

But what about birth control? Jean silently argued back. Young people were far more sophisticated about contraceptives than older generations ever were. These days, Trojans were sold as openly on drugstore counters as toothpaste. Surely Rachel wouldn't be dumb enough to have unprotected sex. Not in this day and age.

The little voice said nothing. It didn't have to. It was only the week before that Jean had read the depressing statistics on adolescent pregnancy in a *Newsweek* cover story about unwed teenage mothers.

She was hit with a violent urge to pull off at the next exit, swing the car around and speed home to confront Rachel. What stopped her was the memory of where their last confrontation had led—to Rachel's three-day disappearance, the single worst period of Jean's adult life.

Wrestling with her anxiety, she finally managed to subdue it. *Rachel pregnant after dating a young man for just a month? And such a well-mannered, buttoned-down young man to boot?* It was simply too improbable. Surely she was just panicking, Jean told herself, imagining the worst—an understandable (if slightly hysterical) reaction, given her recent troubles with Rachel.

But those troubles were a thing of the past. Jean felt sure of it.

Feeling much better, she reached down and switched on the radio, catching the tail end of Perry Como's rendition of "Have Yourself a Merry Little Christmas."

37

THE THREE SWEAT-SLICKED BODIES LAY SIDE BY SIDE ON THE big, dark bed, the young female wedged between the two males. Gazing up through heavy lids at the mirrored canopy, the girl regarded her two lovers, their powerful bodies pale against the black satin sheets. Simon was stretched on her left, eyes closed, his thick cock lolling on one thigh. To her right lay David, staring up at her, languidly stroking himself to another erection. She smiled into the mirror at him. It excited her to compare the cocks of the two men, father and son.

Reaching down with his free hand, David placed it between her legs. She parted her thighs for him.

"You're leaking," he said into her ear.

She removed his hand, held his glistening middle finger to her lips and licked. "I'm very full," she said softly. Both men had come several times inside her.

Turning toward Simon, she reached up a forefinger and traced the eye-shaped tattoo around his left nipple. His eyes opened slowly. Sliding her fingertip along the deep cleft that separated his pectoral muscles, the girl jiggled the suede pouch that Simon had taken to wearing around his neck. Dangling from a leather thong, the little sack bulged in a peculiar way and gave off a faintly offensive smell, like spoiled meat.

"What's this?" she asked.

Simon tucked in his chin and gazed down, the corners of his mouth creasing into a deep frown, as though he had forgotten that the pouch was there. Then his face brightened and he laughed loudly.

"A relic," he said happily, reaching around his neck with both hands and undoing the knot. "I acquired it on Thanksgiving." Hooking his forefingers into the mouth of the little sack, he spread it with a yank, tilted it upside down over the girl's chest and shook out its contents like a prospector emptying his nuggets onto an assayer's tray.

A whitish lump hit her chest and slid down her sweaty

breastbone, coming to rest on her belly. Propped on her elbows, she stared down at the thing, her nose wrinkled in distaste. David leaned over and stared too.

It was a pale, bony knob, one end so smooth and round that it might have been a blob of melted wax—except for the stunted, thumblike growth poking up from the flesh. And the shard of white wristbone that jutted from the blackened clots at the opposite end.

The girl reached down and swatted the thing off her belly onto the sheets. David picked it up and inspected it closely.

"It belonged to an unfortunate young lady who seemed remarkably untutored in spiritual matters," Simon said pleasantly. "It fell to me to instruct her in the precepts of her own faith." He paused for a beat while David and the girl looked at him quizzically. "Matthew 5:30," Simon continued, his voice brimming with amusement, as though he were enjoying a delicious private joke. Reaching across the girl's body, he took the little stump from David's hand and popped it back into the sack. "And if thy right hand offend thee," Simon intoned in the exaggerated accents of a tent show evangelist, "cut it off."

Abruptly, his heartiness evaporated. He turned his fierce gaze to the girl. "We've had enough," he commanded. "Leave us now."

Pouting, she rose to all fours and climbed over David, who leaned up and licked at one nipple as it dangled directly above his mouth.

David kept his eyes on the globes of the girl's perfect buttocks as she sauntered from the room. A pearly flow, the consistency of gruel, dribbled down the back of one thigh.

When she was gone, David rolled his head on the pillow and looked over at his father. "Very sweet, that one," he said, grinning lewdly.

"Like all young flesh," answered Simon. "She's learned her body's power."

"You're the one who's taught her."

"As I once taught you," said Simon. He reached out a hand and, with the lightest of touches, ran it down the length of David's belly, letting it come to rest just above the black tangle of his pubic hair.

The two men exchanged a look that spoke of shared secrets in the past. A full minute passed in a silence so complete that when Simon finally broke it, his voice sounded artificially amplified.

"How is the girl?" he asked, removing his hand from his son's body.

"Rachel?" said David, looking very pleased with himself, like a man who has been waiting for the perfect moment to deliver a wonderful surprise. "She's pregnant."

"You're certain?" Simon seemed unsurprised.

"She missed her period. And she's been puking every morning for a week." David stretched languorously and let out a yawn.

"Excellent," Simon said quietly, tapping his lips with a fingertip.

"When will the offering take place?" David asked.

"The instant of birth. I will take its first cry, fresh from the breeder's womb. Eight months from now. On the first day of August."

"Lammas Day," said David.

"Yes. The day of the harvest."

David frowned. "But you can't be that precise, Simon. What if the infant doesn't arrive on schedule?"

Simon gazed at the overhead mirror, his lips curling into a smile. "It will."

38

THE STONEHAM HISTORICAL SOCIETY WAS THE GRANDILO-quent name of a converted storeroom at the rear of the town library. Its walls were hung with old county maps and sepia-toned photographs of Stoneham village from the days when the roads were rutted dirt and the stores along Grace Street had hitching posts out front. The few pieces of furniture—a battered wood desk, several oak filing cabinets, glass-fronted bookcases—looked as antique as the photographs. Every available inch of space was crammed with stacks of yellowed newspapers, cartons spilling over with town records, and dusty volumes on the history of New

York State, Westchester County, and Northampton township.

Presiding over this ramshackle collection was Mr. William Kittredge III, seventy-nine, a lifelong resident of Stoneham. A walking encyclopedia of local history, Mr. Kittredge, whose wife of fifty-five years had passed away the previous winter, arrived every weekday morning at nine and spent the next several hours hunched over the desk, laboring at his magnum opus, a definitive history of Stoneham village from its founding by Quakers in the late 1600s until the present. Or rather, until that point in the not-so-distant past, roughly the early 1950s, that Mr. Kittredge considered the last golden moment in the history of American civilization.

Mr. Kittredge knew little and cared less about the contemporary world, which had sunk, as far as he was concerned, to a level of barbarism unequaled since the fall of Rome. And one of its most deplorable features was its complete indifference to history and tradition. Mr. Kittredge knew this to be true from his own disheartening experience. No one seemed particularly interested in the trove of historical documents he had so lovingly assembled. Every so often, the door to the archives would fly open and a flashy young couple would breeze in, curious about the background of some hundred-year-old house they had just purchased in town. Mr. Kittredge would generally oblige, dredging up the information from the vast fund of local lore he carried around in his head. Then weeks, sometimes months, would go by without another visitor to his archives.

And so, when the white Japanese compact pulled to a stop at the rear of the library on the morning of Friday, December 16, Mr. Kittredge naturally assumed that the driver had made a mistake. The window facing his desk overlooked the tail end of the library parking lot, and most cars that drove into his view were simply making a U-turn. This one, however, did not. It slid into a parking space, the driver's door swung open, and out climbed a pretty young woman with black hair burnished to a high shine by the bright winter sunlight.

Slamming the car door, she walked briskly to the rear entrance of the library, disappearing from view as she rounded the corner of the building. A moment later she stood in the doorway of the musty little archives, squinting into the dimness while her eyes readjusted after the early morning glare.

"Come in, come in," Mr. Kittredge commanded.

Navigating around various boxfuls of old ledgers, she stepped across the floor. The old man half rose from his desk chair, right hand extended.

"Mr. Kittredge," she said, shaking his hand with a firmness that surprised him. "Marianne Byrne. I called a few days ago. Remember?"

"Of course I remember," he grumbled. He was trying to place her face—he had seen her somewhere before. "Senile dementia hasn't set in quite yet."

"Sorry." She looked abashed. "I didn't mean—"

"Just a little joke, young lady," he said. "Have a seat." He motioned to an old straight-back chair at the side of his desk. "Let me see. You called about . . . ?"

"A police matter."

"Oh yes, yes." That was it. He had seen her patrolling around town in her uniform. He had always been struck by her prettiness. "So this is official business?"

"Let's say it's a problem I have a particular interest in."

"Go on."

"I'm trying to track down a certain place. I don't even know that it's located in Northampton, but I thought that would be the logical place to start."

"And exactly what kind of place is this?"

She exhaled an embarrassed sigh. "That's the problem. I'm not really sure. I believe it's a house, known by an old family name."

"And what is the name?"

Marianne made a sheepish face. "Sorry. I don't really know that either. It's Vande-something. Something that sounds like VandeCamp."

Pulling off his eyeglasses, Mr. Kittredge fogged each lens with a moist, heavy breath, then rubbed them clean with a yellowed handkerchief he extracted from a pants pocket. With his heavy frames removed, she could see his eyebrows raised at her vagueness.

"Not very much to go on," Mr. Kittredge said. "The name is Dutch, of course. I assume you know that they settled in great numbers in these parts. And south and north

230

of us. All the way up through Dutchess County. Greene County too, for that matter."

She looked dismayed. "That's a lot of territory."

"True. On the other hand, the majority of those old Knickerbocker places are long since gone. Torn down by the end of the last century. What people call progress," he added dryly. "Of course, if this place is still known by its ancestral name, we can assume that it must be relatively imposing—an estate, perhaps, or one of those big summer places built along the river by financiers and businessmen from the city."

"Then you think you can help?"

"Well, now," said Mr. Kittredge, sitting up straight in his chair. "I'm involved in a personal project of my own, which occupies a good deal of my time." A thick stack of white paper lay before him on his desk. As Marianne looked down at the topmost sheet—which was covered with crabbed, slightly shaky handwriting—the old man reached out and patted it as lovingly as if it were a dozing kitten. "Tell you what," he said after a moment, removing a blank index card from the center drawer of his desk and passing it across to Marianne, along with a ballpoint pen. "Why don't you leave me your phone number and I'll see what I can do."

Marianne wrote out the information in her neatest printing. "This is my home number up in Hoffmann's Falls. I've also put down the number of the police station. You can always leave a message for me there."

Mr. Kittredge held the index card close to his glasses to make sure he could read it. The little card trembled slightly in his gnarled hand.

"I imagine you people down at the station house are pretty frazzled these days, what with all the unpleasantness that's been going on lately." He shook his head. "Never thought I'd live to see such dreadful doings in this town."

"It's been pretty awful all right," Marianne said, shooting a covert glance at her wristwatch. It was getting late.

"Of course, this isn't the first time that Stoneham has been blighted by murder," he continued. "But that was many years ago. Most people nowadays have completely forgotten about it, if they ever knew about it at all."

"Oh yes," Marianne interjected quickly. "The killing at

231

the country club back in the fifties. I've heard about it."
She rose to her feet and reached her hand across the desk.
"Mr. Kittredge, I'm sorry but I've got to run. I'm late for
work. I'm grateful for any help you can give me. I wouldn't
trouble you if this weren't a matter of extreme urgency."

Watching her as she strode to her car and slid behind the
wheel, Mr. Kittredge puckered his mouth in displeasure.
Another youngster in a rush, just like the rest of them, he
thought. Not a moment to spare for the past. Always racing
headlong into the future. Mr. Kittredge knew exactly what
his own future held in store, and he was in no great hurry
to reach it.

He hadn't intended to tell her about that absurd business
at the country club at all—a trivial, sordid affair as far as
he was concerned. No, the incident he was referring to was
far more gruesome than that—an honest-to-goodness, old-
fashioned horror story, the kind that didn't happen in the
modern world anymore. She might even have learned something from it.

Too bad, he thought. It's her loss, not mine.

Turning from the window, he gazed around the crowded
room, thinking about Officer Byrne's visit.

All at once, a ripple of excitement ran through him. His
sprawling collection of books and documents, his heaps of
history volumes, old newspapers, ledgers, surveys, deeds,
tax records and phone directories, lay before him like a
vast field before the eyes of a hungry prospector. Somewhere buried deep inside, waiting to be discovered, was a
single small but invaluable nugget, the solution to Officer
Byrne's problem.

Here was precisely the kind of treasure hunt that Mr.
Kittredge most loved but hadn't experienced in more years
that he cared to, or could, remember. Just thinking about
it made him feel younger, as if he'd been injected with a
miraculous new megavitamin.

He looked out the window, but Officer Byrne's car was
gone. A sudden feeling of warmth for the pretty young
police officer suffused him. He had been offended by the
abruptness of her departure. But she had left him with a
wonderful gift—a nearly impossible but irresistible
challenge.

39

SEATED AT HIS DESK, DICK WAYLAND RUMMAGED IN HIS trousers pocket for a fresh roll of Tums. Ripping off the foil end, he popped a pair of the chalky tablets into his mouth and swallowed them down with barely a chew. The three mugs of steaming black coffee he had guzzled since arriving at the station house an hour before had curdled inside him. The burning lump lodged in the pit of his stomach felt like a white-hot charcoal briquet.

This goddamned case will eat an ulcer into me yet, he thought bitterly.

The Prince tragedy had been the single worst episode of his entire professional life. He would have to live forever with his failure to save the kidnapped baby. His failure to save the life of Anna Prince too. And even young Kevin Peterson, for that matter.

Three failures.

Still, he had been able to take a certain amount of comfort from the mere fact that the case was closed. No more harm could be done; the worst had already happened. The little town of Stoneham, whose security he, more than any other individual, felt directly responsible for, was on its way back to normalcy. Wayland had seen it himself, strolling around the town's tiny shopping district and driving up and down the residental streets: the look of relief in the faces of the mothers, the carefree children at play. The good citizens of Stoneham had begun to breathe easily again, to sleep peacefully in their beds at night without waking in terror at every creak of the floorboards or rattle of windows.

The Prince case had ended badly, but at least it had ended.

And now here he was, just a few days before Christmas, staring disbelievingly at the letter he had received that morning from Jack Byrne, the craziest fucking thing Wayland had ever read.

If it wasn't so sick, it would almost be funny, all this

cockeyed stuff about devil-worshiping priests who lived forever by sacrificing newborn babies to . . . He checked the name again. *Belphegor.* He sat there gazing at the word for a moment, the look on his face as sour as the taste in his mouth. How the hell do they come up with these goddamned names? he wondered. First it was Baphomet the horned Satan. Now this one—Belphegor the soul-stealer. What would it be next? Barfbag the stomach-turner? Bullflop, the king of utter crap?

He shook his head in disgust. *Who dreams up this stuff anyway? And what kind of headcases actually believe in this shit?*

He had to admit, though, that there wasn't anything funny about the second page Byrne had sent, a Xeroxed illustration from some old book on Satanism. There was something genuinely creepy about the Hell-fired scene: a devil-tailed priest shoving a sack over the head of a struggling infant while a bunch of buck-naked men and women looked on, leering like hyenas. For all its crudeness, the picture had a weirdly disturbing power, no doubt about it. Staring at it, Wayland could almost hear the cackling of the priest, see the aroused spectators lick their lips as they watched the baby smother.

Wayland massaged his forehead with the fingertips of one hand, as though trying to rub away the wrinkles. He didn't know what to think.

Sighing, he buzzed Evelyn on the intercom and told her that he didn't want to be disturbed. Then, with a glance at Byrne's letter, he reached over and punched up the number to Queens.

Wayland was about to hang up on the sixth ring when the receiver was lifted at the other end.

"Yeah?" said a gruff voice.

"Jack? It's Dick Wayland. Catch you at a bad time?"

"No, no. Just a little frazzled. I've got a shitload of stuff to take care of before I leave tomorrow."

"Going somewhere for the holidays?"

"Delaware. My yearly visit to my sister. What's up? You get my letter?"

"That's what I'm calling about." Wayland hesitated for a moment, debating which tack to take. He hadn't really worked it out in his head before making the call. He decided to be direct. "Jack, all this stuff in your letter about the dog and the Prince baby and Simon Proctor. No offense, Jack, but you really believe all this shit?"

"I think what I wrote is that they *may* be connected," Jack answered, sounding a little miffed to Wayland's ears. "You look closely at that woodcut I sent?"

"The picture? Yeah, I saw it. I guess people liked looking at scary pictures in the old days too. Nowadays we got *Friday the 13th* movies. So what does that prove?"

"Notice the dog?"

Wayland reached down for the Xeroxed sheet and held it up to the light. "The dead animal lying in front? So?"

"According to Marianne, that retriever you found up there was mutilated in the same way."

Wayland squinted at the drawing. The creature had obviously been butchered; its throat gaped and a bubbling mess of guts showed through its split belly. And there was a peculiar marking on its flank too, something that may have been a missing patch of hide. But then again, maybe not. The picture wasn't realistic enough for Wayland to tell. Hell, he couldn't even say for sure if the animal was a dog.

"Your daughter's quite a gal, Jack," he said after a moment. "A real ball of fire. But she kind of has an overheated imagination."

"A little imagination isn't necessarily a bad thing in a cop," Jack answered dryly. "Listen, all I'm saying is that there's enough here to justify some more investigating. We know Proctor was into Satanism. We know he was capable of murder and mutilation. He killed one of his own cult members and cut out his fucking tongue, for Chrissake. There's a good probability that he was responsible for other murders too.

" 'Good probability' is stretching it, Jack. That accusation came from Anna Prince, period. It was never confirmed by the New Mexico police. And she didn't know *what* she was saying. Even her husband thought she'd gone off the deep end." Wayland's voice grew softer. "Not that anyone could blame her."

"Still, there's always the possibility she was right," Jack insisted. "Look, don't get me wrong, I don't necessarily agree with everything Marianne believes. But the fact is that Proctor has disappeared and no one's been able to find him. Maybe the Prince woman wasn't as crazy as you think. Maybe Proctor *was* in your area. And here's an even scarier possibility," Jack added quietly. "Maybe he still is."

"And maybe," Wayland answered, unable to contain his exasperation, "all this devil-worship stuff is just pure bull-shit, plain and simple. Why the fuck do we need to look for dog-carving, baby-sacrificing boogeymen when we already have the Peterson kid's confession?"

"No reason," Jack said calmly." Except maybe it's true."

Wayland realized that he was gripping the phone much harder than he needed to, so hard, in fact, that his fingers had begun to cramp. He could feel the veins throbbing in his temples too, and had a vivid image of the blood shooting up into his head like the mercury in a cartoon thermometer. His anger was quickly reaching the boiling point.

But as he sat there seething, it suddenly struck him that he wasn't really angry at Jack Byrne. He was angry be-cause he couldn't dismiss Byrne's suspicions as easily as he could Marianne's. Wayland and Jack went back many years. They weren't friends, exactly, but they were good enough acquaintances for Wayland to know that Byrne was a serious man, not given to hysterics. He also knew—it would be hard to find a cop in the New York metropolitan area who didn't—what had happened a few years before to Jack Byrne's partner, Sam Turner. However bad things had been in Stoneham lately, they were nothing compared to what Byrne had been through. He had come close enough to pure evil to be scorched by it, closer than Wayland ever wanted to come. Of course, that kind of experience can leave a man pretty paranoid, and maybe Byrne had just started seeing Satanists behind every tree. But Wayland understood that there is sometimes a fine line between para-noid craziness and watching your back. And when you're a cop, watching your back isn't crazy at all.

"All right, all right," he finally said with a little groan of resignation. "I'll have some of my men poke around. See if they can dig up anything on Proctor's whereabouts. And I'll have them do some more checking on the Peterson kid too."

"Good," Jack said, then paused in a way that made Wayland think there was something else on his mind.

"That it?" Wayland asked.

"No," Jack said.

"Go ahead."

"About Marianne. I want her kept out of this."

Wayland's eyebrows rode up a few inches on his forehead. "Why's that?" He really didn't need to ask; he knew the answer already.

Wayland could hear Jack let out a long breath. "I hope to hell Marianne's wrong about everything," he said after a moment. "Nothing would make me happier. But if she isn't, if there really is a cult operating up there, I don't want her anywhere near it. It's no place for—" he hesitated ". . . for a rookie cop."

Wayland had the distinct impression that Jack had started to say something else: "for my child." It was a sentiment that Wayland could appreciate. He was always amazed at how protective he continued to feel about his own grown-up daughter.

"I hear you, Jack," he said, smiling for the first time that morning. "It's a tall order, though. Your daughter has developed some kind of fixation about this case."

"That's what worries me."

"Worries *you?*" Wayland laughed. "Shit, Jack. Dealing with devil-worshipers is one thing. But telling your kid she's off this case—now *that's* what I call scary."

After hanging up, Wayland sat back in his chair for a few minutes, tapping his steepled fingertips against his chin. Sunlight slanted through the big window behind him. He could feel the sun on the back of his neck, as pleasant as a warm compress on his knotted muscles.

But Wayland could take no comfort from it. One week left to go before Christmas, and he was about to plunge back into the nastiest mess he'd ever confronted.

Buzzing Evelyn again, he told her to send Patrolwoman Byrne in to see him as soon as she arrived from her morning shift. Then he pulled the topmost file from his "in" box and turned his attention to other matters.

He was scanning a report on a routine break-in when he heard a knock on his open door. Glancing up, he saw Mari-

237

anne standing there, coat unzipped, cap dangling from one hand, a large manila envelope clutched in the other.

"Come in, Byrne," Wayland said, tossing the report onto his desktop. "There's something I have to talk to you about."

"Me too," she said, stepping into his office.

"And what's that?" Wayland asked, knitting his fingers and resting them on his belly as he leaned back in his chair.

Dropping her cap onto the chair that faced his desk, she undid the metal clasp on the manila envelope and removed a single sheet of white paper, which she carefully laid on the blotter in front of Wayland.

Wayland leaned forward, squinting at the paper. It was a pencil sketch of a big, curly-headed man, completely naked except for some kind of Superman cape around his shoulders. Between his legs, an enormous cock rose straight into the air, its surface dark and nubby, as though it were encased in a leather condom. Wayland frowned in distaste.

"So what do you think?" asked Marianne.

Wayland raised his eyes in her direction. "What do I think? I think you need a steady boyfriend, Byrne. Your fantasy life is getting real strange."

"Funny, Chief. I didn't draw it."

"No? Glad to hear it. Who did?"

Marianne crossed her arms and smiled. "Kevin Peterson. I found it stashed in his room."

Wayland shook his head. "That was one fucked-up kid."

"You're missing the point, Chief."

"Yeah?"

"Look at the face," said Marianne, pointing. "Who does it look like to you?"

Wayland studied the drawing for a full fifteen seconds before answering. "My wife's uncle Ernie?"

"Come on, Chief," Marianne pleaded. She reached into the envelope again and pulled out another item, which she placed on the desk beside the pencil sketch. It was a full-face mug shot of Simon Proctor. "Look. It's the same person. The man in that drawing is Simon Proctor." Her voice rang with excitement. "Don't you see? This is the link we've been looking for!"

Wayland compared the two images for a moment, then

238

shrugged. "Hell, Marianne, the guy in this drawing could be almost anybody. The face is too small to tell."

Marianne shook her head vehemently. "It's Proctor. I'm sure of it. And I'll tell you something else. I called the Taos P.D. again yesterday. Had a long talk with Lieutenant Garrison. He said it's their belief now that Proctor never intended to remain in Santa Fe. They think he took a room there just to throw them off the track. They think he could be in New York."

Wayland sat forward. "They said *that?*"

"Well . . ." Marianne hesitated. "They said he could be anywhere."

"I see." Wayland's cheeks ballooned as he whistled out a long sigh. "I'll tell you what, Marianne. I want you to give me a detailed report on all the facts you've discovered relating to this cult business. If you want, you can tack on a section at the end explaining your theories."

Marianne's eyes lit up. "Got it," she said eagerly.

"And then . . ." Wayland picked up a pencil by its point end and drummed the eraser against the desktop. "And then I'm taking you off the case."

Marianne gaped. "You're *what?*"

"You're officially off the case when you hand in the report," Wayland repeated firmly.

Marianne looked so bewildered that for a moment Wayland's heart went out to her. He wished he'd broken the news more gently. "Sorry, Marianne. This is the right decision, one I would have made on my own anyway. You're letting yourself get too carried away by this case. You're—"

"What do you mean 'on my own'?" Marianne interrupted.

Wayland could have bitten his tongue. He hadn't meant to refer to his conversation with Jack Byrne. But now that he'd brought it up, he wasn't about to lie. "I had a talk with your father. He feels the same way I do."

"My *father?*"

"Yeah. It shows how seriously he takes all this Satanic stuff. He's worried about you, okay? Wait'll you have kids."

Marianne glared at him, her blue eyes bright with anger. "No offense, Chief, but I think this is shitty," she said. "I'm the one who's been pushing this angle all along. Half the information in this case comes from me. I'm the only

239

one who's been pursuing the leads. Everyone else has had their head up . . . has had their head in the sand.''

"You're out of line, Officer Byrne,'' he said angrily. Bad as he felt for her, he wasn't about to stand for any insubordination. He didn't like her tone one bit.

"This is not fair,'' Marianne said, swallowing hard.

"Sorry, Marianne,'' Wayland repeated, his tone softening. "But this is the way it's going to be. I want that report by tomorrow afternoon.'' He regarded her for a moment as she stood there rigidly, lips drawn tight, head shaking slowly back and forth as if she couldn't believe what he was telling her. "Look, Marianne, you've got your whole career ahead of you. There'll be plenty of other cases. More than you'll want, take my word for it. And you're not even being completely shut out of this one. You'll be informed of what's happening. Any suggestions or ideas you have, I'd be glad to hear.''

"Great,'' she said bitterly. Grabbing her cap off the chair, she turned on her heel and strode from the room.

Marianne headed straight for the lunchroom, hoping that it would be empty. It was. She plunked herself down at a table and began shredding a styrofoam cup into confetti. Minutes passed before she felt calm enough to come to a decision. By then, she was holding nothing in her hands but a ragged disk of Styrofoam.

She had no choice but to do what Wayland asked, up to a point. She would give him most of the information that he wanted. But she wouldn't give him everything.

Orders or no orders, she'd be damned if she'd give up on this case. She had no intention of telling Wayland about her visit to the Historical Society or about the house she'd asked old Kittredge to help her locate. That was her baby.

She'd be damned if she'd tell her father either. She'd been planning to, until this morning. She'd intended to call him tonight, before he left for his visit to her aunt. Now she didn't think she could speak to him at all without getting into a terrible fight. She couldn't remember ever feeling so furious with him.

40

"WELL, LOOK AT THIS," JEAN PEARY EXCLAIMED, PULLING open the front door. "It's snowing again." She sounded delighted. "A real, old-fashioned white Christmas."

She and her departing guests stood in the front hallway, peering out at the night. In the glow of the porch lamp, the powdery fall looked as heavy as a blizzard. The flagstone walkway, which Jean had shoveled clean earlier in the day, was already overlaid with a thick carpet of white.

"I'm glad we don't have any driving to do," Ruth Wagner declared. The Wagners, both in their seventies, lived just up the hill in a pine-sheltered little Tudor as trim and charming as a fairy-tale cottage.

"Are those boots of yours good for the snow?" Jean asked.

"Oh, I think so, Jean. They got me here in one piece, at any rate."

"Have no fear," Ruth's husband, George, proclaimed grandly. "You shall have this stout arm to lean upon."

Jean looked at him dubiously. He was four years older than his wife and had been making very free with the Bordeaux throughout dinner. His right forearm, held aloft as though he were Sir Walter Raleigh rendering assistance to the queen, looked impossibly frail, even under the padding of his Harris Tweed coat.

"I'll help too," offered Julie Houghton, the Wagners' youngest granddaughter. Fifteen years old, she had flown in from Chicago to spend Christmas with her grandparents while her mother and father treated themselves to a long-delayed second honeymoon in St. Croix.

"For heaven's sake," Ruth protested, laughing. "You'd think I was an invalid! Thank you, dear," the old lady said as Jean leaned her cheek down to her lips. "It was lovely. Where's Rachel? I want to say good-night."

Jean called into the kitchen and a moment later Rachel appeared, sipping ginger ale from a mug.

Ruth kissed her good-bye, then raised a hand—liver-spotted

241

but as delicate as a child's—and touched the girl's cheek. "Get some rest, dear," she said, her voice tinged with concern. "You look a little peaked."

"Good night! Good night!" the departing trio cried. "Merry Christmas all!" Their voices rose and fell as they slowly made their way up the walk, furrowing a ragged path through the snow. The flakes were falling so rapidly now that, within seconds, the shoulders of their overcoats looked as though they were draped with glistening white shawls.

Jean watched until they were out of sight beyond a hedge, then shoved the door closed. Rachel had gone back into the kitchen—she could hear water running and dishes clattering. "Don't worry about cleaning up!" Jean shouted. "We'll take care of it later!" It was still early, just a few minutes before ten.

Returning to the living room, Jean cleared a space on the coffee table, moving aside a bottle of Grand Marnier, several brandy glasses, and two small crystal bowls, one brimming with mints, the other with assorted nuts. A pair of plump macadamias perched on top of the pile seemed to call out to her, but she resisted their siren song. The waistband of her white skirt already felt uncomfortably tight.

She did splash a finger or two of Grand Marnier into a snifter before kicking off her pumps and settling back on the sofa, her crossed feet propped on the coffee table in the place she had made for them. She gazed around the room, sighing contentedly.

Jean loved Christmas and had spent the last week decorating the house to a fare-thee-well, as Ruth Wagner might have said. The mantel was crammed with Christmas cards, but on every other available inch of space—bookshelves and side tables, the top of the stereo cabinet, even the window ledges—she had arranged balsam boughs, pinecones, red candles, choiring cherubs, and miniature sleighs drawn by prancing reindeer.

The branches of the fat Douglas fir were dripping with ornaments, many rich in family memories, and dotted with delicate points of pure, white light, emanating from a hundred tiny bulbs. (Jean disapproved of blinking, multicolored Christmas tree lights, regarding them as garish—"as tacky as a neon tavern sign" was the way she'd once put it to

Rachel.) The gossamer wing tips of the trumpeting angel hovering at the apex of the tree brushed lightly against the living room ceiling.

Jean had even cajoled Rachel into crawling into the attic and dragging out the carton containing their hand-carved crêche. In sharp contrast to her childhood, when Christmastime had thrown her into such an acute state of excitement that she had trouble sleeping at night, Rachel seemed strangely disengaged from the holiday this year. Setting up the crêche—arranging and rearranging the figures of the Holy Family until she got them just right—had always been her favorite part of the preparations. This year she had seemed absolutely indifferent, as though the little manger with its wooden figurines were a child's toy she had suddenly outgrown.

At one point, however, while Jean was tiptoeing to hang a spangled ball from an upper branch of the tree, she had glanced down and spotted Rachel with the blue-robed Madonna clutched in one hand, staring at the Holy Mother with a peculiar intensity.

Now, sipping from the snifter, Jean gazed at the flaming logs snapping and popping in the fireplace and wondered, for the thousandth time, about her daughter's health. Perhaps Rachel hadn't grown too sophisticated for the innocent pleasures of Christmas after all. Perhaps her apparent apathy was simply a function of physical listlessness, another symptom of the mild but obstinate virus she had been suffering from all month. After all, Rachel had certainly not seemed distant tonight. On the contrary, she had played the perfect hostess, helping to serve dinner and clear afterward, chatting politely, even warmly, with their guests.

Jean turned her head and looked up from the sofa, aware that Rachel had entered the living room. "Come sit down, sweetie," she said, thumping the cushion beside her with her free hand.

Rachel stepped to the sofa and flopped down at the far end, putting as much distance between herself and her mother as possible. Jean turned slightly on the cushion so that she could look at her daughter without getting a crick in her neck.

In her black velvet dress, with her blond hair spilling over her shoulders, Rachel looked particularly fetching to-

243

night. But Ruth had been right—Rachel also looked drawn. There was an air of tension about her too, as she sat wedged in her corner, staring down at the carpet and sucking on her lower lip.

"Did you have a good time tonight?" Jean asked, reaching out to twirl a strand of Rachel's hair with a forefinger.

"I guess," Rachel answered, jerking her shoulders in a gesture that was either a shrug or a flinch, Jean couldn't tell which. But she withdrew her hand anyway.

"What did you think of Julie?"

"She's all right," Rachel replied indifferently.

Jean had been delighted when Ruth had called to ask if she could bring her granddaughter along to Christmas dinner. Julie was only a year younger than Rachel, and Jean had thought that her daughter would be grateful for a dinner companion her own age. But the difference between the two girls had been striking—and depressing. In contrast to Julie, who still acted like an eager-to-please, bubbly little girl, Rachel seemed amazingly sophisticated, almost world-weary. Studying the two as they sat together making strained, sporadic small talk over dinner, Jean had experienced a complicated emotion, compounded of loss, regret, and guilt. Rachel had grown up far too fast, and Jean held herself partly—no, largely—to blame.

Now, Rachel let out a deep sigh, not of sadness or weariness, but of determination, as though she were steeling herself for an unpleasant task.

Jean regarded her intently. "Something wrong, sweetie?"

"No. Well, yes. At least, you'll probably think so." For the first time since she sat down, she turned her large, hazel eyes to meet her mother's.

"Try me."

"I'm pregnant."

Jean gaped at her. A full five seconds passed before she was able to respond. "You're joking."

Rachel shook her head. Then, shooting a glance at Jean's drink, she said, "You're going to spill that."

Jean glanced down. The snifter was trembling in her hand. Leaning forward, she carefully set it down on the coffee table, then drew in a deep breath and turned to face her daughter again. "How in God's name did this happen?" she asked hoarsely.

244

"The usual way," Rachel answered airily. "I had sex and—"

"*Rachel!*" Jean's booming voice silenced her daughter. She couldn't remember the last time she had raised her voice to such an angry volume. Maybe that was part of the problem, she thought. Maybe she should have done a little more screaming.

Breathing hard, she clamped her eyes shut and struggled for control. It took her a long moment before she had calmed down enough to look at her daughter and speak again, though her voice quavered slightly even so. "How far along are you?"

"A month."

"A month!" Jean scoffed. "You can't tell after a month."

"Yes you can," Rachel insisted. "They have these kits in the drugstore. And besides, I've been having morning sickness."

Jean knew it was true. She had known for the past few weeks but had simply refused to believe it. "Is it Tim?" she asked.

"Yes."

"My God, Rachel," Jean cried. "You've only known him a few weeks."

"Seven weeks and four days," Rachel said. "What difference does it make? I'm in love with him and I'm going to marry him."

"Marry him? *Marry him?* My God, Rachel, you're not thinking of having this baby?" For a moment Jean had to close her eyes again. The room had done a sudden, crazy spin, as if the sofa were a seat on a carnival Tilt-a-Whirl.

"I told Tim you'd react this way," Rachel mumbled bitterly. "If you won't give your consent for us to marry, I'll have the baby anyway. Is that what you want, to have an illegitimate grandchild?"

"You are *not* going to have this baby," Jean said, her voice rising.

"Oh, yes I am!" Rachel yelled. "I want this baby and you can't make me have an abortion! You can't! You *can't! You can't!*"

The violence of her outburst propelled Rachel halfway

off the sofa. Now, she sank bank onto the cushion, panting loudly, her soft face flushed from chin to forehead.

Desperation flooded through Jean. An image of her daughter stomping out the door again, this time in the wind-driven snow, flared in her brain. She knew she had to exert some control over the situation before the crisis got completely out of hand.

Taking a deep breath, she began to speak calmly and rationally about what having a baby at sixteen would mean: about the interrupted schooling, the grinding responsibility, the loss of spontaneity, of freedom, of youth. She pointed out that seven weeks and four days was not long enough to really get to know someone, that Tim would be forced to abandon his college plans for a mediocre job to support his young wife and infant, that the difficulties of starting a family at such a tender age would put intolerable strains on what seemed, at the moment, like an ideal relationship.

Rachel listened to her mother's speech patiently, waiting until Jean was finished before replying in equally reasonable tones. "First of all, I'll be seventeen by then. And second of all, I love him and he loves me. We want to get married, and we're going to have this baby."

Jean opened her mouth to object, but no words emerged. She had run out of arguments, out of energy, out of hope. She turned away from her daughter's face and gazed at the fire, stunned into silence.

"I have something else to tell you, Mom." Rachel's voice was firm and confident. "I'm moving in with Tim. To his apartment."

Jean slid the heels of her hands into her eye sockets and shook her head slowly. When she looked up again and began to speak, her voice remained steady but her face looked haggard. "Rachel, surely some part of you must realize how crazy this is, how ill-equipped you are to be a mother or a wife. Or even"—her voice took on an edge of bitterness—"some young man's live-in companion."

"I'll be a better wife to him than you were to—" Rachel stopped, but the unfinished sentence hung crackling in the air like a high-voltage power line left dangling by a storm.

Jean actually had to force her hand down into her lap. For the first time in her life she felt like slapping Rachel hard across the face.

But what would be the point? she thought. She would not win that way. Nobody would.

A whoosh of sparks shot up the flume as the last of the logs collapsed in a burst of embers. Wearily, Jean told Rachel to go to bed. Her daughter nodded, rose from the sofa, bid her mother good-night, and walked out of the room with the stride of a victor.

For a long time Jean felt unable to move. The fire died, and the room grew colder. But Jean sat motionless until her chilled hands and feet had turned as numb as her heart. By the time she managed to haul herself off the sofa, dizzy with fatigue and heartsickness, she had decided on the only course of action that seemed available to her, short of shipping Rachel off to a convent.

She would cut her daughter some slack. Time, Jean believed, was on her side. Rachel was only a month pregnant, at most. They still had several months before a decision had to be made about the fate of the baby.

Fetus, Jean corrected herself grimly.

Would a boy as young as Tim really want to be saddled with such responsibility? Jean found it hard to believe. With a little bit of luck, one of them, if not Rachel, then surely Tim, would wake up in time and realize how insane it would be to let this pregnancy run its course.

As she moved mechanically around the living room switching off lights, Jean almost stumbled over the little crêche set up on the floor near the Christmas tree. She paused for a moment to look down at it, and as her gaze fell on the heavenly infant swaddled in its bed of straw, misery rose up in her breast in a great billowing wave so thick and bitter that, for a moment, she thought she might choke on it.

41

STEPPING UP TO THE STATION-HOUSE ENTRANCE, MARIANNE exhaled a cloud of breath as thick as cigar smoke. She would have smiled with relief as she shoved open the heavy glass doors, but her face muscles felt frozen into immobility. The tip of her nose, too, had passed from pain to icy numbness. Pausing in the lobby to stomp the snow from her boot soles, an image from her childhood came to her, a Disney cartoon in which a sinister Jack Frost—a crook-backed old ogre with fingers like frozen twigs and a great jagged nose dripping with icicles—chased a trio of terrified kittens across a bleak, winter landscape. Marianne had been haunted by it for years.

Though the station-house thermostat was set at an energy-saving sixty-six degrees, the air felt positively tropical compared to the temperature outside, where a savage wind made the subfreezing weather almost impossible to bear, even for a short time. And Marianne had been out in it for nearly an hour, standing in the right lane of Route 28, waving a bright orange signal flag to detour oncoming traffic around a disabled heating-oil truck that had fishtailed on an ice patch and skidded half off the road into a ditch. The truck was still there when Sam Ferris finally arrived to relieve her. "Wayland says to take a break," he had said, grimacing as wind-driven snow peppered his cheeks like bird shot. For once Marianne had been grateful for Wayland's paternalism.

Pulling off her gloves as she headed for the coffee machine, she reached up and touched her nose, just to make sure it was still there. Her fingertips came away wet. She reached for a hankie. Either her nose was running badly or else it really had turned into an icicle and was beginning to melt in the warmth.

Inside the lunchroom, Mike Holson and Roy Auslander sat hunched over a table, so deeply engrossed in an argument over Super Bowl possibilities that they barely glanced up to acknowledge her presence. Helping herself to some coffee, Marianne stepped to the window, the cup clutched in both hands and held close to her face. For a while she stood there without taking a sip, simply gazing out toward Grace Street and inhaling the fragrant steam gratefully, like a convalescent breathing healing mist from a vaporizer. —

Stoneham was in the grip of a ferocious cold wave that had roared down from Canada four days before. The last heavy snow had fallen on Christmas night. By now the storm had subsided to flurries, though the wind was as brutal as ever. As Marianne watched, a howling gust whipped the branches of the tall spruces in front of the station house, sending thick clumps of snow tumbling from the treetops. Grimacing, she turned away from the window and carried her brimming cup toward an empty table.

As she passed the double row of wooden pigeonholes that served as the departmental mailboxes, Marianne spotted a small, yellow memo slip shoved inside her slot. She plucked it out with fingers still tingling from the cold. "Call Kittredge," it read. Below, scrawled in Pete Rydell's chicken-scratch handwriting, was the number of the Stoneham Historical Society.

She could feel her heart begin to race, and made an effort to control her quickening excitement. It could be nothing, she told herself. She didn't want to be disappointed. Blowing the steam off her coffee, she forced herself to take a few slow sips. Then waving to Holson, who had paused long enough in his lament on the Giants' fading chances to flash her a friendly smile, she headed for the report room, where she slipped behind a vacant desk, grabbed up the phone and punched in Kittredge's number.

"I believe I may have found what you're looking for," Kittredge said after the two had exchanged greetings. Marianne could hear the deep self-satisfaction in his voice.

"You get results fast, Mr. Kittredge," she said.

"Well, Officer Byrne, I was raised to believe in the quaint notion of doing a job correctly. Used to be a time when all Americans were brought up that way. It was one of the qualities that made our country great, respected throughout the world . . . "

"Uh-huh," Marianne said, doing her best to convey polite interest. She herself had been educated by the nuns to

249

believe in certain old-fashioned virtues, one of which was respect for the elderly.

"But you don't want to talk about that," Kittredge went on. "You're a police officer and you have your work to attend to. As a taxpaper, I am philosophically opposed to wasting the time of our public officials with trivia."

"I appreciate that," Marianne said, struggling to mask her impatience. The old man was certainly putting her parochial-school training to the test. "So you've found the house?"

"The house?" Kittredge said. It seemed to take him a moment to remember why he had contacted her in the first place. "Oh, yes. Vanderdam."

"Vanderdam?"

"I believe that's the place you're looking for. Does that name sound right to you?"

"It certainly could be," she said excitely, pulling open the long center desk drawer and rummaging for a pen and notepad. She flipped open the pad and clicked the ballpoint into readiness. "Please go on."

"I was right—the house isn't located in Stoneham at all. Not even in Westchester County. It's quite a ways up north in Dutchess County, near a town called Stottsburg. Small town on the east side of the Hudson, a good seventy miles away from here."

"Stottsburg," Marianne repeated slowly, printing out the name as she spoke.

"Now, this house dates back to the 1840s. It was built, as I surmised, as the summer residence of a New York financier. Horace Vanderdam was the gentleman's name. From what I gather about Mr. Vanderdam—you see I believe in uncovering the whole history of something, Officer Byrne, not just the impoverished facts—he died a disappointed man. Only two of his children survived into adulthood. Both were females and neither ever married."

"Mr. Kittridge, where—" Marianne began, but now that the old man had gotten started, he wasn't about to be sidetracked.

"No one to carry on the Vanderdam name into future generations, you see. The old man himself outlived his wife by twenty years. Died in his seventies. Afterward, his daughters—a pair of eccentric spinsters, no doubt—made

250

the house their permanent, year-round residence." Marianne listened with half an ear as the old man recited the whole history of the house and its various ill-fated owners, tuning in when he finally returned to the present. "The place stood empty until a year ago. It had become almost prohibitive to heat. Then it was purchased by its present owner, a rather mysterious party who, rumor has it, has done some massive restoration," the old man finished.

" 'Mysterious party'?"

"That's what I'm told. No one has actually seen him. Or her. Or them. They don't come into Stottsburg. The renovations have evidently been handled by contractors and construction crews from a different part of the state. Windows in the house are all shuttered. I gather from the realtor I spoke to that there is a general air of, let us say, inhospitability about the place."

"Were you able to find out the name of the owner?" Marianne asked, barely daring to breathe while she waited for the answer. *Proctor, Proctor,* she repeated soundlessly.

"It was purchased in the name of a corporation," Kittredge answered. Marianne could hear paper rustle again. "Something called the Xerrot Corp."

Marianne made a disappointed face, though she hadn't really expected to establish such an obvious connection to Proctor. "So you really think this is the house?"

"It's the only possibility I could find," Kittredge answered, sounding slightly irritated. "There *are* a few other places around still known by their ancestral names. But nothing that sounds even close to VandeCamp. What do *you* think?"

Marianne hesitated for only a moment. "Mr. Kittredge, I think you're a genius. How can I thank you?"

"I'm too old by thirty years for a proper thanks," he replied with a dry chuckle, then added quickly, "Forgive me, Miss Byrne. No impropriety intended. I consider myself amply rewarded by the work itself, another obsolete attitude, no doubt. I enjoyed the digging. And the discovery, of course. That's payment enough."

"You're a peach, Mr. Kittredge. As my grandmother used to say."

"I obtained directions to the house, by the way. I thought you might like to make a trip up there."

Marianne copied them down carefully as the old man dictated.

"Now if you need anything more from me, young lady, you'd better call me right away," Kittredge said. "I leave for Florida on New Year's Day. Go there every year on January first for four months of rest and recreation. Good for my arthritis. Good for my state of my mind too. Seeing all those retired old fogies withering away in the sun like prunes reminds me of why I continue to work."

Hanging up, Marianne stared down at the information Kittredge had given her, her mouth widening into a smile. The lingering doubt she'd voiced to the old man had evaporated, replaced by a sense of absolute certainty. She had done it. She had gotten a fix on the mysterious place she had known only as Vandesomething.

She had found the lair of Simon Proctor.

Marianne felt like whooping with triumph but settled for pumping her fist in the air like a celebrating athlete.

"You hit the Lotto jackpot or something?" someone said behind her.

Swiveling in her seat, Marianne saw Holson looming in the doorway. She sprang up and pulled him into the little room, swinging the door closed behind him.

"What's up?" Holson asked with a little laugh.

Marianne wrapped both her hands around his big right bicep and squeezed. "Mike, I found it!" she whispered excitedly.

"Found what?"

"Where Kevin Peterson's cult's been meeting!"

Instantly, Holson's expression turned serious. "Kevin Peterson's *what?*"

"Cult," Marianne repeated. Quickly, she filled him in on the relevant facts—her growing conviction that Kevin Peterson had not acted alone in the Prince kidnapping, that the abduction had been carried out by a cult, and that the mastermind behind the crime was none other than Simon Proctor. She described the contents of the small wooden chest she had found cached in Kevin's bedroom, and sketched in the obscene practices of the Belphegor cult, which would account both for the baby's abduction and the peculiar mutilations on the body of the butchered dog that had turned up on Woodland Drive.

252

"You're telling me that there's one of these Belfry—whatever cults operating around here?"

Marianne simply stared back at him.

"What about that babysitter? Rachel. You think she's involved too?"

"I don't know," Marianne said. "Maybe."

Holson frowned. "So where's this place supposed to be?" he asked.

"A town called Stottsburg, up in Dutchess County," Marianne said, keeping her voice low, as if the little room might be bugged. "In a house built a long time ago by a guy named Vanderdam."

"Christ," Mike Holson breathed. "How'd you find out about this place?"

"Jerry Waller. Remember? The teacher at Willow Brook, the one who found the dog's tongue nailed to the gazebo? The Peterson kid was a student of his. They were real close."

"Yeah," Mike said slowly, "I remember the chief saying something about that in his briefing."

"Kevin came to see him just before he died. He started to tell Waller about this place but then thought better of it. After Kevin turned up dead, Waller showed up here."

Holson's eyes narrowed suddenly. "Hey, I thought Wayland ordered you off this case."

Marianne bridled. "I spoke to Waller before Wayland took me off."

Stroking the tip of his moustache with a forefinger, Holson gazed down at the floor for a long moment, seemingly lost in thought. Finally, he looked up at Marianne again. "So what're you going to do? Tell Wayland?"

She snorted. "Give me a break," she said. "The first thing I'm going to do is make absolutely sure I'm right. Then I'm gonna serve Simon Proctor up to him on a platter."

Holson looked amused. "And exactly how're you going to do that?"

"I'm going up to the Vanderdam house," she announced.

"You're crazy."

"Wrong. I'm the only one in this place who sees what's really going on."

253

"No offense, but this is a truly dumb-ass idea, Marianne," Holson declared.

"Still, that's what I'm doing."

He gazed at her tensed jaw and defiant eyes. Finally, he shook his head and sighed. "Want company?"

Marianne smiled. "You're sure? The chief might be real pissed when he finds out."

Holson smiled back. "I already told you once. You're not in this alone."

Touched, Marianne reached up and squeezed his right arm again, awkwardly this time. "Thanks."

Holson patted her hand gently where it rested on his arm. "So when are you planning to do this?"

"Right away," she said, removing her hand from his arm. "Tonight."

He shook his head. "Can't. It's Betty's birthday. How about tomorrow?"

"I'm on tomorrow until four."

"We'll do it then," Mike said. "I'm off work early. How about I pick you up at your place at five? That enough time to get home?"

"Yeah."

As she stood there in the closed-off little room, staring up at Holson, Marianne suddenly became aware that she was fighting back an impulse to throw her arms around his neck and kiss him. Taking a step back, she perched on a corner of the desk. "You're sure about this?" she asked him again. "Your ass could end up in a sling."

"What are friends for?" he said with a shrug.

They exchanged a long look, then Mike turned and reached for the doorknob. Just as he was turning it, Marianne rose from the desk and placed her hand against the door.

"Mike," she said. "Not a word about this to anyone. This is my baby, and I want to be the one to deliver it. Promise?"

Turning around to face her again, he raised his right hand to shoulder level, pinkie and thumb curled together, three remaining fingers stuck straight up into the air.

"Scout's honor," he swore.

42

MARIANNE NAVIGATED, READING THE DIRECTIONS BY FLASH-
light, while Holson drove.

"We're getting close," she said, squinting through the
windshield. "There!"

Off to the right, illuminated by the high beams of Holson's '89 Buick, a pair of snow-topped stone pillars loomed
at the edge of the woods like sentry boxes. Cruising slowly
past the pillars, Holson steered onto the shoulder, cutting
the headlights as the car rolled to a stop in the snow.

"Hope we don't end up in a ditch," he muttered, switching off the ignition.

Closing the car doors quietly behind them, they trooped
back toward the columns, their flashlights aimed at the
ground. The packed snow of the narrow lane leading up
into the Vanderdam property was rutted with fresh tire
tracks. There seemed to be a number of different sets,
though it was impossible to tell how many.

"No noise from here on in," Holson whispered, zipping
his black, lamb-fleece collar up to his chin. His breath came
out in puffs of vapor.

Marianne nodded. She was already shivering, and not
only from the cold. Much to her chagrin, she felt far more
apprehensive than she'd expected to. "Mike," she whispered. "Thanks again. For coming up here with me." In
the warm car she had realized how safe she felt in his
company, the way her father had always made her feel
when she was a kid. Mike was a big man, and a far more
experienced cop than she. "To tell you the truth, I really
didn't want to do this alone."

She raised her flashlight beam toward his chin, so that
she could see his face without blinding him. In the yellow
glow—shadows mottling his features like camouflage paint—
Holson wore an expression Marianne could not read.

"Come on," he said after a moment. "We'd better get
going."

Their boots crunching on the hard-packed snow, they

made their way up the narrow path, sweeping the ground ahead of them with their lights. The deep woods pressing around them made the darkness feel solid, as though the pathway were a tunnel through the night. Emerging at the far end, they found themselves at the edge of a cleared slope bathed in the spectral glow of a nearly full moon. They snapped off their flashlights. The snow-blanketed hill-top gleamed silver-blue. Straight ahead, on the crest of the hill, the big house hulked in the moonlight.

The winter night felt as silent and cold as the ocean; poised there, feeling the thudding of her heart, Marianne had the oddest sensation, as though she were standing not on the rise of a hill, but on the floor of the sea. The looming house seemed as dead as a shipwreck. She looked over at Holson, who was staring straight ahead, wiping his nose and moustache with the back of one gloved hand. He seemed to become aware of her gaze. Nodding toward the house, he crouched slightly and slipped quickly up the path, Marianne following close behind.

A large parking area had been shoveled clear at the side of the house. Marianne counted eight cars. Bending low, she switched on her flashlight and moved down the line, aiming the beam at the license plates. All the cars were from New York. She decided to take down the numbers. Undoing the side pocket of her parka, she pulled out a notepad with a ballpoint stuck through the spirals. Holson hunkered down beside her.

"Leave that for later," he whispered. "We can't call them in now anyway."

Returning to the front of the house, they began to make a slow, counterclockwise circuit, looking for a window to peer through. The heavy, outside shutters had been closed and latched with metal eyehooks. Reaching up, Marianne undid one of the shutters, swung it open, and peered in. Only her reflection glared back at her, like a genie's face inside a magic mirror. Heavy black curtains blocked the window from the other side.

"These folks like their privacy," she whispered to Holson.

He raised a forefinger to his lips to say, *Listen*.

From somewhere deep inside they could hear the throb

of strange music, less a recognizable melody than a steady, drumbeat pulse.

Grabbing Marianne by the forearm, Holson pulled her back a few steps. He put his mouth close to her ear and whispered, "Something's going on in there, all right."

"Proctor's in there," she said.

"You don't know that. Shit, it could be a frat party, for all we know. Some local kids warming up for New Year's Eve." He shook his head. "We're going to have to go in."

"Go in?" she said. "I don't know, Mike. Maybe that's not such a great idea." She hadn't expected to feel so unnerved by the great, dark house. All her boldness had turned faint in its presence.

Holson hugged himself against the cold. "Hey, Marianne, what the fuck did you drag me up here for anyway?"

Even in the refrigerated air Marianne could feel the warmth flood her cheeks. She felt angry and abashed in equal measure.

"All right," she said grimly. "How do we get in?"

"Let's try the back door."

They stole around to the rear. "Hold this," Holson whispered to her, passing her his flashlight. She shone the beam at the door lock. Yanking off his right glove with his teeth, Holson reached into his hip pocket for his wallet, pulled out a credit card, shoved it between the door edge and jamb and began working it fiercely.

"Dead bolt," he muttered after a moment. "Shit!"

Grabbing his flashlight from her hands, he swept the beam along the foundation. "Maybe there's a basement window," he whispered.

"What's that?" Marianne said, using her own light as a pointer. A few feet from where they stood, the snow was piled higher against the house, as though the ground beneath it rose up in a little slope. Kneeling, Holson began to scoop away the snow with one hand. It took him less than a minute to expose the lid of a slanting wooden bulkhead.

"This must lead to the cellar," he whispered excitedly, continuing to shovel away the snow. Before long he had uncovered a rusted metal hasp. There was no padlock through the staple. Holson flipped open the latch and, using it as a handle, lifted back the heavy wooden door. The

257

creak of the hinges made Marianne wince. She pressed close to Holson as he aimed his light down into the bulkhead. A narrow wooden staircase that looked impossibly rickety descended into utter darkness.

"You're packing, right?" Holson asked.

Marianne nodded. "I've got my backup too," she said, aiming her beam at her left ankle. She hoped her voice didn't sound as shaky as she felt.

"All right. Let me go first."

They went down cautiously, Holson leading the way. There was no railing on the stairs, only the cellar wall on their right. Putting out her hand to steady herself, Marianne could feel the raw, hard-packed earth through her gloves.

Worms, she thought, snatching back her hand reflexively.

Did worms live through the winter? She had no idea. It wasn't a question she was prepared to dwell on either, particularly not at that moment. The dank smell of cold earth choked her nostrils, and a sound like the slither of a thousand nightcrawlers filled the inside of her head. She wanted out of there fast. Moving too quickly, she missed the lowest step of the ladder and came stumbling down against Mike.

"You okay?" he whispered.

"Yeah," she answered weakly. She felt like an utter fool.

Standing at the foot of the ladder, they swept their beams around the cellar. Rotting crates and moldering cardboard boxes were piled in the dark. "Jesus," Mike said, aiming his flashlight into the space behind the staircase. An old-fashioned rat trap, canopied with cobwebs, was shoved into the far corner. A heap of remains—mummified things of dried fur and jutting bone—lay on the bottom of the rusted little cage.

"Come on," Marianne urged.

Cautiously, they made their way forward. The cellar was surprisingly large. Much to Marianne's relief, the earth walls soon gave way to stone, the dirt floor turning to concrete. Ahead of them an enormous furnace suddenly rumbled to life. Marianne ran her light over it as she tiptoed past. In the darkness it seemed as big as a battleship engine.

The cellar turned a corner. Peering around the edge of the wall, they aimed their lights into the void.

258

"Look!" Mike whispered. A white enamel freezer chest squatted against the far wall. Beside it a narrow wooden staircase stretched upward from the cellar floor.

"Up there," Holson said, shining his light over the closed door at the top of the stairs. "That's our way in."

They stepped quickly to the foot of the staircase. Pulling off her right glove, Marianne unzipped her parka and reached into her waistband for her .357 Ruger. In spite of the cold, her palm was sweaty against the hard rubber of the Pachmayr grip.

"Here we go," Holson said. He too had his gun in his hand—a Smith & Wesson 9mm autoloader.

"What's the plan?" Marianne asked.

"See what we can see. Hear what we can hear. Ready?"

Marianne nodded, heart racing.

Holson led the way up the creaking stairs. At the top he turned the knob, opened the door a crack, and peered out. Then, with a little nod over his shoulder to Marianne, he pulled the door wide and quickly slipped through.

Marianne sucked in a deep breath and followed.

They were in a long, narrow corridor nearly as dark as the basement. Holson's beam, sweeping around the black-papered walls, looked like a miner's light in a coal shaft. Only a crack of light glowed dully from the bottom of a doorway, a few yards to their left.

After the frigid cellar, the hallway seemed suffocatingly close. That big furnace must be working overtime, Marianne thought. The air stank too, though of what Marianne could not readily tell. The stench was a mixture of sickly sweet and foul odors—a kind of perfumed corruption. Marianne tried breathing through her mouth, afraid that the smell would make her sick. Her head was already swimming from the darkness, the stifling heat, and the fear.

Back pressed to the wall, Holson began to move along the corridor commando-style, right arm cocked at a ninety-degree angle, pistol pointed straight into the air. Marianne stood frozen, watching him slip closer to the door.

Forcing herself to move, she hurried down the hallway at a crouch. She came to a stop beside Holson, flattening her back against the wall.

The pounding music was louder now. It was coming from

259

the room behind the door. Marianne could feel the wall behind her vibrating to its beat, as though from the thumping of a monstrous heart.

Her own heart was knocking hard against her chest. She was sweating too, and breathing as noisily as if she'd run a mile.

Suddenly, Holson took a quick step toward the door and pressed the side of his head against it. He stood that way for a moment, listening.

As Marianne watched him, her simmering anxieties suddenly raged to a boil. The whole plan had been a mistake! What were they doing there, anyway? Breaking and entering, that's what! If they got caught, they'd be finished—discharged from the force, kicked out on their butts.

She stepped beside Holson and, tiptoeing up, put her mouth to his ear. "Let's get of here!" she whispered frantically.

And then Holson did something strange. He stood up straight, turned slowly toward her, and said, not in a whisper but at a perfectly normal volume, "It's too late."

Marianne took a step backward, staring, though she couldn't really see his face. She was utterly bewildered, not so much at his words as at his tone. There was something inexplicably smug, almost gloating, about it. She opened her mouth to ask him what the hell he was talking about.

Only then did she realize that they were not alone in the corridor.

She could not see the others, of course. They had approached her from behind. But she felt their presence in the instant before her arm was grabbed and twisted sharply up behind her back, her gun pried from her grip.

"Mike!" she gasped.

Marianne saw his lips curl into a smile as he turned his flashlight on her, pointing it straight into her eyes, blinding her. *What's he . . . ? Why isn't he . . . ?* Behind her a chorus of voices whispered and tittered.

Marianne tried turning away from the light. A powerful hand snaked over the top of her head, clutched the hair at her widow's peak and yanked. She yelled.

She still expected Holson to leap at her attackers.

"Mike!" she cried out again. "Help me!" But Holson did not leap at her attackers.

Squinting through his light, Marianne saw him take a step back as the heavy door slowly swung open and a man emerged into the hallway.

He was big, taller even than Holson. With one hand he clutched a crimson cloak around his body. The other held aloft a silver candelabrum bristling with flaming black candles. Holson's flashlight clicked off.

Marianne's breath caught in her throat. She was staring into the leering face of Simon Proctor.

"Welcome, Marianne Byrne," he said, his deep voice ripe with mockery. "Did she give you any trouble?"

"Not really," Mike said, holstering his pistol. "Acted pretty chickenshit, though." He snorted. "Big tough cop. Better check her right ankle. She's wearing a backup."

Someone crouched at her feet. Glancing down, she was able to catch a glimpse of a young man's naked, muscular back before the hand twined through her forelock pulled her head back with a savage jerk. She felt her pants leg being hoisted and heard the tearing sound of Velcro as her ankle holster was removed.

Marianne struggled against panic. She tried to think clearly but could not make sense of what was happening. Why didn't Mike draw his gun and arrest Proctor? Why was he acting as though he and Proctor knew each other?

The top of her scalp felt as if it were being ripped from her skull. Trickles of sweat from the pain, the stifling heat, and the desperation tearing at her heart ran down her forehead and stung her eyes. She was afraid she might begin to cry.

Proctor stepped toward her, bringing the candelabrum so close to her face that she could see the dribbles of wax sliding down the dark candle shafts like black tears.

"I see the question in your pretty face, Officer Byrne. Your colleague, Michael, is one of us. A most valued member of our little group."

"Liar," Marianne said.

"Oh yes," Proctor replied with a little laugh. "The father of it." He glanced around at Holson. "You've done well, Michael. I think you'll enjoy your reward."

Proctor motioned with his candelabrum. "This way."

Turning, he disappeared through the doorway, his satin cape sweeping behind him.

As Marianne was pushed past Holson, she twisted her head and tried to spit in his face. But nothing came out. "Bastard," she rasped. Holson only smiled back.

Rough hands shoved her inside the black chapel. Behind her, she heard the heavy door swing shut.

43

"OPEN UP, MARIANNE, OPEN UP." THE GYNECOLOGIST sounded amused. What am I doing here, anyway? Marianne wondered. She didn't need an examination.

Above her the heads of his assistants floated in the darkness, whispers and giggles muffled by their strange, full-face masks.

It was hot, so hot in the shadowy examination room. It smelled bad too, as though some previous patient had lost control of her bladder during the examination. Marianne could feel rivulets of sweat streaming down her body. Her eyes stung with perspiration. She would have reached down to wipe them, but something tight cut into her wrists whenever she tried to move her hands. Her arms felt funny too, floppy and useless.

The doctor was pushing at her knees, shoving her legs as far apart as they would go.

"Come on, Marianne. Open up. That's our girl. That's our little girl."

She could feel his fingers inside her, slipping in and out. She was wet, embarrassingly wet. Voluptuous warmth radiated from her clitoris up through her pelvis. Someone else, one of the nurses, began examining her breasts, massaging them gently, rubbing smooth fingertips over her nipples, making them hard. She had to concentrate to keep from squirming with pleasure.

"Isn't that nice, Marianne? Doesn't that feel nice?"

They had given her a cupful of medicine to drink before stripping off her clothes. She remembered that. She hadn't wanted to drink it. It smelled awful, like a public urinal, and the cup had a creepy, bleached-white look, like the cap of an animal's skull. She had squeezed her lips as hard as she could and tried to turn her face away as the reeking drink was lifted to her mouth, but one of the male nurses had pinched her nose tight and squeezed the sides of her jaw until she'd opened wide. "There, there," the doctor had cooed as he forced the medicine down her throat. "Nice warm piss."

"It won't kill you," one of the nurses had said.

Someone else had laughed. "We're clean. No AIDS."

"There's a special treat in it too," the doctor had said. "Make you feel good."

The warm stinking medicine had tasted foul, foul. She had started to gag but the male nurse had grabbed one of her ears and twisted until she'd shrieked with pain. "If you throw it up, we'll just make your drink more," he had threatened. She had kept it down. After a few moments wooziness overcame her, her eyelids drooped, her limbs went rubbery. The room had spun, blackened. Later, she had half opened her eyes and found herself naked and strapped to the table, her examination already under way.

Something was happening between her legs. She tried to fight against the pleasure. What if she had an orgasm during her examination, with everyone watching? The thought mortified her, and yet the feelings were so sweet. Raising her head with a struggle, she looked down the length of her sweat-soaked body. One of the nurses had lifted off her mask and had her face buried between Marianne's legs. In the hush of the examination room, Marianne could hear the wet sounds of the girl's eager lapping.

Marianne flopped her head back on the black-draped table and let the liquid pleasure flood through her. With a groan of surrender, she began to grind her open vulva against the girl's hungry mouth and tongue.

Opening her heavy-lidded eyes, she gazed up at the doctor, who was looking down at her face, laughing soundlessly. She'd never seen a physician who wore a bright red gown before. It was open in the front too, and she could see his hard, naked body underneath it, with strange eyelike markings on his chest. She let her gaze wander down the length of his body. He was so big between his legs.

She wanted to reach out and clutch him, stroke him, make him feel as nice as she felt.

"You like that, don't you, Marianne?" the doctor said. "You want to come, don't you?"

"Mmmm." She closed her eyes and ran her tongue over her half-opened lips. The pleasure was building, her orgasm was coming on. "Yes," she whispered. "That. Do that."

With shocking suddenness the sensation stopped. Marianne let out a cry of disappointment All around her, laughter and mocking cries of sympathy issued from the hovering masks.

Marianne looked down between her legs. Grinning lewdly, the naked girl stood straight, wiped her smeared mouth with the back of one hand, then replaced her mask over her face, Snow White with apple-red cheeks and a simpering smile.

The doctor turned his head and addressed someone behind him. "She is yours to enjoy first, Michael."

Michael? The name filtered through the cottony haze of Marianne's drugged consciousness. She forced her sagging eyelids open. At the foot of the table Mike Holson loomed over her, naked, his hard-muscled body slick with sweat, as he had sometimes appeared to her in her most secret dreams.

A lulling voice crooned inside her head: *This is a dream, just a dream.*

But the look on his face, sneering and malign, was unlike any he had ever worn in her dreams.

"I've been waiting a long time for this," Holson said thickly.

Marianne moaned as he drove himself into her. Grunting savagely, he rammed at her womb as though he were trying to rupture it. Marianne looked up pleadingly. All around, the spectral masks leered down at her, their frozen grins as ghastly as the smiles on a circle of skulls.

A jolt of terror surged through Marianne's brain. Her consciousness surfaced like a foundering swimmer fighting his way up for air. "Bastard!" she shrieked. "Get off! Get off!" Fingers curled into claws, she strained at her bonds, fighting to get at Holson, to tear at his face, rip out his eyes.

One of the cult members shoved a handful of fingers into

her mouth, forcing her head back onto the table. Panic flooded through her as she struggled to breathe. She felt the table list violently beneath her, like a capsizing life raft. Then she plunged into the swirl of semiconsciousness, the drugs dragging her back down like an undertow.

The violent pounding between her legs ceased. As she sank into the bottomless darkness, she heard a man's husky voice from very far away: "Bitch." The man spat noisily, and she felt something splat against her belly. Then a different voice spoke, a voice rich in command and authority—her doctor's voice.

"The rest of you. Enjoy her as you wish."

The blackness overcame her.

Later, she resurfaced. Someone was whispering to her. She could feel the hot, wet breath against her ear. "Wake up, Marianne. Wake up."

She mumbled something.

"What?" Proctor asked.

"Fuck . . . Fuck you," she croaked.

"No, my dear. It is you who has been fucked. Many times. Did you enjoy it?"

Marianne opened her mouth to speak but her voice failed her.

"Save your strength," Proctor said tenderly, stroking the damp hair from her forehead "There is one more lover you must satisfy tonight. The sweetest of all, Marianne. You will be his bride. You will lie in his cold chamber and feel the power of his embrace. He will kiss you deeply, Marianne. Oh yes, he will smother you with kisses, so sweet and deep."

He leaned forward and touched his mouth softly to her cracked lips.

She floated out into the darkness.

The throbbing ache between her legs brought her partway back. It hurt so much. And she could feel something leaking down there. Was she bleeding? Why didn't her doctor help her? She could hear him conferring with his associates.

". . . something that will wake her up . . ."

". . . wedge it open . . ."

". . . a stick . . . like the dog . . ."

Someone was tugging at her jaw, pulling her lips apart. Marianne willed her eyes to open. The doctor was shoving some kind of stick inside her mouth. A tongue depressor? But he was inserting it wrong, wedging it straight up and down. It hurt terribly, cutting into the soft tissue underneath her tongue and digging into the flesh of her upper palate. She tried to protest, but the only sound she produced was a desperate gurgle.

The doctor disappeared for a moment, then loomed over her again, something long and slender dangling from one hand. Marianne struggled to focus on it.

"Open wide, Marianne," he said, lowering the object toward her mouth.

He was going to take her temperature. But as his hand drew nearer, Marianne—terror burning the fog from her brain—saw that the thermometer was horribly pink and slick. And it wiggled, like something alive.

"Open wide, Marianne," he repeated. "That's my little girl."

A gurgling scream, raw and primal, tore its way up from the center of her being as Simon Proctor slid the earthworm onto Marianne's tongue.

44

STEPPING OUT OF HIS '84 PONTIAC AND ONTO THE NARROW driveway alongside his house, Jack Byrne gritted his teeth against the cold. The early morning air was frigid enough to test the devotion of the most resolute Christian. Just a day after returning from his Delaware vacation, Jack had risen with the first light, thrown on his clothes, bolted down a cup of black, instant coffee, and made it to church in time for the six A.M. mass, along with half a dozen other hardy souls.

Jack had become a much more regular churchgoer since Peggy's death. He was surprised at the solace he derived from his weekly attendance. His years as a cop had left him little doubt that Hell existed; the evil that had reared up and consumed his closest friend could have sprung from no other source.

He was less certain about the existence of Heaven, but

the beauty of the service and the warming words of Father Rafferty's sermons had the power to persuade Jack that God's Heaven was real. And that was a comforting thought, particularly during the holiday season, when his loneliness felt even more piercing than usual. It did his soul good to imagine Peggy residing somewhere above, gazing down at him.

Jack closed the car door carefully behind him. The block was so still at that hour, the houses so steeped in slumber, that a slamming door would have seemed as loud as an explosion. As he approached his front stoop, a sound shrilled abruptly from inside his own house, causing Jack's heart to do a little flip. The telephone was ringing. The sound would have been harmless enough at any other time of the day. But at that early hour—Sunday, seven A.M.— it was as nerve-jangling as a triggered alarm.

Moving as quickly as he could across the ice-glazed side-walk, Jack hurried up the stairs, keys in hand. Maybe it's Marianne, he thought as he undid the locks. He hadn't been able to reach her when he got back the night before. And they needed to mend some fences. She had been very cool when he had called her on Christmas day.

He knew it wasn't Marianne, though, before he was half-way across the living room. The phone had rung at least ten times, and his daughter was too impatient to wait that long for an answer. Frowning deeply, he grabbed up the handset.

"Yeah?"

"Jack. Dick Wayland."

Something in the tone of Wayland's voice stopped Jack from making a crack about the earliness of the hour. "What's wrong?"

"You better get up here right away."

"Is it Marianne? Is she hurt?"

There was a long pause, as if Wayland were steeling himself to deliver unspeakable news. "He's got her," he finally said.

Jack felt his throat constrict with dread. "Who's got her?"

"Proctor," answered Wayland with a tremor in his voice that terrified Jack more than any sound he'd ever heard in his life. "For the love of Christ, Jack. Just hurry. We haven't got much time."

267

45

THE BIG WALL CLOCK OVER THE FRONT DESK WAS JUST HIT-
ting the half-hour mark when Jack burst into the station
house. He had made the trip to Stoneham in record time,
tearing up the empty parkway at ninety, fighting to keep
his mind as blank as the asphalt zooming by beneath his
wheels.

"Where's Wayland?" he demanded, barging past the
young desk officer, who quickly rose to intercept him.

"Mr. Byrne?" the officer said, sinking back onto his
chair as Jack nodded in acknowledgment. The young man
looked ashen-faced, and he spoke with a hoarseness that
Jack recognized immediately as the sound of bad news—a
tone of voice he associated with hospital waiting rooms and
phone calls that shatter your sleep at three in the morning.

The young officer nodded over his shoulder. "They're
back there. In the chief's office. Watching the tape."

Tape? Jack thought wonderingly. *What the hell?* And
then he was pushing through a door into an office crammed
with men, at least a dozen of them, some in uniforms,
others in civvies. A few were perched on a conference
table, others were sitting stiffly in chairs. Most were on
their feet, and all of them had their backs to Jack, their
faces turned to a TV monitor on a high, metal rack. The
air was hazy with cigarette smoke. Most of the screen was
blocked from Jack's view. As he strode toward the group,
a few of the men glanced over their shoulders.

"It's Byrne," he heard one of them say.

"Turn it off," somebody else commanded. It was Dick
Wayland's voice. The television screen went dead. Then
Wayland detached himself from the group and came toward
Jack, both hands extended as though he meant to embrace
him. The other men swiveled to look. Jack had a quick
impression of a crowd of haggard faces. Then Wayland was
standing in front of him, leaning close, clutching his shoulders as though to steady Jack for a terrible shock.

"Where's my daughter?" Jack asked.

Wayland shook his head. "It's bad, Jack."

Jack's heart slammed once against the wall of his chest. "Is she dead?"

"No. At least, we hope—Jesus, Jack, this is—"

"How do you know?" Jack pressed. "How do you know she's not dead?"

"We got a tape," Wayland said. "It was dropped off here early." He pointed with his chin toward a balding cop sitting hunched on an office chair, legs crossed tightly, right hand cupped over his mouth. "Nash found it lying just inside the doorway when he came in around quarter to seven. It was wrapped inside a message."

"What kind of message?"

Taking Jack gently by one elbow, Wayland led him toward his desk as the others stepped aside to let them pass.

Lying on the center of the blotter was an unfolded white sheet, creased across the middle, a little tab of Scotch tape sticking up from the top. Jack leaned down to read the words neatly printed in black ink. HOPE YOU ENJOY THIS EPISODE OF "AMERICA'S FUNNIEST HOME VIDEOS."

He looked up into Wayland's face. "Let me see it," he said grimly.

Wayland's eyes were veined with red, his breath sour. "Jack, I gotta warn you. This is bad stuff."

"Let me see it," he repeated.

Wayland nodded at Nash, who rose quickly and stepped away from the chair. Unbuttoning his topcoat, Jack seated himself in Nash's place, the chair turned toward the VCR and monitor.

"Lights," Wayland said to the cop standing closest to the wall switch. The room went dark. Wayland leaned over and hit the play button on the video machine. Just then two more men opened the office door and wedged their way into the room. "Lyle, Greg," Wayland said to them. "Get up here. We need your ideas." Then he stepped away from the equipment and positioned himself behind Jack, placing one strong hand on Jack's right shoulder. Jack felt Wayland give a firm squeeze.

Then, as the videotape started up, he forgot that Wayland and the other men even existed. He forgot that he was sitting in a darkened office inside a suburban police station.

269

His world consisted only of the small, glowing screen, where absolute horror began unfolding before his eyes.

At first the images moved crazily, jerkily, as if the cameraman were hiking over rutted ground. Barren trees and snowbanks joggled by. The light was very poor. Then a voice, as unnaturally hearty as a game show emcee's, began to speak: "Sunday dawns. Soon, good Christians everywhere will be rising to their devotions. Except for one, who has been through a very long night of worship already and is undoubtedly looking forward to a nice, long sleep." Several voices sniggered in the background.

Abruptly, the unseen cameraman came to a halt. The camcorder moved in a slow semicircle. Jack felt his heart go cold at the sight.

He was staring at a tiny graveyard, surrounded by a tumbledown stone wall. Ancient, weather-scarred tombstones poked up from the snow, some of them tilted at crazy angles, others shattered across the top as though they had been vandalized with a sledgehammer. A few lay toppled facedown in the snow.

The pivoting camcorder came to rest on a tall figure, posed by the crooked trunk of a dead-white tree. Slowly, the camera panned up from his high leather boots to his black leather topcoat, belted at the waist, and up to his head, which was completely encased in a dark, woolen ski mask. As the camera zoomed in toward the mouth hole, the tall man began to talk in the same, deep, mocking voice that had spoken a moment before.

"Welcome to our ceremony," he began, his words issuing from the mouth hole in little puffs of steam, like smoke signals. "Sorry we couldn't invite all of you to join us here this morning. We know how disappointed some of you must feel, especially the father of the bride. But at least you'll be receiving this videotaped souvenir, sure to be a treasured keepsake in the years to come."

More laughter. The camera moved again, resting briefly on a dozen figures clad in heavy jackets, winter pants, and snow boots. Their faces were concealed behind cheap Halloween masks of movie monsters and cartoon characters. Jack recognized Dracula, Betty Boop, and Popeye. The light was better now: watery rays of sunshine were trickling over the dilapidated stone wall. From somewhere in the background came a strange, rhythmic sound—a dull, thudding crunch.

All at once every part of him froze, as though the cold fear building up in his heart had suddenly caused it to burst, flooding his body with ice water. One of the newly arrived men standing beside him gasped aloud. The other whispered, "Sweet Jesus." Jack bit down on his lower lip to keep from crying out.

He was looking at his daughter.

She stood there shivering in the cold, a plaid blanket tossed loosely over her shoulders, her naked legs exposed, her eyes vacant and unfocused. Her face was swollen and bruised, and her hair stuck to her cheeks in matted clumps. She seemed dead to the world around her. Jack's eyes followed the camera as it traveled down the length of her body. There was something dark running down the inside of one thigh. It looked like blood.

"We think she's in shock," he heard Wayland say softly behind him. "Or drugged. Or both."

As Jack watched with agonized helplessness, his daughter's knees buckled and she started to totter. A figure in a grinning donkey mask grabbed her roughly by one arm and shoved her around so that she was facing the camera, which zoomed in for a close-up. "Smile, Marianne," came a sneering voice from behind the mask. "You're on 'Candid Camera.' "

Stepping into the frame of the picture, the tall man in black placed an arm around Marianne's shoulders and drew her close to his body. "Poor baby," he said soothingly. "What a long night you've had." Reaching up a black-gloved hand, he tickled her under the chin with his forefinger. "Well, you'll be sleeping soon. We're getting your bed ready right now. See?"

Still clutching her around the shoulders, he half led, half dragged her through the snow.

"See?" the black figure repeated, motioning downward while the camcorder pulled back to show where he was pointing. "They've been at this half the night. Preparing your honeymoon suite."

"Oh Christ," Jack moaned. His vision darkened for a moment, and he clutched the seat of his chair with both hands.

271

At the base of an old, gray headstone, worn to the smoothness of slate, a pair of men in sweaters and ski masks stood back to back, deep inside a long, trenchlike hole. Visible only from the shoulders up, they were digging with mechanical regularity. Dirt clumps flew from their shovel blades, showering onto a high mound piled at one side of the hole. Muffled grunts accompanied every downstroke of their shovels.

They were opening one of the graves.

The tall man pulled Marianne closer to the edge of the hole. Suddenly, she seemed to become aware of what was happening. She began to struggle feebly, beating the tall man's chest with limp, half-curled fists, trying to push him away.

Hugging her tighter to his body, he laughed delightedly, as though she were a child who had just performed an adorable trick. "You aren't upset about something, are you, Marianne?" he asked with mock concern. "Just think how lucky you are. After all, how many people get to watch their own funerals?"

From deep inside the excavated grave came the distinct sound of metal scraping against wood. One of the diggers looked up and said, "I think we can get it out now. Let's have the ropes."

One of the masked figures standing nearby stooped and tossed two thick coils of rope down to the diggers, who caught them in midair, then ducked into the grave, disappearing from view.

Minutes passed. Still cradling Marianne under one arm, the tall man slid the opposite hand under her blanket where it lay open at her chest. The blanket began to move slowly, rhythmically, as though he were massaging her right breast. But Marianne was completely oblivious. Mercifully, she seemed to have sunk back into her stupor.

Then the two diggers were handing up the rope ends to four of their comrades, who had positioned themselves on either side of the grave, two at the foot, two by the headstone. Then the diggers clambered out of the hole and sat down heavily in the snow.

The four men strained at the ropes, hauling the coffin out of the earth. Slowly it rose into view—a plain wooden box, its slatted sides warped and worm-eaten. They laid it down

272

in the snow by the side of the grave. Then one of them grabbed up a shovel, worked the blade under the rotted lid and levered it off with a single downward thrust of the handle.

"Oh, shit," one of the female cult members exclaimed, tittering behind her Bambi mask. Two other masked figures who had bent over the coffin backed away.

With a grotesque tenderness, as though he were assisting an invalid, the tall man led the unresisting woman toward the open coffin. "Look, Marianne, look," he cooed, like a father pointing out a pretty flower to a toddler. "That's what you'll look like soon." Turning his head, he called to his followers, "Take it out."

Two of the cult members stooped, one at either end of the coffin, and lifted out a skeletal thing in a moldering white gown. The camcorder moved in for a close-up of the corpse's shriveled face—hollow eye sockets, gaping nose hole, lipless mouth stretched into an obscene grin. Wisps of wiry gray hair sprouted from the top of the parchment-colored skull.

"Make her kiss it," a woman's voice urged, and the others took up the cry.

Jack heard his name spoken from somewhere high above him. He struggled to listen. It was Wayland's voice, choked with pain and rage. "Jack," he was saying, "maybe you shouldn't—"

"I have to," Jack mumbled. "I have to see it."

The two cult members holding the corpse lifted it toward Marianne, while the tall man forced her head forward until her blue lips were pressed against the skull's leathery cheek. Marianne did not struggle or cry out. She only flinched slightly at the touch of the mummified flesh. Nothing more. The circling figures mocked and hissed.

"Put the two of them in the coffin together," a male voice sang out, and the others responded with approving cheers.

The tall man shook his head. "No. She must wait for her lover alone." With a sudden sweeping motion, he ripped the blanket from her shoulders like a stage magician revealing a miracle.

"Belphegor Satanis!" he cried.

A fearful roar went up from the assembled group, as

though from a single, monstrous throat. It hung in the frozen air for a moment while the tall man boomed a chant in a guttural language that Jack did not understand.

At a nod from their black-clad leader, a half dozen of his followers hurried forward, seized Marianne, and bundled her toward the coffin.

The rest happened very quickly. Marianne, awake but seemingly lifeless, was loaded into the narrow box. The slatted lid was fitted back in place and the coffin swiftly lowered. Then two of the huskier figures picked up the shovels and began covering the coffin, while the others scooped up handfuls of earth and flung them into the grave, squealing gleefully as they did so, like a bunch of preschoolers at play in a sandbox.

Jack felt as cold and hollow as a carcass in a butcher's meat locker. They're burying her alive, he thought numbly. *My child.*

When the grave was completely refilled, the tall man stepped to the center of it and reached both hands under his long, leather coat. Jack heard the metallic rip of a parting zipper. Feet planted wide, the man began to urinate, the heavy stream splashing noisily onto the grave. Rezipping himself, he stretched his arms high over his head and let out a loud yawn. "Come, my children," he said, turning to his followers. "Let us leave Sleeping Beauty to enjoy her bridal night in peace."

Suddenly he paused, head cocked to one side, right hand raised high, as though to say, Listen.

In the early morning stillness, a faint, smothered cry, like the keening of a lost soul, seemed to drift from the ground beneath his feet.

The tall man drew back his head and barked out a savage laugh.

Abruptly, the picture went dead, dissolving into a buzzing storm of static.

Someone reached forward and switched off the TV. The overhead lights snapped on. Jack looked around him dully. He felt a profound sense of unreality, as though his pain-deadened soul had detached itself from the frozen shell of his body and had drifted off to another dimension. He seemed to be observing the roomful of stunned, silent men from somewhere far, far away.

274

One of the younger cops jumped from his chair, sending it clattering to the floor. He rushed from the room, face drained of color, Adam's apple bobbing spasmodically, as though he were going to be sick. His frantic departure seemed to act as a detonator. All at once the room exploded in a din of curses, cries, shouts for action.

Dick Wayland ran to the front of the room, hands raised high, pleading, "Come on! Come on! We need some ideas!"

Jack turned his gaze on a dark-haired cop with a moustache, who was calling out, "The motherfucker doesn't show you anything. A few trees, some fucking headstones—"

"No, wait!" It was one of the late arrivals, the man Wayland had called Greg, a thin cop with nervous hands. "I think maybe I recognized something. But I need to look at the tape again."

"How the fuck can you tell anything from that tape?" the moustached cop demanded.

"Shut up, Mike," Wayland said. Then, facing Greg again, he asked, "Want to see the whole thing?"

"No, no. Just the part where you first see the graveyard."

Wayland rewound the tape to the beginning, then searched until Greg called out, "There!"

Wayland hit the pause button while Greg leaned forward in his chair, squinting.

Wayland watched his face intently. "Well?" he said after a long moment.

Greg's head began to nod, slowly at first, then hard and emphatically. "Yeah," he exclaimed. "That's it. I'm almost positive."

"How do you know?"

"Ellen and I were there in the fall. She's taking a course, a drawing course at Mercy. She had this assignment to sketch something in the country. We went walking down this road and we stumbled across an old graveyard. Ellen wanted to go in. It's about half an hour north and then over east a ways. Close to the Connecticut border up 322, off a road called Broad Bottom. You can't forget that."

"You sure?" Wayland asked.

"Definitely," Greg said. "Look." He pointed at the

screen. Every eye in the room focused on the spot he was indicating. There, lying half buried in the snow, was a small, gray object that looked like a little stone bed.

"What is it?" asked Lyle Kimball.

"A baby's grave. The headstone is shaped like a cradle with the blankets all rumpled and pulled back, like the kid was snatched away during the night. That's what Ellen picked to draw. She got so teary-eyed over it, she almost couldn't—"

Before he was finished, the room surged into motion, the seated cops leaping to their feet, others heading for the door.

"Cosgrove, get on the horn to the nearest station up there," Wayland barked. "Then notify the troopers and EMS. We'll need an ambulance and paramedics. A doctor too. Tommy, grab some shovels from the supply room." He slapped Greg on the shoulder. "Good job, kid. Let's get going." He turned toward Jack, who was still sitting frozen in his chair.

"Jack—" Wayland began.

Jack looked up at him dully. "The tape," he said in a choked voice. "What time . . . ?" He was having trouble breathing, as if he too were surrounded by a suffocating blackness.

Wayland crouched by Jack's chair. "It had to've been dropped off here around six-thirty. If Nugent's right, that means it was probably around six when Marianne was . . ." He left the sentence uncompleted. He couldn't say the words.

Jack's gaze drifted to the wall clock. "Two hours," he said. "And another twenty before you get up there. Assuming Nugent's right."

Wayland put a hand on Jack's leg. "There's got to be some air in there. It's not vacuum-sealed. If she's breathing shallowly, maybe . . ."

The two men exchanged a long stare. Then Wayland said firmly, "Jack, every minute—"

Wayland's words hit Jack like an electric jolt. His deadened heart surged to life as if it had been jump-started.

"You're right." Shoving himself from his chair, he reached out a hand to Wayland and pulled him to his feet. "Let's go get my daughter."

276

46

SIREN SCREAMING, ROOF LIGHTS FLASHING, WAYLAND'S cruiser hurtled up Highway 684 under a pale sun that peered blindly through the scuttling clouds. The rest of the caravan followed close behind, three more squad cars with a wailing ambulance bringing up the rear.

Wayland drove. Seated beside him in the passenger seat, Jack kept his eyes fixed straight ahead, his ears tuned to the exchange going on behind him. Greg Nugent and Mike Holson were squabbling in the backseat. Their voices were heated but low.

"Fuck you, Mike," Nugent said angrily. "I already told you I was sure. What do you want me to do? Sign a fucking affidavit?"

"You've never been sure of a goddamned thing in your life," Holson muttered. *"Shit!* This is a mistake. If you're wrong, we're gonna lose her."

"Keep a lid on it, Mike," Wayland growled. Turning the wheel sharply, he swerved north onto 322, then looked over at Jack apologetically. "Holson was real close to Marianne. They were buddies."

Jack twisted around in his seat to look at the moustached young officer, who met his gaze briefly, then turned away. His face looked tense and surly.

They missed Broad Bottom Road the first time and had to retrace their route. Jack glanced anxiously at the dashboard clock. They had lost nearly four minutes. Terror chewed at his heart and he realized with some surprise that he'd been praying all along. *Please God, please God, let her be alive.*

Wayland hung a sharp left onto the narrow, unpaved road, the squad car rattling like a jalopy as it jounced uphill through the barren woods. Fresh tire tracks rutted the snow straight ahead of them.

Nugent leaned forward. "It's about three-quarters of a mile on the left. You'll see a big old oak. There!"

A pair of patrol cars from the Town of Whitfield P.D.

277

were parked at the base of an enormous tree. Jack could see that the local cops had only just arrived. They were huddled over their open car trunks, passing around shovels and picks.

Wayland cut his siren and slid his cruiser beside the two patrol cars. Behind him the other vehicles braked to a stop up and down the hill.

Jack was out the door before Wayland's car had stopped moving. "Pop the trunk!" he called over his shoulder. Grabbing a shovel, he turned to Nugent, who was still half in, half out of the car. "Where?" Jack rasped, then followed Greg's pointing finger.

He ran over the crusted snow. Straight ahead, on the crest of the hill, he saw the low, crumbling wall and, directly beyond it, the little field of gray headstones.

He hurried through the gateway and stopped dead. There were footprints here, lots of them. Heart hammering, he began to scan the little graveyard for landmarks. Behind him he heard the echoing shouts of the others. "This way!" "Move it!" Wayland, hampered by his big belly and a chestful of cigarette sludge, was puffing his way up the road behind the two paramedics.

Holson suddenly materialized beside Jack. "Wait for the others," he said.

Jack shook his head. "It's got to be right near here," he said, nodding toward the dead, gnarled tree he recognized from the tape. He looked around frantically. Then froze.

Thirty feet away, in an area of heavily trampled snow, lay a plot of raw earth, a weatherworn tombstone sticking up from one end like a granite tongue.

Sprinting across the snow, Jack tore off his topcoat, flung it over the headstone, and set to work with his shovel on the freshly dug grave. Within seconds three other men— Nugent, Stew Markowitz, and Roy Auslander—were digging beside him. The rest of the cops fanned out across the cemetery, scouring the ground for clues. Wayland shouted directions, while the paramedics, crouching by the stretcher, readied their equipment.

Wayland thought he recognized one of the paramedics, a grim-faced black man with a linebacker's physique. It took him a few seconds to identify the man. It was Camp-

278

bell, the paramedic who had been at the Prince house the night the baby was stolen. Gazing down at him, Wayland couldn't believe how faraway that evening seemed. The kidnapping had occurred just two months before, almost to the day. But for Wayland it seemed to belong to the distant past, marking the exact point in his life where the world had changed forever, from a place of daylight and stability to an ever-darkening nightmare.

"Campbell," Wayland called down to the paramedic. "Where's the doctor?"

"Should be here any sec," Campbell answered, looking up over his shoulder. "Got a man coming up from Westchester Medical Center."

Wayland nodded. The icy air was making his nose leak badly. Wiping it with the back of a leather-gloved hand, he turned his attention to the diggers.

In spite of the cold, they were already sweating heavily, particularly Jack, who was going at the ground like a man possessed. His breaths were emerging in loud wheezes. Five cops stood by the graveside, ready to relieve the workers at the first signs of strain.

"Jack," Wayland called down. "Let someone else take over." At the rate Byrne was going, Wayland was afraid he might keel over any minute.

Jack paused, chest heaving. It seemed to take him a second to understand what Wayland was saying. Then, nodding, he passed his shovel up to a broad-shouldered young cop, who immediately leapt into the deepening hole as Wayland reached down a hand and hauled Jack up to the surface.

On the far side of the stone wall a half-dozen men and women had already gathered in a cluster. They were craning to see around Tommy Reardon and Sam Ferris, who were holding up their hands to keep the little crowd back. Wayland marveled at how quickly the curiosity-seekers had appeared, way out there in the middle of nowhere. It must have been the sirens that brought them running, he thought bitterly, the way a whiff of fresh carrion draws vultures.

The loosely packed earth came up quickly. Just fifteen minutes after the first bladeful of dirt had been shoveled from the grave, Roy Auslander's spade struck the top of the coffin. A few minutes more and the lid was completely exposed.

"Give me a crowbar or something!" Auslander called up to the huddled crowd at the graveside.

Someone produced a twelve-inch pry bar and tossed it down to Auslander.

Jack dropped to his knees and bent over edge of the grave, straining to see around the men kneeling on the coffin lid. He could hear a metallic scraping as Auslander worked the pry bar under the slats of the coffin lid, then the soft splintering of old wood.

"She's in here!" Auslander called.

"Is she alive?" Holson called from somewhere behind Jack.

"I can't tell."

"Get her out!" Wayland cried. "Get her out!"

Jack rose to his feet, holding out his arms as his daughter's white, naked body was lifted out of the grave. Cradling her under her waist, he helped lay her gently on a heavy blanket that had been spread out on the snow. "Move aside, move aside," shouted Campbell, shoving through the crowd and covering Marianne's body with another blanket. At the same moment, his partner stepped forward with a medical bag and knelt by the body.

Jack, his heartbeat galloping, stared intently at his daughter's face. Her lips were blue and slightly parted, her eyes shut tight. Her hair seemed strangely white, as if it were frosted with snow. Jack bit down hard on his own lower lip, which had begun to tremble badly. He had never seen anyone who looked deader.

At that moment his heart gave a sudden leap. He had seen his daughter's shoulder move slightly! But no. It was only a motion caused by the young paramedic as he wrapped the band of his blood-pressure gauge around Marianne's limp right arm.

Jack gazed around him and saw the confirmation of his own worst fears in the stricken faces of the others. Beyond them, at the entrance to the little cemetery, he glimpsed a slender man in a long, tweed coat hurrying forward, something clutched on one hand.

Jack squeezed his eyes tight and prayed more desperately than he'd ever prayed in his life. When he opened them again, the paramedic was staring up at him, beginning to speak, and Jack, looking down into the young man's face, knew what he was going to say. Sinking to his knees, he threw back his head and opened his mouth wide, a howl boiling out of him as the paramedic made his pronouncement.

"I'm sorry, Mr. Byrne. She's dead."

Part Three

Demoniac

47

SEATED AT HIS FORMICA-TOPPED KITCHEN TABLE, JACK
Byrne took a hesitant bite of his turkey-on-rye and forced it
down his gullet with a swig of scalding Lipton tea. Doctor's
orders, he thought grimly. He had lost twenty pounds in
the past few months, and Herb Woolf, his family physician
and old friend, had started issuing stern warnings.

"You're wasting away, Jack," Herb had said recently.
"What the hell are you running on, thin air?"

Jack knew the answer. He was running on rage, his heart
fueled by a hatred so fiery that he half expected flames to
spew from his throat whenever he opened his mouth to
speak. But he didn't want to waste away, not yet, anyway.
Not until he had wasted Simon Proctor, body and soul.

He finished his sandwich while leafing through the morning's *Daily News*. A six-year-old Brooklyn girl had been
gunned down in front of her tenement when rival crack
dealers exchanged blasts from their automatic weapons. In
lower Manhattan a nineteen-year-old coed had been raped,
mutilated with a hunting knife, and thrown to her death
from a rooftop. And then there was the headline story—
PRIEST SLAIN IN CHURCH HOLDUP.

Jack sipped the last of his heavily sugared tea and shook
his head in disgust. Just your average March day in the
city of the damned, he thought. Pushing himself away from
the table, he carried his cup to the sink, rinsed it, and stuck
it in the empty dish drain. On the wall above the sink hung
last year's calendar, a giveaway from the neighborhood dry
cleaners. It was still opened to December. The full-color
illustration showed a picture-perfect, Norman Rockwell
family gathered around a twinkling Christmas tree. Reaching up, Jack tore the calendar from the wall and tossed it
into the empty garbage can under the sink. Then he turned
off the overhead light and headed down the hallway.

The house seemed ghostly, inhabited by nothing but shadows. Jack had spent little time there in the three months
since that unspeakable morning at the graveyard. Mostly,

he'd been living at Marianne's empty apartment, making it his headquarters. Every week or two he would drive back down to Queens to make sure his house was still standing and to pick up a few things.

What he was looking for now was down in his office. Switching on the stairway light, he descended into the basement. The big, unheated room, full of books, magazines, and cartons of mimeographed pamphlets, was musty with the smell of mildewing paper. Jack headed directly for a locked, two-drawer file cabinet in the far corner of the room.

Pulling his key ring from his pocket, he crouched before the cabinet, unlocked the bottom drawer and slid it out. It was empty except for a single object—a small, velvet-wrapped bundle, bound around the middle with a black-satin ribbon. Reaching into the drawer, he lifted out the little bundle, undid the ribbon, and carefully parted the purple velvet.

Inside lay an antique straight razor, its heavy silver handle ornamented with occult markings—a crescent moon, a coiled serpent, a cluster of five-pointed stars. Jack stared down at the folded razor for a long moment, then wrapped it back up in its velvet covering, retied the ribbon, and headed upstairs, shutting the lights off behind him.

Back in his living room, he checked his watch: 12:47 P.M. Visiting hours began at two. It was time for him to go.

He was just slipping into his overcoat—the velvet-wrapped razor stowed carefully in a side pocket—when the phone began to ring. The sound echoed hollowly in the deadness of the house. He walked back to the kitchen and lifted the handset from the wall near the dishwasher. "Yeah?"

"Jack?" It was Dick Wayland. "I thought you might be there. You coming up this afternoon?"

"What else? I just drove down to check on the house."

"Everything okay?"

Jack gazed out at the enveloping gloom. "Oh, yeah. Just great."

Wayland cleared his throat, then made a hawking noise, as if he were coughing up into a hankie. "Sorry. Can't seem to shake this fucking cold. So when am I going to see you?"

286

"I'm heading up now. I was figuring on dropping by around four."

"I'll be here."

A few minutes later Jack was backing his car out of the driveway. He switched on the radio and punched the "scan" button, stopping when he heard the voice of Lena Horne, his favorite singer. He had hit on a whole program of her music. For a while her singing calmed him. But as he headed northward, his mind replaying for the thousandth time the events of the last three, nightmarish months, the music lost its hold on his heart. Rage blazed up inside him like hellfire.

Ten days after Marianne's frozen body had been pulled from the earth, Jack had sat facing Wayland across the chief's big, cluttered desk. The sacks under Wayland's eyes had a bluish tinge, as if covered by eye shadow. He looked like a man who had lain awake every night for a week, staring into the darkness. Jack knew that look very well; he saw it every time he glanced at himself in a mirror.

"So?" Jack had said quietly to Wayland.

"So what?" Wayland answered, stubbing out another cigarette. He had already sucked down two since Jack's arrival fifteen minutes earlier.

"So are you going to help me?"

Wayland fixed Jack with a hard stare. "Officially, I can't condone any of this," he had said sternly. "You're not a cop anymore, Jack."

Very deliberately, Jack leaned back in his chair, placed his interlaced hands behind his neck and regarded Wayland through narrowed eyes. "Tell me this," he said softly. "You're a family man. Father of a grown daughter. What would you do in my place?"

"What would I do?" Wayland chewed on the insides of his cheeks for a while before answering. "I'd do everything I could to get my hands on that bastard," he finally said. "Then I'd cut out his heart with a fucking kitchen knife and feed it to my dog for supper."

"Good," Jack said, sitting up straight in his chair. "So tell me what you've got." He smiled grimly. "Off the record."

There wasn't much to tell. So far, the investigation had

287

gone nowhere. A dozen detectives, some assigned from Grasslands, were working full-time on the case, running down rumors, following up on tips, trying to pick up the scent of Simon Proctor's stone-cold trail. But every lead had steered them to another dead end.

Jack had listened silently, then thanked Wayland, who promised to keep him informed of any developments.

Then Jack had driven up to his daughter's darkened apartment.

It was the first time that he had allowed himself to enter it since their lives—his as well as hers—were destroyed. Just a glimpse of her meager belongings—her thrift-shop furniture and closet hung with simple clothes—brought his despair crashing down on him like a great, black wave. Seated on the edge of her rumpled bed, he had buried his face in his hands and given himself over to grief. After a long while, he had finally gotten hold of himself. Hauling himself from the mattress, he had set about searching the apartment for clues.

In the bottom dresser of her bedroom bureau, he had discovered a small wooden box with a pentagram etched on its lid. Inside were a wolf's-head amulet on a golden chain, a vial of brownish liquid, a pair of ivory figurines locked in an obscene embrace, and a parchment scrap inscribed with a ritual formula.

He found her yellow legal pad tucked away in the drawer of her night table and immediately began poring over it. At three A.M. he was seated at her kitchen table, still mulling over the significance of Marianne's scrawled notes, when exhaustion overtook him. Laying his head down on his folded arms, he fell into a fitful sleep.

He was already wide awake at seven when the call came in from Wayland.

"How soon can you get here? I think we may have a break. Not a big one, but something."

Half an hour later, Jack strode into Wayland's office and heard the news. Jerry Waller, a teacher at the local elementary school, had shown up at the station house at 6:45 that morning, so agitated that he was nearly hyperventilating. Waller hadn't known anything about the tragedy until the day before. He'd been vacationing in England for the previous two weeks and had only heard about the tragedy when he got back. He'd been up half the night, horror-struck at the news.

Waller then repeated the information he had passed along to Marianne—the business about Kevin Peterson and the Dutch-sounding name he had learned from the boy.

Jack waited until Dick had given him the whole rundown before responding. Wayland was right. It wasn't much, but it was their most solid lead so far.

Wayland had immediately assigned five of his men to tracking down the name Waller had given them. For the next few weeks they contacted scores of real estate agents within a hundred-mile radius of Stoneham.

In the meantime, Jack paid an unofficial visit to Kevin Peterson's mother. He got nothing from the brittle-looking blonde except a brazen once-over and permission to search her son's bedroom. The room revealed nothing either. But Kevin's little brother had. The spiky-haired nine-year-old told Jack about the secret hiding place in his dead brother's bureau and the "creepy thing" Marianne had found hidden inside. That cleared up one mystery, anyway—the source of the sinister little treasure box that Jack had turned up in Marianne's dresser.

The mystery of the Dutch name took longer to solve, but the effort finally paid off. In the second week of February, Wayland's team managed to locate the old Vanderdam residence.

The raid took place on a gray Wednesday morning. Jack accompanied Wayland and a dozen, heavily armed officers to the dark old house in Dutchess County. Even before they broke open the front door and spilled inside, pistols and assault rifles at the ready, they knew they would find nothing. The house had been abandoned. Except for the kitchen equipment—a few appliances, some drawers full of cutlery, and a cabinet stacked with department-store china—it had been completely stripped of its furnishings and decor.

Wayland's men spent the next few hours lifting prints and doggedly gathering bits of physical evidence: blood and hair samples, fragments of fabric, even some scraps of human tissue. Most of this material came from the cavernous black room on the main floor. The room smelled faintly but foully. "Jesus Christ," Greg Nugent had hissed, holding his nose in disgust. "What's that stink?"

"Smells like something died in here," Roy Auslander muttered.

"This is the place, all right," Jack said, so softly he might have been speaking to himself. "This is Proctor's lair." Lost in thought, he didn't notice Dick Wayland's eyes on him. Jack knew the smell. It had fouled his nostrils before, in another stinking den he had stumbled upon five years earlier, a place of unspeakable worship where he'd first come face to face with true evil.

Their efforts to trace the owners of the Vanderdam house, officially listed as the Xerrot Corp., had been unavailing. It had taken weeks to extract from Swiss banking authorities the names of the officers of the small organization, whose assets consisted largely of the house in Dutchess County and the hundred acres surrounding it, all worth a little under one million dollars. There were four officers in Xerrot—a German, a South African, a Belgian, and a Taiwanese. Weird conglomeration, Jack had reflected, his suspicions aroused.

Those suspicions were confirmed a few days later when Wayland called with the latest bad news: the South African had never existed and the German was a former Luftwaffe officer who had been dead for the last forty years. Investigators hadn't turned up anything on the other two names yet, but they assumed that this pair was just as phony.

Wayland was so frustrated he was almost spitting, but Jack was unsurprised. He'd discovered that the organization was a black joke just the evening before. He'd been settled on Marianne's sofa, staring at his notes in the warm light of her ginger-jar table lamp. At the top of the page, he had printed the name of the company in big block letters. Suddenly, he let out a curse. He knew that occultists were fond of backward spelling. Why hadn't he seen it earlier?

XERROT CORP

PROC TORREX

290

Proctor Rex. Proctor the King. I bet the fucker had fun dreaming that one up, he thought bitterly, fighting back the impulse to rip the notebook page to shreds.

Jack had pursued other leads. In late February he called on David Prince. He knew that Anna Prince had suspected Simon Proctor of engineering her baby's abduction. Perhaps her husband might have something useful to say. But Jack's knock had been answered by a sleepy-eyed Filipino housemaid who informed him apologetically that Mr. Prince was out of the country on an extended business trip. She couldn't say exactly when he would return.

"Is there some way to reach him overseas?" Jack had asked. "This is urgent."

"I don't know, mister," she had said.

"He didn't leave any telephone numbers or addresses or travel schedule?"

She gave a helpless shrug. "He didn't tell me nothing."

Jack had walked away, shaking his head. Wayland had told him that Prince had farflung business interests. There was no way of telling when the man might return.

Jack had also spent some time trying to track down the girls in the dirty Polaroids Marianne had found in Kevin Peterson's bedroom, on the chance that they might be members of the cult. But that line of inquiry had also led nowhere. Evidently, the girls weren't from Stoneham. So far, no one in the surrounding towns had identified them either.

He *had* found out one interesting fact. When he'd made a trip to Stoneham High School to question Kevin Peterson's teachers about the boy, Jack had been told again and again that Kevin didn't seem to have any friends. "He was a real loner," Bill Perlin, Kevin's science teacher, had said. "He was troubled too. You could see that. And it was getting worse. He wouldn't talk to anybody about it. I tried myself a number of times."

And then Perlin had added something that caused Jack's ears to prick up. The only person he had ever seen Kevin deep in conversation with was a pretty, junior girl with long, blond hair who'd been caught up in some bad business herself at the start of the school year.

Rachel Peary.

Jack, of course, knew the name very well. Marianne had

mentioned the Princes' former babysitter on several occasions, and he'd come upon an entire page of notes devoted to the girl in Marianne's legal pad.

That would be his next step, Jack had decided—questioning Rachel Peary. As his car approached the exit on the Sprain Brook Parkway, the final strains of "Stormy Weather" fading into silence, he resolved that he would visit her tomorrow.

Jack flicked the lever of his turn signal and exited, heading for the Westchester Medical Center. Four minutes later he was maneuvering his car into a vacant space in the visitors' lot. As always, he lingered a moment before opening the door, fighting down the feelings of hopelessness and dread that arose in him every time at the mere sight of the hospital.

Sucking in a deep breath, he stepped outside. The white building towered before him as bleak as a glacier in the sharp winter sun. It was colder up here in Westchester, and the needle-sharp wind stung his face as he hurried across the parking lot and into the main entrance. He nodded to the uniformed guard seated at the information desk. Jack knew the man well by now. Striding into a waiting elevator, he punched the button for the fifth floor. The elevator carried him swiftly up.

In the Intensive Care Unit, there were no visitors, only nurses and doctors, an orderly pushing a cart full of tinkling, sterilized bottles. The hospital odor—an offensive mixture of soiled linen and disinfectant—hit Jack like a blast from a nasal inhaler. Dr. Hecht came hurrying by.

"Hello, Doctor," Jack said, trying to stretch his mouth into a smile.

"Catch you later, Mr. Byrne," the young doctor said. "Got an emergency."

Jack nodded at the nurses seated behind their semicircular counter. Then, steadying himself with another deep breath, he walked into Room 517, just a few yards away from the nurses' station.

There was never any change. She lay motionless in bed, her hollow eyes closed, her fragile heartbeat registering on the monitor above her. Gray-haired and so gaunt that her skull showed through her face, she looked like a wizened old woman, kept alive by an IV hookup and a feeding tube stuck up her nose.

Removing his overcoat and laying it carefully across the foot of her bed, he pulled up a molded plastic chair and, as he did every day, took her limp right hand gently into both of his own. Then, leaning close to the comatose woman, he began to whisper softly in her ear.

"It's me, baby. Daddy. Can you hear me, Marianne?"

48

WHEN NEW ACQUAINTANCES ASKED DR. STUART HECHT, AS they occasionally did, what in the world had impelled him to do his residency in Anchorage, he sometimes answered, only half jokingly, that he had been inspired by the 1960 Duke Wayne movie, *North to Alaska*. He still knew every word of Johnny Horton's rousing title song by heart. Certainly, that rip-roaring adventure film had worked a spell on the imagination of the thirteen-year-old city boy who, for months afterward, had fallen asleep every night in his family's cramped Brooklyn apartment fantasizing about the glorious vastness of America's last real frontier. And so, as soon as the opportunity presented itself, he had headed off for the north country to live out his wilderness dreams.

The reality had turned out to be a good deal less romantic than the fantasy. The beauties of the landscape had never failed to elate him. But he had also seen nature's brutality firsthand—in the blue and bloated faces of the drowned, the mauled limbs of hunters, the shattered corpses of climbers who had missed a toehold on the rock. After four years in Alaska, he had returned to New York with a feeling for nature's power that bordered on awe. And he had brought back something else too. Dr. Stuart Hecht had become an expert on the effects of extreme cold on human physiology.

During his stint in the Emergency Room at Anchorage General, hardly a week went by when he wasn't confronted with at least one case of accidental hypothermia, usually suffered by a newcomer to the state who had underestimated the savagery of the Alaskan cold. Always a conscientious student, Dr. Hecht had sought out every available book and article on the subject of hypothermia. Some of the more dramatic cases he had read about seemed almost miraculous.

Throughout the 1970s and '80s, British and American medical journals reported on remarkable instances of men, women, and children who had been brought back to life after being frozen—apparently to death—by prolonged exposure to the cold. In 1979 a forty-two-year-old electrotechnician, skiing in the Swiss Alps, was caught by an avalanche and buried for over five hours under seven meters of snow and ice. A few years later another Alpine skier, a twenty-four-year-old registered nurse, plunged into a deep crevasse and lay immersed in frigid water for several hours. One of the most astonishing cases of all occurred on June 10, 1982, when a two-and-a-half-year-old girl toppled into a creek near Salt Lake City. Late spring runoffs from a heavy mountain snowpack had lowered the water temperature to under five degrees centigrade. The child's submerged body was not discovered until sixty-six minutes after she disappeared into the creek.

And in another tragedy, a nineteen-year-old woman was raped, beaten unconscious, and left to die of exposure in a stretch of frozen woodland, her nude body half buried in the snow.

In all of these cases, the victims showed no vital signs when rescuers finally recovered their bodies—no respiration, audible heartbeats, or detectable pulse. Their muscles had stiffened to the hardness of rigor mortis. Their pupils were fixed and dilated. Their body temperatures had dropped below twenty degrees centigrade. From all available evidence, they appeared to be dead.

In reality, however, the cold had not killed them. On the contrary, it had helped to preserve them by plunging them into a kind of suspended animation. Through the use of modern-day medical procedures—peritoneal dialysis, irrigation of the chest cavity with warm fluids, extracorporeal circulation by means of a heart-lung machine—each of them was restored not only to life but to fully normal functioning.

In 198′ Dr. Hecht had a chance to put his theoretical knowledge of hypothermia into practice as part of a team that worked to save the life of a local sportsman who had plunged into a mountain lake during an ice-fishing expedition. When the man was wheeled into the operating room, he was clinically dead—without a pulse, limbs flaccid, pupils fixed, and a rectal temperature of nineteen degrees centigrade. The head surgeon, Dr. William Thomas, gave a little gasp of surprise when he opened the man's chest and laid a finger on the dead-still heart. It had been frozen as hard as a rock. Continuous bathing of the chest cavity was begun at once with a warm saline solution.

One and a half hours later, the patient's core temperature had been raised to thirty-six degrees and his softened heart was successfully defibrillated. When he was discharged from the hospital, fourteen days after he'd fallen through the ice, he had made such an astonishingly complete recovery that he might have been going home after a routine appendectomy. It would have been hard for anyone who didn't know the truth to believe that, just two weeks before, the man had been clinically dead.

Stuart Hecht would never forget that experience. And he would never forget what Dr. Thomas had said to him as they'd walked away from the operating room, exhausted but elated.

"My boy," Dr. Thomas had said, draping an arm around Stuart's shoulder. "You've just witnessed the confirmation of an old truism: When it comes to profound hypothermia, there's only one valid criteria for diagnosing death, and that's if the patient doesn't respond to resuscitation. An ice-cold patient, even when he shows not a single sign of life, may not be as dead as he seems. At those kinds of temperatures, clinical death isn't synonymous with biological death. In other words, Stuart—don't assume a person is dead unless he's *warm* and dead."

Dr. Thomas's axiom had remained etched in Stuart Hecht's memory. And so it happened that, when the call came in to Westchester Medical Center about a young police officer who had been buried in frozen ground, Dr. Hecht had hurried up to the crime scene primed and ready for the emergency, as though his long years of training had been preparation for precisely this moment.

He had arrived just as the paramedic was pronouncing Marianne Byrne dead, but he'd needed only a quick check of the young woman's condition to see that she still stood a chance. Packed into the frozen ground, the simple pine coffin had turned into an icebox. In effect, Marianne's body had been refrigerated.

The doctor began external cardiac massage during the breakneck ambulance ride back down to the hospital. In the operating room Marianne was immediately linked to a heart-lung machine, which began to warm and recirculate her blood.

Less than an hour after the procedure was begun, Dr. Hecht walked into the jammed waiting room. It was fogged with cigarette smoke from the crowd of rumpled-looking cops and newsmen, who stood around in clusters of three or four sipping coffee from styrofoam cups and talking in tense, hushed whispers. As the men fell silent, Dr. Hecht approached Marianne's father, who sat slumped in a chair, his face a pale mask of despair. The stillness in the room was so complete that when Dr. Hecht quietly delivered his news, his words rang out as if he'd spoken them over a bullhorn.

"Mr. Byrne," he had said. "Marianne's heart has responded to defibrillation. It's beating again. Your daughter is alive."

The other men, even a few of the reporters, broke out into joyful whoops. Some of the cops pounded their fellows on the back, while others exchanged bearlike hugs. Marianne's father was too overcome to speak. Red eyes brimming, he rose slowly to his feet and embraced Stuart Hecht as though the young doctor were his long-lost son. Hecht felt his own heart leap with a triumphant joy. Gazing into Jack Byrne's face, he saw the most profound look of gratitude he ever expected to be blessed with in his life.

But that had been almost three months ago. Now, sitting in his office on this raw March day, Dr. Hecht felt a terrible weariness descend on him. It was a feeling that had grown depressingly familiar over the past several weeks. The exultation of that unforgettable morning had gradually given way to a sense of helplessness and defeat. Removing his wire-frame glasses, Dr. Hecht pinched the bridge of his nose and squeezed his tired eyes tight.

Something had gone wrong with Marianne Byrne's recovery.

In every case he had studied, patients who had been

resuscitated from states of extreme hypothermia had made complete and dramatic recoveries, regaining full use of their physical and mental capabilities. But, though Marianne Bryne was alive—heart beating, blood flowing, lungs drawing in and exhaling air without the aid of a respirator—she had never awakened from her deathlike slumber. She remained submerged in a deep coma.

Dr. Hecht didn't know how to account for her condition. Perhaps she had been sent into profound shock by the sheer horror of her experience, a trauma so severe that her black hair had turned streaky white. Dr. Hecht had been permitted to view the unspeakable tape of her living interment and had found parts of it impossible to watch.

Or perhaps the young police officer had suffered some indeterminate neurological damage during her hellish night in the clutches of the devil cult.

Whatever the reason, the young woman had remained completely unresponsive to the outer world since the morning she had been pulled from her frozen grave. First days, then weeks, and now months had gone by, but still she showed no signs of consciousness. With every passing hour, the chances that she would make a full recovery grew slimmer. Spring would be here soon, the season of rebirth, and Dr. Hecht prayed that Marianne would return to the world of the living. But he was beginning to doubt that she ever would.

Indeed, he had started to wonder whether, by restoring her to a state that was neither life nor death but some shadowy zone in between, he had done her, or her father, a kindness after all.

49

LATER THAT NIGHT, A HUNDRED MILES NORTH OF THE DARKened hospital room where Marianne Byrne lay sunk in perpetual sleep, Simon Proctor stepped off the porch of his new, country hideaway and walked out into the moonlit front yard. An icy gust buffeted him as he made his way toward the hulking shadow of the barn, but he reveled in the rawness of the wind, inhaling it deeply, as though it were the living breath of night.

He had come outside to cool down the fury that was boiling up inside him. The light from the unshuttered windows behind him fell in yellow patchwork on the ground. Out here there was no need to block off the windows. The farmstead—one of several upstate properties owned by his son—was surrounded by more than two hundred wooded acres. It was even more remote than the place he had been forced to abandon.

As always, the darkness soothed him, and his anger ebbed to a less dangerous level. Inside the house, several of his followers lay entangled on the rug before the crackling fire. Others were diverting themselves on the cushions and sofas. Mike Holson was one of them. It was the sight of Holson, seated naked on a sofa, mouth hanging slack in an expression of stuporous pleasure while the dark-haired girl, Sammi, buried her face between his legs, that had caused Proctor's rage to soar. Only by the greatest effort had he resisted the impulse to step up behind Holson with a razor blade, open his throat, and watch the man's blood spurt to the rhythm of his orgasm.

Simon had fought back the temptation by reminding himself that the big cop was no good to him dead. He still had important uses for Officer Holson.

Simon hadn't been happy about dismantling his sanctuary and moving away from Vanderdam. He recognized the necessity, but he resented it and held Holson largely to blame. Holson should never have allowed the meddling Byrne bitch to get so close to their clan. True, Simon had been delighted to play host to the young woman. He still looked back on that long night of pleasure with deep satisfaction. He even felt a strange satisfaction in having been driven north by his enemies. History repeats itself, he thought, his mind floating back to the far-distant past, to another lifetime, long, long years ago.

Still, Holson had fucked up. He had better not do so again.

By the time Simon reached the barn, he felt much better. Moonlight flooding through the open doors and windows shone on the cavernous interior, still redolent of the animals who had once lived there. Simon nodded in satisfaction. It would do well for a new chapel.

Simon heard a frantic scrabbling on the floorboards. As he stood there, squinting into the shadows, a small animal darted out of the barn and dashed between his feet. With surprising swiftness for a man of his size, Simon stooped and grabbed the creature by the scruff of the neck. Lifting it, he saw that it was a small cat—or rather, a half-grown kitten. A gray tabby. Simon had seen the animal before, stalking field mice and sparrows in the withered grass around the barn.

Simon lowered the cat into the crook of his arm and reached down to stroke the animal's head. As he did, the cat lifted a paw and swiped at his thumb. Simon put his thumb between his lips and tasted blood. Smiling, he regarded the cat speculatively. In the white moonglow, the cat's eyes seemed to glint with insolence.

Inside the old stone farmhouse, Holson squeezed his eyes shut and let out a deep, fluttering groan as his fluids squirted into the kneeling girl's throat. When he looked up again, Simon Proctor was looming in the doorway, cradling something in his arms. Sitting up straight on the couch, Holson saw that it was a small cat, mewling plaintively in Proctor's grip.

Patting her mouth daintily in a parody of tea-party etiquette, the big-breasted girl rose to her feet and approached Simon.

"Here," said Simon, holding out the cat. "A pet."

Sammi took the cat from Simon and cradled it under her naked breasts. Suddenly, she grimaced. "What's wrong with its eyes?" she asked, staring down in disgust. A trickle of fluid, like egg white streaked with blood, ran from the cat's tight-squeezed lids.

"It lost them in the barn," Simon answered. "Poor thing."

Sammi dropped the cat as though it carried a communicable disease. The animal slunk across the floor, colliding with a table leg, then crawled into a dark corner, where it continued to mew piteously.

"Maybe it can go hunting for the three blind mice," one

299

of the naked young men by the fireplace said. The others laughed softly.

"Yes." Simon smiled. "Very good." Then his smile vanished. Turning to Holson, he crooked an index finger at him. "Come with me," he said softly. "We need to talk."

Holson got to his feet, grabbing his jeans and denim shirt from the floor. Pulling them on hurriedly, he followed Simon up the creaking stairs.

By the time he reached the landing, Simon had disappeared into one of the darkened rooms that lined the long, narrow corridor. Suddenly, an orange glow flared to life from inside the farthest room.

Holson walked down the hallway and entered the room, ducking his head as he passed under the lintel. Simon stood in one corner, holding a pewter candlestick and motioning toward a three-legged stool. Behind him the black glass of the window shone with reflected candle glow.

"Sit," Simon ordered.

Holson stepped across the wide, low-ceilinged room and seated himself on the stool. Though he'd never been inside it, he knew that this was Simon's bedroom. It was as stark as a monk's cell and devoid of all furnishings except for an old-fashioned bed shoved against the opposite wall. The bed was enveloped in shadow, but Holson thought he could make out someone lying on it, back propped up against the headboard. He looked up at Simon questioningly.

Slowly, Simon walked over to the bedside and lowered the flickering candle toward the prostrate figure. Holson's eyes widened slightly. On the left side of the rumpled double bed lay a shriveled female corpse, its wiry gray hair spread across the pillow. Holson realized at once that it was the body whose place in the grave Marianne had taken. The corpse's white gown had been stripped off, and the skeletal thing lay completely exposed. Most of its flesh was gone—Holson could see its backbone disappearing into the black cavity of its rib cage, though here and there some desiccated skin still clung to its skull, limbs, and pelvis. A small tuft of gray hair poked up between its bony legs.

Simon swiveled his head and stared at Holson, the orange candlelight transforming his face into a carnival mask. "This is what I want her to look like."

"Who?" Holson said.

300

"Your colleague. Miss Byrne."

"She's a fucking vegetable, Simon. She can't do us any harm."

"I want her dead," Simon repeated. Gazing back down at the corpse with a strange, dreamy expression, he lowered his free hand between its gnarled legs and held it there for a moment. Then, lifting his fingers to his nose, he asked, "Do you want to fuck it?"

"Jesus, Simon," Holson said, rising quickly to his feet. "All right. I'll take care of it. But it's hard right now. Shit. Her room's only a few feet away from the fucking nurses' station."

"Do it." Simon commanded softly. "Soon."

Holson nodded and headed for the doorway. Before he reached it, Simon stepped around the bed and grabbed at his shirtsleeve. "There's something else."

"What's that?" Holson asked.

"The one who gave Marianne the information about our house."

The schoolteacher? Waller?"

"Yes. The schoolteacher. It's time he was taught something himself."

Holson stared into the indecipherable blackness of Simon's eyes. He hadn't been scared of any man since he was thirteen, but Simon made him very nervous.

"Yeah?" Holson asked. "What?"

"He needs to learn how very dangerous it can be to meddle in other men's business," Simon answered, his lips curling into a smile. "He needs to learn the wisdom of an ancient proverb."

"And what proverb is that?"

"A fool's mouth is his destruction," Simon said slowly. "And his lips are the snare of his soul."

50

JACK FOLLOWED THE MAÎTRE D' ACROSS THE FLOOR OF THE crowded restaurant, threading his way between tables that were occupied mostly by middle-aged men in business suits and parties of smartly dressed women. Toward the rear of the second room, a woman wearing a gray-and-white-checked jacket and gray linen skirt looked up as they approached. She was seated alone. Jack's guide, holding out the chair opposite her, murmured, "Enjoy your lunch."

"Mr. Byrne?" the woman said, holding out her right hand. Jack liked her face. It was sensible and open, more handsome than pretty, with pleasant features and lively, intelligent eyes. "It is *Mister* Byrne, right? Not Detective?"

Jack nodded. "Right. I'm retired. But call me Jack. Thanks for agreeing to see me, Mrs. Peary."

"Jean," she said, smiling. "My pleasure. I'm just sorry you had to do all the driving. It's hard for me to get away from the office for very long."

"You're in real estate?" he said, moving his chair an inch closer to the table.

She made a sound of dry amusement. "Theoretically. These days, I seem to spend most of my time at my desk only daydreaming about clients."

"Hard times ahead."

"They're already here, I'd say." A cloud of concern drifted over her face. "Mr. Byrne, Jack, I can't tell you how sorry I was to hear about your daughter. Is there any improvement?"

"No." He shrugged. "Well, that's not what the doctors say. She opens her eyes a little now. Apparently, there's some kind of activity going on inside her head. They call her condition an alpha coma. Just what she's aware of is anybody's guess. She's still not responding to anything external. But the specialists say they're hoping to get her into a wheelchair soon, maybe even send her home." He was doing his best to sound upbeat, but he couldn't keep the bleakness from his voice.

"And"—she hesitated for a moment before pressing on—"do they think she might get better?"

He shrugged. "God knows. The doctors certainly don't."

A gloomy silence settled over them, which was broken by the timely arrival of the waitress, who handed them menus and recited the specials of the day. When she returned a few minutes later, Jack ordered the veal with mushrooms and Jean the blackened swordfish.

Waiting for their salads, Jean tore off a chunk of her hard roll, smeared the underside with butter and took a bite. Jack, who liked women with healthy appetites, looked on with a smile. Much to his surprise, he caught himself thinking how attractive Jean Peary was, and instantly felt a twinge of guilt. This was the first time since Peggy's death that he'd been out to a restaurant with a woman, and though he'd come there on the hope of contacting Jean's daughter, whom he'd been unable to locate, he felt as though he were committing some vague act of betrayal.

At first their conversation stuck to formal matters, but by the time they were halfway through the meal—and more than halfway through the carafe of house white they were sharing—they were chatting like friends. Jack talked about Peggy and their happy years of marriage. Jean countered with wickedly amusing stories of domestic disasters with ex-husband Bill.

Jack was so unused to feeling good that he was shocked to find himself smiling, laughing, loosening up. True, Marianne was never far from his thoughts, even now. All he had to do was blink and the specter of her ravaged face would float before his eyes. But Jean Peary's company made him feel better than he had in many months.

As though she had sensed his thoughts, Jean turned serious. "I met her once, you know," she said. "Marianne. She came to my house to talk to Rachel."

"Yes," Jack said quietly. "I've read her notes about the meeting."

Jean grimaced. "I don't suppose she had very nice things to say about me. I'm afraid I acted pretty unfriendly."

"She liked you very much," Jack said.

Jean leaned forward, resting her arms on the table. "She

struck me as such a strong, mature young woman. I remember wishing that my own daughter . . ." Her voice trailed off unhappily.

Jack could feel his own sadness return like a relapsing fever. "She is—was—" He swallowed hard. "She's something, all right."

Seeing the pain on Jack's face, Jean reached out and laid her hand on top of his. "I'm sorry."

"No," he said firmly. "No. It's all right. I have to be able to talk about her." He gave his head a quick shake, as though he were trying to throw off his sorrow before it got a stranglehold on him. He looked across the table into Jean's clear blue eyes. "I'm glad you brought up Rachel," he said, his voice turning more businesslike. "You said she's not living at home anymore. Can you tell me where she is, Jean? I need to talk to her."

Jean leaned back and readjusted the linen napkin on her lap. "She's moved in with her boyfriend," she said, her voice taking on a sharp note of bitterness. "She's pregnant. She told me on Christmas."

"I see."

"She was only a month pregnant then, and I kept thinking if I didn't come down too hard on her, if I didn't try to force her into anything, she'd see the light and get an abortion." She made a face that seemed to say, So much for *that* bright idea.

"Who's this guy she's living with?" Jack asked.

"A college boy at the state university. His name's Tim Rutherford. Nice, clean-cut kid. I was ecstatic when she started going out with him." She gave a little snort that conveyed the irony of the situation.

"Sounds pretty bad."

"It's terrible. She's only sixteen and he can't be much older. I think he's just a freshman."

"I'm sorry, Jean."

"Believe me, it gets worse." She took a deep breath. "She's dropped out of school. Stoneham High has been bugging me and bugging me, as if there were something I could do about it. It's terrible," she repeated. "She's ruining her life."

"Where are they living?"

"Franklin. In an apartment near the college. I'm not sure

exactly where. She doesn't even have a telephone. They have no money. She won't let me give her any, and Tim apparently won't accept any from his parents either."

"How do you talk to her if she doesn't have a telephone?"

"She calls me. From pay phones, usually from a laundromat near their apartment. She's pretty good about calling two or three times a week. And she's come by to see me a few times. Once at work. We had a fight. It was a mistake. She didn't call again for almost two weeks." She had become increasingly agitated as she spoke. Rolling the stem of her wineglass back and forth between the fingers of one hand, she glanced up at him with a look compounded of anger, grief, and mortification. "It's an impossible situation," she said hoarsely.

A long moment passed while Jack looked at her in silence. He didn't want to add to her burden by laying another worry on her. But if Marianne's suspicions were right, then Rachel Peary's situation was even worse, much worse, than Jean imagined. And something had to be done about it fast.

Reaching into the inside pocket of his tweed sport jacket, Jack pulled out several photographs and passed one of them across the table as though he were dealing Jean a playing card. "Do you know this boy, Jean?"

Eyebrows knit, she examined the photo for a moment before shaking her head. "Nice-looking young man. Who is he?"

"Kevin Peterson."

"Kevin Peterson?" Her eyes widened. "The boy who kidnapped the Prince baby and then killed himself? Your daughter asked about him too—that day she came to see Rachel. And Rachel told her she didn't know him!"

"Yes. Well, that's not true, Jean. I've spoken to some of the teachers at Stoneham High. Apparently Kevin and your daughter were acquaintances."

"I don't know what to think," Jean muttered. "Why would Rachel lie about that?"

Seeing the dismay in her eyes, Jack hesitated for a moment before handing her the two remaining photographs. "How about this man, Jean. Do you recognize his face?"

"No," she said after studying the pictures. "I'm sure I'd remember it."

"His name is Simon Proctor. Ever hear of him?"

Jean gave an apologetic shrug. "No. Who is he?"

Jack gazed at the photographs for a moment. When he looked up at Jean again and spoke, his voice was as hard as the expression on his face. "Simon Proctor is the man who destroyed my daughter."

"My God," Jean gasped.

Choosing his words carefully, Jack explained, "He's an ex-con. He was released from prison in New Mexico last fall. Years ago, he was the leader of a commune that started getting into some very dark, dangerous areas."

"Like what?" Jean asked.

"Satanism."

"Satanism," she scoffed nervously. "You don't really believe all that stuff about devil cults."

"Yes, Jean, I do. I believe in it completely." He paused for a moment, then added quietly, "Six years ago, my partner Sam Turner was murdered by Satanists." Jack was surprised to hear himself saying the words. He hadn't intended to mention Sam.

Jean looked shocked. "What happened?"

Jack stared back at the bright, attractive woman sitting across the table from him. A peculiar sensation came over him—a sense of absolute certainty that this was a person he could trust and confide in. But as he sat there listening to the noises around him—the lunchtime chatter, the clink of wineglasses, the convivial laughter of the businessmen, he decided against telling her. This wasn't the time and it certainly wasn't the place.

"It's not the most suitable mealtime story," he said.

"I'm sorry," she said, reaching out her hand again and patting his where it lay on the table. At that moment their waitress showed up and began removing their empty plates from the table. Jean waited until the young woman was gone, then said, "Tell me more about this Proctor person."

"He's a very dangerous man, Jean. A sociopath with a brilliant mind and a highly charismatic personality. He was in jail for murdering one of his followers." Jack decided to censor the part about the tongue mutilation. He saw no need to go into the gruesome details.

"I still don't understand what this has to do with me— or Rachel."

As gently as he could, Jack told her. "We believe that Simon Proctor is now living somewhere in this area. We believe he's formed a new group and that its members have been recruited largely from around Stoneham."

"And you think . . . ?

"People like Proctor prey on vulnerable youngsters, Jean."

"Like my daughter, you mean," Jean said bitterly.

"I think that's a possibility, yes. So did Marianne." Jean was shaking her head, but Jack pressed on. "Please. Hear me out. The police are now working on the assumption that Proctor was responsible for the kidnapping of the Prince baby. Now it's my theory that this cult is into a very obscure kind of worship, focusing on a demon called Belphegor. What this demon—"

"Belphegor?" she interrupted. "Did you say Belphegor?"

"Yes. Do you recognize the name?"

Jean's face had turned nearly as white as the tablecloth. "Oh, God," she wailed. Other diners turned to look at them. She buried her face in her hands. "Then it's true. My baby's one of them!"

"Why? Tell me, Jean!"

It took her a moment to get hold of herself. Leaning forward on her forearms, she whispered hoarsely, "I found some things in her room."

"Like what?"

"There was a piece of paper with writing on it, some strange language that looked a little like Latin. And it mentioned something about Belphegor."

Jack's heart was pounding. "Did you find anything else?"

Jean's head darted up and down. "A dagger. And a tiny bottle. It had something in it that looked like blood—"

"It *was* blood. Kevin Peterson had one hidden in his room too. I had it tested." Reaching behind him, Jack pulled his wallet out of his back pocket, flipped it open and carefully removed a folded piece of paper from one of the compartments. "I copied this from a parchment sheet Marianne found in Kevin's bedroom. Is it the same language?"

307

She unfolded the paper and read the message swiftly. "Oh God, it's more than that. It's the same exact message!"

"Are you sure?"

"I've read it dozens and dozens of times. I'm sure."

He studied her deathly pale face. "You knew, then? You knew Rachel belonged to one of these groups?"

"No," she said miserably. "She swore it was nothing. She promised me. And I was stupid enough to trust her." She rose suddenly, overturning her wineglass, which spilled the last of its contents onto the tablecloth. "I've got to get out of here!"

It took Jack a few minutes to settle the bill. He thought Jean might be long gone by the time he got outside, but she was waiting there, leaning against a car in the parking lot, her pale face tilted up to the gray, lowering sky. She looked almost haggard out there in the daylight, as though the things he had told her had aged her ten years.

As he approached, she turned to him and said, "You think this man Simon Proctor has my daughter, Jack?"

"I think she might be a member of his cult, yes."

"And is she in danger?"

Is she in danger? Jack thought. *Shit yes, lady*. But what he said was, "If you mean, do I think Simon Proctor will do anything to her that he hasn't already done, no. You've seen her recently. She was in one piece, right? But that doesn't mean she hasn't gotten herself into a very scary situation."

Tears welled in Jean's eyes. "I'm going to get her away from that son of a bitch," she rasped. "I'm going to—"

"Jean," Jack said urgently, taking firm hold of her right upper arm, "don't say anything to Rachel about Simon Proctor. If you do and it gets back to him—and it will, Jean, I guarantee it—he'll kill her. I said she wasn't in immediate danger, and she isn't, unless you force his hand."

"Or hers?"

He nodded.

Squaring her shoulders, she wiped the end of her nose with the heel of her hand, hardly aware of what she was doing. "What should I do, then?"

He told her what he wanted while he drove her back to

her house in his car. She was in no condition to go back to the office. He dropped her off at the foot of her driveway, promising to call soon. Then he swung his car around and headed for the parkway.

As he turned the car onto the road that led to the parkway entrance, he passed a roadside billboard advertising U.S. savings bonds. Looking at the chubby, dimpled baby in the ad holding out its arms to college, to the future, to whatever life had to offer, he thought about what Jean had told him about Rachel's pregnancy, working out the arithmetic in his head.

The baby would be born in August.

The realization jolted him so hard that he nearly missed the entrance ramp. Jack knew that on the first of August, Satanists celebrate one of their most important holy days—Lammas, the harvest festival. Rachel was more central to Simon's plans than he had thought while speaking to Jean. Simon Proctor, he realized now, intended to harvest Rachel's baby on Lammas.

51

JACK COULDN'T SLEEP THAT NIGHT. LYING AWAKE IN THE dark of Marianne's bedroom, he stared up at the ceiling until the blackness dissolved into a murky half-light in which his thoughts swirled before him like ghosts.

He saw a pregnant blond teenager being used as a breeder to produce a baby for Simon Proctor's sacrifice. Saw the bright, pleasing face of Jean Peary, who had aroused a mix of feelings in him that he could not afford to be distracted by right now.

And he saw Sam Turner, his partner for seven years, a soft-spoken black man with a teamster's physique and a gentle way of smiling that made you feel he could still perceive the beauty in life, in spite of all the ugliness around him. That was how Jack liked to think of Sam, as he had seen him a thousand times, a strong, serious man whose

309

daily exposure to the extremes of human depravity had not, miraculously, killed off his capacity for joy.

But it was hard for Jack to keep that image in mind for very long.

Always the other image rose up to displace it, the way a familiar face will turn suddenly monstrous in the midst of a bad dream. No matter how hard Jack struggled to hold on to the good memories of all those years, he would end up with the same unspeakable vision in mind—Sam, the way he looked at the very end, the last time Jack laid his disbelieving eyes on him. . . .

Seven years before, a long investigation into a drug ring called the Camarilla had led to the arrest of the leader, a thirty-seven-year-old sociopath named Adolfo Benitez. When the police broke into the gang's lower Manhattan headquarters, they made a horrific discovery. Sitting on the stovetop in the reeking kitchen was big cast-iron pot containing a witch's brew of coagulated blood, clumps of human hair, animal bones, the charred shell of a large turtle, and a human heart that the coroner ultimately identified as that of a preadolescent male. The Camarilla, it turned out, was not just another band of big-city drug dealers. It was a Satanic cult that had progressed from animal to human sacrifice. Benitez had bound his followers to him by persuading them that his black rituals would protect them from their enemies, even make them invulnerable to police bullets.

Sam had been more directly involved in the case than Jack. Several years before, he had investigated the ritual murder of a drug dealer, which he was then able to link to the cult leader. It was Sam's riveting testimony that had finally convicted Benitez.

Led from the courtroom in cuffs after the verdict was read, Benitez paused by the bench where Sam was standing and chatting with Jack. The cult leader's tangled hair was caked with filth, and his black eyes glinted with madness. When he grinned at Sam, he displayed a mouthful of yellow teeth, each filed to a sharp point. "See you soon in Hell, dead man," he croaked before the officers shoved him down the aisle.

Sam had simply shrugged when Jack had warned him to be careful. "He's history. So's his group." He slapped his belly and grinned. "And I feel like getting me some lunch. What do you say to some Szechuan, my friend?"

"Just watch your back," Jack had answered as they'd headed from the courthouse.

It wasn't long before Jack put the Benitez affair out of his mind. He and Sam had other matters to attend to, other drug cases, other murders.

Exactly two months after the Benitez trial ended, the phone woke Jack at two A.M. "Better hurry up if you want to save the nigger's skin," a husky voice said. Jack heard a low, snuffling laugh in the background. Then silence.

"Jack, what's wrong?" Peggy had asked, sitting up in bed beside him.

"It's Sam," he'd answered grimly. Fighting back his fear, he quickly dialed Sam's number. When no one answered by the tenth ring, he threw on his clothes, grabbed his service revolver, jumped in his car and sped toward Flatbush.

Sam lived by himself on the second story of a two-family house. The owners of the building, an elderly Jewish couple who occupied the bottom floor during the spring and summer months, were away in Florida.

The side door leading up to Sam's part of the house was open. Jack could see lights burning upstairs. Pulling his gun, he edged through the door and slowly climbed the stairs, hugging the wall.

He leapt onto the landing at a crouch, then straightened up slowly, sweeping his gun around in a wide arc. There had been a violent struggle up here—much of the furniture was overturned, table lamps lay shattered on the floor. But he saw no sign of Sam.

Jack found him in the bedroom, spread-eagled on his blood-soaked mattress, his wrists and ankles bound to the wooden posts at the four corners of the bed. And still alive.

His face, though contorted in agony, hadn't been touched. But the rest of his body, from his neck down to the ankles, looked as if it had been dipped in blood. Something terrible had been done to him, though at first Jack could not, or would not, comprehend the truth.

He hurried to the side of the bed and bent close to his friend, who was making torturous moans from deep inside his chest. Without thinking, Jack laid a hand gently on

311

Sam's chest, then jerked it back in revulsion, staring down disbelievingly at the horror he had not wanted to face—the twitching muscles, the cordlike tendons, the fibrous bundles of exposed meat.

Sam had been skinned alive.

He died moments later while Jack, his hand shaking so violently he could barely hit the buttons, phoned police emergency.

After dropping the handset back into the cradle, Jack had stumbled into the bathroom to throw up. When he looked up from the toilet bowl, he noticed the dark, limp things draped over the shower rod. For a second he flashed on a familiar image—Peggy's freshly washed panty hose, hanging up to dry in the bathroom.

Only Sam wasn't married, and the hanging strips were not hosiery.

They were the dark, dripping pieces of his skin.

Many hours later, after the swarm of investigators and newsmen had thinned out, Jack had staggered back to his car and collapsed into the driver's seat. As he leaned forward to turn the ignition key, he caught sight of something out of the corner of his eye. It was lying on the floor of the passenger side. Cautiously, he bent down and picked it up. It was a old-fashioned straight razor with an elaborately decorated silver handle.

No one had to tell Jack that he was holding the weapon that had been used on his friend. Or to help him interpret the message it was meant to convey: Beware. You could be next.

Jack had taken that message to heart. He had followed the advice that he had tried, in vain, to communicate to Sam. He had watched his back very vigilantly. And he had been deeply relieved when word reached him eight months later that Adolfo Benitez had been killed in prison, knifed to death in the shower by a fellow inmate to whom he had made an unwelcome homosexual pass. A few weeks after Benitez's death, the remnants of his gang were gunned down in a shootout with police.

So much for Satan's promises, Jack had thought when he heard the news.

That same night, Jack quietly removed the silver-handled

312

razor from the precinct-house evidence locker and brought it home with him to Queens.

Jerking himself upright, Jack swung his legs off Marianne's bed. He sat there for a while, perched on the edge of the mattress, waiting for his heart to stop pounding. Sam's death never failed to give him palpitations, even after all these years. As soon as he felt a little calmer, he switched on the reading lamp, got up, and walked across the room to Marianne's pine dresser, which now held some of his clothes.

Pulling open the top drawer, he removed the silver-handled razor he had brought with him from his basement office. For all these years, he had kept it. He wasn't sure why. He'd always thought that it served him as a concrete reminder of the evil power he had pledged himself to fight. Now, he realized that he had been saving it for another purpose all along.

To fight fire with fire.

He stepped over to the bedroom closet, slid open the door, and slipped the heavy razor into the outer pocket of his sport jacket.

From now on he would carry it with him always. One day he would come face to face with Simon Proctor. And when that day came, he would finally put the razor to use.

52

BY THE TIME JERRY WALLER FINISHED GRADING THE geography exams, preparing the next day's lesson plan, and checking the terrarium to make sure that the hermit crabs had received their minimum daily requirement of shredded lettuce, the rain was falling so heavily that he could hear it thudding on the rooftop a full floor above his vacant classroom. All the other teachers had been smart enough to clear out before the storm really got going. Grabbing his trench coat from the closet, he stuck a few papers into his briefcase and headed out the door, turning the lights off behind him.

The empty corridors and stairwells echoed with the sound of his footsteps as he made his way down to the front entrance. The only other person he passed was the hollow-chested janitor, Billy Brennan, who glanced up from his mop bucket with rheumy eyes and croaked out a listless "G'night."

Standing just inside the front doors, staring out at the storm, Jerry muttered a curse. The thick April rain cascaded in sheets, exploding off the sidewalk. What made matters worse was the blustering wind, which blew the rain in all directions. Jerry saw at a glance that his umbrella would be useless.

The rain suited the dreariness of his mood, though. Taking care of his last-minute chores hadn't been the real reason he'd lingered at school long after everyone else had gone home. He'd hung around because the prospect of going home so depressed him. Unlike his pupils, who often acted as if school were a prison from which they'd be sprung at three, Jerry dreaded the end of his workday. Stuck in a hopeless marriage, he found his only refuge in his classroom. His home had become something worse than a prison; it had become a cage holding two hostile creatures who spent all their time circling each other warily when they weren't exchanging angry snarls.

With no one there to hear him, Jerry let out a loud, despondent sigh. Oh well, he thought. No use putting off the inevitable. Setting his briefcase down between his feet, he pulled on his shapeless Maine fisherman's hat and turned up the collar of his trench coat. Then, grabbing his briefcase by the handle, he pushed open the door and sprinted out into the rain.

It hit him like a gale at sea. Before he'd run six yards he was drenched. "Shit!" he shouted aloud, rounding the corner of the school building. His car was two hundred yards away, on the far side of the parking lot.

Keeping his head lowered, his eyes on the streaming pavement, Jerry didn't notice the blue-and-white Northampton P.D. car parked alongside his old Toyota until he was almost on top of it.

Jerry wondered what the cops were doing there. But at the moment his main concern was getting out of the rain. Moving between the squad car and his Toyota, he pulled open the front door of his car, tossed in his briefcase, and was just about to get behind the wheel when the passenger window of the other car slid down and someone called him by name.

Bending over, Jerry peered into the police car. There was only one person inside, a powerful-looking young policeman with a dark, neatly clipped moustache. He was leaning across the front seat, his head cocked to one side so he could look up at Jerry.

"Mike Holson, Mr. Waller," said the cop. He was almost shouting. Even so, Jerry had to strain to hear him over the pounding of the rain on the car roof. "I tried calling you at home, then took a chance you might still be here."

"You found me," Jerry shouted back. "What can I do for you, Officer?" The rain pouring off his hat brim was making it hard for him to see. "I'm in danger of drowning here."

"We've got some questions we need to ask you, sir. We think you might be able to help us."

"Is this about Marianne Byrne?"

"Yes, sir. If you'll get in, I'll drive you on over to headquarters."

"I've got my own car," Jerry said, nodding toward his Toyota.

"You won't need it, sir," the officer said. "I'll drive you back."

Jerry felt the cold rain running off his hat brim down the back of his neck. He pulled open the passenger door of the police car and ducked inside.

53

IN A SMALL, LOW-CEILINGED BEDROOM ON THE SECOND FLOOR of the farmhouse, Rachel and David lay together in bed, sheets thrown back, bodies damp from the exertions of their lovemaking. The warm April breezes made the drawn shades flutter. Rachel would have liked to feel the soft air on her skin, but David had asked her to lower the shades, and she had done it unprotestingly. Like his father, David felt more comfortable in the dark.

Still, the room wasn't completely dark. The afternoon sunlight filtering through the shades created a cozy, sexy dimness that reminded Rachel of the times during her childhood when, lazing in bed on a bright weekend morning, she would draw the top sheet over her head, tenting it with her knees, and pretend she was nestled inside a secret hideaway—a safe, warm, magical place where the outside world couldn't touch her. It was the way David always made her feel.

As she snuggled against him, nuzzling her head against his chest, he ran his hand over her breast, gently brushing his fingertips over her puckered nipples. "Your breasts are getting bigger," he whispered.

"I like the way they feel," she murmured.

"Me too." He slid his hand down her swelling belly and onto the moist tuft of her pubic hair. She parted her thighs slightly.

"You feel different inside," he said.

"Mmmmm," she answered. "How?"

"Creamier."

Eyes closed, she smiled and hummed with pleasure as David continued to massage her.

She came again under his ministering fingers. Reaching up, she took his face in both her hands and pulled his mouth to hers. They kissed hungrily for a long moment until David pulled away. "I don't think I can fuck again," he said with a laugh. "Not yet."

Rachel, pouting, closed her eyes and pillowed her head on his chest. A few moments passed while they lay together in silence. Then David said, "Now tell me about this thing with your mother."

"Do I have to?"

"Yes."

"Oh well," Rachel sighed after a moment. "I think she's getting suspicious. The last two times I called, she asked me all these questions about Tim—you know, what he's studying, what his major is, shit like that."

He laughed. "Mothers are supposed to ask questions like that. That's their job."

"I know. Maybe it's nothing." She trailed her fingers up

316

and down his chest. "But I wouldn't put it past her to call the university and check up on Tim. She's been bugging me for months about bringing him over to dinner. *And* asking to see my apartment."

He thought for a while. "Maybe it's time you moved up here, Rachel."

"Really?" Her face was bright with pleasure. "You mean it?"

"Sure."

"I'd still have to call her, though."

"Maybe not. We could work that out. Would you mind not talking to her anymore?"

"Are you kidding?" she asked scornfully. "But what about Tim?"

"He can move up here too—there's plenty of room. Or maybe he can go back to his old place."

"Oh, David," she said. "I'm so happy. And we'd be together?"

"Not all the time. I still have other things to do. But a lot."

Rachel sat up and began kissing his face softly, then slowly moved down his neck and chest, her soft tongue flicking over his nipples. Getting to her knees, she licked down the center of his hard-muscled belly. Taking his swelling penis inside her mouth, she suckled him until he was stiff again. Looking up at him, she smiled and said, in a low, throaty voice, "Think you can fuck again now?"

Afterward, still straddling him, she reached down and stroked the sweaty strands of his hair away from his forehead. "David," she said, her own forehead creased into a frown. "What's going to happen to the baby?"

"You know," he answered flatly. "You're not getting second thoughts, are you?"

"No," she said hastily, not wanting to anger him. "But it's just a *baby*."

"That's the whole point," he said.

"You know what I mean."

"Listen, Rachel," he said gently, placing one hand on the side of her face and stroking her cheek with his thumb. "It's a vessel, that's all. A container. When Simon performs the rite, it'll be like he's drinking spring water from

317

a bottle, or inhaling perfume. The bottle doesn't know anything. It doesn't feel anything."

She squeezed her eyes and lips tight. "I don't know," she said after a moment.

"Rachel, this is your gift to me, remember?" he said.

Looking down again, she gazed at her lover's face and thought how much she adored him, how happy he made her feel. She couldn't bring herself to deny him anything. She wanted nothing else in life but to lie in his arms, to be his special woman, to be loved.

"I just feel funny about it, that's all," she said meekly.

He pulled her down onto him, hugging her to his chest, rocking her from side to side, whispering into her ear. "Rachel, the night of the ritual is going to be the most exciting night of your life. And mine. We'll be bound together forever."

"You mean it?" she asked, her faced pressed into the crook of his neck, her voice muffled.

"It'll prove that you really love me."

"How can you doubt it?"

"Well, when you start asking questions like this . . ."

"I won't anymore, David," she said quickly, a trace of panic in her voice. "I promise I won't say anything about it again."

"That's my baby," he cooed into her ear. "That's my sweet baby girl."

54

DOME LIGHTS FLASHING, THE NYPD PATROL CAR NOSED ITS way along West 128th Street, the vehicles in front moving aside with infuriating slowness in spite of the siren's blare. Though it was just a little after seven on a Friday morning, a jostling crowd had already gathered on the sidewalk by the rubble-strewn lot. A half-dozen patrolmen, a few armed with megaphones, struggled to keep the onlookers at bay. Shouting taunts and curses, several teenage boys clambered onto the roof of a double-parked delivery van and craned to get a better look at the lot where the police forensic unit was busily at work.

Pulling up beside the van, the patrol car slid to a stop. The rear door popped open and a stocky little man with bushy gray eyebrows and a gray moustache stepped out into the gutter. Flanked by two detectives, the gray-haired man in the rumpled business suit pushed his way through the crowd, watching where he stepped as he made his way across the lot, around piles of dog shit, shattered beer bottles, and heaps of rotting garbage that seemed to have been dumped straight down from the windows of the flanking tenements. The man—Herbert Schaitkin, Chief Medical Examiner of the City of New York—counted a dozen empty crack vials scattered on the ground.

At the far end of the lot, a cluster of police officers stood beside a sprawling heap, along with two photographers who snapped pictures. Other officers moved slowly around the cordoned-off area, crouching occasionally to sift the littered ground for clues. As Schaitkin approached, one of the uniformed men in the little group, Detective Sergeant William Farr, turned, and spotting the pathologist, called out, "Wait'll you get a load of this one, Chief."

"What've we got?" Schaitkin asked as the men parted for him.

"One for the books," answered Farr. He nodded at the body on the ground. "Couple of kids found it this morning. Saw a foot sticking out of a pile of cardboard and shit. Probably dumped here a few days ago, judging by the stink."

As Schaitkin knelt beside the body, one of the cops behind him said, "Looks like some kind of drug hit. Colombians, probably. They get real creative."

The victim was a big man, dressed in a torn plaid flannel shirt and soiled khaki trousers. He had a headful of bushy dark hair and a salt-and-pepper beard that could have used trimming. His hands were tightly bound behind his back with a loop of wire.

Something awful had been done to his mouth. It took Schaitkin a few seconds to realize what he was looking at. He had never seen a man killed that way before.

Wedged deep inside the corpse's gaping jaws, like an apple shoved into the mouth of a suckling pig, was a dirty greenish ball. Sucking in his breath, Schaitkin leaned closer. There was printing on the ball. *Wilson 5*, it said.

"Sweet Jesus," Schaitkin hissed, straightening up.

"Can you believe it?" Farr asked over his shoulder. "Shoved a fucking tennis ball down his throat. Guy choked to death on a tennis ball."

Schaitkin reached down a thumb and gently lifted the tip of the man's nose. Crusted matter, yellow-brown in color, clogged the corpse's nostrils.

"Find any identification?" he asked.

"Guy's wallet was still in his hip pocket. Got a driver's license, couple other things. Cash and credit cards gone, of course."

Rising stiffly from his crouch, Schaitkin brushed the dirt from his knees before turning to Farr.

"Have it to me by this afternoon," he said, tilting his head toward the corpse. Nodding to the two detectives he had come with, he turned and trudged back to the waiting car.

Later that day, in the autopsy room, the ball was pried from the rigid jaws of the cadaver. Schaitkin placed it in a plastic bag and had one of his assistants carry it upstairs to the toxicology lab. When the results came back several hours later, they confirmed what the chief examiner had already surmised.

The report indicated the strong presence of the emetic ipecac. When his children were growing up, Schaitkin, like many parents, had always kept a small bottle of ipecac in his medicine chest at home in case of accidental poisoning.

The tennis ball had been soaked in the emetic before it was forced into the victim's mouth cavity. The dead man, whose driver's license identified him as Jerry Waller, had drowned in his own vomit.

55

On a cloudless morning in mid-spring, Saturday, May 11, Marianne Byrne returned to the quiet house in Queens she had grown up in.

Her father rode beside her in the rear of the private ambulance, gently clasping her frail, limp hands, which lay folded in her blanketed lap. "We're going home, baby," he said softly, leaning closer to make himself heard over the motor's rumble. From time to time her eyes would drift in his direction, and he would search them eagerly for some sign of awareness. But there was none. Her gaze stayed as blank as a mannequin's.

Pulling into Jack's driveway, the ambulance backed over the bright pink-and-white azalea bushes lining the edge of the concrete. Peggy's azaleas. Jack was glad she wasn't there to see them crushed.

Or to see her child's dead, ghostly face as the attendants lifted her wheelchair down and set it gently on the sidewalk.

A gray Volvo station wagon that had accompanied the ambulance down from Westchester drew up at the curb. A moment later Jean Peary stepped out into the gutter, resettling her sunglasses on her nose. "Can I help with this part, Jack?" she asked, walking around her car toward the front stoop.

He had bounded up the stoop, propped open the screen door, and was groping in his pants pocket for his key ring. "We can manage," he said, undoing the deadbolt. His voice dropped. "Unless you can figure out a way to get these people to move on."

Jean glanced over at two little boys in Simpsons T-shirts, a stoop-backed old man lugging a plastic grocery bag in each hand, and a teenage girl in designer jeans pushing a baby stroller—all of them frozen in their tracks, gawking at the wheelchair as the heftier of the two paramedics maneuvered it along the sidewalk. "Neighbors?" she murmured.

"The kids live down the block," Jack said. "The others . . ." He ended the sentence with a shrug. "Never mind. Let them look." Goes with the territory, he thought bitterly. In all his years as a cop, Jack had never gotten used to the rubberneckers. On the streets of New York they flocked around ambulances like autograph hounds around a star's limousine.

The two steps leading up to the front porch had been overlaid with a wooden ramp. Jack had also hired a mason to raise the the level of the stoop so that it was nearly flush with the door saddle.

Taking the handles of the wheelchair from the paramedic, Jack rolled his daughter to the small room at the rear of the house opposite his own bedroom. When Marianne was a baby, the room had served as her nursery. Later, after she had been moved upstairs to the larger bedroom under the eaves, Peggy had converted it into a sewing room.

Traces of the nursery still clung to the walls. Running around the perimeter of the room, just underneath the ceiling, was a narrow wallpaper border, old-fashioned and faded by the sun—lambs and butterflies frolicking in an eternal spring. Seeing it now, Jack was glad he'd never gotten rid of it. It would give Marianne something pleasant to look at, maybe stir up some happy memories, assuming she was capable of remembering anything at all.

With the help of the big paramedic, Jack eased Marianne into the hospital bed he had purchased. Stooping, he worked the crank until his daughter was lying in a half-upright position. After seeing the paramedic out and watching the curiosity seekers drift away—*th-th-that's all, folks!*—he returned to Marianne's bedroom, where Jean was raising the venetian blinds on the windows.

The afternoon before, Jack had bought several dozen red tulips, Marianne's favorite flower, and arranged them in vases all around the room—on the dresser, the night table, the bookshelves and windowsills. Now, in brilliant light that flooded the room, the flowers glowed like gemstones. He looked over at Marianne, whose vacant gaze was fixed on the opposite wall.

As suddenly as if a plug had been pulled from his heart, all the pleasure he'd felt at bringing Marianne home drained out of him, leaving his insides hollow. Maybe they were

322

right, he thought miserably. Maybe I should have put her in a nursing home.

Jean, who was standing by the dresser, unpacking Marianne's hospital bag, turned toward him, holding out a hairbrush. "Is this hers?"

He nodded.

"Can I brush her hair? It looks tangled."

"Please."

Jean stepped to the bedside and perched on the mattress beside Marianne. "It might be best to cut it really short," she said, running the fingers of one hand through Marianne's thick hair. "Or else you ought to keep it braided. Otherwise it'll be a real mess." She began to brush the hair with long, loving strokes.

She continued to brush as she spoke, her voice calm and comforting, as though ministering to a catatonic young woman were simply a normal part of everyday life. The bristles caught in a snarl, jerking Marianne's head slightly. Jack saw Jean wince.

Marianne didn't even blink.

A memory stabbed at him—his daughter, five years old, bursting out of the bedroom where she and Peggy had been enduring the nightly ordeal of "neatening" the raven-black hair that cascaded halfway down the child's back. Tears in her eyes, Marianne had thrust the brush at Jack, who was settled in his easy chair, trying to read the *Daily News*. "You do it, Daddy. Mommy doesn't do it right."

Shaking the memory from his mind, Jack cleared his throat and said, "Jean, thank you for this. And for coming down here today."

Jean smiled up at him, and he saw the moisture welling in her lower lids. So she wasn't so calm after all. "You don't need to thank me, Jack. It's nice having a daughter to take care of."

Jack's eyes narrowed. "How long has it been since you heard from Rachel?" he asked.

"Nearly three weeks." Her voice faltered and she drew a deep breath. "I don't want to burden you with this, Jack," she said. "Not today."

"Don't be silly," he answered, taking the bentwood rocker that stood in a corner of the room and moving it closer to the bed. "What did she have to say?"

"Not much. She said she'd call again, that she was just very busy and she couldn't use the phone at the Laundromat any more." Jean lowered the hairbrush and shrugged hopelessly. "But I don't think she's going to." Rising slowly from the mattress, she stepped around to the opposite side of the bed, and the gentle brushing began again. "It's odd, but I think she suspected something. I mean I think she realized that I know she's been lying to me."

He frowned. "What makes you think that?"

"Nothing I can put my finger on. I'm just pretty sure, that's all. I think that's why she hasn't called." She stopped brushing again and looked at him pleadingly. "Jack, if she does cut me out completely, if she disappears, what then?"

For a moment he didn't respond. He was wondering if Jean was right, if Rachel did suspect something. Finally he answered, "Don't worry. We'll find her."

"Really?" Her voice was both doubting and hopeful.

Looking at Jean seated beside his daughter, Jack was hit with the conviction that he could love this woman. Immediately, however, he put the thought out of his mind; right now, his feelings for her could only get in the way of the task ahead.

Rising to his feet, he stepped to the bedside, reached out a hand and touched Marianne's slack cheek with the back of his fingers.

"I couldn't save her," he said, so softly that he might have been speaking to himself. "I tried, but I couldn't."

Jean laid her free hand on his forearm and gave it a gentle squeeze. "Jack, you can't blame yourself for what happened."

For a moment she wasn't sure that he had heard her. He was staring into the distance, focused on something no one else could see.

Then he turned to Jean. "I know who to blame," he said grimly. His eyes had a look she had never seen in them before, and it frightened her. "He got my daughter, Jean. But I promise you I won't let him get yours."

56

ENGROSSED IN HIS WRITING AS HE WAS, WILLIAM KITTREDGE knew perfectly well that someone had entered his sanctum. He had heard the door to the Historical Society creek open and caught a whiff of the sweet spring air that had accompanied the visitor into the musty room. But Mr. Kittredge had no intention of looking up from his notebook until he had completed the passage he was working on, a rousing description of the great Stoneham fire of 1912, which had incinerated three homes and six business establishments along Grace Street, including the First Bank of Stoneham and Bardwell's General Store.

It took him another few minutes to craft the concluding sentence before he looked up. Smiling with satisfaction, he capped his fountain pen, closed the marbleized cover of his notebook, and, swiveling his chair, gazed up at the bearded stranger who loomed above his desk.

Normally, William Kittredge would have been happy to see the somber-looking, middle-aged gentleman. He looked like a serious individual, not one of those flighty young pups who would barge into the archives for a quick consultation and then breeze out again without so much as a fare-thee-well. But Mr. Kittredge had recently grown intolerant of any interruption of his labors. During the winter, he had suffered through a very bad case of the flu, which had lingered in his system for nearly two months. In another few weeks he would turn eighty. Never before had he felt such a strong sense of urgency. He still had decades to cover in his definitive history, and he feared he was running out of time.

All at once the visitor's face contracted and he let out an explosive sneeze. "Sorry," he said, dabbing his nose with a hankie. "Dusty in here."

"The past gives off its own distinctive atmosphere, Mister . . ."

"Byrne. Jack Byrne."

"Mr. Byrne. Unfortunately, many people seem highly

allergic to it. To me, it is the very breath of life." He lowered his head and glanced at Jack over the top of his eyeglasses. "What may I do for you, sir?"

Reaching into the inside pocket of his sport jacket, Jack pulled out a small, folded square of white paper, opened it, and laid it face up on the desk. "I'm hoping you can explain why my daughter had this in her possession, Mr. Kittredge."

The old man picked up the paper and held it to the light trickling in from the window over his desk. His full name—William Kittredge III—was written in neat, flowing script above the phone number of the Historical Society.

"And who is your daughter?" Kittredge asked, returning the paper to Jack.

"Her name is Marianne. She was a policewoman—"

Kittredge's sharp intake of breath cut Jack off. "Of course, of course. I knew the name Byrne sounded familiar." Slowly removing his reading glasses, he looked at Jack with commiserating eyes. "I was so terribly sorry to learn of your daughter's misfortune. I didn't hear about it until I returned from my winter vacation in Florida. I spend several months down there each winter, you know. I met your daughter shortly before I left. She came here to see me."

Jack nodded toward the folding chair at the side of the desk. "Do you mind?"

"Please," Kittredge answered.

Undoing the middle button of his jacket, Jack sat down and said, "I didn't know anything about her visit. I just happened to come across that sheet the other day, stuck inside one of her books." He paused for a moment, fighting back another sneeze. "Excuse me," he said, pulling out his handkerchief again and blowing his nose. "Mr. Kittredge, I'd like to know what my daughter came to see you about."

The old man leaned back in his chair. "She wanted to know the whereabouts of a certain house. She didn't give me much to go on, just part of a name." He allowed himself the tiniest smile of self-satisfaction. "But I managed to locate it."

"What sort of house?"

"An old summer residence built back in the 1840s by a wealthy financier, a Dutch gentleman named Vanderdam."

Jack tugged at his lower lip. "So that's how she found it," he muttered under his breath.

"Beg pardon?" Kittredge asked.

"Nothing," Jack said, shaking his head. "Please go on."

"I'm afraid there's very little more to tell. Your daughter never explained why she was interested in the place. I was curious, of course."

Jack hesitated for a moment, then said, "She was trying to locate a certain group of individuals who may have been involved in some very serious crimes here in Stoneham."

Kittredge's eyes widened. "Are you referring to the Prince kidnapping?"

"Among other things, yes," Jack answered. "We believe these people may be involved in cult activities."

"Do you mean devil-worshipers?"

"Something like that, yes," Jack said. "We have reason to believe that they are under the control of a very dangerous, very deranged individual."

"Fascinating," Kittredge said, picking up his reading glasses and tapping his lips with one earpiece. "And who, may I ask, is this person?"

"His name is Proctor," Jack said softly. "Simon Proctor."

Kittredge felt suddenly weak, as if he'd just been hit with a relapse of the flu. He must have looked as bad as he felt, because his visitor leaned forward and asked, "Are you all right, Mr. Kittredge?"

"Yes," Kittredge said, closing his eyes for a moment. When he opened them again, Jack Byrne was staring at him worriedly. "No cause for alarm, Mr. Byrne. Just a momentary dizzy spell. I've been a little under the weather in recent weeks."

His mouth had gone dry. Pouring himself some springwater from the thermos beside him, he took a slow sip before turning back to his visitor and asking, "Did I understand you to say 'Simon Proctor'?"

Jack's eyes narrowed. "That's right. Why? Have you heard the name before?"

"Oh, yes," Kittredge said. "Most assuredly."

Jack sat up straight in his chair. "What do you know about him, Mr. Kittredge?"

327

"Many rumors," the old man said. "A handful of facts. But one thing I know for certain."

"Yes?" Jack asked, leaning forward in anticipation.

Kittredge laid down his plastic mug and fixed Jack with a steady look. "The last time Simon Proctor was seen in these parts was over two hundred years ago."

There was a long moment of silence while Jack tried to make sense of Kittredge's statement. Finally, he said, "I'm afraid you'll have to explain that to me, Mr. Kittredge."

"Strange," Kittredge said, more to himself than to Jack. "I was on the point of telling her about Proctor in December, but she dashed out before I had a chance." Settling back in his chair, he launched into his story, as though delivering it from lecture notes.

"Not many years after the founding of our village, back in the mid-1700s," Kittredge began, "a stranger arrived in Stoneham. From the sparse accounts that have come down to us, he was a striking individual. The average man, you know, was of much shorter stature in those days. If you've ever taken a tour of a Colonial dwelling, such as the historic restorations over in Tarrytown, you will have noticed how low the ceilings are. A man of your height would have to duck to clear the door frames. But Simon Proctor was big even by today's standards—a tall, powerful, darkly brooding man. Accounts vary as to his profession—some say tanner, others peddler or apothecary. One early chronicle of our village suggests that, at some point in his life, he had pursued the vocation of itinerant preacher. Another describes him as a medical man, what they used to call a leech. All accounts agree on his unusual degree of erudition. The wagon he arrived in was, reputedly, laden with several trunkloads of ancient, leather-bound volumes.

"Proctor settled in Stoneham, though he remained aloof from the community, inhabiting a small cabin somewhere on the outskirts of town, apparently in the vicinity of what is now known as Borden Hills. Even today it is a relatively undeveloped area. At that time, of course, it was sheer wilderness.

"Within a short time of his arrival, dark rumors began to circulate about the mysterious stranger. In spite of the great strides in scientific knowledge taking place during the so-called Age of Reason, it remained, in many regards, an intensely unenlightened time. Though perhaps," Kittredge added dryly, "no more so than our own. In any event, according to local gossip, Proctor passed the evenings in the gloomy solitude of his cabin poring over his volumes of occult lore by candlelight. At midnight, so the stories went, he would trek into the dark heart of the wilderness and there perform unspeakable rituals, conjuring up demons and consorting with the spirits of the dead.

"Superstitious rubbish, of course. And yet, in 1773, there occurred an atrocity which confirmed the villagers' worst apprehensions about Proctor." Leaning forward, Kittredge lifted the thermos-top cup to his lips and moistened his mouth again before continuing. "One sweltering Sunday at the very end of July, the sons of the Reverend Silas Graves, twin boys of seven, disappeared from a field near their home, where they had gone to amuse themselves following the family's Sabbath dinner. Suspicion immediately settled on Proctor, and a party of men, led by the Reverend Graves, marched out to his cabin to question him. He made furious denials and chased them from his property with a muzzle-loader. Shortly afterward, a foot traveler journeying to the village from an outlying farm stumbled upon the corpses of the two boys in a shallow grave not far from Proctor's place. The children had been mutilated in an unspeakable manner which the histories only hint at. An enraged mob of locals, heavily armed at this time, set out to arrest Proctor. But by the time they arrived, he had disappeared."

"Where did he go?" Jack asked.

Kittredge shrugged. "Who knows? Melted into the wilderness. It was easier for people to vanish in those days.

"Several years later, however, stories began drifting down from upstate, from the Mohawk Valley, stories about a renegade white man, in league with the devil, who had become the leader of a ferocious band of Iroquois warriors. They had half the valley terrified—plucked babies from their cribs and children from their own backyards, slit their throats and worse. Of course, documentation in the eighteenth century wasn't what it is now, so many of the accounts were undoubtedly apocryphal. Still, there *was* a certain plausibility to the stories. The Iroquois were furiously angry at most white men at that time."

329

"Why?" Jack interrupted.

"Why? Because of what George Washington had done to them."

Jack Byrne looked perplexed.

"It's not the kind of thing our history books like to dwell on, of course. Not quite in keeping with our exalted image of the Founding Father and all that." Kittredge drew in a deep breath and exhaled it as a sigh. "The Iroquois fought on the British side in the Revolutionary War. To punish them, as well as to eliminate any future threat, Washington sent General James Clinton on an expedition to wipe out all their villages in the Mohawk Valley. He burned their dwellings and fields and slaughtered their livestock. That was in 1779. Most of the Iroquois Nation was destroyed and dispersed. The ones who remained in the Mohawk Valley would certainly have been ripe for vengeance."

Jack could see how it would fit. A charismatic stranger offering the Indians a chance for revenge, while bending them to his own dark purposes.

"And this man was supposedly Proctor?"

"According to the rumors."

Jack leaned back in his chair and shook his head. "It's a fascinating story, Mr. Kittredge. Truly. But of course, the Simon Proctor I'm looking for is alive today."

"Yes. I know," Kittredge said.

His voice had grown weak and faltering, perhaps from all the talking he'd done, though to Jack's ears the shakiness sounded like fear.

Clearing his throat, Kittredge said, "There was one more rumor about Simon Proctor you may be interested in knowing."

Jack raised his eyebrows. "Yes?"

"They said that he had been alive for hundreds of years and that he would go on living forever. They said that he would never die as long as he kept sacrificing human victims, especially very young ones, to the devil."

A few minutes later, after thanking Kittredge for his time, Jack bid the old man good-bye and walked out into the sunlight. He paused for a moment on the concrete stoop, his eyes aching from the sudden brightness, his

330

brain spinning from the extraordinary story he'd just been told.

From somewhere in the distance, the faint shouts of children came drifting across the parking lot. Gazing to his left, Jack could make out the Gothic spires of Stoneham Junior High and, off to the right, the fenced-in schoolyard, packed with students on their lunchtime break. The high, happy sound of their voices pierced him with a longing for an innocent pleasure, a sense of sweet contentment at simply being alive in a world that he knew was lost to him forever.

Sighing, he trudged down the stairs and headed for his car. He decided there were only two logical explanations for the facts he'd learned from Kittredge. Jack knew that Simon Proctor—the Proctor of the present, the madman he was hunting—was well-versed in the arcana of the supernatural. Perhaps, in his readings, he had come across accounts of the eighteenth century Satanist and, for reasons unknown, had adopted his name. Perhaps, in his insanity, he even saw himself as the reincarnation of that demoniac killer.

Or maybe, less likely but still conceivable, he was an authentic descendent and namesake of the original Proctor.

As Jack leaned down to unlock the car door, he could feel the sun's warmth lying across his shoulders like a heating pad. But all the warmth in the world couldn't touch the seed of coldness that Kittredge had planted in his heart.

Try as he might to shake it, there was, he knew, one other possibility—the one he had seen reflected in Kittredge's anxious eyes, heard quivering in the old man's age-roughened voice.

Years before, after the horror of Sam's murder, Jack suffered from brutal nightmares that woke him every night in a puddle of sweat. He had been sent for a few sessions of counseling to a therapist, Dr. Stein, a mousy-haired woman with piercing brown eyes magnified threefold by the thick lenses of her glasses. And this surprising woman, so unremarkable in other respects, had said something he had never forgotten.

At one point during their second session, she had asked

331

him why he had volunteered to work on the Camarilla investigation, what had attracted him to the case.

Jack had never given the matter a moment's thought. He answered with a shrug. Dr. Stein then asked him about his religious beliefs, and Jack had told her about his devout Catholic upbringing.

"So you believe in the devil?"

It took Jack a while to answer. "I believe in evil, sure. But if you mean do I literally believe in Satan . . ." He had paused again. "Not since I was a child," he finally answered.

"You know, Detective Byrne," Dr. Stein had gone on to say. "Buried deep inside our minds, all of us have hidden fears left over from our childhoods. Now, one of the things psychology teaches us is that human beings tend to control their fears in one of two contradictory ways. Take a person who has been in a car accident as a child and develops a deathly fear of traveling at high speeds. That person may grow up and never set foot inside an automobile again. Or conversely, he may grow up to be a professional racer."

Jack had chewed that over for a few moments before answering. "I think I get the point. Becoming a racer is a way of conquering his fear."

"Exactly."

"Interesting. But I'm not sure what this has to do me."

"What I'm suggesting," Dr. Stein said, "is that your attraction to the occult may be a way of managing your own fear."

"What fear is that?"

"Your fear that the devil may be real."

Now, as he slid behind the wheel of his car, Jack recalled Dr. Stein's words. With his rational mind, he knew the very idea was utterly ludicrous—that the psychopath he was hunting and the madman of two hundred years ago were one and the same. But there was another part of his mind, very old and not rational at all, that didn't find the notion very funny at all.

Reaching across the car seat, Jack popped open the glove compartment and pulled out his map of New York State.

In the end, he thought as he unfolded the map, it didn't really matter. Human or devil, Proctor would be destroyed.

He would do the job with his own hands. But first, of course, he had to find him.

Now, thanks to Kittredge, he finally had a lead. On the crinkled surface of the map, Jack's fingers traced the route leading from Stoneham to the area the old man had indicated.

Starting tomorrow, Jack would search upstate. He would travel to the Mohawk Valley.

57

RAY-BANS SHIELDING HER EYES, WALKMAN EARPHONES clipped to her head, Rachel lay flat on the green plastic webbing of the chaise longue, her face tilted up to the noonday sun. Behind the dark lenses her eyelids were closed. A syrupy warmth seeped through her loins as George Michael crooned the soundtrack to the slow-motion fantasy playing inside her head like a pornographic music video—David and she fucking languorously on a tropical beach, then bathing their sweat-soaked bodies in the crystal-blue ocean.

A purring moan started deep in her throat as she slid a hand under her oversized cotton T-shirt and ran it over her swollen belly toward her left nipple, which had become exquisitely sensitive in recent weeks. Suddenly she frowned. Her fingers had brushed across her belly button—formerly hollow but now poking up from her middle like a hard, fleshy knot. Her eyelids snapped open.

Yanking off the headpiece in frustration, Rachel propped herself on her elbows and glanced around. She was alone in the big, grassy yard behind the old farmhouse. Reaching down, her forearms crisscrossed over her belly, she grabbed the bottom of the white cotton tee, drew it up over her head and tossed it onto the grass beside the lounge chair in a single motion. Maybe her stomach would look a little less gross if it were tan, she thought. Replacing the earphones on her head, she settled back on the chair, hoping no one would come out of the farmhouse and see her fat body exposed.

The warm sunshine felt good on her skin. Before long

333

her insides began to warm up again too, as she lay there thinking about David. He had been gone for nearly a week, and she missed him terribly. She was also beginning to go a little stir-crazy. Right now, for instance, what she wanted more than anything else—besides seeing David again—was to have someone drive her to the nearest Burger King and treat her to a double cheeseburger, large fries, and a strawberry shake.

It doesn't seem like so much to ask, her inner voice grumbled. But Simon had made it clear to her that leaving the farm was out of the question. She couldn't risk being spotted by someone who knew her, even up here in the boondocks, so far away from Stoneham.

It wasn't that she felt ignored or mistreated. Far from it. The others had been exceptionally considerate, indulging her every whim. All she had to do was ask. Just a week before, she'd expressed a longing for Ben & Jerry's Heathbar Crunch. The next day, three quarts of the ice cream had materialized in the freezer. If anything, she was beginning to feel a little like an overstuffed holiday goose.

No. It was the isolation that was getting to her, especially during those bleak stretches when David was away on business. That and the agonizingly slow passage of time, the endless sense of waiting, waiting, waiting, with all those eyes constantly on her.

Sometimes she would burst out crying for no apparent reason. All someone had to do was look at her sideways and the tears would flow as though a spigot had been turned on behind her eyes. At those times, her heart was filled with such a confusing mix of feelings—loneliness, longing, frustration, and something else too, piercing but elusive—that she couldn't begin to sort them out.

A tattered-looking cloud drifted directly overhead, blocking the sun for a moment and pimpling her skin with goose bumps. Rachel shivered and hugged herself across her swollen breasts.

There were many things she did not want to think about.

She turned the volume of her Walkman a notch higher and tried to make her mind a blank.

She had just began to relax again to the rockabilly beat of "Faith" when she sensed a hovering presence. She opened her eyes. Above her loomed a man-shaped silhou-

334

ette, backlit by the high sun. A white-rayed corona seemed to emanate from its head like a saint's halo. Embarrassed by the open display of her distended flesh, she stuck her hand under the arm of the chair and groped in the grass for her T-shirt.

The man reached down and grabbed her arm. With his other hand he gently pucked the earset from her head, shaking it free of her long entangling hair.

"No, no," Simon Proctor said, bending close. "Let me look at you, Rachel. Your body is very beautiful."

She knew there was no point in protesting. Submitting, she lay back on the chair, her hands folded primly over her belly.

"Your underpants too," he said.

She hesitated for a moment, then raised her hips and shimmied her white cotton panties down, kicking them off her left ankle over the end of the chair.

A long moment passed. She could feel her face grow warm, not from the sunshine, but from the intensity of Simon's stare. She did not know what he wanted.

He laughed gently. "You're embarrassed. I can see it in the way you're holding yourself." Perching himself on the chair beside her, her reached up one powerful hand and laid the palm caressingly on the right side of her face. "Don't be ashamed, Rachel. Your body is beautiful this way, blossoming with new life." He told her how radiant her flesh looked, as sweet as ripening fruit.

Rachel felt herself relax as Simon spoke. He could be so kind and understanding, as if he were looking right inside your head, reading your thoughts. He always seemed to know just what to say to make you feel better.

Head tilted sideways, she gazed down the chair at him. He was dressed in a pale, cotton robe. She noticed the bulging in his lap and smiled, wondering if he wanted to fuck. The thought suddenly seemed appealing to her. She reached out her hand and laid it on his thigh.

Laughing softly, he lifted her hand and kissed it tenderly on the palm. "No, child, no. I don't want to disturb the sleeping life inside you."

As he spoke, he laid a hand on her belly. Almost immediately the baby gave a little kick.

"He's strong with life."

"It might be a girl," Rachel said, smiling. It now occurred to her that the child she was carrying might well be Simon's. She always thought of it as David's.

"It feels like a male," Simon said contentedly.

Patting her cheek again, he began to rise from the chair. As he did, Rachel reached out and held on to his wrist. "Simon," she began, then seemed reluctant to continue.

"Yes, child?" he said, reseating himself. "What's worrying you?"

"Simon, what if the baby doesn't come on Lammas?"

"It will."

"How can you be sure? I mean, what if I don't go into labor at the right time?"

He regarded her thoughtfully, then, taking her right hand in both of his, gave it a reassuring pat. "If it doesn't come by itself, Rachel, there is something we can give you to induce labor and ease the baby out. That would better for you anyway. No pain."

"And I'll be okay?" she went on, her voice still tight with worry. "I mean, having the baby out here like this instead of in a hospital?"

"Rachel," Simon answered soothingly, "women have delivered babies without hospitals for many centuries. Even today, many women prefer to give birth at home, attended by midwives. It's nature's way."

"But we don't have a midwife here."

Simon chuckled soundlessly, as though she'd said something amusing. "You have someone better than a midwife," he said, indicating by his look that he meant himself.

"You've done this before?"

His smile broadened. "Many times."

Rising again, he kissed her hand. "I promise you, child. By the next morning you won't even remember that you've given birth. There will be no pain, not even any discomfort. Nothing."

Turning, he strolled off slowly in the direction of the house, his pale robe swaying.

Knitting her fingers behind her head, Rachel stared up at the sky. Simon had allayed her concerns about a few things—her body, the rigors of labor.

All at once she felt another sharp movement deep in her

336

belly. She laid a palm over the spot where the baby had kicked.

She still hadn't gotten used to the sensation. It was slightly creepy to her, the idea that there was a living thing growing inside her. But along with the squeamishness, she felt something else—an unexpected surge of tenderness toward the tiny being floating within her. That, she realized, was the other part of her anxiety. She was worried that she might feel terribly guilty after she gave birth, and the baby was—

She could never even finish the thought. And there was no one here she could really confide in.

As desperately as she missed him, she couldn't even unburden herself to David, not after the way he'd reacted the last time she'd brought up her feelings about the baby.

She needed badly to talk to someone. She had never felt so alone in her life.

58

LATE IN THE AFTERNOON OF THE LAST SUNDAY IN MAY, Jack Byrne sat on his living room recliner, gazing through the wide-open window. Just outside his house, the branches of one of the big Norway maples that lined his tree-shaded street stirred peacefully in the warm breeze. From down the block he could hear the playful cries of children as they clattered along the sidewalk on skateboards.

This being Sunday, Marianne's nurse, Mrs. Pitmann, was at home with her own family, so Jack had spent the day tending his comatose daughter by himself. Though her utter helplessness continued to fill him with despair, he was glad to be at home. He had spent the week on a fruitless search of the area around Pattersonville, a small town in Schenectady County, just northwest of Albany.

He had just closed his eyes for a moment when he heard a car pulling up to the curb directly in front of his house. The motor died, a door swung open, then closed with a solid thunk. Heavy footsteps approached the front stoop, then, after a brief pause, moved in the direction of the side

337

door. The wooden ramp made the front entrance unsuitable for anyone not on wheels.

A moment later the door buzzer sounded.

"Coming," Jack called, rising to his feet and heading toward the hallway. He was expecting the visitor, who had phoned earlier in the day to ask if he could drop by. Jack undid the lock and pulled open the side door.

Dressed in jeans and a denim workshirt unbuttoned halfway down his chest, Mike Holson loomed in the doorway.

"Come on in," Jack said, motioning Holson inside with a sideways jerk of his head.

Holson stepped into the house. "Thanks."

Leading his visitor into the living room, Jack nodded toward the plastic-covered chintz sofa, then resettled himself on his recliner.

"Good of you to come," Jack said.

"Yeah, well, like I said on the phone, I've been meaning to get down here on one of my days off." Leaning forward on the sofa, Holson stared at Jack, his brow furrowed with concern. "How's she doing anyway? The chief says there's been some improvement."

Jack studied his visitor for a moment before answering. Holson was sitting with his elbows on his thighs, his hands clasped like a supplicant's. Jack could see that the young man was feeling tense; his fingers were so tightly clenched that the knuckles seemed to shine. He had also fortified himself with drink before coming. Jack had caught a sharp whiff of beer when he'd greeted Holson at the door.

Jack was unsurprised. Most of his visitors seemed nervous nowadays, especially the ones who hadn't seen Marianne in a while and weren't sure what to expect.

"What I told Wayland is that she seemed a little better to *me*. But you'd have to spend lots of time with her to notice it. She still doesn't do any of the important things. If you drove all the way down here expecting to have a conversation with her, forget it." Jack suddenly felt a hundred years old. "It's going to be a long time before she's able to talk," he said, massaging an eye socket with the heel of one hand. "If ever."

Holson looked down at the floor. "Shit," he muttered bitterly. "From what the chief said, I was hoping . . ." He

338

finished the thought with an angry shake of his head. "Can I see her now?" he asked, glancing back at Jack.

"Sure," Jack sighed, pushing himself to his feet. Motioning for Holson to follow, he led him down the main hallway to the little bedroom at the rear of the house. Classical music issued softly from the room. Jack kept the radio on for Marianne throughout most of the day. In the evenings he wheeled her into the family room, where they watched TV together for several hours.

Pausing on the threshold of the bedroom, Jack glanced over at Holson, who seemed to be struggling to find the right expression. Jack understood. Even the neighbors who saw Marianne nearly every day on her fresh-air outings with him or Mrs. Pitmann had to strain to keep the distress from their faces whenever they bent over her wheelchair to say hello. And the young man hesitating so anxiously in the doorway had been Marianne's special buddy on the force.

Jack knew what it was like to have something horrible happen to a buddy. It wasn't hard for him to imagine what Holson must be feeling.

"Go on in," he said gently. "She's begun looking at people when they talk to her. That's one of the ways she's improved. Whether she'll actually recognize you or not . . ." Jack shrugged, as if to say, God knows.

Holson looked at him doubtfully, then, drawing a deep breath, stepped into the room and approached Marianne's wheelchair.

Jack had clothed her in a cobalt-blue, sleeveless dress that emphasized the porcelain whiteness of her face and arms. But the dress also deepened the blue of her large eyes. In her drawn, pallid face, Jack could see the ghostly afterimage of the beautiful young woman his daughter had been.

Ignoring the bentwood rocker Jack had placed beside the wheelchair, Holson hunkered down in front of her. "Hey, Marianne," he said softly. "It's Mike—your buddy. Remember me?" He stared into her face for a long moment, then shot Jack a quizzical look over his shoulder. "Think she hears me?" he asked.

Jack had stepped over to the dresser and lowered the

339

volume on the radio. Now, he studied his daughter's face intently. "She hears you," he said. "Keep talking."

Turning back to Marianne, Holson rested his hands on the armrests of her wheelchair and leaned an inch closer. "Hey, Byrne," he said in a mock-reproachful tone. "The guys gave me a message for you—they said you should quit malingering and get your ass back to work."

It was a strained attempt at humor. Holson seemed acutely uncomfortable. But Jack's attention remained riveted on his daughter.

When Holson first addressed her, her eyes had flickered in his direction. She had been responding that way for a few weeks now. Sometimes, when she shifted her gaze toward Jack, he could swear she recognized him. But it was hard to tell. He tried not to indulge in wishful thinking.

Now, however, as Holson continued his clumsy joking, Marianne's eyes widened slightly. A liquid sound, the kind a baby makes to voice its frustration, began to gurgle deep in her throat. Suddenly, her fingers twitched spasmodically on the arms of her wheelchair.

"Jesus," Jack exclaimed. "She knows you!"

Still squatting on his heels, Mike moved back a few inches from Marianne's face. "Think so?"

"Yes! Yes!" Jack said excitedly. "She hasn't reacted like this to anyone!" Hope surged within him. Maybe Dr. Hecht was right, maybe Marianne really was on the road to recovery. "She knows you!" he repeated. "Look at her!"

A trickle of saliva drooled from one corner of Marianne's mouth as she tried to form the guttural sounds into words. Her struggle was painful to see. Her whole body quivered with the effort.

Hurrying toward her, Jack knelt at her side. "Marianne, it's me, baby, it's Daddy." Reaching up with one hand, he stroked her thick hair back from her forehead. "Don't worry, baby," he soothed. "It'll come. It'll come."

Gradually she quieted down. Jack could feel her agitation subside under his touch. After a few moments her eyelids closed and her breathing grew calmer.

Jack became aware of the wetness refracting his vision. Squeezing his eyes closed, he rubbed away the welling tears with his fingertips, then slowly rose slowly to his feet.

340

Reaching for his hankie, he dabbed Marianne's chin dry, kissed her gently on her widow's peak, and turned away.

Holson had already stepped away from the wheelchair. He stood by the open window, gazing out over the small backyard screened from the neighboring houses by the tall slatted fence Jack had installed years before.

Jack could see that the young man had been unsettled by Marianne's reaction. Holson was looking worriedly out the window, nervously snapping and unsnapping the metal wristband of his Seiko. Jack put his hand around Holson's broad shoulder and squeezed.

"Sorry," Holson said, turning toward Jack. "I didn't mean to upset her."

"No, no," Jack said. "You were terrific. She recognized you, I'm sure of it. And did you see the way her fingers moved? That's a very encouraging sign, Mike."

"How come?" Holson asked.

"Once she begins moving her fingers, its only a matter of time before she'll be able to control them. That's what the neurologists say. And you know what that means."

Holson stared at Jack without responding.

"She can learn how to manipulate things again, maybe even learn how to write again." Jack clapped Holson on the shoulder like a man celebrating a victory. "She'll be able to communicate!"

"That's great," Holson said, though to Jack's ears he sounded somewhat dubious.

Jack noticed that the young cop's brow was beaded with sweat. "Looks like you could use a cold one," he said.

Holson nodded. "Hot in here."

"Yeah," Jack said. "I guess this room does catch some afternoon heat. But between the windows and that"—he jerked a thumb toward the ceiling fan swirling lazily overhead like an idling biplane propeller—"it stays pretty comfortable most times. My wife never could stand air-conditioning. Said it made her feel like a side of beef in a meat locker."

"Where is your wife?" Holson asked.

Jack turned his gaze toward the new grass carpeting the backyard. "She died a few years ago." A silent moment passed before he looked around again at Marianne, who was still sitting with her eyes closed, her breathing soft and regular. "Come," he said, clasping Holson's upper arm. "Let's give her a chance to rest. She's had a lot of stimulation for one day."

On the way back to the living room, Jack detoured into the kitchen to grab two bottles of Rolling Rock from the refrigerator. He handed one to Holson, who took a seat on the sofa. Jack took his customary place on his recliner.

Holson polished off the beer in a couple of gulps, wiped his moustache with the back of one hand, and set the empty bottle down on the marble-topped coffee table. His cheeks ballooned out, then quickly deflated as he hiccuped up a tight-lipped belch. "You really think she's getting better?" he asked.

"Definitely," Jack said. "It might not look like much to you, Mike. But believe me, what you saw in there was a big step for her."

Holson nodded slowly. Then, as if remembering another appointment, he raised his left wrist and checked the time. "Got to go," he said, getting to his feet.

Jack rose too. "Thanks again for coming, Mike."

"Well, if you really think it did some good, maybe I'll drop by again."

"Any time."

Walking Holson outside, Jack shook his hand warmly, then stood on the sidewalk watching him drive away.

The afternoon was shading into early evening. The children had been called inside to wash up for dinner. Jack was alone on the block. Standing there in the suppertime silence, listening to the leaves stir in the trees, he thought about Holson and Marianne.

He felt sure now that there had been more to their relationship than simple friendship. He knew Holson was married. But he also knew something about the feelings that could develop between male and female coworkers. Christ, even he had once indulged in a heavy flirtation with a good-looking precinct secretary named Joanne McCarthy. True, it had never come to anything. But if his devotion to Peg had been less than complete . . .

Turning back to the house with a long sigh, he wondered whether his daughter and Holson had been lovers.

59

LISTENING TO THE LATE MAY DOWNPOUR PELTING THE ROOF, Sheila Mulford—a plump, plain-faced widow of sixty-three—wondered, for the thousandth time in her life, where the expression "raining cats and dogs" came from. As a child she had sometimes stood by her bedroom window and stared out at the rain, trying to visualize the falling water as a downpour of household pets. At other times she wondered if the expression was meant to suggest the violence of a big storm, the way it raged like scrapping beasts.

Neither explanation seemed very convincing to her.

Oh well, who knows? she thought, shrugging. Whatever it means, it's sure doing it now.

Turning away from the stove, and a small aluminum pot into which she'd just emptied a can of Campbell's cream of mushroom, she took a step toward the sink and nearly tripped over her dog, a three-year-old black Labrador named Cisco, who lay pressed to the floor, front legs splayed, tail thumping expectantly on the linoleum.

"Don't go looking at me with those soulful eyes," Mrs. Mulford scolded. "You ain't going out in this weather. Get all soaked and muddy, come back inside tracking your mess over this brand-clean house."

Mrs. Mulford had never seen such a dog. Even in the heaviest downpour, Cisco loved to romp outside in the rain. Sometimes Mrs. Mulford would let him, but she had spent the morning waxing the floors and had no intention of letting him undo her hard work.

"You don't want to go out in this kind of weather anyhow," she said, casting a glance at the kitchen window, which seemed curtained with streaming, liquid gray. "It ain't a fit day out for man nor beast," she added, paraphrasing her late husband, Bill, a lifelong W.C. Fields fan, who never failed to come in from a storm without mimicking the comedian's immortal line.

By late afternoon, however, the sky had lightened and the deluge had dwindled to a sprinkle. Mrs. Mulford was

343

relaxing in her easy chair, leafing through the latest *Reader's Digest*, when Cisco patted up, nuzzled his head under the magazine and laid one paw in her lap. Looking down at him over the top of her half-lens reading glasses, she clucked her tongue, then sighed. "Okay, dog, you go ahead—but don't you come back here if you get dirty!"

Twenty minutes later, as Cisco headed northward, the sun broke through the clouds. By then the rain had stopped completely and the only moisture from above came from the soaked branches that shook their fat droplets onto him whenever he passed through the trees. But out in the meadows the tall grass was drenched, and by the time he was in sight of the stream, Cisco's black coat was slick with water.

Pausing on the crest of the little hill that led down to the stream bank, Cisco shook himself violently, the drops spraying off in all directions, catching the light like a shower of tiny prisms.

Cisco was especially fond of this stream because he could occasionally flush a water rat out of the thick weeds lining the muddy bank. Some of them were too fast for him and he lost them as they slithered into the stream. But every now and then he managed to sink his teeth into one of them. Cisco was always hungry. Anything he caught he ate.

That afternoon, though, was not one of his lucky days. Not only did he fail to turn up a single water rat, but he scratched his nose on a thistle plant as he sniffed along the bank.

Heading home again, he chanced upon a rabbit munching clover in a meadow. Cisco gave chase, but the rabbit disappeared underground. After trying futilely to dig out the rabbit, Cisco flattened himself by the hole, waiting. The smell of the warm rabbit made him salivate. But the rabbit stayed put, cowering in its burrow.

By the time Cisco had given up, the sun was low on the horizon and his stomach tight with hunger. His path led past the place with the big house and the old barn, which still smelled of the farm animals that had once inhabited it. The house had been abandoned for many years, but humans had recently moved back into it. Still, the presence

344

of the new occupants hadn't kept Cisco away from the place. No one had ever bothered him.

This time, however, as he trotted across the yard in front of the big, empty barn, Cisco heard a sharp whistle, then a man's voice calling out to him. Pulling up short, Cisco cocked his head in the direction of the sound. A tall man was standing by the barn door, holding something high in the air.

Cisco was a friendly dog, big enough not to be afraid of anything he had met so far in life. Still, he wouldn't have gone out of his way to approach the stranger. But the object dangling from the man's outstretched hand was a big chunk of meat, and it smelled too good to resist.

Barking once, Cisco headed over to the man and, tail wagging, bolted the meat down in a few bites. As he chewed, he felt the man take hold of his leather collar with one strong hand and, with the other, begin to stroke his head. This was fine with Cisco. He liked to be caressed, and the man had given him the meat.

After a few minutes, though, a strange tiredness began stealing over him. Suddenly he wanted desperately to be at home, stretched out on the floor beside the woman's feet. Whining, he tried feebly to pull away. Above him the man laughed, a nasty sound that made Cisco struggle even harder. But with every passing second, his limbs were growing weaker.

The man tightened his grip on Cisco's collar.

60

ON SCREEN, THE LOCAL TV ANCHORWOMAN—A BLOW-DRIED blonde with the whitest teeth this side of a Crest commercial—ran through the routine horrors of the day. In Brooklyn, a gang of white teens armed with tire irons and baseball bats had set upon a pair of black passersby, beating one of them to death. A few hours later, a thirty-year-old white stockbroker had been killed by a gang of teenage blacks in a street mugging in lower Manhattan. And then there was the seventy-year-old grandmother in Queens, found raped and strangled in her bedroom. The apartment showed no signs of forced entry. Apparently, the victim had known her killer. The police were in the process of questioning an eighteen-year-old neighbor, a boy she had known all his life.

Sitting on the family room sofa, Jack grimaced at the TV. Why the hell do they call it "news"? he thought. It's just the same old shit, day after day. Scraping the last of the ice cream from his bowl, he stuck the spoon in his mouth and sucked it clean. Looks like we're in for another long, hot summer in the city, he mused, the look on his face as sour as if he'd just swallowed a spoonful of brine.

He watched until the weather report was over, then rose and snapped off the TV. The forecast for the next day, Saturday, June 4, called for cloudy skies but no rain until the evening. He was grateful for that. Tomorrow morning he would be heading up north again, to a small town called Minaville. Mrs. Pitmann was due promptly at seven A.M. and had agreed to stay until eight at night. If he made good time traveling, he could count on maybe seven hours of searching. That wasn't a lot of time, but at least he wouldn't be slowed down by a storm.

In the kitchen, he rinsed out the spoon and bowl and stuck them in the draining rack. For the past few weeks, ever since the warm weather started in earnest, he had been eating two scoops of ice cream every night while watching the eleven o'clock news. He had no particular craving for ice cream, any more than he had for other foods. Most evenings, as he sat there spooning it down, he barely tasted it. If someone had asked him what flavor he was eating, he would have had to glance down at the bowl. But his search required energy. As far as Jack was concerned, the double mound of frozen sweetness he consumed every night was nothing more than concentrated fuel.

He'd actually begun buying the stuff for Marianne, who'd been addicted to ice cream all her life. During the most weight-conscious years of her adolescence, her struggles to resist the temptation of a hot fudge sundae had been painful to behold. A month ago he had walked to the supermarket and brought home a quart of Häagen-Dazs chocolate chocolate chip. Since then, he had been giving her a scoopful every evening, tucking a paper napkin under her chin and feeding her tiny bitefuls, the way he'd fed her Gerber's tapioca pudding when she was a baby.

At the feel of the spoon on her lower lip, she would open her mouth just wide enough for him to insert the tip, then nibble at the ice cream with a strange delicacy. He thought the taste of the ice cream would comfort her, though he couldn't be sure that she even recognized it anymore.

Until tonight, that is. For the first time, she seemed aware of what she was eating. Her eyes had fixed on his, and she'd made a deep-throated gurgle that, to Jack's sensitized ears, at least, sounded like contentment. The corners of her mouth twitched a little too, and he thought that she might be trying to smile.

Slowly but surely she was showing signs of progress. Maybe Dorothy, Jack's sister down in Delaware, was right. Maybe he ought to send Marianne to stay with her. The Dowling Institute, a nationally known clinic for neurological patients, was less than ten miles away from her home, and Dorothy had volunteered to drive her niece back and forth every day for therapy.

When Jack had mentioned Dorothy's proposal to Stuart Hecht a few weeks ago, the sober-faced young doctor had pronounced it an excellent plan. "The Dowling Institute's a first-rate facility," he had said. "It might be a very good thing for her—bring her along quicker. That is, if you can let her go."

That, of course, was the crux of the problem. Jack didn't know if he *could* let Marianne go. On the other hand, if Marianne weren't around, he'd have more freedom to hunt for Simon Proctor.

Turning off the kitchen light, he walked down the hallway and peered in at his daughter. Eyes shut, she lay flat on her back, a light cotton blanket pulled up to her chest. He could see from the soft, rhythmic movement of the blanket that she was sleeping peacefully. In the muted glow of the bed lamp, she looked peaceful and girlish—except for her hair, jarringly white in the lamplight.

Jack always left the lamp burning around the clock. He did not want Marianne to awaken in the darkness and go plunging back into the nightmare of that unspeakable winter night when Simon Proctor had placed her living in the grave.

After he had kissed his sleeping daughter on the brow and given his teeth a vigorous brushing, Jack climbed into bed and fell instantly asleep. Outside, a black '89 Buick turned the corner at the far end of the block and cruised down the street, slowing a bit as it passed by the Byrnes' modest brick house. Continuing down the street, it swung right at the corner and disappeared.

When it reappeared a minute later, its headlights were off. Most of the cars belonging to the houses were off the street, on driveways or in garages, so parking spaces were plentiful. The Buick slid to a stop across from and slightly diagonal to the north side of the Byrne house, in a shadowy spot shielded from the orange glow of the streetlamps by the overhanging branches of a big maple.

The motor died but, though the minutes ticked by, no one emerged from the car. From the outside the windows looked as solid as the black-enameled body.

Seated behind the steering wheel, Mike Holson watched and waited.

From where he sat, he could see the dull glow of a lamp coming from a rear window of the house. He couldn't tell if the source was the bitch's bedroom or her father's. He leaned his skull back on the headrest and waited.

After a while he began to sweat. The night was cool for June, but Holson was wearing black Reeboks, black Levi's, and a long-sleeved black turtleneck.

He reached down to the window handle and rolled the glass down a crack.

The light was still burning. Holson lifted his left wrist close to his face and, with the forefinger of the opposite hand, squeezed the little button on the watch rim that illuminated the dial. It was close to twelve-thirty.

Fifteen minutes later he decided that the light must be coming from Marianne's room, and that it was probably kept burning all night.

Reaching into his right pocket, he pulled out a pair of black kidskin gloves and slipped them on his hands. Then, stepping quietly from the car, he closed the door carefully, leaving it slightly ajar. He had already adjusted the switch on the roof lamp so that the light would stay off, even with the door open.

Hurrying across the street, he made straight for the rear of the house.

Even if she had been able to speak, Marianne couldn't have described the sound that woke her. It was not something she was accustomed to hearing—an odd, metallic scraping noise coming from the window across from her bed.

She was used to the quiet revolutions of the fan above her head. They had become an ingredient of her sleep, like the feel of the pillow beneath her head. But her sleep was not as sound as her father thought. A burst of canned laughter from the TV, the sudden gush of water from the bathroom taps, the rumble of her father's voice as he spoke on the phone—all these things disturbed her sleep momentarily. Her forehead puckered as she struggled, unconsciously, to interpret the noises, to fit them into some remembered pattern. Once she did, she could relax. Thunder would waken her instantly, and for a few moments her eyes would roll with anxiety as she tried to understand the frightening noise. She could not have said "thunder" or "storm." But after a while her mind labeled it "safe," and she was able to drop back into sleep again.

The scraping noise was different, out of place. Her mind could connect it to nothing in her daily experience. Within seconds she began to struggle frantically toward consciousness, the way a panicky diver flounders up toward the wavering light. A sense of alarm was swelling within her, propelling her out of her sleep, but the sea of darkness that engulfed her was as heavy as tar and, try as she might, she could not seem to fight her way to the surface.

By the time her eyes fluttered opened, Mike Holson had forced the window screen open and was standing inside her room, at her bedside.

She knew him immediately—this time not just his face, but his name as well. Her heart contracted violently inside her, and she gasped with fear and pain. She could see his mouth moving and hear words coming toward her, words she could not decipher.

Suddenly the pillow beneath her head was yanked away.

She could see it in his hands and began to roll her head from side to side, to thump her feet beneath the sheet and blanket. Her arms were frozen at her sides, fingers jerking.

Then she heard him whisper clearly: "Let's do it in the dark, baby."

An instant later the light was gone, the light she had clung to so desperately for months. Next she felt an enormous weight straddling her chest and the smothering mass of the pillow as Holson forced it down on her head.

But by then her head had turned, fast, toward the space where the light had been, and that saved her.

She shrieked with rage and panic and, at the same time, her arm muscles came to life. Her right hand swept clear of the bed in a broad arc and struck the ceramic lamp, which teetered on the edge of the night table for an instant, then plunged to the floor and shattered.

In his dream, Jack was back on the force, chasing a gang of teenagers down a dark, crooked street. Though he was running hard enough to feel his chest tighten, the gang was moving at a casual lope, like the members of a high school football team jogging onto the practice field.

All at once the twisting streets vanished. The young men were outside in a bright meadow, their torn jeans and black leather jackets replaced by strange scarlet uniforms—ballooning sweatpants and long, flowing jerseys. Above their heads, they tossed a football-sized projectile, laughing and shouting as they hurled it back and forth. Jack squinted hard at the object. It was a female doll, its lifeless features painted onto its white ceramic face—red puckered lips, saucer-eyes as shiny as mirrors. Jet-black bangs hung down to its eyebrows.

The dozen young men cackled and jeered as they played catch with the doll. Suddenly, someone was standing beside Jack. It was Jean Peary. "That's my baby. They have my baby." Jack looked again. The doll's arms and legs were waving frantically as it flew through the air into the hands of the tallest of the team members, a long-haired blond whose broad-shouldered back was turned toward Jack. Slowly, the young man swiveled, his lips twisted upward into a mocking grin. With both hands, he raised the struggling infant high over his head.

350

Jean let out a desperate shriek as the young man flung his hands downward, hurling the infant to the solid ground, where its porcelain skull shattered with a sickening crash.

But even as it happened, Jack's slumbering mind stirred with the consciousness that the startling noises—the high-pitched scream and accompanying crash—were coming from outside his head.

It took him a few moments to wrest himself awake. A confusion of sounds that his sleep-fuddled brain couldn't make sense of filtered into his awareness. Footsteps? The sliding of a window sash inside its frame?

His eyes shot open. Leaping from his bed, he saw at once that something was wrong. The stretch of hallway just outside his door, normally illuminated by the light spilling from Marianne's perpetually burning bed lamp, was black.

He was across the hall in an instant, hitting the wall switch just inside her bedroom as he dashed through her door.

Blinking in the sudden, sharp light from the ceiling fixture, he saw her lamp in pieces on the floor and the pillow beside it. Marianne was sprawled half off the mattress, her lower body entangled in the bedclothes, her left arm flailing in the air as though she were trying to beat off an invisible assailant. The sounds coming from her throat were raw and guttural—primal grunts of rage, desperation, and pure animal fear.

Jack leapt to the bedside, scooped her in his arms and began rocking her gently back and forth, as he had when she was a newborn.

"Sshhhh," he soothed. "It's okay, baby. It was just a nightmare."

Her hair was soaked with sweat and he stroked it back from her forehead until she quieted. Somewhere outside, a motor revved and a car screeched away from the curb. The sounds registered in Jack's mind, but he was too focused on Marianne to pay them much attention.

Suddenly she began to struggle against him, as though to free herself from his embrace. He loosened his hold and, lowering her away from him, saw the urgency in her eyes and the frantic movement of her lips. She was trying desperately to speak.

351

"What is it, baby?" he pleaded. "Tell me."

She was making sounds, but her mouth couldn't form them into words. After a while she gave up, squeezing her eyes and lips tight in frustration.

Abruptly, she opened her eyes again. Raising her right hand, she stuck out the forefinger, which jerked up and down like a seismograph needle registering an earthquake.

Jack stared in astonishment. He could feel his heart do a little flip as the realization dawned on him. She was signaling that she wanted to write.

"Yes," he said excitedly. "I understand."

He ran back to his room and returned a moment later clutching a legal pad and felt-tip pen. He helped her curl the index finger of her right hand around the pen, then held the pad before her. His own hands were shaking too, and it took some effort to hold the pad steady.

Marianne raised the pen to the yellow paper and attempted to write, though her hand tremored badly. Several times the pen slipped from her grasp and Jack had to put it back in her hand.

After a few moments of struggle, Marianne dropped her hand to her side, as though she were exhausted from the effort.

Jack held the pad up to the light. The top sheet contained a few scratch marks that bore only the vaguest resemblance to letters. He thought he could make out an H and a L— was she trying to write HELP?—but he couldn't be sure.

Still, she had tried! Looking down at her face, he could see the bitterness of her disappointment. Tossing the pad aside, he bent to her again and took her back into his arms.

"Don't feel bad, Marianne," he whispered fervently. "Don't you see what a breakthrough this is? How well you're progressing? You just need some more time. And a little help."

Yes, he told himself. She's begging you for help. And you can't do that job by yourself.

Blinking back the moisture that had seeped into his eyes, he reached his decision.

As much as he hated to be parted from her, to relinquish control and entrust his child to the care of others, he was not acting in her best interests by keeping her with him at

352

home. What his daughter needed at this point, even more than the love and reassurance he could provide, was intensive treatment by professionals, people who would know how to give the world back to her.

He would take his sister's advice. He would send Marianne to live in Delaware.

61

LAUREN KELLY, TEN YEARS OLD, HAD STAYED HOME FROM school for three days with a sore throat, headache, and dizziness, so when her little sister, Suzie, woke up on Thursday morning complaining of the same symptoms, Mrs. Kelly wasn't surprised. Not that she necessarily believed that the younger child was really sick. For the past two days, seven-year-old Suzie had trudged off to school whining about the unfairness of life. "How come *she* gets to stay home all the time?" Still, Mrs. Kelly wasn't the type of mother who took chances with her children's health. And so, though the timing couldn't have been more inconvenient, she found herself, on the morning of June 9, with both her children on her hands.

Normally, she wouldn't have minded, but today was a different story. Her article for the PTA newsletter—about the recent fourth-grade trip to the Teatown Lake Reservation—was due that afternoon, and she didn't want her kids in her hair while she worked on it. She needed some way to keep them occupied for a few hours.

Well, she thought as she loaded the breakfast dishes into the KitchenAid, that's why God invented VCRs.

When she told the girls that she was running into town for a few minutes to pick up a tape for them to watch, each had a different request. Lauren asked for *Look Who's Talking,* while Suzie begged for *The Little Mermaid.* But Mrs. Kelly had her own ideas. For a long time she had wanted her girls to see one of her own favorite films, *Harvey.* Mrs. Kelly had first encountered the movie on TV when she was around Lauren's age and had adored it ever since. To her mind, it was the greatest feel-good movie of all time. Just thinking about it made her smile. And given all the traumas their little town had suffered since the start of the school year, smiles weren't so easy to come by.

Spring had been robbed of its sweetness by the still-unsolved murder of Jerry Waller. Like everyone else she knew, Mrs. Kelly had been deeply shaken by the news of his death, and even more stunned by its circumstances. The police hadn't made all the details of the murder public, but the word around town was that he had run afoul of drug dealers and been killed in some particularly brutal way. Though neither of her girls had been students of his, Mrs. Kelly knew him from PTA meetings. She also knew his reputation as one of the most caring and dedicated teachers at Willow Brook.

Still, it was obvious from the way he looked and dressed that he had something of a hippie past, which would help account for his involvement with drugs. And according to local gossip, his marriage had been in serious trouble. Perhaps the poor man had been driven to extremes by depression.

Whatever the case, she couldn't imagine a better medicine for her girls than a heartwarming dose of the old Jimmy Stewart movie.

The day was gloriously bright when Mrs. Kelly stepped into her car for the three-minute ride into town. She bypassed the local video shop and headed directly for the library, where she had seen *Harvey* listed in the catalogue. Luckily, the movie was available. "You're the second person who's asked for it this week," the librarian, Mrs. Blanford, said. Apparently the tape had been returned just the day before by a good-looking teenage boy Mrs. Blanford had never seen before. Mrs. Blanford, who evidently loved the movie as much as Mrs. Kelly did, had been delighted to see that a teenager had been interested in watching *Harvey*. "Young people nowadays tend to go in for such trash," she clucked as she stamped the due date on the checkout card.

Back home, Mrs. Kelly popped the tape into the VCR and left Lauren and Suzie seated side by side under a comforter on the family room sofa. Then she prepared a cup of instant coffee in the microwave and settled down with her legal pad at the kitchen table.

In the background she could hear the playful lilt of the soundtrack music, and then Jimmy Stewart's gentle drawl as he offered his card to a complete stranger and invited him to dinner. Seconds later Mrs. Kelly was lost in her writing.

She was so deeply immersed in it that it took a while for her to become aware of something strange gnawing at the edge of her consciousness. She lifted up her head and listened. It was the movie. The whimsical music had changed into an ominous throbbing, and Mrs. Kelly thought she could hear something that sounded like chants. Her eyebrows furrowed as she concentrated on the peculiar noises.

Suddenly screams and horrified cries of "Mommy! Mommy!" burst from the other room. Leaping up, Mrs. Kelly dashed into the family room, freezing at the sight that confronted her on the TV screen. For a moment she simply could not make sense of what she was seeing.

When she finally realized what it was, Mrs. Kelly began to scream too.

62

"YOU SHOULD'VE SEEN THIS WOMAN," WAYLAND WAS SAYing. "She comes running in here holding the tape by one corner, arm's length, like this"—he stuck out his right hand, the index finger and thumb forming a little tweezer—"like it had been dipped in shit or something." He expelled a sharp, humorless snort. "Which, in a manner of speaking, it was."

Jack focused hard on Wayland's words, struggling against the memory that threatened to overwhelm him. Just being there in Wayland's office with the video setup looming before him was giving him sweaty palms. The last time he had stared at that screen, it had shown him the worst horror he'd ever been forced to look at in his life. Now he'd been invited to a private screening of Simon Proctor's latest home video, and he was doing his best to steel himself.

Wayland popped open the black plastic case and removed the cassette. "It's clean of prints, of course," he said, holding it out so that Jack could see the back edge of the cartridge. "See that?" Wayland asked. The little space where the safety tab had been removed was covered with a strip of Scotch tape. "They taped up the hole and just re-recorded over the movie. Mom goes to the library to take out a nice film for the kiddies, and—surprise!"

"What movie?" Jack asked.

"Harvey, that old Jimmy Stewart comedy about the guy with the giant rabbit."

Jack nodded. "Good movie. Very funny."

"Not this version," Wayland said grimly, shoving the cassette into the machine. Leaning back against his desk, he hit the remote and started the show.

For a half minute or so the black-and-white movie sped across the screen, the actors miming spastically. Then a curtain of static lowered itself over the movie. When it rose again, something very different was going on.

Inside a shadowy, cavernous space murkily illuminated by candlelight, a cluster of young bodies—maybe ten in all—lay entwined on a carpeted floor. Jack assumed that he was looking at the same group of people he had seen once before—only then they had been outside in the snow, their bodies concealed beneath parkas and jeans. Now they wore nothing but a slick glaze of oil, though Jack could see that their features were hidden beneath satiny half-masks that covered their faces above the mouth.

Jack wondered briefly what Mrs. Kelly's children had made of the writhing mass of bodies, their mouths between each other's legs, buttocks grinding and squirming. The orgy continued for several minutes, the camera moving in occasionally to focus on a girl's lips tightening into an O as her climax came on her, or to focus on a jet of sperm arcing onto a belly.

After a while the activity subsided. The cult members rose shakily to their feet and moved to a long black-draped table, arranging themselves around it. Jack looked hard at the screen, searching for telltale body marks—scars, tattoos, anything that might serve as a lead. All the cult members looked very young, except for a couple of the males, whose bodies, though well-muscled, had the fleshiness of full maturity. He checked the women closely for one who might be pregnant. But the girls all looked as flat-bellied and slim-hipped as the boys.

Out of the throats of the coven rose a shrill, exultant chant, whose words Jack could not make out. Then a big man, his naked body greased and his face masked by a grinning death's-head, emerged from the shadows and approached the satin-draped table, cradling a black Labrador retriever that hung in his arms like fresh kill. Stooping, the tall man lowered the limp dog onto the table. As he did, Jack caught a glimpse of two strange, almond-shaped markings tattooed around the man's red-tinted nipples like dragon's eyes.

The death's-head leered up into the camera, then looked back down at the dog. Suddenly, the man thrust his left fist straight over his head, crying, "Belphegor!" Something flashed in the darkness. Jack saw that the man was clutching a sharp-pointed dagger.

Immediately, a tall boy with slicked-back blond hair leaned forward and pried open the dog's jaws with both hands. The tall man stuck his right hand inside the dog's mouth and took hold of the tongue. Reaching down with his dagger, he shoved the tip of the blade into its underside, where it was attached to the floor of the mouth. Then he began to cut.

Jack had assumed that the dog was dead—until he saw its legs begin to twitch spasmodically and heard its high-pitched whine as the man continued to work away at its tongue.

"Shit," Wayland hissed. Jack glanced up at him. Wayland's mouth was pulled into a tight grimace. By the time Jack turned back to the screen, the tall man had finished with the tongue, which lay in a bloody lump on the table, and had set to work between the male dog's legs.

The butchering took a while. The last part of the operation involved the removal of a large square of hide from the left flank of the animal. By then its legs had ceased twitching, and the tall man's hands were coated with blood up to the wrists. Most of the young men and women clustered around the table were speckled with dark droplets, which had sprayed from the dog's severed throat.

When the skinning was completed, the camera moved in slowly for a close-up of the grinning skull mask. All at once the tall man reached up and shoved the mask up onto the top of his head. Jack jerked forward on his seat, feeling his heart tighten up like a clenched fist.

He was looking straight into the face of Simon Proctor.

No, Jack thought, staring hard into Proctor's mocking eyes. Nothing supernatural there. Evil, yes. But human evil. Evil that can be stopped.

Proctor's lips began to move. "The great sacrifice draws near," he gloated. "The offering of the supreme gift. You see our preparations. Nothing can interfere."

Guess again, scumbag, Jack thought.

"The darkness will swallow you all," Proctor sneered. Abruptly, his face dissolved into a crackling snowstorm. When the screen cleared up, the darkness was gone and the picture had reverted to a bright-lit world of dotty old maids and a madman as lovable as an overgrown rabbit.

Wayland switched off the machine and let out a loud whoosh, as though he'd been holding his breath for a while. "So?" he asked, turning toward Jack.

"He's taunting us," Jack said.

"Sick fuck," Wayland said, lighting up a cigarette. "What'd you make of that 'supreme gift' bullshit?"

Jack leaned back in his seat. "Remember those pages from that old book on Satanism I sent to you? The ones with the engraving?"

"Yeah," Wayland said. "I remember."

"He's getting ready for another sacrifice," Jack said. "That's what he's planning to do with that dog hide. Make a pouch. To smother a baby." Jack drew in a deep breath, then exhaled it slowly. "Only this one will be fresh from the womb. He wants the first breath it takes. That'll be the gift. The uncorrupted soul of innocence. He's planning to do it on August first."

Wayland stared at him through narrowed eyes. "How do you know that?"

"I know. Marianne did too." Jack shook his head. "She was right all along. About everything."

Wayland glanced down at the smoking cigarette between his fingers and didn't say a word. Then he shot Jack a quizzical glance. "But how the hell can the asshole arrange that? He can't—" Wayland's eyes widened abruptly in realization.

Jack nodded. "That's right. A little amateur surgery. A do-it-yourself cesarean."

Wayland stared at Jack in silence for a moment, then muttered, "Jesus, Jack. We gotta stop that motherfucker."

"Yes. We do," answered Jack, not even conscious of the silver-handled razor clenched in his fist, deep in his jacket pocket.

63

THE DELICATE MEAT, GLOSSED WITH RED, SEEMED TO MELT beneath his knife edge. Jack speared a bite with his silver fork and raised it to his mouth.

"How's the duck?" Jean asked, smiling.

Jack finished chewing before he answered. "Great. Never had it with cherry sauce before." He contemplated the few remaining slices, arranged in a little fantail in the center of his plate. "The portions are very, ah, elegant."

Jean smothered the laughter that would have seemed out of place in the hush of the Bedford restaurant that she had chosen for her date with Jack. Around them the muted talk of the other dining couples filled the small, candlelit room with a warm, conspiratorial sound, intimacy made audible.

Jean took a sip of Chablis. "They want you to save room for dessert. Don't worry, Jack," she said, peering at him over the rim of her wineglass. "I won't let you leave here hungry."

Jack smiled back at her. In the candle glow, her complexion looked as warm as a bride's. But he could see that the months of worry had deepened the lines in her face—across her brow, under her eyes, at the corners of her mouth.

He wondered how she would look if she knew the whole truth.

He had continued to keep it from her, of course—the unspeakable peril her daughter was in. She knew how urgently he was searching for Simon Proctor. But she knew nothing about Lammas or the monstrous ritual he was sure would be performed on that day.

359

Though they had seen each other only occasionally in the months since they first met, they spoke frequently on the phone. Jack could feel their friendship deepening in ways that, under more normal circumstances, sometimes lead to love. He wanted badly to protect her. By now his unrelenting hunt for Simon Proctor was driven as much by a desperate desire to save her child from destruction as it was by his own hunger for revenge.

"Still no word from Rachel?" he asked.

Jean shook her head forlornly. It had been over two months since she had last heard from her daughter. Tim Rutherford, too, had dropped out of sight. The police had been unable to turn up any record of a student by that name registered at Purchase. The only Tim Rutherford currently within the state university system was a twenty-three-year-old, black theater-arts major at Albany.

Jean had stopped eating. The cheerfulness she'd been trying to sustain since the start of the dinner had evaporated in an instant. She placed her fork—a plump, curried scallop impaled on the tines—onto her plate and lowered her head.

"I'm so terrified that . . ." She left the sentence dangling, afraid to speak the words.

Jack reached across the table and squeezed one of her hands. "She's not dead, Jean," he said. "I can guarantee it."

She looked up at him quickly. "How can you be sure?" she asked. She wanted desperately to believe him. He could see the hope in her eyes. But her voice was full of suspicion. Jean Peary was nobody's fool; Jack knew that as well as anybody. She could tell that he was holding something back from her.

He leaned toward her earnestly and said, "I know Proctor. How he thinks. Rachel is too important to him."

For a long moment Jean sat there, searching his eyes, saying nothing. Then, as though she'd made a conscious decision that what she didn't know wouldn't hurt her, she smiled wanly and nodded, relaxing back in her chair.

They said nothing for a while, until Jack picked up his utensils and resumed eating. "Those scallops okay?" he asked, gesturing with his fork.

Jean glanced down at her food as though she'd forgotten

that she had ordered any. "Just fine," she said, clearing her throat. "Here . . ." She lifted her fork and held the pearlescent lump toward Jack's mouth. "Taste."

"Delicious," he said, chewing. "You shouldn't let them get cold."

"You're right," Jean said, squaring her shoulders and getting back to the business of eating.

"Tell me how your search is going," she said a moment later, as Jack refilled her wineglass. "Any progress?"

"Not much," he confessed, though he tried to keep his tone undiscouraged. "I've eliminated some possibilities, but . . ." As he finished the meat, he filled Jean in on the details of his most recent expeditions upstate.

Armed with police photographs of Proctor, a snapshot of Rachel provided by Jean, and a Hagstrom road map of the region, Jack had spent the past few weeks checking out several towns on the north side of the river. He had followed his usual procedure—stopping at gas stations, groceries, post offices, pharmacies, liquor stores, and whatever real estate agencies he could find.

One shaggy-haired 7-Eleven clerk in Jonesville thought he remembered an "old dude" who looked like the man in the mug shots come into the store with a cute blond girl, "a real cheerleader type." But when Jack pressed him for details, the young man picked at a zit on his chin for a moment, as though that were an integral part of his thinking process, then said, "It was sometime last summer. Yeah, I'm positive. I remember, 'cause I'd just started working here like a week before they came in."

Proctor, of course, had still been in prison at that time.

"And that was my *best* lead," Jack said wryly. "But I'll find them," he asserted, sounding more confident than he felt. "Especially with so much more time to devote to the job. Now that Marianne's away."

"You miss her, don't you?" Jean said gently.

"You bet. But this is definitely the best thing for her. No question."

"How's she doing?"

"Just great. So far, most of the stuff that's gone on at the institute has been diagnostic. The real therapy will start next week. But Dorothy says she's getting stronger by the day. She says that—hey, you with me?"

Realizing that Jean was no longer listening, Jack had looked up from his plate. He saw that she was staring at something behind him.

"What's wrong?" he asked.

"That man," she said.

He turned his head in the direction of her gaze.

"It's David Prince," she said. "I'm sure of it."

A tall, tanned, dark-haired man in his forties stood at the front of the restaurant, chatting like an old acquaintance with the balding maître d'. Nestled in the crook of his right arm was a striking redhead in a simple black dress held onto her body by spaghetti straps. The man wore a loose-cut suit that even Jack, notoriously oblivious to fashion, recognized as one of those fancy designer outfits whose names he could never remember.

Beaming at some pleasantry Jack couldn't hear, the maître d' gestured in Jack and Jean's direction, toward an empty corner table in the rear. Then, at Prince's nod of approval, he turned and led them across the room.

Glancing quickly back at Jean, Jack could see in her face that she intended to speak to Prince.

As the little procession passed by the table, Jean reached up and lightly touched Prince's arm. "Excuse me," she said. "Mr. Prince?"

Pausing, Prince glanced down at her quizzically. "Yes?"

"I'm Jean Peary, Rachel's mother. We met once, at your house. That horrible night."

"Of course, Mrs. Peary. I remember you. How are you?"

Jean made an "I've-been-better" face, which immediately turned somber. "But how are you?" she asked. "I don't have to tell you how sick I was to hear about—"

"I know, Mrs. Peary," Prince cut in, as though his tragedies were still too painful to talk about. "I appreciate it."

Prince's date and the maître d' had halted a few feet away and were looking on with polite smiles.

"It was nice seeing you again, Mrs. Peary," Prince said. "Please give Rachel my regards." Nodding at Jack, who had been studying his face intently, he began to turn away.

"Mr. Prince," Jack said quickly.

Prince stopped and looked in Jack's direction.

"My name's Byrne," said Jack, half rising from his chair and holding out his right hand. "Jack Byrne."

As the two men shook, Jack thought he saw something flicker in Prince's eyes, perhaps a spark of recognition, perhaps something else. Jack couldn't tell. Whatever had gleamed there was gone in an instant, leaving nothing but a look of mild curiosity.

"I know this is an inconvenient moment, Mr. Prince," Jack went on, keeping his voice at a discreetly subdued level. "But the Northampton police have been trying to contact you for months."

"Are you a policeman, Mr. Byrne?"

"Retired," Jack said. "NYPD."

"Then what's your interest in this matter?"

"Personal," said Jack. "My daughter was a member of the Northampton force."

Prince studied Jack's face silently for a moment before saying, "I seem to remember that my wife received a visit from a young policewoman named Byrne. You said 'was.' Did something happen to her?"

"You don't know about it?"

"Sorry. I've been out of the country for the past few months. What happened?"

Jack looked hard into his eyes. "She fell into the hands of Simon Proctor."

Jack thought he saw Prince stiffen. At that moment the redhead made a soft, throat-clearing sound.

"Mr. Byrne, if you please. I've already told the police all I know about Simon Proctor. I think the whole thing's a fantasy."

"What happened to my daughter is no fantasy, Mr. Prince. What happened to your baby isn't either."

"Simon Proctor had nothing to do with that," Prince said.

"We have good reason to believe that he did."

Jack felt rather than saw Jean turn her head to stare at him. But his eyes remained fixed on Prince.

After a moment's hesitation, Prince turned and flashed his date an apologetic look, then nodded at the maître d', who led the young woman to the corner table.

Prince pulled out one of the vacant chairs at Jack and Jean's table and seated himself.

363

"Thank you, Mr. Prince," Jack said, settling back into his chair. "I won't keep you long."

"No," Prince answered. "You won't. What, specifically, can I do for you, Mr. Byrne?"

"It would be a great help to the investigation if you could supply us with a bit more information—the names of all the people who were members of your commune back in the sixties, for example. The one Proctor headed."

Prince's face darkened. "You know about the commune?"

"I'm working closely with Dick Wayland," Jack said.

"Good luck," Prince snorted.

"Mr. Prince, you have no idea how important this is. More lives are at stake."

"Mr. Byrne, as far as I'm concerned, this matter ended with the suicide of that little prick, Peterson. As I explained to your incompetent friend Wayland on various occasions, this stuff about Simon Proctor is pure bullshit. But if it will make you feel better . . ." He pushed his chair away from the table and rose to his feet. "I'm leaving again for Europe tomorrow evening." Reaching inside his jacket, he extracted a small leather case, flipped it open and removed a business card. "Call my secretary in a couple of days. She'll have a list of all the names I can remember." He handed Jack the card, then nodded at Jean. "Now, I'd like to have my dinner," he said, then turned and walked away.

Jack glanced at the card, pulled his wallet from his back pocket and stuck it away in a side compartment. When he looked back up at Jean, her face had gone so white that, had the maître d' noticed it, he would have hurried to her side, frightened that the food had made her ill.

"Jean?" Jack asked, reaching across to her again. He knew what had happened. As he'd remarked to himself earlier, she was nobody's fool. She hadn't missed his remark about Simon Proctor and David Prince's baby. Now the implications were clicking into place.

"Jack," she said, sounding utterly stricken. "Babies? They kill babies?"

"We don't know for sure, Jean," he answered. "It's possible."

"And Rachel?" she said hollowly. "She was part of it?"

"I just don't know, Jean," he repeated gently. "She may

364

be perfectly innocent. Men like Proctor prey on the innocent, use them for their own purposes."

For a moment Jean seemed to take some comfort from that. Then her eyes widened, as if another, even more horrific thought had just occurred to her. "Rachel's child," she gasped.

"I swear to you, Jean," Jack said quickly. "I won't let anything happen to them. Rachel *or* the baby."

He spent the next several minutes soothing her, and finally she seemed to get a grip on herself.

"Jack," she said fervently. "You have to promise me that you'll do everything in your power to get her back for me."

"You know I will," he swore. Glancing over Jean's shoulder, he saw David Prince and his date leaning toward each other over the small, linen-draped table. As Jack watched, the woman picked up Prince's right hand with both of hers and kissed it tenderly on the palm.

Just then the waiter reappeared to ask about dessert.

"You go ahead, Jack," Jean said, unsnapping her purse and fishing out a Kleenex, which she used to dab her eyes.

"Just coffee for me," Jack said to the waiter. "Regular."

The waiter turned back to Jean. "Perhaps a liqueur for the lady?"

"Ah yes," Jean said with a humorless little laugh. "A drink. What a clever idea."

64

AT MIDNIGHT ON THURSDAY, JULY 2, THE HERKIMER County town of Barnesville (Pop. 263) lay sleeping under a star-spangled sky. The handful of houses bordering County Road 39A, most of them slightly tumbledown, with sagging front porches and fenced-in yards dominated by towering sunflowers, had been dark for hours. The tiny commercial district—Barnesville Paint and Hardware, Cafferty's Dew Drop Inn, Williams' Pharmacy, All-Pro Septic, and Knabel's General Store—had been dead since dinnertime. Northerly winds had swept the sky free of clouds, and the air was chilly for July.

At five minutes past midnight a battered Chevy pickup whooshed through town at eighty. For the next half hour the road remained dark and empty. The night was absolutely still, save for the noises of the crickets and the echoing throb of a bullfrog in a nearby lake. Then a motorized hum could be heard in the distance, growing steadily louder. A few minutes later a small sport car—a Mazda Miata—appeared from the north, weaving slightly as it moved along the blacktop, as though its driver weren't fully in control.

Slowing as it reached the little shopping district, the car turned into the unpaved parking area at the side of Knabel's General Store and came to a stop. The lights died, the driver's door swung open, and a very pregnant Rachel Peary squeezed herself out from behind the steering wheel and, glancing around nervously, stepped into the night.

Closing the car door quietly, she made her way around to the side of the little store, a low-roofed wooden building with a dusty display window and a "Live Bait" sandwich board set up outside. The bright, three-quarter moon lit her way. Bolted to the wood-shingled wall was a single pay phone. Rachel had never used it, but she knew it was there. Knabel's was the place where the other members of Simon's little group came to make their phone calls. There was no telephone at the farmstead. Even if there had been, Rachel would not have used it.

Not to make this call.

She had daydreamed about doing this for weeks, though she hadn't thought she'd have the courage to go through with it. Tonight, almost impulsively, she had put her plan into motion, slipping out of bed after the others were asleep, cautiously removing Tim's key ring from his bureau drawer, then tiptoeing out of the house and taking off in his car.

Once she was on the road she had thought, fleetingly, about simply driving on until the gas gauge hit empty, then hitching the rest of the way to Stoneham. Except for the change in her pocket, she had no money at all.

But she knew she would never make it that far. Simon

366

would get her before she reached home. Nothing escaped him.

Even now, as she hunched in the shadows by the side of the store, she felt terrifyingly exposed.

Drawing in deep breaths through her nose to calm herself, she fished for the change in the pocket of the jeans jacket she had thrown over her summer frock.

She lifted the handset from its cradle and reached for the coin slot, but her hand was trembling so badly that the coins spilled from her fist.

"Shit!" she exclaimed under her breath, then knelt painfully in the dirt to grope for the coins.

Something moved in the darkness behind her.

Her heart gave a jolt and a sob caught in her throat. Then she heard the scrabbling of claws, a metallic rattle, and a frantic rummaging—the noises of a nocturnal scavenger, a tomcat or raccoon, digging in the garbage cans at the back of the store.

It took her a moment to calm down sufficiently to resume her search. Finally, she managed to find most of the coins. Grunting, she labored to her feet.

Her hands were still quaking badly, but this time she was able to get the the quarters into the slot. Above her the silhouetted treetops shook against the sky as though nature itself were infected with her fear.

She leaned her face close to the push buttons and punched in her mother's number.

The fifth ring finally roused Jean to consciousness. Groping in the darkness for the telephone, she knocked a tumbler off the night table. But her carpet was safe; she'd drained the last of the Jack Daniel's before falling asleep, and the glass contained nothing but melted ice water.

Leaning on one elbow, she squinted at the glowing red digits of her clock—12:46—and croaked, "Hello."

The voice on the other end sounded frail and shaky. "Mom?

Jean was fully awake in an instant. "Rachel," she gasped. "My God! Are you all right?" Her tongue felt thick and cottony. It was hard to form words. "Where are you?"

"I'm okay, Mom," Rachel said, her voice barely louder than a whisper. I'm sorry I haven't called for a while but—"

"Rachel," Jean said urgently, her heart slamming. "You've got to come home."

"Mom . . ." Rachel said, her voice taking on an edge of irritation.

Jean could hear the annoyance in her daughter's voice, and shook her head to clear it. She knew she had to proceed carefully. She wished she hadn't drunk herself to sleep. Her mind felt as fuzzy as her tongue.

"Where are you, sweetheart?" she said, her tone softening. "Tell me and I'll come get you."

"I don't need you to come get me," Rachel said, her voice firmer now. "I don't want you to. I just want . . ." Her voice trailed off.

"What?" Jean asked gently. "What do you want, Rachel?"

"I just . . . I guess I'm a little scared about having a baby." Jean heard the quaver return to her voice. "I mean, does it hurt a lot when the baby comes out?"

"Rachel," Jean said, struggling to stay calm. "Why don't you come home and have the baby here, where I can help you?"

"It's not that easy," Rachel said. "Tim's very possessive—"

"Tim!" Jean exploded. "Don't tell me about Tim. I know who you're with." The words were spilling out now. She couldn't stop herself. She'd been forced to contain her fear and her worry and her anger for too long. "I know all about Simon Proctor."

Instantly, she knew she'd made a terrible mistake. She heard Rachel gasp at the other end of the line.

Jean hurried on desperately. "Rachel, sweetheart. You've got to get away from that man." Her voice cracked and she could feel the tears welling up in her eyes. "Please baby, you're all I have. He's a terrible man, much more dangerous than you think. There are things you don't know about him."

As soon as Jean had mentioned Proctor, a stunned Rachel had held the handset out at arm's length. She had no idea how her mother had found out about Proctor. But she knew that this call had been a terrible mistake.

Pleading desperately, struggling to hold back her sobs, Jean heard the line go dead.

368

65

JACK HAD BEEN DRIVING WITH ONE EYE ON THE GAS GAUGE for the past twenty minutes. His nerves were already badly frayed, and the sight of the needle hovering near empty didn't help. So his tense grip relaxed a bit on the steering wheel when he spotted the hand-painted, roadside billboard reading GAS—STRAIGHT AHEAD.

Squinting down the two-lane blacktop, Jack could see a couple of old frame houses a quarter mile up the road and a red Texaco star sticking into the air. He glanced down at his road map, spread out on the passenger seat beside him. He was approaching a little Herkimer County town called Hinton.

He'd been combing Herkimer County for the past nine days. No, he corrected himself, calculating the dates in his head. Ten. He'd spent these days the same way he'd passed the last three months, and with the same results. Driving around the countryside, asking the same questions, getting the same answers. *No answers at all.*

He could feel his frustration take on the tinge of despair, and he fought against it. The dashboard clock read 5:27. The date was July 31. He could not afford to succumb to hopelessness. In another few hours, Lammas would arrive.

He had concentrated the final days of his search in this area, partly through the process of elimination—he had already scoured much of the Mohawk Valley—but mostly because of his intuition. During his years as a cop, he had learned to trust his hunches.

This time he was afraid his intuition had failed him. He knew what the consequences of that failure would be. His frown grew even darker at the thought.

In less than eight hours a newborn would be slaughtered to appease a madman's bloodlust. And Jean Peary would surely never see her daughter alive again.

The thought made him accelerate unconsciously, so that when he pulled into the gas station, he sent the driveway gravel spinning through the air. The station was a shedlike

369

garage with a couple of ancient pumps out front. Jack cut the motor and pushed his door open. Stepping out of his air-conditioned cocoon into the sunlight was like entering a steambath. The heat was so oppressive, even up here in the country, that Jack was instantly carried back to those suffocating summer days in the city when the weather itself seemed to drive men to murder.

From inside the darkness of the garage he could hear a loud metallic clank. A few seconds later the noise stopped abruptly and the station owner emerged from the shadows, wiping his hands on a filthy rag. He was a skinny man, maybe fifty years old, with a smudged, sunburned face and dark sweat stains under each armpit of his dirty, blue grease-monkey outfit. The name patch on his chest said BILL. From the way Bill was eyeing him, Jack could tell that the station didn't service many strangers.

Nodding at Jack, the scrawny mechanic drawled, "Hot enough for you?"

"Pretty damned hot," Jack answered. "Fill her up. Super." He handed the man his car keys, then stepped around to the passenger side, opened the door, and stooping, took a large manila envelope from the seat.

Jack removed two photographs and held them out to the man. "Ever see either of these people around here, Bill?" he asked. "Stopping for gas or maybe just cruising through town?"

Locking the trigger on the gas nozzle, Bill reached for the pictures. He examined them closely one at a time, staring for so long at the snapshot of Rachel that Jack felt a tiny sprout of hope stir to life inside him. But in the end Bill just shook his head and said "Nope."

"You sure? Not even the girl? She'd be pregnant now."

"I'm sure." Bill grinned, exposing crooked, yellow teeth. "I wouldn't forget a pretty young thing like that."

Jack's cheeks puffed out with disappointment. "Right," he sighed, sticking the photos back inside the envelope. "You got a working toilet?" he asked, nodding toward the little office abutting the garage.

"Around back," Bill said. "Key's next to the register. Hanging on the wall."

The tiny office was furnished with a small metal desk and a wooden folding chair. On the wall above the desk hung a calendar from Bachmann's Feed and Supply Company showing a buxom blond farm girl wearing nothing but tight denim cutoffs. She was posing in a barn, perched on a stool, leaning forward, her hands on the teats of a Holstein cow. Her own enormous breasts hung down nearly to her thighs. The caption beneath the photo read, "Milkin' Time!"

An ancient cash register with a crank on the side sat in the center of the desk. Beside it a rotating fan whirred away. Jack ducked around the curling strip of bug-covered flypaper that dangled from the ceiling and reached across the desktop for the rest-room key, which hung on a hook beside the wall calendar.

The buzzing of flies filled the foul-smelling little bathroom. Jack tried breathing through his mouth while he straddled the bowl. The walls of the stall were covered with crudely scrawled graffiti—sex organs, swastikas, and brutal slurs against blacks, women, homosexuals, and Jews. He shook his head as he rezipped himself. So much for the pastoral innocence of the countryside.

Back inside the office, he returned the key to its hook, then shoved open the screen door, gratefully sucking in fresh air. The station owner was feeding the last few drops of fuel into the tank of the dusty Pontiac.

Jack's mouth felt parched from the heat and from his own tension. An old soft drink machine stood a few feet away, next to the office window. Fishing some change from his pocket, he stepped over to the machine, only to find that it was out of order.

Figures, he thought, glancing idly at the window. Taped to the inside of the dusty glass were various notices—drive-in schedules, auction announcements, hand-lettered "For Sale" flyers.

Among them, more sun-faded than the rest, was a mimeographed circular that caught Jack's eye.

LOST DOG, it said in large, neatly printed letters. Jack's eyes raced over the rest. "Male black labrador, 3 yrs old. Disappeared from home near Barnesville, May 28. Answers to name of Cisco. Generous reward. Call Sheila Mulford, 581–6718."

Spinning on his heels, he hurried over to the station owner, who was replacing the nozzle in its boot. "Say,

Bill," Jack said. "You know that sign in there about the missing dog? Taped to your window?"

The man squinted quizzically toward the window, as if he weren't sure what Jack was talking about. "That dog over to Barnesville? Thought I took that old poster down." He shook his head. "Bad business," he said. "Found the animal lying on the roadside, all butchered the hell up. Papers never did release all the details. Folks around here think it was outsiders, probably come up from the city." He gave the last words a particular emphasis, as though Jack himself might be a suspect in the crime. Then, glancing at the money indicator, he said, "That'll be $13.25 on the nose."

Jack quickly pulled out his wallet and handed him a twenty.

The station owner ambled to his office, rang the sale up on his cash register, and carefully picked the change from the drawer, counting the amount out loud.

When he lifted up his head again and turned toward the door, the stranger's car was gone.

66

THE BIG SLIDING DOOR HAD BEEN LEFT OPEN A CRACK, AND a shaft of sunlight cut into the gloom of the barn. Dust motes swirled in the yellow light like the single-cell creatures that swarm in the scum of ponds. Seated cross-legged on the carpeted floor, Simon Proctor stared at the teeming motes.

Except for the white cotton pouch between his legs, affixed to his loins by slender chords, he was naked. He had just completed his daily regimen of exercise, and his torso was slippery with sweat.

The dust-polluted beam filled his vision. The light-shaft was like an X-ray illuminating the invisible contagion of the air. Corruption, Simon knew, was all-pervasive. Every breath was the inhalation of filth.

Even at this moment, he could taste the foulness in the corrugations of his tongue, feel it settle like a sediment in the deepest chambers of his lungs. It had been too many months since he had performed the purifying ritual.

Tonight, a new life would suffuse him.

He thought of the exaltation to come—of sucking the uncontaminated breath from a being just sprung from the womb. A thrill of pleasure rippled through him, like that of a wine connoisseur imagining the first sip of a rare and costly vintage.

Tonight he would sip the soul of a newborn. He would drink a pledge to his lord and master, Death.

Simon Proctor worshiped death because it was the one thing he feared.

Like other desperate seekers after truth, he had scoured the sacred scriptures of the world for a consoling belief. But his questing had only persuaded him of the futility of hope. The afterlife, he saw, was nothing but a cunning myth designed to lull the weak-willed into resignation.

With the dawning of the sixties, he, like millions of others, had turned to drugs as a gateway to the ultimate. But his searing visions only strengthened his despair. Staring up at the desert air, his powers of perception magnified to infinity by mescaline or LSD, he saw the perfect blue sky shatter like crystal. Behind it lay nothing but an endless expanse of blackness, the profound and illimitable domain of death.

For a long time he had sought transcendence in the intoxications of sex. He and his group had settled in La Cruz by then, and all of them, male and female, were available for his pleasure. But in the end the sex also deepened his sense of mortality. The sweet flesh of his followers, so delicious at first, finally left a bitter taste in his mouth. He was close to forty by then and far past the freshness of youth, in spite of his strength and vitality. Even in the midst of an orgy, entangled among bodies half his age, he could feel the shadow of encroaching decay.

He understood then that death ruled the universe. And he saw that his only hope was to find a way to appease death, to serve as its priest. Perhaps if he paid homage to death, he might somehow earn its forbearance.

He remembered very clearly when the revelation struck. He had always slept very little, and on that special night, as was his custom, he was lying awake at three A.M., immersed in one of his many volumes on occult lore—a dusty history of demonology he had picked up in a secondhand bookshop in Taos. He remembered that when his eye fell on the page, he had emitted such an astonished gasp that the two teenage girls curled on either side of him stirred in their sleep.

It was the sight of his own name that had brought the exclamation to his lips. Excitement pulsing through him, he had pored over the story of his eighteenth-century namesake, the mysterious necromancer who had marshaled the powers of darkness to his cause.

At first he took the coincidence of their names as a portent of his own destiny. Only later did he come to believe that he and the other Simon Proctor were, in fact, the selfsame being, and that the body he now inhabited could remain alive forever.

The book was infuriatingly vague about the precise nature of Proctor's dark practices, but it was clear that child sacrifice was involved.

The pregnant runaway who had shown up one morning at the commune offered Simon his first opportunity. She had lived with him until her daughter was born, and for several months thereafter. The sacrifice itself took place on the last day of April—Beltane, the ancient festival of the planting.

The ceremony had filled him with the greatest sense of power he had ever known in his life. Still, it was, in many respects, a clumsy affair. At the time, he did not yet know the correct ceremonial procedure. He had slit the mother's throat first, then used the skinning knife on the child. For months its flayed pelt had hung from the wall of his adobe.

It was only when he sensed that the law was closing in on him, after the traitor McKluskey had alerted them, that he took the skin down and burned it. The police, who had been seeking the missing runaway for months, turned the commune upside down, but Simon had taken special care with the remains of the girl and the baby. The desert was an ideal place for such disposals. The police could never locate the bodies.

Venting his rage on McKluskey had been a mistake, and Simon had paid dearly for it. The decades of his imprisonment were the darkest time of his life—a living entombment. And yet, he had turned that ordeal into triumph. In the weight room of the prison he had hardened his body into its present state of perfection. And it was during this period that he had discovered the revelations of Belphegor.

He had his son to thank for that. Dutiful as ever, David had supplied him with the books he needed to continue his studies. And it was in one of these volumes, the *Ritualis Satanis* of Johannes Portas, that he had finally discovered the Way.

By then his son had become a wealthy and powerful man. And so it was not difficult for David to put Simon's commands into effect. When the day of Simon's deliverance finally arrived, all was in readiness.

David had even make the ultimate offering—his own child—for Simon's first oblation to Belphegor. Of course, Simon understood that David had grown tired of the burden of his family by then. His wife was a beautiful woman, but already nearing middle age. In a world full of succulent young bodies, she could be nothing but an impediment.

The sacrifice he had performed on All Hallow's Eve had filled him with an ecstasy that nothing else in his life—not drugs or sex, not even the earlier blood rite in New Mexico—had ever made him feel. Only one experience could conceivably surpass it. And for that Simon had required a breeder.

Tonight the breeder would fulfill her own role in the sacred drama. And his destiny would be fulfilled.

Getting to his feet, Simon raised his hands high over his head and stretched. Then he stepped over to the altar table at the far end of the barn.

A small ebony box sat on the table. Simon lifted the hinged lid and peered inside at the contents for a moment. Then, reaching in, he removed the topmost object, a knife with a ten-inch blade of slightly curved steel, similar to a filleting knife.

There was no need to test the keenness of the edge. Simon knew that it was as sharp as a scalpel. He had honed it himself only the day before.

He reached inside the box again and stroked the surface of the second item, a black pouch, folded in half. One side was lustrous satin; the other was animal hide, a section of the coat of a black Labrador retriever.

Replacing the knife on top of the pouch, he closed the ebony lid and turned toward the barn door, smiling as he gazed at the deepening glow of the sun shaft.

Simon needed no watch to tell him the time. Darkness was on its way. He could taste it.

BARNESVILLE WAS SO TINY THAT JACK HAD ALREADY SPED through the town before he realized that he had passed it. Braking, he swung a U-turn on Route 14, a cracked and buckled roadway with weeds sprouting from its potholes, and drove slowly back to the little cluster of weatherworn houses that sat on either side of the asphalt

The town post office was nothing but a converted parlor at the front of one of the little frame houses. The postmaster, a deaf old man who kept fiddling with the volume control of his hearing aid, told Jack how to get to Sheila Mulford's place.

It was just after six when he rolled to a stop in front of the white clapboard house four miles north of town up a dirt road. Jack had passed another house about a mile before. Gazing up the road as far as he could see before it disappeared over the crest of a wooded hill, he could spot no other houses.

Jack climbed out of his car, manila envelope in hand, and gazed at the front of the trim little house, which was flanked by fat hydrangea bushes heavy with blue flowers. The air was perfectly still except for the buzzing of grasshoppers and the rise and fall of the cicadas' song. Climbing onto the creaking front porch, he rang the bell and listened intently for any sounds from within. Hearing nothing, he rang again.

He was just about to step down off the porch and circle the house to see if there was a buzzer in back when the front door opened.

He found himself staring up at a short, plump woman

376

wearing a calico apron and clutching a crumpled paper napkin in one hand. He could see that he had interrupted her supper.

Eyeing him suspiciously, as though he might shove a foot in the door and try to hard-sell her on a year's supply of biodegradable laundry detergent, she swallowed her food, wiped the corners of her lips with the napkin, and said, "Can I help you?"

"Mrs. Mulford," Jack said, stepping back onto the porch. "My name is Byrne. Sorry to bother you at dinnertime, but I saw a sign about your missing dog."

"You must've seen an old sign," the woman said brusquely, "He was found a long time ago." She began to shut the door.

Jack stuck his right palm on the door to keep it open. "Mrs. Mulford, please. I need to ask you some questions. It's very important."

Peering around the edge of the door, she looked at him questioningly. "You a policeman?"

"Yes," Jack lied, hoping she wouldn't ask for any identification. "From downstate a ways. There've been a few other cases like this south of here. I'm doing some investigating."

"Other cases?" she asked.

"That's right."

Mrs. Mulford blinked rapidly and turned her face away from him. "These other cases," she asked, her voice cracking a bit. "Were they—were the animals all . . ." The tears started to flow and she dabbed at her eyes with the napkin.

"I'm sorry to upset you," Jack said gently. He waited quietly for a moment until she regained some control.

"It's still a hard thing," she said at last. "That creature was all the company I had." She drew a deep, shuddering breath, then said, "What can I help you with, Mr. Byrne?"

"It would be helpful to know exactly what condition your dog was in when they found him."

Blowing her nose into the napkin, Mrs. Mulford said, "He was mangled up something awful. Some of it was the birds, of course. He'd been dumped on Billings Road, and the crows was at him when they found him. But it wasn't any crows that chopped out his tongue. Nor cut a big piece of hide from his belly."

Jack's heart began to palpitate. "This piece of hide," he said, "was it any particular shape?"

"Yes, sir," she said firmly. "Shaped like a rectangle. I didn't see it myself, of course. Cisco, that was my dog's name, was disposed of before I even found about it. But the sheriff told me all there was to know. Said the cut was 'neat as a sewing pattern.' His words exactly. 'Neat as a sewing pattern.' "

"Mrs. Mulford," he said carefully, his heart racing, "do you have any idea who might have done such a terrible thing?"

She smiled grimly. "Well, the sheriff, he thinks maybe some kids did it. You know, rowdies from a different town."

"But you don't?" he asked.

"No, sir. I do not." She shook her head emphatically. "I believe I know those responsible."

"Yes?" Jack said.

"Those new folks who bought the old Parker place about six months ago," she said, lowering her voice, as though her accusation might carry across the open countryside. "Could be they did the ones you were talking about too, south a ways. They hardly ever come into town. The sheriff, he thinks I suspect them just because they're newcomers." She shrugged. "Well, he can be stubborn. There's a whole bunch of them living over there, you know. Couple of times I've caught a glimpse of them driving through town. They're mostly young people."

Jack's mouth had gone dry from his excitement. He pulled out his photographs and handed her the one of Rachel.

"Could this be one of them, Mrs. Mulford? She'd be pregnant now, maybe much heavier."

She took a step out onto the porch to examine the snapshot by daylight. "Never seen her," she said after a moment, handing it back.

Frustration stabbed at him. "What about this man?"

She studied the picture carefully, frowning hard. Finally she raised her eyes and nodded slowly. "Yes, I believe I have seen this individual. The last time I was driving down by Hobb's Road, maybe four or five weeks back. I passed

378

a car turning up the path that leads to the old Parker place. The passenger up front was a big man, long-haired, like one of those hippies from way back. I stared at him real hard through the windshield, and the look he gave me could have shivered glass. I didn't catch but a quick look at his face. But this could be him, all right."

"Are you sure?" Jack asked.

"Never claimed to be perfect, Mr. Byrne," she said. "But if this ain't the face I saw, it sure could be his brother."

Jack noticed that his hands were trembling slightly as he replaced the photos in the envelope. But his voice remained steady when he spoke again.

"Mrs. Mulford," he said, "may I use your telephone?"

68

CLOTHED IN A SHIFT OF FINESPUN WHITE LINEN, RACHEL LAY atop her mattress in the second-story bedroom, staring out the wide-flung window at the distant hills. The sun had already sunk below the treetops, and the cloudless sky was smeared with red. The shadow of the wooded hills was darkening the meadowland. Night was hurrying near.

Rachel could feel the nervous dampness of her palms as they lay flat on the crest of her mountainous belly. Wiping them dry against the linen, she turned her head away from the window and tried hard not to think of the ceremony to come.

At Simon's suggestion, one of the other girls in the group—a tall brunette named Sonya, whose mother was an obstetrician—had taught Rachel some basic Lamaze techniques. Rachel was supposed to use them during delivery to ease the pain. But she found that the shallow, rhythmic breathing helped calm her, and she concentrated on it now.

The bedroom door suddenly swung open and David stepped into the room. Rachel let out a sob of relief and flung her arms around his neck as he bent to kiss her cheek. "David!" she cried.

"Ssshhh," he murmured, disentangling himself from her embrace. Holding himself at arm's length, he stared down at her face, smiling tenderly. "Let me just look at you for a moment. You've never looked more beautiful."

Rachel gazed up at him gratefully.

Seating himself on the edge of the mattress, he stroked her damp hair back from her forehead. "I'm so proud of you," he said. "Rachel, I'm never going to forget what you're doing for me today. No other woman has ever given me as much."

Tears came to her eyes. "David, I'm scared."

"Don't be, sweetheart," he said softly, then lowered his head and planted a kiss on her belly. "You're not going to feel anything. And it all will be over with very quickly."

There was a knock on the door, and Julia stuck her head in. "Rachel? Can I come in?" She walked to the bed and took Rachel's hand in both of hers, squeezing. "Oh, you look so beautiful! You're so lucky, Rachel—to be able to bring this gift to Simon. I wish I'd been chosen. I was jealous at first. But I'm so happy for you now."

"I'm a little scared," Rachel began shakily.

Samantha had come in the room too. "Why?" the girls cried in unison. "It won't hurt you, Rachel."

"That's what I've been telling her." David smiled down at her. "I'll be back later, sweetheart," he said, kissing her on the brow, then rising from the mattress. "Why don't you girls stay with her awhile?"

Rachel let them fuss over her for a few minutes, then sent them out of the room. She was too nervous to talk to them. They kept repeating how blessed she was. She *knew* that.

Others came and went calmly, happily, hushed, nearly reverential in her presence. She lay on the bed, waiting for David to return, watching the light die outside the window. From time to time a gust of wind blew through the open window and stirred the delicate fabric on her legs.

Gradually the air turned cooler. Rachel fought back her mounting apprehension by trying to think of the good things to come—shedding the grotesquely fat belly she had come to detest, regaining her firm, lithe body, spending voluptuous afternoons again in her lover's arms.

She did not resume her breathing exercise. Instead, she began reciting a soundless incantation, her lips working rapidly as she mouthed the silent words.

It will be over soon. David and I will be together again. It won't hurt. David and I will be together again. It will be over soon.

69

THE TRAFFIC IN THE FAST LANE CLEARED OUT OF THE WAY as the quartet of police cruisers raced up the Taconic. Nick Pasaglia handled the lead car, while Dick Wayland navigated. They were less than ten miles south of Albany. The time was 7:33 P.M.

Wayland shot a glance at the speedometer—ninety-two mph. He reached for the mike and pushed the talk switch. "We'll be exiting in a couple of minutes. Keep close." The acknowledgments of the other three drivers—Sam Ferris, Lyle Kimball, and Tommy Reardon—crackled over the transceiver. In their voices Wayland could detect both tension, and something else too, exhilaration. He knew what they were feeling. The investigation that had gone nowhere for nearly a year was finally leading somewhere, to a little upstate town called Barnseville.

Wayland grumbled something under his breath.

"Can't hear you, Chief," Pasaglia said.

"I just hope those local guys don't fuck up," Wayland said again, louder this time. After Byrne had called with the news about Proctor, Wayland had notified the town sheriff and the Herkimer County police. They were all supposed to rendezvous with some state troopers in Barnesville.

"We've got to catch him while the sacrifice is happening," Wayland said, more to himself than to Pasaglia. "We haven't got shit on Proctor except cruelty to animals. And maybe kiddie porn."

"What about Marianne?" Nick suggested. "She can testify against him when she's better."

"She's never gonna be that better," Wayland muttered.

Mike Holson stirred in the backseat. "I still can't believe this shit," he muttered. "What the fuck have we got to go on, anyway? Another goddamned butchered dog. Jesus. This guy Byrne, cruising around all over New York State—the guy's gone off the deep end. And we're going along for the ride."

Wayland felt his back jolt as Holson gave the front seat an angry shove. Turning, he stared curiously at his young officer. All the men had been surprised when he had called them together to fill them in on Byrne's news—surprised and then, an instant later, hopped up for action.

Holson's reaction, though, had stopped at surprise. In fact, he had looked almost stunned by the news. He had appeared to be lost in some kind of daze as he'd gotten into the squad car.

Wayland was still puzzled by his reaction. "What's your problem, Holson?" he asked.

"Shit," Holson scowled, "I didn't even know we were *doing* an investigation upstate."

"*We* weren't," Wayland snapped. "I explained that to you already. Is that what's eating you? You worried someone else is going to get the glory? Or you pissed because I dragged you in on your day off?"

"Nah," Holson mumbled. "I'm glad you caught me. Two minutes later and I would've been gone."

"Yeah, I thought you'd want to be in on this," Wayland said.

Nick interrupted. "Here's the exit, Chief."

"Okay. Head west at the end of the ramp." He looked out the rear windshield to make sure the other cars were close behind, then bent over his road map, trying to calculate the remaining mileage. The last glimmers of daylight were nearly gone.

"Where is Marianne now, anyway?" The voice from the backseat was still tense with suppressed emotion of some sort, but Wayland had too much on his mind to give the matter any more thought.

"Byrne sent her down to live with his sister," he said abstractedly, staring down at the map. "In Delaware, I think. She goes to some kind of clinic down there. For therapy."

382

Wayland looked up from his map. Still fifty-plus miles to go, at least half of them on two-lane country roads.

Pasaglia popped on the headlights, and the beams lit up the road. Wayland hoped to hell that Byrne was right about the ceremony, that it wouldn't get started until midnight.

If it took place at nightfall, Rachel Peary's newborn was already dead.

70

FOLLOWING MRS. MULFORD'S DIRECTIONS, JACK HAD NO trouble finding the turnoff to the old Parker place. He continued past the turnoff for a dozen yards until he found a good spot to pull off, a small grassy patch sheltered by a stand of pine. Cutting the engine, he reached beneath his seat for his heavy-duty flashlight, then swung himself out of the car. There was no time to lose. The daylight was draining fast.

He jogged back along the edge of the blacktop until he arrived at the turnoff, then cut left onto the narrow dirt road that disappeared into the trees. According to Mrs. Mulford, the Parker place was set back a quarter mile from the main road. Jack moved quickly up the rutted path, listening intently for the sounds of others. Except for the evening chorus of insect noises, the world was steeped in silence.

He emerged from the trees onto the crest of a little hill. Looking down, he could see a massive brown barn and, just beyond it, the porch end of a gray-shingled farmhouse. He crouched in the tall weeds and scanned the premises, getting the lay of the land. No one was in sight.

Staying low, he moved around the hilltop, then hurried down the grassy slope toward a clump of bushes a few yards from the back of the barn. Breathing hard, he hunkered behind the bushes and peered over the foliage. He'd been worried about encountering dogs, but nothing moved or made a sound.

From where he crouched, Jack could see most of the house. A few of the ground-floor windows were lit up, and lamplight glowed from an upstairs room. But he could see no signs of movement inside. There were no cars either, unless they were parked on the north side of the barn.

He squatted there for a few minutes, listening and watching the windows.

In the deepening twilight nothing stirred except the cloud of gnats swarming around his head. He slapped them away, then edged over to the far end of the bushes. No sense in waiting any longer. Drawing a deep breath, he scurried toward the house in commando fashion and flattened himself against the wall, just below one of the brightly lit windows. Slowly, he raised his head and peered over the lintel.

He was looking into a living room that seemed recently vacated. Two empty tumblers, an uncapped bottle of Jack Daniel's, and a paper plate littered with sandwich scraps sat on a battered coffee table. Magazines lay scattered on the floor. A big crystal ashtray overflowing with butts perched on the arm of the sofa.

Except for its air of desertion, there was nothing even vaguely odd about the room, and a rush of panic swept through him.

He knew from long experience how unreliable a witness the average person could be. If Mrs. Mulford had misidentified the face in the picture, then several dozen police officers were now converging on the town of Barnesville for nothing. And somewhere else in the state, Simon Proctor was about to consummate an unspeakable ritual.

He made a complete circuit of the house, looking into the uncovered windows, confirming that no one was inside. From the northeast corner of the porch, he could see that there were no cars parked beside the barn. In the deepening gloom he trotted toward the barn, moving openly now that he realized he was alone.

Slowly, he slid the big door along its track. Metal screeched, and he froze at the sound. He clicked on the the flashlight, but the yellow beam was too weak to illuminate the far end of the cavernous barn. Jack thought he could make out some peculiar objects, though he couldn't be sure. But a thick odor assaulted his nostrils, and the stench alone told him all he needed to know.

Mrs. Mulford had been right after all.

The air smelled both fetid and cloyingly sweet, as if incense had been burned to mask the stink of decay. This was Simon's lair, all right. It carried his scent as surely as the old Vanderdam place had.

He stepped into the barn, keeping the light low. The floor of the barn was carpeted, and an image flashed into his mind—the orgy that had preceded the dog sacrifice on the videotape he had viewed in Wayland's office.

Carefully, he moved across the floor, the flashlight cutting through the murk ahead of him. As he approached the far end of the barn, he saw the altar. Stepping close, he saw a black satin altar cloth blotched with clotted brown stains, and remembered the blood that had poured from the black dog's butchered mouth and genitals.

Suddenly he felt a primitive dread rising inside him. Something large was hovering over his head. He could sense it, floating high in the reeking darkness. Slowly, he swung the beam toward the rafters.

"Sweet Jesus," he said aloud.

His mouth went dry as he gaped at the life-size effigy nailed to the massive wooden cross. A freakish wig of some sort had been affixed to its head. The long, stringy hanks framed the agonized face of Christ. He ran his light down the length of the torso, cringing at the desecration committed on the figure. A grotesque brassiere of some sort, with fishhooks dangling from the tips, had been tacked across the chest. Holding the flashlight higher, Jack squinted hard at the leathery-looking chest band, then gasped aloud as he realized that he was staring at dried human flesh.

Whose? he wondered, fighting down the sickening mix of fury and revulsion that roiled inside him. He wanted desperately to tear down and destroy the abomination, but he had no time.

He contented himself with using the butt end of his flashlight to smash the framed blasphemies hanging on the wall behind the altar.

Then he hurried from the barn and stood in the moonlight for a long moment, drinking in great gulps of air to clear the stench of sacrilege from his nostrils and mouth, his mind racing.

He should have known that Proctor would not conduct the Lammas ceremony indoors. Why else would he have moved so far out into the country? The bastard wanted isolation, enough space and privacy so that he could commit the outrage in the open, under the blackness of the midnight sky.

But where? In his mind he saw once again the old engraving of the Belphegor cult from Portas's history of Satanism—a clearing in the woods, illuminated by a hellish blaze. Jack had read the accompanying description so many times that he still remembered some of the words: "When these members of the devil are met together, they light a foule and horrid fire."

Jack flashed his beam on his wristwatch. Nearly nine. Wayland and the others should have rendezvoused by now. Jack didn't know how long he could expect them to sit tight, awaiting his return, before they got antsy and started roaring around the countryside.

Keeping the light trained on the ground, he raced back to his car.

He forced himself to drive slowly, creeping along the backwoods roads. Twice during the next thirty minutes cars came up behind him. Pulling as far to the right as possible, he stuck his flashlight out the window and waved them around his car. Then he resumed his agonizing search, straining to peer into the blackness. Proctor was out there somewhere.

The night air had turned cool, but a dribble of sweat ran down into his left eye, stinging it. He rubbed his eye socket with the back of his hand. The night search was affecting his vision—slithery shapes swam before him and light-sparks glimmered in the blackness of the woods.

It took him a second to grasp that the gleams were real.

Jamming on the brakes, he cut the headlights, flung open the door, and leapt out of his car, wildly scanning the woods.

Nothing. *Fuck!* his mind screamed. Maybe he had hallucinated the yellow gleams after all.

He clambered onto the hood of the car and strained to see into the looming mass of the forest.

There!

Fire glow quivered over the treetops, maybe a quarter mile east of the road.

He hammered the air with his fist. "Got you, you motherfucker."

Leaping off the car, he jumped behind the wheel, gunned the Pontiac to sixty and roared through the night toward Barnesville.

71

LYING FLAT ON THE MAKESHIFT TABLE, RACHEL STARED UP at the infinite blackness of the sky. Beside her the roaring bonfire gave off a seething mass of sparks that scattered into the darkness. All around, the masked and naked worshipers swirled and writhed, their bodies drenched from the heat of the fire and the frenzy of their orgy.

She could not tell whether Michael Holson had arrived. She had heard David discussing his absence with Simon before the ceremony began. Some police emergency must have detained him, they had decided. Simon would have preferred holding the ritual with the entire coven present, but the sacrifice could not be delayed. The ceremony would have to proceed without him.

Rachel's tongue felt like a thick wad of flannel. She tried to moisten it with saliva, but the fear had completely dehydrated her mouth.

Something loomed at the foot of the table. Lifting her head, she gazed above the enormous bulge of her stomach. Simon towered over her, glaring down, his face livid in the firelight. Suddenly he raised both hands high over his head in the gesture of invocation. "Belphegor Satanis!" he cried.

The moment had arrived.

Terror turned her bones to ice, and her limbs began to tremble. Twisting her head, she watched as two of the men moved to the fireside and dipped the cloth-wrapped ends of two wooden torches into the blaze. Raising the flaming torches high over their heads, they stepped to either side of Simon.

The rest of the coven circled the table, bending close.

She cowered from the inhuman faces—monkeys and vultures, asses and goats—and cried out sharply, "David! David!"

A grinning hyena mask lowered itself over her face

"Keep your mouth shut," David's voice hissed.

"I'm scared!" she wailed in a little girl's voice.

"Keep quiet," he said again. "Your part in this is nearly over."

The boys flanking Simon lowered their torches. Gasoline fumes drifted over her like night mist, stinging her eyes, choking her. *Everything is wrong*, she thought frantically.

Stooping, Simon shoved her white linen shift over her upraised knees and bunched it onto her belly. She was naked underneath, and the heat from the torches stung her bare flesh.

She flinched as Simon placed both his hands on her huge, swollen belly. "Belphegor, Soul Devourer," he intoned. "We have bred this gift for your pleasure."

His prayer rolled on, but Rachel was concentrating only on her own body. *Nothing is happening inside! Nothing!* She could feel no cramps, no contractions, nothing to indicate that she was ready to deliver.

"Simon," she gasped, reaching up to him with a trembling hand. "Something's wrong. I don't think the baby is ready to come out yet! I don't feel anything!"

He seemed not to hear her. His eyes had a glazed, faraway look.

"You said you were going to give me something if I wasn't ready!"

His distant gaze came into focus on her face. "Yes, child," he said, smiling. "I have it right here."

Reaching inside his full cloak, he nodded to the surrounding acolytes. "Hold her," he commanded.

Instantly, Rachel felt strong hands seize her wrists and ankles.

"David!" she screamed, struggling helplessly to break free.

The hyena's face appeared above her again. She opened her mouth to cry out to him. In that instant, David reached down and shoved a balled satin cloth into her mouth.

Her terrified scream gurgled deep in her throat as she

388

gaped at the glinting object Simon had pulled from the folds of his cloak—a shining knife with a long, narrow blade.

"Belphegor sanctus!" he shouted.

Placing one hand on the top of her belly, as though it were a melon he was preparing to slice, Simon stuck the knife point just above her pubic region. Rachel felt it stab into her flesh. The world swirled and darkened. She tried to scream again but the sound was choked off by the smothering gag.

Just then an echoing bang, like a cherrybomb exploding, sounded somewhere behind her. An amplified voice crackled an order, something crashed from the woods, and Rachel felt the handholds loosen from her wrists and ankles as the votaries of Belphegor began to scatter and shriek.

72

CONCEALED BY THE TREES, THE TWENTY-ONE POLICE OFFICERS armed with assault rifles and handguns had awaited Wayland's signal. Jack was there too, along with a pair of paramedics summoned from Herkimer General. The second the sacrificial blade touched the flesh of the prostrate girl, a sniper fired a shot over Proctor's head, Wayland barked out a command on his bullhorn, and the two dozen men burst from the woods.

One of the cultists, a big man in a hyena mask who'd been positioned at the head of the altar table, instantly broke for the forest and disappeared into the blackness. Mike Holson, Ruger in one hand and a flashlight in the other, immediately took off after him, followed closely by Lyle Kimball.

For an instant the other cultists simply froze in place, like deer caught in the headlights. By the time they tried to flee, they were already surrounded by a dozen cops. Herded into a circle, they shouted and cursed. Some hunched to hide their nakedness, placing protective hands over their groins. But a few of the girls, drugged and defiant, thrust out their chests and giggled lewdly at the grim-faced officers.

Simon found himself encircled by six cops with assault rifles, muzzles leveled at his naked chest. Smiling thinly, he turned from one man to the next, looking each in the eye, then let his knife slip from his fingers and drew his cloak slowly across his body.

Wayland strode over to the party of officers ringing the teenagers. "Get some clothes on those people," he barked to Greg Nugent, who immediately trotted off up the dirt path leading to the clearing. Two of Wayland's men had scouted out the path an hour before and discovered a string of parked cars, their open trunks pulled with the discarded clothes of the cultists.

By the time Jack pushed his way through the crowd of cops surrounding the altar table, the paramedics were already attending to Rachel, whose gag had been removed. She lay there sobbing convulsively into her hands while one of the men bandaged the small cut on her lower abdomen. Jack watched for a moment as the paramedics helped her off the table and onto the wheeled stretcher they had rolled into the clearing.

Then Jack turned and wedged himself between two of the officers surrounding Simon Proctor, until he stood face to face with the quarry he had been hunting for so long.

Simon stared at Jack curiously for a moment, then broke into a broad, mocking smile. "Sleeping Beauty's father, isn't it?" he sneered, his face flushed in the glow of the bonfire. "How is the little corpse feeling nowadays?"

Jack struggled to subdue his fury. He could feel his shoulder muscles twitch with the effort. Reaching inside his pants pocket, he wrapped his right hand around the coolness of the smooth, silver handle.

Wayland, spotting Jack, strode up quickly beside him. Glancing over at his friend, he saw a face rigid with hatred. Then he noticed Jack's hand thrust deep inside his pocket, as though he might be getting ready to whip out a little .25 autoloader and start blasting.

Wayland laid his own right hand on Jack's forearm. "Jack," he said gently. "Let it go."

For a moment Jack seemed not to hear him.

"Jack," Wayland said again, as if calling his friend back from someplace far away. "It's over."

Jack hissed out a sigh as the tension siphoned from his

body. He slowly withdrew his empty right hand from his pocket, nodded at Wayland, then took a step closer to Simon.

"Your master isn't going to like this, Simon," he said, his voice even.

Simon's sneer held for a moment, then wavered, then vanished. His mouth tightened into a thin line.

"You've failed him, Simon. You know what the punishment for failure is, don't you, Simon?"

Staring intently into Simon's face, Jack saw something flicker in his eyes. The tip of Simon's tongue skimmed nervously across his lips.

Jack gave a little snort, then spun on his heels and pushed his way out of the circle of policemen.

Legs scratched and bleeding, David Prince stumbled through the forest, one hand cupped over his exposed genitals. He had flung away his mask, and the low-hanging branches lashed his face, opening cuts on his cheeks and across the bridge of his nose.

His foot hit a tree root and he went sprawling into a little clearing. He lay panting on the forest floor for a moment. Then, pushing himself to all fours, he crawled for cover behind a nearby clump of bushes, dried pine needles sticking to his sweat-soaked chest and belly.

If only he could make it back to the farmhouse! There were fresh clothes hanging in the closet and a walletful of cash he had left in his bureau drawer. It was too late to help Simon and the others, but he could still save himself. He could be out of the country by morning, living off the assets he'd stashed in banks around the world. He could start a new life in another country.

Someone was headed his way; he could hear the man crashing through the undergrowth. Cowering behind the bushes, David peered through a small break in the branches.

Across the small clearing a light bobbed in the darkness. Then a tall man stepped out into the clearing. Enough moonlight filtered down through the treetops for David to make out the man's face.

It was Holson!

Relief flooded through him. He leapt from his hiding place and called out in a hoarse whisper, "Mike!"

Three things happened simultaneously. An enormous boom filled the air, a bright orange fireburst blossomed in Holson's right hand, and a blow hit David squarely in the center of his chest with the force of a sledgehammer.

Holson managed to get off a second shot before David hit the ground, the .357 slug tearing through the naked man's left shoulder

But by then David Prince was already dead.

The shots brought Lyle Kimball running. Holson was crouched beside the body, his flashlight aimed at the big hole in the middle of the dead man's chest. Kimball came up beside Holson, gun drawn. He gazed down at the body for a moment. "Is he dead?" he finally asked, sounding slightly stunned.

"Looks pretty dead to me," Holson said, rising from his crouch.

"How'd it happen?"

"Crazy fuck came at me with his right hand stuck out. Like he had a knife or something."

"Did he?" Kimball asked.

Holson shook his head. "Sure as shit looked like he did, though."

Kimball stared at Holson for a moment, then turned his light onto the dead man's face. He let out a little gasp.

"What?" Holson asked.

"Look!" Kimball exclaimed. "Don't you recognize him?"

"Shit," Holson said, staring down. "The baby-snatching. It's the father."

"Prince," Kimball said. "Christ." He continued to gape at Prince's face for a moment, then glanced over at Holson. "I'd better get the chief."

"Yeah," Holson said. "I'll wait here."

Reholstering his pistol, Kimball turned and hurried back in the direction he'd come from.

He and the others were back in ten minutes. Holson heard them coming noisily through the woods. Wayland and Jack Byrne were right behind Kimball. They had brought Simon with them. He was wearing clothes now, loose-fitting khakis and a long-sleeved white shirt. His wrists were cuffed behind his back and he was flanked by a pair of state troopers.

"Fucker jumped me from the bushes," Holson began explaining as Wayland strode up. "Like he had a knife."

"Yeah," Wayland grunted. "I heard." He aimed his beam at the corpse's face. "Jesus," he muttered. "It's him all right."

Jack took one look at the face and sat down heavily on a big fallen log nearby.

Wayland gestured to the troopers, who led Simon up beside the corpse. Wayland kept his light on Prince's face.

Simon shook his slowly and gazed over at Jack. "So the punishment has already commenced," he said flatly.

Jack looked up at him. Simon's face was masked in shadow. Jack could not read his expression. "What do you mean?" he asked.

"Your daughter's suffering has been repaid," he replied in the same emotionless tone. "With the life of my son."

"Son!" Wayland exclaimed.

"No more words," Simon said. "I will speak no more words." Turning, he took a few steps away from the body, the troopers keeping close on either side.

Wayland spoke something urgently to Holson, but Jack could not hear, though he was sitting only a few feet away. His mind was whirling. *David Prince. Of course. Proctor Rex—Proctor the King. Son of the king. So Rachel was doing this for Prince, not Proctor. Was it his baby she was carrying, not Rutherford's? And the wife's suicide? Probably a setup. She must have begun to suspect.*

The puzzle that Marianne had been struggling to fit together had finally fallen into place. Jack saw the picture clearly now.

But as he perched on the log, elbows propped on his knees, forehead pressed into his palms, he couldn't shake the nagging sensation that a crucial piece was still missing.

He was still trying to fill in the blank a half hour later when Wayland walked up to him and said, "Time to go."

They were back in the big clearing by then. The blaze had burned down, and a dozen more officers had arrived, along with a pair of police photographers. One was shooting pictures of the altar table and close-ups of the sacrificial knife and dog-hide pouch. The other was off in the woods, snapping photos of David Prince's corpse from a half-dozen angles.

The news media had already gotten wind of the story. A small flock of reporters, including a few cameramen, was gathered at the far end of the clearing, clamoring for a look at the crime scene. Five of Wayland's men were trying hard to keep them at bay. Jack could picture the morning headlines: SAVED FROM SATAN! MIDNIGHT RAID ON DEVIL RING! COPS BREAK UP CULT SACRIFICE!

The teenage coven members, all of them clothed and cuffed, a few of them crying, were being herded into squad cars for the drive back to Stoneham. Simon stood apart from the others, still guarded by the two impassive troopers. Holson, who was hovering nearby with Kimball, kept glancing over at Proctor, whose eyes remained shut, his expression blank and unreadable.

"How're you doing?" Wayland asked Jack.

"Feeling good," Jack said, smiling wanly.

"You should be," Wayland said, clapping him on the shoulder. "You did it. You got the job done."

"Yeah," Jack said quietly.

Wayland looked at him curiously. "What's up?"

"Nothing," Jack said after a moment. "Just tired, I guess."

"Come on. We'll go back and have a drink in my office to celebrate. I want to be there for the bookings."

Holson suddenly materialized beside them.

"You want me and Lyle to drive him back to the station house, Chief?" he asked with a little nod toward Simon.

Wayland glanced over at Proctor. "Yeah, why don't you go ahead. I've still got to straighten out a couple of things with Rayburn." Bill Rayburn was the local sheriff. He had a big mopping-up job to oversee, and he didn't seem entirely thrilled by the responsibility.

Wayland waved Kimball over. "Lyle," he said. "Make sure you sit right next to that fucker the whole way back."

"I know the drill, Chief," Lyle said.

"Good. See you back there soon."

Jack watched as Holson and Kimball took custody of Proctor from the troopers. Grabbing him by the elbows, they hustled him out of the clearing and toward the waiting car while one of the news photographers, craning for a shot, fired off flashes in the darkness.

394

73

"TALK LOUDER, JEAN," JACK SAID INTO THE MOUTHPIECE. "Things are pretty wild around here."

He was perched on the corner of Wayland's desk, telephone receiver pressed tight to one ear, left hand muffling the other. Their connection was weak, and he was having trouble hearing her over the noise of the station house.

Jean's voice, thick with emotion, rose a notch in volume. "The doctors say she's all right," she repeated. "I wanted to let you know right away."

He could hear the exhaustion in her voice. He was not surprised. It was nearly five-thirty in the morning. Glancing out the big window behind Wayland's desk, he could see the first glow of sunrise bleaching the night from the sky. Jean had driven straight to the hospital west of Albany as soon as she got the call from Pete Rydell. She had arrived there about the same time Jack got back to Stoneham.

He told her to check into a motel and try to get some sleep.

"I'm too tired to sleep," she answered. She paused for a moment, then said, "Jack, how will I ever be able to thank you?" He could tell she was close to tears. Her husky voice quavered with the effort to hold them back.

"You don't have to thank me, Jean," he said. "Just take care of yourself. Things are going to be rough for a while. I'll do whatever I can to help."

"I know you will, Jack," she said. "I've come to rely on it."

They spoke a few more words before Jack gently replaced the handset in its cradle.

Outside Wayland's door, Tommy Reardon let out a whoop as he exchanged a high-five with Sam Ferris. "We got the bastards!" Reardon exulted.

Glancing over at Jack, Ferris shot him a triumphant thumbs-up. "You did good," Ferris said, grinning broadly.

Jack smiled back and nodded.

Wayland, who'd been out in the lobby trying to deal with

the growing mob of reporters, appeared in the doorway. "Keep it down," he chided. "We've got people here whose lives are falling apart. You guys looked around? Get out there and see what you can do."

Jack knew what Wayland meant. He'd been circulating around the station house before Jean's call came in. The place, normally as sleepy as the town library, was a madhouse. Cops were crammed into every office and cubicle, questioning prisoners, taking fingerprints, typing out arrest forms in triplicate. And then there were the parents, dragged out of bed at dawn. Most of the women seemed stunned and stricken, their faces gray under the harsh fluorescent lights. Their husbands, dressed carelessly in old polo shirts and slacks, hovered nearby, looking bewildered. A few of the men—bankers and CEOs clearly unused to being kept waiting—milled around making huffing noises, while their patrician wives shot indignant looks at every passing officer. The family lawyers had begun arriving too. Some consulted quietly with their sorrowing clients, while others blustered at the desk sergeant.

Wayland, his heavy jaw shadowed with stubble, plopped down heavily in his chair with a groan. He massaged his red eyes with the heels of his hands, then looked up at Jack. "Do I look as tired as you?"

"I don't know how the hell I look," Jack said, standing up from the desk corner and stretching. "But I feel like I could sack out for a week."

"Same here," Wayland said. "I feel happy as hell, though, about nailing that fuck Proctor. You should too."

Jack, rubbing the back of his neck, gazed down at the floor and didn't respond.

"You worried about Holson and Kimball?" Wayland asked.

Jack glanced over at him. "Everyone else is back."

Wayland frowned. "I'm not going to worry yet. Shit, Sam just drove up about ten minutes ago. Maybe they ran into a snag. You get stuck behind a few farm trucks on one of those country roads and that'll slow you down pretty good."

It was what Jack had been telling himself too, without really believing it. Something continued to gnaw at him, though he still couldn't say what it was.

All the way back to Westchester he hadn't uttered a word. The other men in the car were flying so high that they hadn't noticed.

Huddling silently in the backseat, he could feel the silver razor, folded and worthless, in his left pocket. He had hoped that fate would give him the chance to use it, but that hope had turned out to be pure wishful thinking. So Simon's punishment would be left to the courts.

Jack was sure that Proctor would spend the rest of his days behind bars. Still, he couldn't help feeling cheated of his vengeance.

But there was something else eating at him too.

In the darkness, as the car rushed through the rolling countryside, he had racked his brains to figure it out. The answer seemed maddeningly close. The harder Jack tried to snatch at it, the further it seemed to retreat from his grasp.

Something that happened back there in the woods, something to do with David Prince . . .

His ruminations were interrupted by Wayland. "Let me buzz Rydell and have him get them on the radio." He reached for his intercom to call the front desk.

He never got the chance.

Just as he hit the button, there was a sudden commotion in the hallway outside—cries of outrage and distress. "Shit no!" Jack heard Tom Reardon shout disbelievingly.

He and Wayland turned toward the doorway just as Pete Rydell, his face waxen, pushed his way past the men crowded outside and staggered into the office.

Wayland half rose from his seat. "What—"

"Chief," Rydell said, his voice unsteady. "It's Lyle."

"What about him?"

"He's dead! Shot!"

Wayland fell back in his chair as though he'd been clubbed from behind. "Where?" he said hoarsely. "How?"

"They found his body in a rest area off the Taconic," Rydell said. "I just got a call from the highway patrol. Some salesman stopping to take a leak found him dumped in the bushes."

"What about the others?" Jack asked urgently. "Proctor and Holson."

Rydell shook his head. "No sign of them. The car's gone."

Wayland seemed paralyzed. He stared sightlessly at his desktop, then began to mutter aloud. "How could it happen? The fucker was shackled. Lyle swore he'd stay right on top of him. And Holson's a fucking bull. How could Proctor take both of them?"

Staring over at Wayland, Jack expelled a sound as though he'd been poked in the solar plexus. The answer he'd been groping for had just struck him with the force of a physical blow.

Holson. Holson was one of them.

It all made sense now. The way Marianne had fallen so easily into Proctor's hands. Holson must have set her up! The bastard had kept Proctor informed every step of the way. That's why the cult had cleared out of their Dutchess County quarters a few days before the raid. And why Tim and Rachel had vanished upstate just as investigators were closing in on them.

And that's why David Prince had died; he must have said or done something that threatened to expose Holson.

Jack felt the strength ebb from his limbs. He pulled out one of the plastic seats ringing the little conference table and lowered himself onto it.

Now he understood the meaning of those mysterious noises coming from Marianne's bedroom that night back in June. He hadn't dreamed them. And Marianne hadn't been spelling out "Help." She'd been trying to write Holson's name.

A wave of dizziness caused the room to cant suddenly, and he closed his eyes tight. He had to think this through.

Would Holson kill Proctor too, the way he'd killed Prince?

No. He needs Simon. He has nowhere to run. Simon has access to money. And he has the brains.

Opening his eyes, he looked over at Pete Rydell and motioned him out of the room. Then, getting up and closing the office door behind him, he walked back over to Wayland and told him the truth.

Six hours later, near the edge of a sprawling dump outside Oneonta, a local teenager scavenging for usable car

398

parts stumbled upon the abandoned police car. Jack had been right about one thing, Holson couldn't afford to kill Proctor.

But Jack hadn't considered Proctor's position. Simon no longer had any particular need for Holson.

The young cop was slumped on the front seat, his head—or what remained of it—propped against the window. A cloud of flies buzzed around the shattered glass, feasting on the clotted matter that the .357 slug had blown from Holson's skull.

Conclusion

Townshend, Vermont
Friday, August 15
One Year Later

74

JULY HAD BEEN A MONTH OF RAIN, AND JEAN HAD SPENT many a dreary morning staring out the kitchen window at the sodden hills that ringed the rear of her property, wondering if she'd made the right move. But for the past two weeks the southern Vermont skies had looked as clear and pure as the little backyard stream that had attracted her to this piece of land in the first place.

Now, as she bustled around her bright country kitchen, opening cabinet doors and writing up a shopping list, Jean felt infused with new life, as if her heart had been recharged by the sunshine. Her doubts had dissipated with the bad weather, and she was sure, once again, that she had done the right thing for Rachel and herself. And for the baby.

Eight months after the baby was born, in the spring, she had decided to leave Stoneham. Life in the insulated little suburb had become intolerable, both for herself and for Rachel. Too many housewives pausing to stare at her when she shopped at the local Gristede's, too many whispered exchanges between well-heeled matrons when she strolled along Grace Street. And Rachel had become utterly isolated, ostracized at school, the object of cafeteria gossip and homeroom stares. Ultimately, Jean had been forced to withdraw her daughter from school and to hire a private tutor.

It was soon afterward that she made the decision to take Rachel away from Stoneham, to leave the nightmare behind and try to reconstruct their lives. Southern Vermont seemed ideal. Jean loved the area. In the early years of her marriage, before Rachel was born, she and Bill had traveled up there every fall, to take in the foliage and treat themselves to a long weekend at the Newfane Inn. It was close enough to New York for Jean to feel that she wasn't completely severing her ties with the few friends who still mattered to her. And Vermont still had a sleepy, bygone air about it, a sense that it existed out of time, in some spellbound world untouched by the nightmares of modern life.

And so, on the first day of spring, Jean had put her house up for sale. Though the northeast, like the rest of the nation, was suffering through a severe real estate slump, she knew her house would go at the right price. And, in fact, within two weeks, it was snatched up by a young couple with a baby, both of them attorneys, who had decided to trade Manhattan for suburbia and were delighted to have found such a charming "starter house." Her asking price was insignificant by Stoneham standards. But it was more than enough to allow her to purchase a rambling old house and two wooded acres just outside of Townshend and to put something in the bank besides.

Bill had felt guilty enough about his absolute noninvolvement during Rachel's long ordeal to bolster his child support payments voluntarily, by two hundred a month. Between that windfall, her savings, and the profits of the Stoneham house, Jean had enough to get by on. For a while, at least.

Adjusting to her new surroundings had been the hardest part of the move so far. In spite of the loveliness of the landscape, particularly at that time of year, when the summer trees made the distant hills look as soft as forest moss, Vermont could dull the senses of a lifelong New Yorker like Jean. In comparison to Townshed, even Stoneham seemed like a thriving metropolis. Every time she entered the tiny village, Jean experienced the sensation of stepping inside a souvenir postcard—picturesque but absolutely devoid of action.

But of course, inactivity was precisely the point. For Jean no less than Rachel, sedation was, in effect, just what the doctor ordered. With nothing else to distract them, and the days moving along at such a languid pace, she and Rachel had all the time in the world to repair the shredded fabric of their life.

Of course, Jean had help in that task. That was another reason she had chosen that part of Vermont.

Rachel's court-appointed psychiatrist, Dr. Herbert Adler, had agreed with Jean that removing Rachel from Stoneham might be the best thing for her. When Jean mentioned southern Vermont, Dr. Adler's normally deadpan features had rearranged themselves into a look of pleasant surprise. "I was thinking the same thing myself," he said.

As it happened, Dr. Adler's old friend and colleague, a psychiatrist named Gerard Walsh, had a practice up in Brattleboro. "Gerry's just the man for Rachel," Dr. Adler said. A native Californian, Walsh had practiced clinical psychiatry in Berkeley during the heyday of hippiedom and had extensive experience treating drug-damaged youngsters who'd gotten sucked into one or another of the crackpot pseudoreligions that had flourished in that countercultural hotbed. During the early 1980s he had traveled throughout the country as a professional "deprogrammer," undoing the indoctrination of brainwashed teenage cult members.

Exactly one week to the day after the Mayflower moving van had transported all her worldly possessions from 18 McClellan Place up to her new home in Townshend, Jean drove Rachel into Brattleboro for her first appointment with Dr. Walsh.

At her first glimpse of the fortyish psychiatrist, Jean had to suppress a smile, so completely did his appearance match her expectations. An intense, narrow-shouldered man with wire-frame glasses and thinning gray hair brushed straight back into a ponytail, he was a perfect specimen of the aging ex-hippie, a species as common to certain parts of Vermont as the milk cow. But he radiated such an intense combination of acuity and kindness that Jean warmed to him instantly.

Rachel, too, seemed to like him and—even more important—to trust him. Since then she had been seeing him twice a week, Tuesday and Friday mornings at eleven-thirty, in his office, a soft-lit, book-lined room in the back of the little clapboard house he inhabited by himself a half mile outside of town.

Jean added a few final items to her grocery list, then glanced up at the wall clock. It was close to ten-forty. Plenty of time to make it to Brattleboro for Rachel's appointment.

She headed for her bedroom to change shirts. Though the sartorial standards of Brattleboro were infinitely more relaxed than those of Stoneham, the shapeless old Lacoste she liked to wear around the house was grubby even by local norms.

Slipping off the shirt, she reached into her closet for the turquoise cotton blouse she had just gotten back from the cleaners. She tossed the wire hanger onto her bed, buttoned up the blouse, then walked back to the front of the house and out onto the porch, the screen door clattering shut behind her.

The morning sparkled, and the air was aromatic with the greenness of the land. At the far end of the front lawn, Rachel, dressed in jeans and a simple white cotton T-shirt, sat cross-legged on grass, pushing the baby back and forth on the little Fisher-Price swing set Jean had purchased soon after their move.

"Baby goes up," Rachel singsonged as she gently shoved the small plastic bucket seat into which the infant was strapped. "And baby goes down."

In the sunny stillness of the morning, the young mother and her gurgling child made such a happy pair that even Jean could believe, at least for the moment, that everything would turn out all right.

"Rachel," she called after watching them for a moment. "Time to go."

Rachel acknowledged with a little wave, then got to her feet, brushing the damp grass off her backside. Stepping around to the front of the swing, she unsnapped the safety strap, lifted the baby out of the seat, and strolled across the lawn toward Jean.

"Here," she said, holding the baby out to Jean, who took him in her arms. "I just have to use the bathroom."

"Grab my purse on your way out," Jean said. "I left it on the coffee table."

Rachel disappeared into the house. Cradling the baby in her arms, Jean looked down into his face.

Daniel was his name. He was a lovely child, with chestnut hair and bright, dark eyes. Jean puckered her lips and made a soft kissing noise. Smiling, the baby reached up and touched her chin with his fingertips.

She wished she could love him more wholeheartedly.

It would have been easier, she thought, if he bore a stronger resemblance to Rachel. But the tiny face beaming up at her was an infant version of one she recognized clearly, though she had seen it only twice, the last time in a fancy Bedford restaurant just—could it be?—a little more than a year before. It felt like a lifetime ago.

She told herself again and again that this innocent creature could not be held responsible for the sins of his father. But her heart wouldn't listen to reason.

On some deeply irrational level, one she would have been ashamed to admit openly to, since it seemed so steeped in vanity, she also blamed the baby for turning her into a grandmother. She simply couldn't reconcile herself to a status she associated with blue hair and dowager's hump. The word itself seemed so alien to her self-image that she grimaced whenever she thought of it.

Hating her ambivalent feelings toward the radiant infant who was, after all, her own flesh and blood, Jean struggled to combat them. Now, she bent her head and kissed the baby on his silky-smooth forehead. His smell was even sweeter than the country air.

It was odd, she thought. On the one hand, being a grandmother made her feel prematurely old. On the other, she hadn't felt younger in years.

She had Jack Byrne to thank for the latter.

The baby squirmed in her arms. "Omma," he exclaimed.

"Yes." Jean laughed, turning to glance over her shoulder at Rachel, who had just emerged from the house with Jean's big leather handbag slung over one shoulder. "Here's Mama."

Jean held the child out to Rachel, who lowered him gently to the ground until the soles of his baby-sized running shoes were planted more or less firmly on the grass. Passing the handbag over to her mother, Rachel took her child's right hand and began to lead him slowly toward the car. He tottered along with stiff, bowlegged steps.

"He's becoming quite a walker," Jean said, reaching down to take his other hand.

Approaching the car, they came to a thick, gnarled tree root poking up from the lawn. Simultaneously, Jean and Rachel lifted the baby up into the air by his hands. He squealed with pleasure as they swung him over the exposed root and set him down on the opposite side.

After harnessing him into his safety seat, Rachel slid into the Volvo station wagon beside her mother. Then Jean backed the car out of the driveway and headed toward Brattleboro.

For a while Jean and her daughter rode in silence, though occasionally Rachel would swivel in her seat and, pointing out the window, say, "Look at the horses, Daniel," or "See the pretty farmhouse?" Approaching Brattleboro, they passed by an old-fashioned covered bridge that spanned a shallow river whose banks were strewn with rocks and boulders, bone-white in the sun.

"We should stop off at Hickin's on the way home," Rachel said. "Pick up some preserves."

"Good idea," Jean said. "Maybe a blackberry pie too. Jack loved the last one I bought."

Rachel shifted in her seat. "What time are they coming?"

"Early," Jean said. "Probably around two. We'll have to hurry back from town."

Rachel made no answer.

It was strange, Jean thought. Rachel seemed genuinely fond of Jack, who treated her with gentleness and understanding. Still, Jean's relationship with him made Rachel intensely uncomfortable. Maybe, Jean sometimes thought, it had to do with the sex. She and Jack had become lovers during the winter, and they made no pretense of sleeping in separate bedrooms when he drove up for his bimonthly visits. Jean knew that even the most sexually advanced teenagers could become prudish when it came to their own parents' love lives.

Of course, there was another, perhaps more plausible reason for Rachel's discomfort. Marianne. Understandably enough, Rachel felt extremely ill at ease in her company.

Jean glanced over at her daughter, who was staring out

the windshield. "Jack says Marianne really loves coming up here," Jean said. "She thinks it's the most beautiful place she's ever seen."

"Mmmmm," Rachel replied.

Jean paused for a moment before continuing. "I know you feel awkward about her visits," she said, choosing her words with care. "But Marianne doesn't blame you. She knows you weren't even there that night—"

"Please, Mom," Rachel said quietly. "I can't talk about it."

Jean nodded. What she'd said about Marianne was true. She bore no grudge against Rachel, only against Simon Proctor. And even he no longer existed as a specific memory for her. In the typical way of trauma victims, she had absolutely no recollection of the terrible ordeal she had suffered at his hands.

Jack had told Jean something about the horrors of that night, though only in the most general terms, and Jean was grateful not to know any more than she needed to.

Just outside of Brattleboro, Jean came to a little turnoff. Slowing, she drove the Volvo up the rutted road that led to Dr. Walsh's house and stopped by his front porch. Parked farther along the driveway, near the rear of the house, was a shiny black Mitsubishi sedan. Jean assumed it belonged to another patient.

"I'll pick you up in an hour, hon," Jean said as Rachel stepped out of the car. "I should be done with the shopping by then."

Rachel leaned back inside. "Be a good boy," she said to Daniel, blowing him a kiss. "Listen to Grandma."

"He'll be fine," Jean said. "He loves riding in the shopping cart."

Rachel gave a little wave, then turned away, slamming the door behind her. Jean swung the station wagon around and headed back toward the main road. Glancing into her rearview mirror, she caught a quick glimpse of Rachel as she disappeared through Dr. Walsh's front door.

75

JACK HAD STAYED OVERNIGHT AT MARIANNE'S APARTMENT
so that they could get an early start. He knew that they
would run into some commuter traffic around Hartford,
where the left lane of the highway was closed for construction, and he was eager to get to Vermont. He hadn't seen
Jean in two weeks, and he wanted to spend as much time
with her over the weekend as possible.

By eight A.M. he had loaded his old Samsonite suitcase
and Marianne's overnight bag into the trunk of his Pontiac,
held his daughter's elbow as she settled herself into the
passenger seat, then maneuvered out of the visitor's slot
and headed north.

As soon as they hit the parkway, Marianne reached down
to her armrest controls and slid the glass halfway down the
window. For several minutes she sat there silently, eyes
closed, one hand flat on the crown of her head to keep her
hair from blowing wildly, a blissful half-smile on her face
as the sweet morning air flowed over her.

Finally she sat up, closed the window, and reached forward to switch on the air conditioner.

"How're you feeling, sweetheart?" Jack asked, reaching
over to gently squeeze her left hand.

She returned the squeeze. "Alive," she said with a little
laugh. "Who could ask for anything more?"

That was how it had been for the past six months, ever
since Marianne had fought her way back to life with the
help of the specialists at Dowling. The smallest things,
things Jack barely noticed—the scrabbling of a squirrel up
a tree trunk, the shadow of a drifting cloud, a spiderweb
beaded with dew—could fill her with a quiet joy. Just the
feel of summer sunshine on her face seemed to be a source
of deep, almost sensual pleasure for her.

Jack thought of her exquisite new sensitivity to the natural delights of the world as God's compensation for the
unimaginable horrors she'd been put through.

One hand on the wheel, he glanced in her direction. She

has regained most of her weight, and her face, though more lined than before, looked as lovely as ever. She had dyed the gray streaks out of her hair. The lustrous blackness seemed duller now, but the hair itself had lost none of its beautiful texture. The only other evident signs of the damage she'd suffered were the way she slurred certain words, and the slight, possibly permanent limp that required her to walk with a cane.

Even the most minor of her impairments made Jack's heart ache. But to a far greater degree than he had dared to hope possible, he had gotten Marianne back. Now, as the car carried him northward toward Vermont and a weekend with the woman he loved, he couldn't have felt any happier.

Well, he thought, correcting himself. There's one thing that would make me happier.

His features must have darkened as he thought it. Or maybe Marianne had read his mind, because, at that very moment, she looked at him and said, "Still no leads on Proctor?"

Jack shook his head. "Hard to believe, what with the FBI hunting him and every department in the country on the alert. He's a slippery son of a bitch, all right." Grim-faced, he nodded slowly. "But he can't hide forever."

Marianne stared out her window for a long moment before sighing, "I hope you're right."

Much to Jack's surprise the anticipated traffic never materialized. He and Marianne continued to zip along at a steady sixty-five, making much better time than he'd expected.

As they neared the northern border of Connecticut, Marianne suggested a pit stop. Just outside of Enfield, Jack exited the highway and pulled into the parking lot of a roadside Big Boy restaurant. He walked around to the passenger side and held out his hand to Marianne, who grabbed it and pulled herself out of the car with the aid of her cane. As she hobbled toward the entrance, an elderly couple emerged from the restaurant and paused to stare at her. Magnified by the thick lenses of her glasses, the old lady's rheumy eyes seemed awash with sympathy. Marianne gave her a reassuring smile as she passed.

They had grabbed a quick bite in Marianne's apartment

before setting off. Now, after making use of the rest rooms, they settled into a rear booth and ordered coffee and Danish. The sunlight spilling in from the big plate-glass window beside them sparkled on the surface of the coffee.

"I've got something to tell you," Marianne said, taking a nibble from her cinammon Danish. "I've decided to go back to school."

Jack looked pleased. "You have? Where?"

"Maybe Purchase or Pace. Maybe John Jay. I've sent away for some catalogues."

"I think that's great. What are you going to study?"

Marianne shrugged. "I'm thinking of going to law school. If I do, I'll need to take some more undergraduate courses first."

"I think it's a terrific idea," Jack said softly. The admiration he felt for her was making it hard for him to speak. "Always thought you'd make a hell of a lawyer."

They chatted for a while about commonplace matters—the lawn work that Jack's backyard desperately needed, Aunt Dorothy's recent back surgery, Dick Wayland's retirement.

Half-consciously, Jack kept checking his watch.

Marianne smiled. "We're going to get there plenty early, Dad."

"I know but—"

"Ah," she sighed theatrically, then gave a little laugh. "Young love."

Jack looked abashed. "I hope you don't feel . . . I mean, I'm feeling a little guilty about—"

"Don't worry," Marianne said, putting down her coffee cup and reaching across the table to pat his hand. "You're not being disloyal to Mom. I think it's great that you feel this way about Jean. She's a wonderful person."

A few minutes later they were back on the road. As they crossed into Massachusetts, Marianne turned on the radio and scanned the FM stations until she hit on a tune she liked. Even Jack, whose familiarity with pop music ended with the era of Perry Como and Patti Page, recognized the song as an early Beatles number. The buoyant harmonies filled the car, and Jack found himself humming along.

The digital numbers on the dashboard clock read 10:41.

"At this rate we'll make it to Brattleboro by noon," Jack said. "Easily."

"Well, that should make you happy," Marianne said. "More time to play."

"Jean probably won't even be back from town," Jack said.

"What'll we do if she isn't?"

Jack shrugged. "Hang around the house and wait for her to get back," he said. "Let's hope she left the front door unlocked."

76

DANIEL WAS CONTENTEDLY GNAWING ON A FAT PRETZEL when Jean pulled into Dr. Walsh's driveway. The shopping had taken longer than she'd expected, and she was ten minutes late to pick up Rachel. She had kept pausing in the aisles to let Daniel admire the brightly colored packages arranged on the shelves. And the checkout counters were jammed with housewives stocking up for the weekend. The line took forever to get through.

She was surprised that Rachel wasn't waiting outside. The last time Jean had run late, she'd found her daughter lounging on the grass, face tilted up to the sun. Perhaps, Jean thought, Dr. Walsh had decided to spend a few extra minutes with Rachel. Jean knew that most psychiatrists kept to strict, fifty-minute sessions. But Dr. Walsh, with his laid-back sixties demeanor, didn't strike her as the kind of man who would be rigid about such matters.

She swiveled in her seat and reached over to tickle Daniel's side. He giggled delightedly, sending a paste of masticated pretzel spilling down his chin. Clucking her tongue, Jean fished inside her handbag for a Kleenex, which she used to wipe him clean.

"You're getting hungry, aren't you, baby?" she said. "Don't worry. Mommy'll come soon."

When another five minutes passed with no sign of Rachel, Jean decided to see what was keeping her.

"Grandma'll be right back," Jean said, sliding out of the

car. She left the driver's door open, so that Daniel wouldn't feel he was being shut up all alone in the car.

Then she walked across the lawn and up onto the wooden porch.

The front door was ajar. Jean pushed it open and stepped into the house.

To the right, a staircase with an oak banister ran up to the second floor. To the left was a hallway that led past a series of rooms to the rear of the house. Jean, who had been inside the house several times before, sometimes wondered why a single man like Dr. Walsh would need such a sprawling place. Perhaps, she thought, he was divorced and had ended up with the house as part of the settlement. Or perhaps he had lots of friends who came for extended visits. She could easily imagine Dr. Walsh hosting *Big Chill* get-togethers of middle-aged survivors of the 1960s.

She moved down the hallway, glancing into the rooms that she passed.

The house was bright and airy, full of antique furnishings— corner cabinets and claw-footed tables and spindle-legged chairs. The walls were hung with a colorful assortment of posters and prints. The atmosphere was so warm and cheery that Jean wondered if Dr. Walsh specialized in the treatment of children as well as troubled adolescents. The decor itself was enormously reassuring.

The hallway ended at the doorway to the den that served as Dr. Walsh's waiting room. The den had an intensely cozy atmosphere with overstuffed sofas and easy chairs, a well-worn Oriental carpet, and a coffee table spread with magazines.

At the far end of the den was a little hall, only a couple of yards long, that led to Walsh's office.

Jean made her way around the coffee table and easy chairs and paused at the end of the passageway, listening intently.

She could hear nothing coming from the office. The house was so quiet that the loudest sounds were the twittering of a bird just outside the wide-flung windows and the stirring of the leaves in the soft summer breeze.

But of course, Jean assumed, Dr. Walsh's office would be soundproof. It wouldn't do to have one's most intimate confessions audible to the people in the waiting room.

She hesitated for a moment, Then, after glancing at her watch and seeing how late it was—almost one o'clock—she walked down the little passageway, took a breath, and knocked.

Nothing.

Frowning, she knocked again, this time more emphatically.

Nothing.

She could feel a clenching in her chest as she reached down to the doorknob, turned it, and swung the door open.

The book-lined room was darker than she'd expected. She took a step inside, squinting. A thick stench hung in the air, as if from an open sewer.

She did not see Rachel anywhere.

Dr. Walsh was seated at his desk in his high-back swivel chair, facing away from the open door toward the window behind him. He might have been staring outside. Except for one thing. The curtains were drawn over the window.

Jean felt her heart thud as stepped across the room.

"Dr. Walsh . . . ?"

Her foot hit something on the floor. She paused, staring down.

It was Dr. Walsh's phone, torn from its wall cord.

Slowly, Jean raised her eyes and looked at Dr. Walsh.

She saw at once what had been done to him. His gaping eyes bulged. In the murky light, his complexion looked purple. His thick tongue jutted obscenely from his mouth.

A length of wire had been looped around his neck and pulled so tightly that it was embedded in the flesh of his throat. The sewer stench surrounded him like a miasma. Jean knew what happened. Dr. Walsh had voided his bowels as he died.

Suddenly, Jean heard a ragged, sobbing sound. It took her a moment to realize that the noise was coming from her own throat. She struggled against her panic.

Only then did she notice the scrap of paper stuck to Dr. Walsh's shirt with a pin.

Reaching out, she tugged the paper free and held it close to her eyes, trying to control the shaking of her hand.

A message was inked onto the paper in bold, black letters. It read:

MY DEAR MRS. PEARY,
A COUNTRY BARTER—
YOUR CHILD FOR MINE.
SEE YOU AT HOME.

SP

Her terror overwhelmed her. An anguished scream tore itself from her throat. Turning, she fled from the house toward her waiting car.

77

JACK WAS RIGHT. HE AND MARIANNE MADE IT TO BRAT-tleboro before noon. They still had a twenty-five-minute drive to Jean's house. But since they were so early, Jack didn't object when Marianne suggested that they stop just outside of Newfane. She had spotted a big roadside gift shop on their previous trip, and she wanted to check it out.

They browsed for fifteen minutes, and Marianne invested twenty dollars in a half gallon of grade-A medium amber maple syrup to eat with her microwave waffles. Then they hit the road again.

Jack didn't mind arriving at Jean's house at one. He felt sure that she would be back from Brattleboro by then, and the idea of having her there to greet him was more appealing than the thought of driving up to an empty house.

And so he was both surprised and mildly disappointed when he pulled into Jean's driveway and saw that no one was home. He drove his Pontiac around to the rear of the house, where the detached two-car garage was located, frowning when he saw the black Mitsubishi parked in front of it.

"Who's that?" Marianne asked.

"Don't know," Jack said. "Jean would have told me if she'd gotten a new car."

He pulled beside the Mitsubishi, turned off the engine, and got out of his car. Marianne swung open her door and maneuvered her legs around until her feet were resting on the grass.

416

Jack made a circuit of the black car, cupping his hands around his eyes to peer inside. He looked toward Marianne and shrugged. Then, turning to the house, he walked softly up the three wooden steps to the little rear landing. The glass-paneled back door, which Jean generally kept locked, opened into a small hallway that led directly into the kitchen.

Jack reached for the doorknob, then froze. He bent closer to examine it. The wood of the door frame was gouged and splintered. He gave the door a little shove and it moved. Someone had jimmied it open.

He hurried back down the stairs and over to the passenger side of his car.

"What's wrong?" Marianne asked, seeing the look on his face.

"I'm not sure," he said. Reaching across her lap, he popped open the glove compartment and stuck his hand inside.

"What are you looking for?"

"Something I keep with me," he said, straightening up out of the car. Marianne caught a glimpse of something long and bright clutched in his hand, but she could not tell what it was.

"Should I come with you?" she asked.

"Just wait here for a few minutes," he said, then turned and walked quickly but stealthily along the side of the house and around to the front.

Jack could move quietly for a big man, especially when he was wearing rubber-soled shoes. He crept up the steps onto the wooden porch and moved cautiously to the front door. He tried the doorknob. As he'd expected, Jean had left it unlocked. Clearly whoever had forced his way into the back hadn't known.

He turned the knob until the latch clicked, and eased open the door.

Then, thumbing open the blade of the silver-handled razor, he slid inside the house.

78

THE TRIP FROM BRATTLEBORO TO TOWNSHEND WAS THE LONG-
est fifteen minutes of Jean's life. She had exerted every
ounce of willpower at her disposal to keep her speed down
to sixty. Not that she feared getting stopped by the police,
for nothing would have made her happier than to attract a
state trooper's attention. But the snaking road was tricky
to negotiate even at the posted forty-five, and it was no
time for an accident.

The Volvo screeched to a stop in the front yard, plowing
deep ruts in the lawn. Jean jumped out, dashed around to
the passenger side, flung open the rear door, and, her hands
trembling violently, unsnapped the baby from his safety
seat. She did not want to leave him alone in the car with
Simon Proctor around.

Snatching Daniel to her chest, she flew up the front steps
and burst into the living room.

Jack Byrne was sitting there, wedged into a corner of
her sofa, his hands hanging limply in his lap. His eyes
seemed to be staring straight at her, and his face was absolutely white. There seemed to be blood everywhere—
splayed across the sofa, spattered over his pants. A puddle
of it had collected at his feet. His shirt was soaked in it,
as though someone had hurled a bucketful of gore directly
at his chest. She could see that all the blood had gushed
from the ugly slit that ran across the entire width of his
throat.

Jean could hear herself begin to whimper. She bit down
hard on her lower lip and squeezed her eyes tight, afraid
that she might pass out.

When she opened them again, Simon Proctor was standing in the room beside the sofa.

"I had no idea you were expecting company, Mrs.
Peary," he said. "How fortunate for me that I was sitting
here enjoying the view through your handsome bay window
when I saw him skulking outside." He reached out one
hand and stroked Jack's livid cheek with the back of his

418

forefinger, the way a lover might caress the face of his beloved. "For all his strength, he was surprisingly easy to kill."

Clutching the child tightly to her breast, she stared hard at Proctor, trying to keep her gaze away from Jack.

She would not have recognized him if she had passed him on the street. In the police photographs Jack had shown her, Proctor looked twenty years younger than his age—a big, broad-chested man with thick, wavy hair. But the man who stood before her looked every minute of his sixty-plus years. His posture was still commanding, but his flesh seemed to have shriveled. His face was hollow-eyed and gaunt, and the lank arms that hung from the short sleeves of his shirt were those of an athlete gone to seed.

She saw that he must have ambushed Jack—snuck up behind him and knocked him out before cutting his throat. This Proctor could never have outfought her lover.

He had grown a wispy beard and his hair was shaven close to the skull. But his eyes had lost none of their intensity.

"Yes," he said, his gaze boring into her. "I am not what I was. It has been His punishment, you see. For the failure of the ceremony." His voice turned harshly imperious. "Give me my child, Mrs. Peary."

Daniel was squirming and kicking in her arms. She pulled him tighter to her.

"You said a barter," she answered, her voice quaking. "Where's Rachel?"

Proctor took a step toward her and lifted his right hand. The polished blade of the straight razor glinted in the sun shaft slanting in through the window.

So reflexively that the action took even her by surprise, Jean shifted her hold on Daniel, grabbing him by both ankles and lifting him as high in the air as she could. The baby swung upside down over the wood floor, yowling.

"I'll drop him," she shouted. "I'll smash his head. I swear I will."

Proctor froze in his tracks, then smiled slowly. "As you wish," he said softly, then turned and strode off down the hallway.

Jean hooked one arm under Daniel's back and cradled him to her shoulder. Then, keeping her eyes averted from the blood-drenched corpse on the sofa, she hurried toward her bedroom.

When she stepped through the doorway, Proctor was standing directly beside Rachel, who was seated across the room in a wooden straight chair. Her mouth had been sealed with a strip of silver insulating tape, and her wrists were bound tightly behind the chair back. Her red-rimmed eyes stared imploringly at her mother. Jean couldn't make out the muffled words emanating from behind the tape. But their panicked, pleading tone was unmistakable.

"Release her," Jean demanded.

"Of course," Simon said pleasantly.

Stepping briskly behind the chair, he cupped his left hand under Rachel's chin, jerked it upward, and in the same movement, drew the razor across her throat. A liquid wheeze bubbled out through the scarlet gash in her voice box.

Jean shrieked with horror. Heaving the baby onto her bed, she lunged at Proctor, fingers clawed. The jetting blood from her daughter's wound sprayed across her face, wetting her lips with coppery warmness.

Proctor swung his razor at Jean, who jerked her arm upward in an instinctive, blocking gesture. She felt the blade slice her forearm to the bone as she tumbled backward onto the mattress where Daniel lay screeching.

Proctor threw himself on top of Jean and slashed down at her face. She twisted her head sideways. The razor sliced through the quilt and sank into the mattress.

Jean's right hand groped wildly. She touched something cold and hard and slender—the wire hanger. She curled her fist around it, the metal hook poking out between the index and middle finger, and slashed upward at Proctor's face.

The hook dug into his left temple, skittered along the side of his head, and sank into his eye socket. Jean felt the cornea pop. Simon roared with agony and fell back, clutching at his ruptured eyeball.

Jean hurled herself off the mattress and bolted from the room toward the kitchen. Behind her, she heard Simon bellow with rage and pain.

Grabbing the handle of the utensil drawer, she yanked it—too hard. The drawer flew out of its slot. Forks, spoons, knives of every size cascaded onto the linoleum floor. Drop-

420

ping to her knees, she rummaged frantically through the sprawling heap of utensils. Her fingers closed around the wooden handle of an eight-inch carving knife just as Simon burst into the room and fell upon her.

She flung herself onto her back in the instant before Simon straddled her. With both hands on the knife handle, she thrust upward at his throat.

At the last moment Simon jerked his head backward, and the knife missed his throat and sank into the fleshy underside of his jaw, passing through the floor of his mouth, piercing his tongue, and sinking into the spongy tissue of his soft palate.

A shrill scream whistled through his pinioned mouth. He yanked his head back and slashed down at Jean, who turned her face sideways to avoid the blow. The razor sliced through her left ear, nearly severing the upper half. Simon grabbed her hair and twisted, shoving the side of her face against the floor.

Simon's right hand swept across his body in a sideways arc, the blade rising over his left shoulder, poised to slash down at her jugular. His forearm brushed against the jutting knife handle, sending a fresh jolt of pain through his skull. He would enjoy watching Jean Peary flop on the floor as her arterial blood spurted. He tightened his fingers in her hair and took aim at her throat.

Two hands reached down over his left shoulder and clamped themselves onto his wrist. He felt a weight on his back, as though a knee were digging into him. Then he felt moist breath in his ear as a woman's voice whispered, "No more, Simon."

He recognized Marianne Byrne's voice, and a current of fear slithered through him. He had assumed Jack Byrne was alone. Marianne must have been waiting in the car, then snuck in through the back door when her father failed to emerge.

He struggled to pull free, then willed himself to relax his right arm. The butt end of the knife handle was pressed into the crook of his forearm. If Marianne yanked backward, the blade would be driven up into his skull. He breathed deeply through his nose and swallowed his own blood.

"That's right, Simon," Marianne hissed, "it's over, you

421

fuck." She tightened her grip, giving his arm a little tug, forcing the tip of the knife blade deeper into his palate. A choking sob gurgled from his throat.

With a sudden desperate motion, his free hand snaked around to grab at Marianne's ankle.

Marianne began to lose her balance.

Through the red film of her fear, Jean saw Simon try to throw off Marianne. Reaching up with both hands, she grabbed the back of his head and, with a savage howl, yanked down with all her might while Marianne held tight to his forearm.

An explosive crunch inside his head was the last sound that Simon Proctor heard. His vision exploded in a nova of incandescent white as the knife blade was driven up behind his nasal cavity and deep into his brain.

Soundlessly—without so much as a whimper—he collapsed onto Jean's prostrate body.

Jean immediately shoved him away and struggled to her knees, her bloody ear dangling.

"My father?" Marianne screamed.

"Marianne . . ." Jean was sobbing now. "Marianne . . ."

Marianne hobbled as fast as could into the living room.

Jean struggled to her feet, cupping one hand over her butchered ear. She had taken only a few wobbly steps when she heard Marianne begin to wail.

By the time Jean reached the living room, Marianne had collapsed onto the couch beside her father and had pulled his slack body onto her lap. She was rocking him back and forth. "Please," she sobbed, as though she might beseech him back to life. "Please."

Jean leaned against the doorway, weeping.

Then, after stumbling over to the phone to dial 911 and sob a message to the police operator, she staggered toward the bedroom where Rachel and the baby waited—the child she had not managed to save, and the child who was all that was left her.